# ELEPHANT WALK

## SECOND BOOK IN THE BRIGANDSHAW CHRONICLES

## PETER RIMMER

# ABOUT PETER RIMMER

Peter Rimmer was born in London, England, and grew up in the south of the city where he went to school. After the Second World War, aged eighteen, he joined the Royal Air Force, reaching the rank of Pilot Officer before he was nineteen. At the end of his National Service, he sailed for Africa to grow tobacco in what was then Rhodesia, now Zimbabwe.

The years went by and Peter found himself in Johannesburg where he established an insurance brokering company. Over 2% of the companies listed on the Johannesburg Stock Exchange were clients of Rimmer Associates. He opened branches in the United States of America, Australia and Hong Kong and travelled extensively between them.

Having lived a reclusive life on his beloved smallholding in Knysna, South Africa, for over 25 years, Peter passed away in July 2018. He has left an enormous legacy of unpublished work for his family to release over the coming years, and not only they but also his readers from around the world will sorely miss him. Peter Rimmer was 81 years old.

# ALSO BY PETER RIMMER

∼

~

# BOOK 1 – SPRING AND NEW BEGINNINGS

# 1

## APRIL 1907

*H*arry Brigandshaw first visited Purbeck Manor when he was twenty-one years old having finished his three years at Oxford University. He was one of the few undergraduates to take a degree in geology and the only student attending Oxford from the Crown colony of Southern Rhodesia. There had been three options for Harry in Central Africa: he could either help to administer the colony through the British South Africa Company that held the royal charter, farm the land, or search for minerals to supply the empire with its raw materials.

The train stopped at Corfe Castle railway station. His friend and fellow graduate, Robert St Clair, opened the carriage door and together they pulled their suitcases onto the platform, while down the far end of the train their trunks were unloaded from the guard's van. They watched the porter, and the guard put the trunks on the barrow. No one got on the train and no one else got off. The stationmaster gave a loud, important whistle, the guard waved a green flag, the train engine puffed up steam, and the train went off on its way to Swanage.

The porter rested the barrow on its stubby legs and looked at them.

"No one to meet me?" said Robert St Clair.

"No one what I seen, Mister Robert. You want to leave the luggage as usual?"

"Thank you. I'll probably come tomorrow. Mrs Pringle well, Pringle?"

"Arthritis. Be better with the summer comin'. Thank you, Mister Robert."

"My friend and I will change in the waiting room. You just keep an eye open." The porter put the shilling in his pocket, the cases on top of the trailer, and trundled off down the platform.

"Change?" asked Harry, not sure what was going on.

"You do have your walking shoes in your suitcase as I told you?"

"I think so."

"Good, we're going to walk to the Manor. It's only seven miles along the valley... So many brothers and sisters and not one to meet me at the station."

"You did tell them when we were arriving?"

"Probably not... One night I spent in the waiting room it was raining too much or was it snowing? The fire was cosy. Pringle told me his life story while we sat by the fire. One of his sons was in your part of the world during the war. Boers didn't give him a scratch. Anyway, it's a nice day today, and just right for a good walk. We'd need sandwiches and a fresh flask of tea."

"And how do we do that?"

"Mrs Pringle. She makes real doorstopper sandwiches, but the bread's always fresh. It's kind of vital. You see, there were too many children coming and going from the Manor to school. We needed a refuelling stop."

"And Mrs Pringle doesn't mind?"

"You'll see. I'll bring her a chicken when I come back for the trunks. In the rural areas, everyone helps everyone else. It's the only way it works. But you should know, coming from a farm."

"Certainly couldn't walk from Salisbury station to Elephant Walk."

"How far is it?"

"Something like thirty-four miles."

"That's a bit far."

"The distance is not the problem, it's the lions."

"Luckily we don't have lions in England. Come on, Harry, can't wait to get home. I did warn you the place is a lunatic asylum."

"More than once, Robert."

"You'll love Mater and Pater, and I know they'll love you."

"And once your family owned the whole valley?"

"I'll show you the castle ruins. Perfect spot for a sandwich and a cup of tea. I'm hungry, but first, let's go and get what we need from Mrs Pringle."


THE VICTUALS and the raincoats were put in Robert St Clair's haversacks with an extra pair of socks each and the friends began the long walk through the English countryside.

"You knew we were going to walk?" said Harry, pulling a haversack onto his back.

"Of course. It's easier to tell the guests when they arrive."

THE CLIMB UP to the ruins on top of the hill took them an hour. Moss and grass had grown over the old stones and none of the walls was higher than a man's shoulders.

"Oliver Cromwell," said Robert. "One of my ancestors fought for King Charles. Unlike Charles, who had his head cut off, he got across to France when Cromwell won the civil war. Cromwell had the old castle smashed to the ground. We came over with William the Conqueror long before that. Our fiefdom was the Isle of Purbeck, and our job to guard the valley from marauders coming from the sea. The castle commands the valley. The St Clairs owned as far as you can see in all directions. Now we have the home farm and I don't think we can last much longer. Let's sit on the grass and have a sandwich. I'm starving... Oh good, she's put some pickles in the sandwich box. I've had this one since I went to prep school... When Cromwell died and with him the Commonwealth, Charles the Second gave my ancestors back their lands. There wasn't any point in rebuilding the castle as the invention of the cannon had made the castle walls obsolete. Must have been bleak up here with the wind from all directions. The manor house was built in the valley, and if you look hard you can just see the chimney pots sticking through the trees. My father sometimes comes up here on his own to talk to our ancestors. It wasn't his fault. Grandfather was a libertine. He loved gambling and women and lived most of his life in London. Aunt Nut says we now live in genteel poverty. Debt is very boring, Harry. I'm sorry... You ready for a good strong walk through the valley? Wow, that sandwich does make me feel a lot better. Tally-ho! I wonder what we are having for supper tonight? We all eat together. Everyone will want to know about Africa, so be prepared. The one golden rule is we all eat first before the food gets cold. Then we talk. Mater doesn't like anyone talking with their mouths full."

THE FIRST APRIL shower was sharp and over before they had time to unstrap the haversacks and put on their raincoats. Rainwater dripped down their faces but did not penetrate their tweed hacking jackets.

Robert had taken the bridle path through the valley, saying the road, which straddled the Purbeck Downs, was boring. By the side of the path ran a brook that murmured and gurgled its way over stones, and round the small, twisting bends. The path had been well ridden by many horses.

Instinctively, from his years in the African bush, Harry pressed into the dung the stick he had cut from an ash tree soon after leaving the railway station.

"What are you doing?" asked Robert.

"Seeing how long ago the horse went by. But it doesn't work. Dung keeps wet for weeks in England if it ever dries out. Force of habit. Like carrying a gun or a stick. In Africa, it is necessary to know what passed by and when. You can read from the ground what happened as easily as if you had sat high on a rock and watched the game. I never walk without a gun. My father was a white hunter before he went farming. The wilderness of Africa, he called it. Long before we English came to settle. Are there any fish in the stream?"

"Minnows and sticklebacks. As a small boy, I spent hours trying to catch them without success, happy as a sandboy. Fred caught one once. It was a stickleback and it pricked his finger. We were using bent pins so it fell back in the water. I was very proud of Frederick for weeks after that. Fred's three years older than me. He took the Indian Civil exam and went out to India. Terrible writer, so we don't hear much, but I always remember that stickleback... We've been walking long enough to deserve another sandwich and a cup of tea. I hope Fred's enjoying India. It's so far away from the brook... Did you hear that! It's a cuckoo. Someone said they come here all the way from Africa but only sing in England. Everywhere else they are silent. Do you have cuckoos in Africa, Harry?"

"Yes. And you're right, they don't sing at home. We can sit under that tree in case it rains again. How much further do we have to go?"

"This is the halfway stop. Why do we grow up? It's such a pity. When I was a child so many small things gave me pleasure. Now I seem to need much more from life to make me happy. Good, there's one more pickle each. What do you think of our valley?"

"It's very beautiful. I can see why your family have stayed here for so many hundreds of years. My maternal grandfather's family came to England with the Conqueror. I wonder if our ancestors were friends? I rather fancy life repeats itself through the generations. Probably all it does do. The same lives over and over again. The rebirth. The only way we are sure of our immortality. From one generation to the next for all eternity."

"Amen. I hope all my ancestors enjoyed their lives as much as I have done."

"And will do."

"Of course. We'll split the last sandwich. One day I want to come to Africa. Harry, will you have me?"

"You will always be welcome."

"Is that an invitation?"

"Of course."

"Poor Father. He says a degree in history is as much use as a man's tits."

"Or the Pope's balls."

"I've told you that one?"

"You have. And I won't repeat it in front of the ladies on pain of death. Without knowledge of history, we have no idea of the future. Someone said that. Just don't ask me who. Put on your raincoat. It's going to rain again. And hard. Even under the tree."

"How do you know? The clouds look the same."

"First I heard it. Now I smell it. And here it comes."

"You chaps from Africa are very clever."


THE SHORT SHARP shower came and went, leaving the sky slate-blue with scurrying clouds on the horizon. A watery sun came out and made no impression on the material of their jackets. Harry wished for an African sun. The grass and trees dripped from the rain and the fresh scents of spring overcame the smell of old, damp cloth. Birds took to singing now the rain had gone. A lark flew off from a field full of black and white cows, the tiny bird soaring up to the heavens, singing as though to burst its heart with joy. Harry watched the bird until it was too high to see with the natural eye. A thrush joined the chorus from a hedge that kept the black and white cows where they were meant to be.

"Your cows?" he asked, nodding his head at the field.

"Not yet. Not for a while yet. All we now have are the few hundred acres around the old house. Without Cousin Potts, we would be in all kinds of financial trouble. Father says in all his life he's never wanted an old man to go on living so much. When grandfather died, Potty, as we kids called him, arrived for a weekend at the Manor and never left. Rumour has it that he and Granny Forrester were more than kissing cousins when they were young. He went away to one of the colonies, and when he came back my maternal grandmother was married to grandfather. I rather think there was a little scandal, and one hols I caught Potty and Granny holding hands looking into the old fish pond. I slunk away without them seeing me. I may be a romantic but those two old people are as much in love as Genevieve with her last boyfriend. If we put a pointed tassel-topped hat on Genevieve and a long white dress down to her ankles, she could walk straight into the court of King Arthur without worrying about the last centuries. Sir Willoughby Potts was governor of some obscure island in the Pacific that had something to do with Captain Cook and Australia, but for the life of me

I can never remember its name. Don't worry, Potty will tell you. He likes talking about the good old days in the colonies. He never married and has a thousand a year from his mother's family. When he retired, I think it was Lord Salisbury who gave him a knighthood and a very nice letter of thanks. Not a penny, poor fellow, so when gramps died it was quite an opportunity for everyone. We had the house and he had the income. Poor old gramps. I hope he doesn't mind. So you see the dilemma. We all watch his health very carefully. It's so beastly not having money. Spoils everything. The one grandfather spent all the money, but the other one popped off rather conveniently, don't you think?"

"How long has Cousin Potts been staying with you?"

"Twenty years. I was one year old."

"How many acres do you farm?"

"Along with the land around the old house, about six hundred in total, I rather think. But there's the rub. None of us knows anything about farming."

"Isn't it time someone found out?"

"The problem, I suppose, is Richard. He's the eldest and inherits everything that's left in the family. There's no point in the rest of us learning to farm when the moment Pater dies, God forbid, Richard inherits what's left of the land."

"Why doesn't Richard learn about farming? Like everything else, you have to know what you are doing on a farm. My father knows more about Elephant Walk than all the employees put together and he's made certain both of his sons have inherited his knowledge."

"You'll see. Poor Richard... I think I'll find a nice prep school in the country and teach history."

"You want to be a junior school teacher?"

"They usually give the masters somewhere to live, even if it is a room next to the common room."

"The pay is terrible."

"Let me know when you think of something better I can do."

"You might like Africa, Robert."

"I would never leave England."

Robert's voice was so emphatic, Harry turned to look at him, but his friend strode ahead with his chin pushed forward. For the next half hour, they were silent as the old house appeared and reappeared through the trees and folds in the land. Intermittently, Harry could see the walls of it were covered in ivy. The windows winked at him through the trees, the spring sun reflecting from the panes. Then a cloud scurried over the sun and sent a cold shiver down Harry's spine, more from premonition than from cold. For the first time in many months, Harry wished he was back on Elephant Walk with his mother and father, his Grandfather Manderville, Aunt Alison, Barend, Madge and Christo. He rather thought he could even put up with his brother George.

"What are you smiling at, Harry?"

"My family. For a moment I was homesick. Maybe watching your excitement as you get nearer to your house. We all crave our roots."

"But your roots are still in England."

"Not anymore. I can see the magic of England, but Africa has a magic all of its own. I think it's the animals. The sudden danger. The vast empty space. But most of all I miss the smell of the wild sage, the smell of rain on old cooking fires in the African bush, the cry of a fish eagle, the bark of a bushbuck, the call of the morning doves. Africa is a place for the future. You don't need a lot to be happy in Africa. A thatched rondavel beside a river. A patch of mealies and vegetables. A good rifle. In Africa, I am free of my fellow man's conventions. Oxford was a wonderful experience but there were so many rules and regulations. All the time I was wondering what everyone else was thinking so I wouldn't offend them by saying something out of turn. I was never my own man, always what the others wanted me to be. We were all trying so hard to conform and be pleasant to each other, we created masks that no one could penetrate. Now, isn't that a false society?"

"I hope you didn't think of me that way."

"Fortunately in life, there are always exceptions. I wouldn't be telling you about it if I thought you the same as the others. Do you know what I am talking about? Sorry. Things like that are best unsaid. A lot of what we think, should stay in our minds if we don't want to upset the apple cart."

"You're right. Too much thinking gives me a headache. Come on. It's still quite a walk. I think I can just make the house without starving to death."

For half an hour they walked in comfortable silence thinking their oh so different thoughts, the signs of spring all around, the first lime-green leaves on the oak trees, the first primrose deep in last year's dark winter grass.

In his mind, Robert St Clair heard the treble call of boys playing cricket, the chock of the leather ball on the bat, the smell of summer in his nostrils. He smiled. A schoolmaster! That was it. Never again having to worry like his father, always a roof over his head, and food on the common-room table. He was good at fitting in and liked being liked, playing the game was more important than winning. And in the hols, long walking tours with a good pair of boots and a strong walking stick, the whole of England, Scotland and

Wales to be explored year after year. And in the winter sitting near a log fire reading his books, so many books, more than he could ever read in a lifetime. He was fourth in line to the barony, no need for progeny, but if a lovely, sweet girl wished to join his woodland walks, he would be happy with whatever life should bring.

The brook dropped into a large hole and went underground for half a mile. The hedgerows still followed the line of the brook and when the water came gushing out, dropping ten feet into a pool, there were no surprises. Regular three-bar gates into the fields allowed him to leave the path whenever he wished, but he always preferred following the water. Robert had counted twelve birds' nests since leaving the railway station at Corfe Castle. Now, in his mind, he could smell the food cooking for his supper. Whatever else happened he was going to be happy for the rest of his life. Suddenly Africa was far too far away, even for his imagination.

"It's very beautiful," said Harry, looking at the tiny waterfall as they stopped for a moment.

Then they walked on in silence.


THE GREAT DYKE stretched most of the length of Southern Rhodesia and Harry Brigandshaw was certain it contained most of the minerals known to man. Copper, nickel, cobalt, iron ore, chromium, the stuff the empire made into machines and power, easing man's burden, taking the drudgery from human life. A pack mule, a prospector's pick, and his knowledge learned at Oxford would unleash the treasure and make certain there was money to govern and prosper the colony. He was going to explore the views of the mountains like his father and Uncle Tinus had explored the country before the Union Jack was raised at Fort Salisbury in 1890. There was more than gold in them hills, he told himself, and involuntarily quickened his pace.

"Are you hungry?" asked Robert.

"In a way, I suppose."

"Here we climb over this gate into our own fields and out straight across to the house... Look. Far over there. That's little Lucinda. It's her birthday tomorrow. She'll be fifteen."

Cupping his hands to his mouth Robert called out, "Cinda it's me. I'm home."


LUCINDA SAT on the wooden bar of the gate, her small feet tucked into the second bar and waited. There were two gates into the pasture, one on either end of the field. In between were the cows looking at the stranger and Robert while they vacantly chewed the grass in their mouths. The cows were fat and full of milk.

"Doesn't anyone milk the cows?" she heard the stranger ask.

"Old Warren will bring them to the milking shed."

"Who milks them?"

"He has two granddaughters. Sort of family business for centuries. Cinda, this is my friend Harry Brigandshaw. He's come to stay with us for a few days and then I'm going to be a schoolmaster."

The stranger was almost six feet tall, slim, his face somehow burnt, unlike any complexion she had ever seen before. Very few boys from their class ever came to Purbeck Manor. From under her long, dark eyelashes, she watched him walk the last of the field towards her. When he smiled at her, she looked away and jumped down from the three bar gate. Then she stood, spreading her elbows on the top bar and resting the side of her face on the long sleeve of her dress. He looked different sideways and could not look into her eyes. This stranger's hair was long, longer than any of her brothers'.

"Where are you from?" she asked.

"Central Africa."

"You are a long way from home."

"You must be the same age as my sister Madge. Her birthday's in August."

"It's my birthday tomorrow."

"I know."

"What else do you know?"

"That I have never met a prettier girl at a three bar gate in all my life."

"Boys always say these things, but they never mean them. Come on. We'll be late for supper. I spied you from my room. I've been watching the path through Merlin's telescope for days. Don't tell Father about being a schoolmaster until after we've all had supper. He'd have a fit. You can each have one of my hands and then we must run."

"You can't run without holding up your skirt," said Harry, taking the proffered hand.

"Then we will go slower and arrive later... Does Mother know you are bringing a friend?"

"Yes she does, and it was wise of Mother not to tell the rest of you girls."

"Are you an explorer, Mr Brigandshaw?"

"My father was. Now we farm. Maize and cattle. We call our farm Elephant Walk. Once every decade or so the elephants migrate through our valley. The migration goes on for days, the earth shaking, the days and nights rent asunder by the trumpeting of the greatest mammals living on this earth. The last time the elephants migrated I was about your age."

"Weren't you afraid?"

"Not really. I was away at school in Cape Town."

"Will you take me to Elephant Walk?"

"It's a very long way away."

"I don't mind."


THE SIBLINGS HAD CALLED him Merlin when he was ten years old and frightened the cat. One minute Tiddles had been lying in front of the fire and next she was hissing and arching her back. When Aunt Nut opened the door to the morning room, she shot past Merlin and Aunt Nut at a speed not seen in years. At first, they put it down to Aunt Nut coming into the room as all the children knew that Great Aunt Nut was peculiar, but it wasn't the aunt at all. All of a sudden the cat had become petrified of Merlin, with or without Aunt Nut in the room, and the name had stuck, as nicknames often will, for the rest of his life. As he grew older, even the dogs growled at him, which was a problem as from an early age Merlin was the best shot in the family, and hunting rabbits with growling dogs gave the game away to the rabbits. To add to the complication, owls and hawks took a liking to newly named young Merlin. But when there was so much going on in the family no one took a particular interest. Merlin brought the telescope he had retrieved from Cinda up to his one blue eye and grunted with satisfaction.

"There they are," he said to his empty bedroom.

Coming down the path between the herbaceous borders was his sister holding a stranger's hand. Behind came brother Robert who was trying to catch up to Cinda's empty hand that trailed, waiting behind her back, but the path was too narrow. Then they disappeared under a long arch of climbing roses devoid of leaf and flower, the old trellis hiding the trio from his sight.

Snapping the telescope back into itself, he watched the path for a moment before shutting his window and drawing the curtains. Then he shivered and wondered why.

Halfway down the staircase, which he'd taken two at a time, he jumped on the banister and came out into the hall at a speed. His mother told him every time it would kill him. Ever since he had scared the cat he had taken to sliding down the banister, quite often frightening himself. As he opened the front door, or more exactly the small door inside the front door, a waft from the kitchen of cooking meat caught his saliva buds and his mouth flooded.

When he reached the edge of the vast terrace to where he could look down the garden, the trio was again hand in hand and walking up the path between the badly kept lawns.

Merlin waved and Robert waved back with his free hand. Cinda broke loose, picked up her long skirt, and began to run.

"Supper's nearly ready," Merlin called.

Behind him, the small door opened again onto the terrace that ran the whole length of the house, and young Barnaby raced across the flagstones that age and many generations of children had worn smooth.

"It's roast lamb," he yelled in his high-pitched voice.

Looking up the terrace at the young man and small boy, Harry Brigandshaw smiled and turned to his friend.

"Don't you St Clairs think about anything else but your stomachs?"

When he looked up again there were more friendly faces waving at them.

"He's very nice," he heard Lucinda call to an older woman who was standing at the top of the terrace stairs.

"That's my mother," said Robert St Clair with great pride.


GRANNY FORRESTER REMAINED inside next to the fire with a shawl over her bony shoulders. Her needlework showed a pheasant in flight, soft brown and dull red, the bird perfectly balanced on the wind. It would cover another footstool that no one would use but it gave her something to do. Her bony fingers worked the pieces of wool into the pattern while her mind concentrated on the distant noises coming from the terrace. There was nothing wrong with Granny Forrester's hearing though she had kept that a secret for years.

Potts watched from his chair and sipped a glass of brown sherry. Officially he allowed himself two every night at exactly the same time and waited for the grandfather clock in the corner of the morning room to chime six o'clock.

"Like a glass of sherry, Nettie?" he would ask every night.

"You know I don't drink, Willoughby, but I'll just have a sip of yours to keep you company."

And every night he poured a glass of brown, sweet sherry, offered the glass to Granny Forrester and watched her take the one big sip that drained the glass. For himself, he preferred a dry, pale sherry, but ever since coming to live at Purbeck Manor, he had changed to the tawny brown.

"That is only your second, Willoughby?" she said, trying not to show her agitation.

"Of course, my dear."

"May I have another sip of yours?"

And every night when they went into supper they were quite tiddly.

When the door opened she pretended not to hear and only when her grandson kissed her on her shrivelled cheek did she smile, her hands still working the snippets of coloured wool.

"I've missed you, Granny," said Robert St Clair next to her ear, and then he stood back to introduce Harry.

"My Grandmother Forrester, Sir Willoughby Potts, this is my good friend Harry Brigandshaw from Oxford."

"Have a glass of sherry, young man. You walked I suppose. If young Robert told us when he was coming they'd have sent the trap, damn it. Knew a fellow called Brigandshaw once. Damn man was a pirate, so they said. Took me out to the Pacific on my first trip. No relation, I hope."

"My grandfather, sir," said Harry.

"Well, have a glass of sherry, anyway. Damn good sailor. But then you'd have to be to be a pirate. Did something to him in the end."

"Made him a baronet, sir."

"Pirate gets a hereditary title and I get a KBE."

"He was very rich and gave a lot of money to the Tory party."

"That makes all the difference. Money talks. Don't you forget it. I wish more of it had talked to me. Go on, Robert, you can pour the sherry and only put a drop in the glass for Lucinda... Isn't it your birthday, Lucinda?"

"Tomorrow, Gramps."

"Don't call me Gramps. You know I'm not a grandfather. There's no respect in this family whatsoever. Barnaby, shut the door. You know your grandmother hates the draught. Ah, there you are, Bess. You'd better have a sherry too. Cold on the terrace. Now, where's the Lord of the Manor?"

"Ethelbert is looking at his pigs."

"Merlin, open another bottle of sherry. I can see from here the decanter's empty."

ETHELBERT, Seventeenth Baron St Clair of Purbeck, had a special rapport with his pigs. Maisey was suckling twelve piglets while she watched him with soppy, adoring eyes. In the next pen, the eight-week-olds were feeding from the trough, ignoring their mother. Then came Hector, the finest boar ever born, and father of them all and countless more that had been well turned into bacon.

The cold draught, creeping up his bottom from the tear in his trousers, reminded him that he was hungry.

"Goodnight, my darling," he said to Maisey. With a light heart and a smile on his ruddy face, Lord St Clair left the pig shed.


BARNABY WATCHED his father go round the back of the old house before letting the curtains fall closed. Outside it was almost dark.

Inside it was warm from the two fires either side of the sitting room. The clink of the glass stopper dropping back into the decanter, the loud tick of the grandfather clock in its corner, the hiss of the gas lamps on the walls that spluttered and moved the shadows, the gentle voices of his family, were all that Barnaby could wish from life. He was the happiest ten-year-old in all of England. It was a fact, yet unrecognised by Barnaby, this well of happiness always overwhelmed him before supper.


HARRY BRIGANDSHAW PICKED up the sweet farmyard aroma of horse manure soon after he sat down with the family in the dining hall. Again, two fires burnt, one at each end of the long room. The end from which was emanating the strange mix of smells of barnyard and roast mutton, was occupied by a large cooked sheep on a spit and Lord St Clair of Purbeck. No one had bothered to introduce them. Absorbed into the chaos of the St Clair family, any introductions would have been superfluous. He had become part of the family the moment he stepped over the threshold.

The baron stood over the crispy cooked carcass with a small sword that had belonged to one of his ancestors. He slashed the blade back and forth across a sharpening iron, his tongue slightly projecting from the left corner of his mouth, his ruddy face screwed tight with concentration. Along with all the grown-ups he was dressed for dinner. For the carving session, Lady St Clair had wisely covered him in a dust coat of the same type people were using to ride in the new-fangled horseless carriages.

On the old table made from a wood long lost in the family history, heaped pots of vegetables, roast potatoes, and sweet roast swedes were methodically being plonked down by an ancient servant that Harry wanted to jump up and help, the weight of the pots almost tripping the old man face down across the table. Next to him, the soft hand of the nineteen-year-old Annabel touched him for the first, but not the last, time.

"James will think he's getting old if you help," she whispered into his ear, blowing gently to finish her warning. Across the table, seventeen-year-old Genevieve glared at her older sister. Under the table, the youngest of the three sisters, Lucinda, was rubbing his ankle with a foot.

The sword stopped flashing in the firelight, and Harry understood the need for the dust coat. His host was a messy carver and between the carcass and the silver salver, most of the juice landed on the dust coat, protecting the stiff white dress shirt from disaster. Stoically, James held out a salver for the cut slices of meat before going around the family. Barnaby's plate was already stacked high with vegetables and potatoes when his turn came to take meat from the salver. Harry smelt the barnyard behind his right elbow as a second salver was slid in front of his eyes.

"You must be Harry Brigandshaw. Welcome to Purbeck Manor. Please don't get up."

It was the first time Harry was served roast lamb by a Lord of the Manor.

"Thank you, sir."

"You can help me muck out the pigs tomorrow. We farmers have to stick together."

When Harry looked up from helping himself to meat, his host gave him a wink.

"Get a move on, Ethelbert," said Lady St Clair. "The food's getting cold. Now, is everyone served?"

Satisfied, she smiled at her husband. "Ethelbert, you may now say grace."

"Thank you, my dear."

"Better put down that dish."

In a brief ceremony, the food was blessed and the whole family tucked in. Having been told by his mother to never finish his food first and to chew at least six times, he was astonished to watch the mounds of food disappear so quickly. Barnaby was the first to finish. Timing his manners, Harry put down his knife and fork just ahead of Granny Forrester and Great Aunt Nut, who came in joint last.

The food had been quite delicious and was followed by plates of battered rhubarb covered in golden syrup. Only after all the food had been eaten did the family begin to talk.

Then, without a word spoken, the women and Barnaby rose from the table, the men moved to chairs closer to Lord St Clair, port glasses and a bottle of port were placed by James in front of His Lordship, who filled a glass, took it from the tray, and pushed the bottle and glasses to Sir Willoughby Potts. Every man poured himself a glass of port.

By the time he found his bed, with the help of Robert, Harry was slightly drunk from the port. When he woke once in the middle of the night he had no idea where he was. Rain was slashing at the closed window. No one had drawn the curtains. A strange keening noise was coming from somewhere inside the old house. An owl, so different to an African owl, hooted despite the rain, and Harry remembered where he was. Secure in his knowledge, he lay back and was soon fast asleep. He dreamed of the Zambezi Valley and when he woke in the early morning with the spring sun streaming through the window, he was smiling.

The house was quiet and Harry pulled the feather-stuffed quilt up to his chin. At the end of the bed, on an old dressing table, a large enamel bowl with a jug the same size stood ready for his morning wash. Under the bed would be a heavy stone potty that his mind tried to ignore; it was cold in the room despite the watery spring sun. The long sash window behind the right side of the bed would look out across an inner courtyard that gave entrance from the main road to the manor house.

The terrace and lawns that he had first seen at the end of his walk from the railway station were on the other side of the house. Across from him the evening suit he had borrowed from Merlin the previous night hung neatly over the chair next to the dressing table.

With the quilt around his shoulders, Harry finally climbed out of the bed and looked down into the cobbled courtyard from the tall window. The sun was shining through an open portal at the entrance to the mansion, sending a shaft of light along a section of the old Purbeck stone walls. Harry let down the sash window a few inches.

A side door opened somewhere below his third-storey bedroom. Birdsong rang through the opening at the top of the window. Into view across the wet cobbles, shining in the sun from last night's rain, walked Barnaby, holding a man by the hand. Slowly the two moved across the cobbles and through the portal into the sun beyond. Even from his third-floor window, Harry could sense that something was wrong. The man pulled back his head and made the sound that he recognised as the keening from deep in the house of the night before. The strange sound, almost laughter, stopped, and the big man holding the boy's hand half turned and looked up at Harry clutching his quilt inside the bay of the third-floor window.

With the sun shining into the man's face, Harry imagined a knight of old in full armour waiting for his horse. Barnaby, not seeing the brief connection between the two men, tugged at the strong arm and led the big man out past the main gate of Purbeck Manor. For the second time since leaving the train at Corfe Castle, Harry shivered as if he'd seen a ghost. Then he understood. The man down below was Richard, eldest son of an ancient family, heir to the barony.

Quickly, Harry washed in the cold water he poured into the bowl from the jug and dressed in the clothes he had worn on the train and the walking shoes he had taken from his bag that was still at the railway station. Then he opened the door to the inner corridor, turned right, away from the end window, and found the central stairs he had climbed the previous night. He was ravenously hungry. Following his nose and the smell of coffee and fried bacon, Harry reached the breakfast room that overlooked the terrace.

"Morning, Harry," said Robert. "Sleep all right?"

"Perfect, Robert."

"Help yourself. We all just come and go for breakfast. The little spirit burners keep the food and coffee hot. We'll take a drive to the station when you're finished and see the Pringles."

"Well I thought we'd go rabbit shooting," said Merlin, coming into the room. "We don't have to take the dogs. The rabbits are making an awful mess of the kale that father so wants to feed to his pigs. I found the burrow yesterday when I was out walking alone. You can shoot a gun, Brigandshaw?"

"I shot my first leopard in self-defence when I was ten."

"Yes, well, I suppose you would in Africa. Do you think a leopard would be scared of me, Harry?"

"I rather doubt it," said Harry.

"I could always try."

"Only once."

"Lucky we don't have leopards in England... Cook wants to make a rabbit stew with shallots and you know how Barnaby loves rabbit stew. Come on. You can ride on over to the railway station in the trap and take Mrs Pringle a brace of rabbits. I'm sure she's sick of our chicken. I might even come with you."

"There won't be room for three in the trap," said Robert.

"Then I won't come. What kind of gun do you want, Brigandshaw?"

"I'm sure you can call him Harry," said Robert.

"Not till I've known a man for a week."

"A .22 rifle," said Harry.

"To shoot rabbits! Rabbits run you know."

"Not if you stay far enough back. Then they don't know who's killing them, and if the shot's clean the other rabbits go on eating. Same with springbok."

"How far back?"

"About two hundred yards."

"You can shoot a rabbit through the head at two hundred yards?"

"I can with my own rifle. I'll have to shoot yours a few times at a target before I use it on the rabbits. Each rifle has its own habits."

"I'll bet you five shillings you can't clean kill a rabbit at two hundred."

"I never bet with friends."

"We're not friends yet."

"Then I'd better take the bet."

"Merlin, from where are you going to get five shillings?" asked Robert.

"You don't have to tell everyone we are poor."

"My father lived in a mud hut next to a river when he first came to Africa. Everything they ate they caught or shot. Uncle Tinus said it was the best days of their lives."

"What kind of a name is Tinus?" asked Merlin, annoyed with himself for having made the bet.

"Martinus."

"Then he was a Boer?"

"Yes. A Boer general, and because he was then living in the Cape, the British hanged a brave man for treason when he was captured."

"Then he wasn't your real uncle."

"He was my father's best friend, his mentor. Oh, he was an uncle all right."

"On which side did your father fight?"

"The British."

"Why?" asked Merlin.

"Because he is an Englishman, which was why Uncle Tinus fought for the Boers. He was a Boer. Wars make a lot less sense from close up. There is nothing pretty about war. I watched him hang."


THE WAY to the kale fields was through the formal garden with its ponds and streams. The ponds were covered in weed. Thick bushes of rhododendron cut off parts of the garden, nothing having been tended for years. To Harry, the riot of so many exotic plants and trees brought an overpowering beauty that he sensed was deeply mixed with melancholy.

On a bench next to a weed-filled lily pond sat the knight without his armour. Barnaby had gone off to catch butterflies with the net he kept under the bench, the netting partly rotten.

Annabel, a sixteen-gauge shotgun under her arm, a green Robin Hood hat on her head topped by a long cock-pheasant feather, stopped at a distance to look at her older brother. Genevieve and Lucinda had preferred to stay at the house.

"From here he looks so perfect," she said, taking Harry's free arm. "Everything on the outside looks perfect. We just can't see into his head where it has all gone wrong. He's the best-looking man I have ever seen. And he's quite useless... What we are going to do when Barnaby grows up is another problem."

"What went wrong?"

"We St Clairs can only marry into the gentry. Over the years we've married into the same families time and time again. You have to change the bull to keep a strong herd. Even I know that, but don't tell my mother I know. He's going to be the last of the direct line according to Aunt Nut."

"He has brothers who will have sons. The title will continue."

"Maybe it would be better to stop with Richard."

"Families. Tribes. People. They don't just stop."

"How do we know if there is no one left to tell us?"

"Is she really nutty?"

"Not at all. They called her Nut as a child as she was sweet as a nut. That's the story. Quite eccentric, but not crazy. But she does have premonitions. She foretold her brother, my grandfather that is, would squander the family fortunes. He was a terrible gambler. When she makes one of her pronouncements we are inclined to take her seriously. Was your grandfather really a pirate?"

"There's a pirate in every man who makes money. Or so my mother says."

"He's rich?"

"He's dead. Left the company to Uncle James."

"None to your father?"

"My father is the black sheep of the family. Ran away to Africa with my mother. Grandfather cut him off without a penny. And there's a lot more to that story I'm not sure about. Mother says there are some things children should not want to know."

"So you're poor. Why did you take Merlin's bet?"

"My father made a lot of money killing elephants for their ivory. He and Uncle Tinus. He's not very proud of it. He says you kill with abandon when you're young and regret it later. We now have a farm."

"Is it big?"

"About the size of all the land once owned by your family. Robert and I worked it out."

"Merlin doesn't have five shillings."

"I know."

"What are you going to do?"

"Miss the first rabbit. Probably the second."

"He will think you were talking big."

"Do you?"

"Not after what I saw what you did to that target... It must be awfully romantic living in Africa. You're a nice man. I like nice people."

"I'm not really nice. Good at giving the appearance, maybe. What people do and think are different. I'm a guest in a lovely home. It was my fault to have boasted. All I had to do was keep my mouth shut and shoot the rabbits, and there wouldn't have been a bet in the first place... Will Richard want to join us?"

"No, he doesn't like guns."

"Then in my mind, he's more sensible than the rest of us."

THE DIRT ROAD ran back along the crown of the Purbeck Hills and gave Harry a wide view of the English countryside. Robert had the reins and the two brace of rabbits hung from the back of the trap, sporadically dripping blood from their dead mouths not a foot above the road. The larks were high in the sky and it was raining over Swanage and the distant sea. Harry could clearly make out the ruins of Corfe Castle on its part of the commanding hill.

Where his trunk would sit when it was picked up from the railway station, sat Barnaby, his legs hanging over the back of the trap between the dead rabbits, his hands holding on firmly against the jolts of the iron wheels running over the ruts in the road. Since leaving Purbeck Manor, they had seen no one, not even a farmer in his fields. There was no hedgerow beside the high road, only a line of great stones two feet high and two feet wide that had lain where they were for centuries. The horse seemed to be enjoying the exercise and kept to a spanking trot until they dipped down towards the village of Corfe Castle when the horse slowed down to a walk for the decline. They passed the Greyhound where an old man was sitting on a bench outside the open door, the handle of a pint of beer gripped firmly in a gnarled hand. The old man watched them for a moment and then dipped his face into the beer, leaving some of the froth on his moustache. Robert called his name and the old man half raised his stick.

Half a mile through the village, Robert found the railway cottage that backed the railway line on one side and the brook they had walked on the other. Climbing roses grew over the arch to the small door that had stood for hundreds of years. The railway company had inherited the cottage when they bought the strip of land in 1840 to build the narrow-gauge railway. The walls of the small house were built from dressed blocks of Purbeck stone, with a black slate roof on top, and chimney pots at the ends of the single roof. The windows were very small.

Barnaby jumped off the back and ran to the central door, which opened before he could reach the knocker. Harry caught a glimpse of the prettiest girl he had ever seen. Hand in hand the children ran off around the back of the Pringles' cottage.

"That child is absolutely beautiful," said Harry.

"'Nd they's goin' to break each other's 'earts," said Mrs Pringle, standing in the doorway. She was a large woman in width but short in stature and still she bent her head coming through the low door. Her Dorset accent was as strong as the smile on her face.

"They're still young, Mrs P," said Robert. "Brought you some rabbits instead of a chicken."

"Your sandwiches are the very best," said Harry for something to say. The woman's arms were twice the thickness of any arms he had ever seen, and they were covered white with flour up to the puffed sleeves. A red apron covered her huge stomach.

"My Tina's goin' on ten. Trouble I say. Can't mix classes. Girl's got ideas too big for 'er boots already. What's more, Mr Pringle agrees with me once in 'is life... Africa? Never been to Africa. Fact is, never been out Dorset. Dorset's good enough for us and ours. There was Walter, of course. Better come in. Made a plum pie from last year's bottled Victorias. Bet those two be in back door by now and straight into the pie. Not too much lead pellets in them rabbits?"

"None," said Robert. "My friend shot them with a rifle from two hundred yards straight through their heads."

"Two hundred yards! Bless my soul. Two hundred yards. Bring 'em in, Mister Robert, but please don't drip on my floor. I like a bit of rabbit myself. And so does Mr Pringle."

"Harry, what a treat. Mrs Pringle's plum pie."

The square table had been made long ago to fit the kitchen and, along with the old wood-burning stove, had never been taken out of the room. There was just enough space between the tables and the wall to fit a bench along each side, the benches polished by the 'slides' into the table of countless Pringles over many generations. When the railway company bought the land and found the cottage, they found Grandfather Pringle and offered him the job of clearing the track of cows and sheep when the weekly train was coming. No one in the family quite knew what Grandfather had done before joining the railways. When a man is in his cottage there is always someone giving him jobs to do. The rent was meant to have been paid to the St Clairs before the railway company came along but Robert thought it doubtful if any money had ever changed hands. A crumbled building at the back of the cottage spoke of long-dead pigs and cows. The small kitchen garden was neat as a new pin. Once, it was said, there were salmon in the brook. What with rabbits and pheasants, a man's family could eat well without having the kind of job people now expected. Robert rather liked the idea of those days. In the summer the fruit was preserved, the wood cut for winter, the wild mushrooms pickled, jams and jellies made from the wild strawberries and blackberries, hazelnuts stored, chestnuts crushed into a paste and pickled with vinegar and last year's sheep wool made ready for making into homespun family clothes. Only when the wars came along were Pringles taken from their tranquillity to fight for King and country. It was the only price they paid. When called by Lord St Clair they had followed for centuries without a word. It was their place, and they enjoyed their place in life, the good and the bad of it. Anyone other than Lord St Clair asking them to fight would have been given a rude awakening. Some people called it allegiance. The Pringles called it mutual protection.

"One of your sons fought in the war?" said Harry.

"That was Walter. Boers didn't give 'im a scratch. Now 'e's gone to Australia with a bloke 'e met in the war. My Maggie's in Australia. It's so far away. Family should stay put. There you are, see," she said triumphantly, opening the oven door. "Put it in oven, I did. Got a big piece out of my pie. That'll be Tina. Off to the river and never stop talkin' unless they're eatin'. Growing kids, I say. Now, Mister Harry, you have a taste of my pie and Mister Robert can 'ang them rabbits in the meat safe. I'm goin' to 'ave a nice cup of tea."

"They're lucky to be such good friends," said Harry.

"Since they was five. There's always a price to pay for 'appiness. Mark my words."

"This plum pie is the best I have ever eaten."

"So it should be... It's goin' to be dark 'fore you get 'ome."

"Jug Ears knows his way in the dark," said Robert.

"Funny name for a 'orse."

"That was Barnaby. We'll pick up the trunks on the way back and be home by supper."

"How many children do you have, Mrs Pringle?" asked Harry.

"Eleven last time I counted. Bunk beds and two to a bed. Tina was my last. Sort of farewell surprise. She's seven years younger than our Edward. Edward was named after the Prince of Wales when he was the Prince of Wales. Gone off to work in Swanage on a fishin' boat. Comes 'ome weekends. They all comes and goes, 'cept the two in Australia and Albert our toff, 'e's a gentleman's gentleman in London. Speaks real posh."

BY THE TIME they retrieved the trunks from the railway station, packed them on the back of the trap and perched Barnaby on top of them, Harry was looking forward to his supper as much as the rest of them. The little girl had once again stood in the doorway. On the way back in the gathering dusk, Barnaby sat as quiet as a mouse.

This time, it was Genevieve who took his hand at the stables and led Harry into the big house. She was carrying a storm lantern to show them the way. The horse had been rubbed down and put into his stable with the feed.

That night at supper there was no doubt in his mind. Granny Forrester was quite tiddly.

"You will stay for the summer?" asked Lady St Clair, when they had all finished eating.

"I'd love to," said Harry, without a thought for his career. If there was anything he wanted to do at that moment in his life, it was to spend the English summer at Purbeck Manor. Under the table, the birthday girl Lucinda, all of fifteen years of age, was again rubbing her slippered feet against his ankle.

# 2

## APRIL 1907

$\mathcal{J}$ack Merryweather had never done a day's work in his life, and after five years of debauchery, he was bored to the point of distraction. He had walked from his club in Pall Mall to 27 Baker Street for the exercise. At the age of twenty-six, he had no intention of ending up fat and pasty-faced.

It was dark. Past midnight and the gas lamps in their triangular cages spluttered and flared. A mist from the River Thames crept through the West End of London leaving the cobblestones wet and shiny. The top hat was firmly on Jack's head of chestnut hair, the opera cloak over his broad, shoulders, the silver-knobbed cane ready to come apart and reveal a three-foot steel rapier that he had never been forced to use. In his boredom (the club had been full of old fogies and not a woman worth looking at in the box he had joined at the opera), Jack rather hoped someone would give him a fight.

The idea of going to a nightclub had come and gone through his mind. For more than a year, drink and women had failed to satisfy Jack Merryweather. Part of his heritage had been envying his great-grandfather for having worked the business that had made Jack rich. He was quite sure Great-Grandfather Merryweather had never been bored.

His first sexual encounter with a woman had been when he was thirteen years old. He still remembered her name, Gloria Marshall; she was the scullery maid at 27 Baker Street. Seven years later his parents had died from a flu pandemic within days of each other. Gloria Marshall, unbeknown to

Jack Merryweather, was the reason he was to prefer women with large breasts.

It had taken a year for Jack to gain control of Great-Grandfather Merryweather's money, all of it, as Jack was the sole heir. The Merryweathers were profuse with money and scant with progeny.

Jack had been sent to St Paul's, a secondary public school, as it was close to 27 Baker Street, and the school took day boys, so Jack's mother would only have to be parted from her son during the day. His mother taking him to school in the family hansom in the morning and picking him up the same way in the afternoon, Jack was the laughing stock of the school to the day he left at the age of seventeen. Being a man of mild disposition he had never minded his mother's whim. He rather thought the drives together to and from school were the only times his mother was happy. Jack's father was a drunk.

Racking his brain for the umpteenth time, Jack tried to think of something to do with the rest of his life and came up empty. When a man was richer than most of his friends put together, ideas of working for a living were pointless.

A shady character with a hat pulled down over his eyes came into intermittent view down the dark road, appearing and disappearing as he approached and left the lamp posts. For the first time all day, Jack's boredom vanished. Gripping the knob of his cane, and the release button ready to flip off the casing to his sword, he watched the man coming straight at him, pace by steady pace, the spluttering lamps unable to reveal his face. The man wore a coat with the buttons open in the front.

'If the man has a gun, I'm done,' Jack told himself. Adrenaline pumped into his brain. The palms of his hands began to sweat. The man was almost upon him.

"Evening, Jack. Bloody awful opera. Bloody soprano sounded as if she was in pain. You need a coat at this time of year. Goodnight."

Jack, speechless, looked at the receding back of his friend, Ernest, and then an idea began to formulate.

ALBERT PRINGLE HAD BEEN WAITING up for his gentleman as he had done every night for two years. The rest of the servants had gone to bed in the three-storey house. Sometimes his gentleman went straight up to bed.

Albert waited in the downstairs maid's sitting room and watched the board. The flap dropped for the main sitting room and Albert picked up the round, silver tray with the single cut glass, the decanter of whisky and the tall syphon of soda. With the tray firmly balanced on the palm of his right hand, he prepared to be of service.

Upstairs the counterpane had been removed from the gentleman's bed, a corner of the sheets and blankets layered back, the carafe of water sat next to the tall glass, the red satin dressing gown laid at the foot of the bed with the slippers on the floor beneath, and the window left open exactly three inches: the gentleman had a fetish for fresh air, even in the middle of winter.

Opening the sitting room door with his left hand, Albert was confronted by a frown, an opera coat thrown on the settee and the cane propped next to the fire.

"You are still wearing your top hat, sir."

"So I am, Pringle. Sit down."

"I'd rather stand, sir."

"We are going to Africa, Pringle."

"Why, sir?"

"To shoot tigers."

"The tigers, I rather think, sir, are in India. In Africa they have lions."

"I believe there is a Colonial Shipping liner leaving for Cape Town two weeks on Thursday. I thought I was going to be attacked and had my finger on the button. Attacker turned out to be Ernest Gilchrist. Frightfully nice chap. Just pack a good trunk. We'll buy all the guns in Cape Town. They'll know all about that sort of thing."

"Have you ever fired a gun, sir?"

"No. But it's very simple. You point the gun and pull the trigger. Elephants are as big as haystacks."

"But they move. Haystacks stay where they are before and after the shot... If you don't mind the impertinence of my asking, have you been drinking, sir?"

"Opera. Bloody awful. Gilchrist agreed. I rather think I had a small whisky at the club."

"May I go home to see my mother before we leave?"

"Yes, of course. You can get some shooting practice. Ask one of the St Clairs. I'll give you a note."

"I've known them all my life. I once had occasion to use Mister Robert's twelve-bore. Nearly knocked me over backwards. You have to keep the butt firmly into the shoulder if you do not wish to sustain an injury."

"Good. You're an expert. I can rely on you, Albert. Tomorrow you shall go and book me a large cabin on the SS *King Emperor*."

.  .  .

FOR A PROFESSIONAL NAME Lily White was something of a misnomer, and by the time she reached thirty, only her old mother knew she was born Lily Ramsbottom, south of Wigan. She had been an only child and the cause of her mother's dishonour. Like other people in life, she had no knowledge of her father, and like them, she kept the fact to herself.

With a face like an angel and large breasts, she had set out for London when she was seventeen years old to leave her sordid past and the Ramsbottom name behind. She had one intention in her life: she was going to trade her body for a husband above her class who was rich.

Her only way into the kingdom of wealth was through the theatre. Many a duke had married an actress. Many a man of high position could trace his mother back to the West End stage, and very few, when they did this, wished to trace their mothers further. Somehow the myth and fantasy of the stage bore a new life and obliterated the past... For Lily, all would have been well if she could act, dance or sing.

By the time she was eighteen, her sights had sunk from dukes and earls to any man who would marry her. If she could have suffered dirty old men she might have had a chance. By nineteen she was a young dandy's mistress, a kept woman, a courtesan. By twenty she had changed hands twice. By the time her large breasts caught the eye of Jack Merryweather she had lost all count of the gentlemen who had passed through her life, some kind, some not so kind. Regularly she sent money to her mother with fictitious descriptions of her life on the stage. The rest she saved and invested in three per cent Consols, money as safe as the Bank of England. If she was not going to marry wealth she was going to make it herself, shilling by shilling. Hard work whatever the kind, she told herself, was always the best way in the end.

Jack came round to the small flat he rented for Lily at eleven o'clock in the morning.

Earlier, Albert Pringle had drawn his bath with the help of the staff carrying buckets of hot water up the stairs to Jack's bathroom where he had soaked for half an hour, intermittently calling for more hot water. Often the idea he took to bed, like quite a few young women, was not as good the next morning as it had been the night before. The great safari, to his great surprise, was alive and well in the morning.

After a good breakfast, he had set off to visit Lily and tell her of his good news.

"Can I come with you, Jack?"

"Don't be silly, Lily. Women don't go on safari. Your beautiful body would turn a nasty brown. Now, aren't you glad for me? I've at least found something to do. We sail for Cape Town two weeks on Thursday."

"You said I wasn't going." Lily tried her best sulk.

"Pringle and I."

"Can't I go as far as Cape Town?"

"And what are you going to do there?"

"Wait for you, Jack," she said in a small voice, shifting her blouse to emphasise her bust.

"We wouldn't be able to travel as husband and wife."

"Oh, Jack. You are so kind. Even a very small cabin."

When going to the colonies, Jack thought to himself in retrospect, it was better to take with you whatever you needed.

WHEN HE LEFT to walk to his club for lunch, Lily smiled to herself. Men are so predictable. Maybe I'll find what I'm looking for in the colonies. She began to hum a song she had once tried to sing in a music hall. As usual, she was out of tune.

THREE SLICES of cold roast pork, a spoonful of apple sauce and a tossed green salad saw Jack through luncheon and into the reading room for his coffee and a read of the day's newspapers. Lily was a nice person for his purpose, but like everyone else in his life, she always wanted something. He didn't mind the money side of the matter, it was the reorganisation that made him wonder if it was all worthwhile. Jack knew as much as anyone that Lily was in it for the money, but that applied as much to his tailor. An allowance, a flat, if small, in the capital of the world, and the girl wanted to go to Cape Town. Why couldn't people be satisfied with what they had, he asked himself, oblivious to the irony.

For half an hour he read the morning newspapers and then settled back in his leather armchair. There was nothing much in the papers, he decided, that hadn't been, since the end of the Boer War. Content that the empire was stronger than at any time in its history, Jack Merryweather put his head back and fell fast asleep in his chair.

When he woke, the coffee was quite cold on the low round table where he had left the club's newspapers. Looking at his fob watch on the end of its gold chain, for the life of him, he could think of nothing to do. He was the only member of the club in the room.

'If you are bored with London you are bored with life' ran through the back of his mind. He had heard it from someone, somewhere... Then he remembered what was in the back of his mind. He would have to send

Pringle a second time to the offices of the shipping company for Lily's ticket... If he had a dog he could take it for a walk in Green Park. He sometimes even wished he could be more like his father. At least when drunk a man doesn't feel the slow passage of time; something he would never admit, not even to himself. He was going to miss the summer season, he thought briefly; racing at Epsom, cricket at Lord's, tennis at Wimbledon. Then he thought of Lily. With a little piece of luck, she might like staying in Cape Town for the rest of her life. He wouldn't mind. She was a nice girl. At least he would then have to spend time looking for another mistress. A young man had to have a mistress, of that much he was quite sure.

Then he got up and looked out of the window into Pall Mall. It wasn't raining. Briefly, a bright sun shone on the wide street. He would go for a good walk in Green Park even if he didn't have a dog. A constitutional walk would do him good. He would think of something to do after he had finished his walk in the park. He had seen every show in London so there was no point in thinking about that idea. Maybe he would meet someone new. He would not think of Africa in case he changed his mind.

THE TALL TREES were mostly bare, the conifers looking old and tired of winter. Under one stark tree, where he was resting for a moment, Jack saw new buds of spring; some leaves, small, lime-green in colour, had broken from the sticky buds. Along the length of Piccadilly on its way into Hyde Park and towards Buckingham Palace, carriages, mostly closed against the chance of showers, were temporary homes to gentlewomen out of their townhouses to sample the sweet fresh air of spring.

One woman stood in the park alone, fifty feet from Jack, covered from high neck to the toes in leather boots, a black silk dress with long sleeves puffed at the wrists, a brown hat cocked front and back and feathered on one side, black ringlets falling past her ears, dark brown eyes burning, the power of stillness defying the movement in the park and on the road, a suffragette sign held aloft in black, gloved hands. Jack read the sign and smiled, the idea of women and parliament absurd to him. The black-clad lady with the burning eyes wanted the vote for women. Women, like Lily, who had never read a newspaper or made other than a personal decision in her life and never would.

'Ah, lovely lady of the placard,' he said to himself. 'Leave the painful job of politics to wise old men who have read and understood the sad, blood-soaked history of man. Oh, sweet lady with the ringlets, don't you understand? They are not interested in women, they are not interested in you. All they want is power.'

For ten minutes he watched the young woman. No one else even looked her way. Like Harry Brigandshaw, far away in Dorset, Jack Merryweather felt an inexplicable disquiet. When he looked back from his shiver the girl and placard had gone. He continued his walk, wishing he had a dog. Somewhere in his mind, he had read a poem about a brown-eyed girl with ringlets down her face. From right past the small orchestra on its stand playing Strauss, to the end of the park itself, he racked his brains.

"When I reach home I will write it myself."

Then he smiled to himself and quickened his pace in the direction that would take him home. Writing poems was something else Jack never told anyone he was doing.

AFTER HALF AN HOUR of playing with words on a sheet of white paper, Jack gave up. What he wanted to do was evoke the burning brown eyes and the black ringlets set against the white, rose-tinged skin, the cheekbones reddened by the spring wind. He had forgotten all about the placard. Like everything else in his life, he was good to a point and then nothing else happened. For most of his life, Jack had been trying to find a talent. Someone had even said collecting stamps could be a talent, but after buying some blank stamp albums and a large box of mixed stamps that he was told by the stamp dealer might just contain a Penny Black, he lost all interest. Trying to sort them into countries had bored Jack to tears, and he would not have recognised a Penny Black if he had seen one. The albums and box full of stamps were still somewhere in the house.

He pulled the cord that would drop a flap in the box in the maid's sitting room telling Pringle to bring up his tea. From down the stairs, he heard the knock on the front door. There was the sound of feet from his downstairs passage and the front door to 27 Baker Street creaked open. He would have to tell Pringle to again oil the hinges. A murmur of voices preceded loud footfalls on his stairs coming up towards his study.

"Jack, I need a drink. May I come in?"

"Come in, Ernest. I've just ordered some tea."

"My dear chap, it's six o'clock and long past drinking tea... What were you doing last night? For a moment I thought you were going to hit me with your cane."

"I rather hoped you were going to shoot at me."

"Whatever for? I would never do something like that."

"I was bored and I didn't recognise you, Ernest, until you said good evening. Fact was, you looked like a bit of a thug with your coat hanging open. Could easily have had a gun."

"Come on, we'll go to the Berkeley. The cab's waiting for us so please hurry... Pringle, for goodness sake, take away that tea. It's past six for heaven's sake... You're not sick are you, Jack?... You'd better put on your coat. I told you that last night. Pringle, be a good chap and get his hat and coat."

"The shipping company was very accommodating," said Albert Pringle diplomatically, the ticket for Miss Lily White propped against the silver teapot.

"For heaven's sake put down the tea tray."

"Thank you, sir. I'll get your hat and coat."

"What shipping line?" asked Ernest Gilchrist. No one spoke. "What's all this about a shipping line?"

"I'm going on safari. Now there's an idea. Why don't you come too?"

"I've never heard of anything so ridiculous in my life. You really do need a drink, Jack. We'll ask Paterson to make us a cocktail."

Deftly, Jack picked up from the tray the envelope with the ticket and locked it in the bottom drawer of his desk. Not wishing Ernest to see his poetry, he crumpled up the sheet of white paper and dropped it into the wastepaper basket under the desk.

THE FIRE WAS BURNING in the large grate away from the windows. The cocktail lounge was small and private with comfortable sofas and coffee tables for the drinks. When Ernest sat down opposite Jack Merryweather across the low, round table his eyes strayed around the room.

"Now there's some luck," said Ernest. "There's Sallie Barker with her mother. You mind if I go across, Jack?" The waiter had taken their order and Ernest went off to a nest of sofas and chairs behind Jack. The drinks came and Jack waited for Ernest.

"Do you mind if we join Mrs Barker and her daughter? Paterson, do me a big favour and move the drinks to the other table and ask Mrs Barker what they are having to drink."

Jack stood up and turned to follow the drinks. Then he stopped. It was the girl with the burning brown eyes and the black ringlets. She still wore the brown hat cocked at both ends with the feather on the one side. The placard was nowhere to be seen. The girl did not recognise him. She was perfect to look at. There was no doubt about that. Jack wondered why it was always when you were going somewhere else you meet someone special. And when Sallie Barker spoke she had a lovely voice.


SALLIE BARKER HAD READ the contempt in Jack Merryweather's eyes back in the park. Nothing was ever what it seemed to be. The only surprise was the rich man her mother had set her up to meet was the same man who had contemptuously stared at her in Green Park.

She was nineteen years old and the only asset left in the family that might be worth anything. She was being sold in a manner of speaking. The genteel called it finding a husband; not any husband, just a rich husband to whom she would belong for the rest of her life. She had only twice before stood in public with a 'Votes for Women' placard. Even though her mother was a staunch suffragette, Mrs Barker knew the value of a rich husband. The contradiction was clear to Sallie. She even understood why they wanted her, Sallie, to hold the placard and not one of the girls with eyeglasses. A girl unable to find a husband would be more likely to want to have the right to independence, a job, a means of supporting herself. A pretty girl was thought to get the message across better to the men as men mostly only took notice of pretty women.

Well, whatever they wanted, she would do their bidding. There wasn't an option. She had no training, other than from Mrs Barker to be a good wife and mother.

When the man she had been set up to meet said he was going to Africa she was quite relieved. She didn't like men who looked down their noses. The man was good-looking but had the personality of a wet dishcloth. He even sipped his drink. Poor Mother. Finding her a rich husband was not easy. And with Father dead and buried six months ago they needed the money. Soon the word would be out that Jim Barker had died bankrupt. Sallie's mother had taken up with the suffragettes soon after his death. Before he died, everything looked very rich. After he died, very poor. The bank had owned the business and the house after they called up the personal surety. Barker and Sons (there weren't any sons, but it looked better on the sign than plain Barker) had been viable when her father was alive. The wool trade was very personal, and the business died with him in the river. Her father had drowned himself. Her mother called it a terrible accident and concentrated on finding Sallie a rich husband. It was their only chance.

Ernest Gilchrist was going on as usual. He was such a bore.

.  .  .

JACK ALWAYS THOUGHT he must look more stupid than he really was. Having inherited Great-Grandfather Merryweather's money, he had also inherited the old man's sense of its value. Left to his own devices, Jack was sure he could have made himself a good living. He rather thought he would have enjoyed making himself a good living. An educated Englishman had the whole empire waiting at his feet. Though he had never bothered taking himself to university (like so many other things in Jack's life, with so much money it seemed rather pointless – you had to do something with a degree if you had one), he had read consistently and well. Reading was one of his passions.

Ernest Gilchrist had never once before asked him to go for a drink in the Berkeley. They had dined together and in company many times but never gone for a drink. They were what people called friends.

"Are your families related?" he said sweetly to Ernest Gilchrist as he sipped his second dry martini.

"Yes. Well. Matter of fact. Yes, I rather think we are."

The girl gave Jack a withering look, and the mother looked uncomfortable. Then he had it. His memory, bad at the social functions, never forgot what he had read in a newspaper.

"I was so sorry to read about Mr Barker," Jack said to the mother.

The mother went white but the girl, to his surprise, smiled. She had a very pretty smile. Ernest Gilchrist crossed and uncrossed his legs and Jack felt sorry for them.

"Why don't we all have supper together?" he said on the spur of the moment into the silence. "There's a place in Soho that serves the best Greek food in London. Do you eat Greek food, Mrs Barker?"

"Yes, I do, Mr Merryweather."

"And Miss Barker?"

"I am partial to the way Greeks cook lamb," said the girl almost laughing.

"Good. Because we don't have to change for dinner. I hate going to change for dinner when I'm having a good time. Ernest, I hope you will not mind if I insist the supper is on me."

"Not at all, dear chap. Very good of you."

The only thing he did not understand was the coincidence of the park. He was about to ask when he saw the girl very slightly shake her head. He was going to enjoy his evening after all.

Jack turned the story of Jim Barker over in his head. Poor sod, he drowned himself in the Thames when he knew he had run out of money. Jack thought having to start all over again would be a lot of fun, but he didn't have a wife and daughter to support.

While they were driving in the cab to the Greek restaurant, Jack racked his brains to remember who in his club had told him Barker was bankrupt. The newspaper had called it a drowning accident. So what, all that mattered was he and the girl knew where they stood with each other. They could have a good evening without all the nonsense. Why were people always after his money? And he wasn't a fool. Only fools were easily parted from their money, he told himself.

THE NEXT AFTERNOON, just before her stint in Green Park, Mrs Barker explained to Sallie the exact details of their predicament. The only salvage from the bankruptcy of Mr Barker was five hundred and ten pounds plus a few shillings her husband had left next to the potting shed at the end of the garden. The gardener and gardener's boy had no idea what was underneath the compost heap.

"If I have to run away, look under the compost heap. There's always brass where there's muck." The last sentence was spoken in the accent of Mr Barker's parents who had made money. At the time, Mrs Barker had cringed at the broad Yorkshire accent. He was drunk on a bottle of port after their guests had left. She had no idea what he was talking about. She hoped her daughter, who had gone upstairs to bed, had not been reminded of Mr Barker's ancestry. She had, of course, married him for his money, ignoring the fifteen year age gap. At that moment of compost heaps and common parents, not even the eleven servants in the house and garden had made her marriage worth its while. She hated her life for always having to be dependent on men.

The servants left altogether a month after the drowning when she was unable to draw money to pay their wages. They had never liked her so that side did not matter. From very rich to digging under the compost heap with a shovel in one month. The cuttings from the autumn's cut-back were quite hot in the centre and the smell was sweet. Determined and desperate, she carried on digging and found a black painted cash box without a lock. Inside was the money but no note. She rather thought her husband didn't like her either.

The money belonged to the bank like all his assets. She pulled up her long skirt and stuffed the notes up inside her knickers. The coins she kept in her hand. She threw the empty black box into the fish pond and watched it sink out of sight. The lilies were thick where she had thrown the box. For weeks she schemed her way out of trouble, even joining the movement for women's rights. All they wanted was money to pursue their campaign so that hadn't been any good to her.

"I'm forty-one, Sallie. Forty-one years old. I was never pretty like you, which is why I married your father. I was well bred if nothing else. It was not meant to end like this. I rather think before the tradesmen make a fuss we had best leave this country. Your father left a box next to the potting shed so we still have some money. A little money. A very little money. I had thought of India, as even quite plain girls have found husbands in India. There are very few white women of breeding who go to India. It is far too hot. Last night that young man gave me our last hope. We will sail to South Africa on the SS *King Emperor*. I have made enquiries. We will take a small cabin together, the smallest in the first class. If needs be, another ship will take us on to India."

"He's not going to marry me, Mother. Please. We'd end up destitute far from our home. Mr Merryweather knows your plan perfectly well."

"He probably does, but he likes you. I was watching you while I ate that delicious roast lamb. In Cape Town, Ernest has a cousin he has never met. They are also cousins of ours. He has written them a letter for me to take to Cape Town. They can't throw a blood relation on the streets. Not in the colonies. There will be no prospects for a penniless widow of forty-one, so I shall take a job as a governess, and no one here will know my shame. You are beautiful. Our cousins will welcome you with open arms. Pretty, well-bred girls are always welcome in the colonies. Now, run along into the park. Mrs Chilcott insists we contribute something to the cause. The rent on this flat is due the day the SS *King Emperor* sails from Southampton. Ernest will escort us to the boat. Such a pity he has no money. He likes you, my dear. I rather think it's why he's been the only one willing to help. Mr Merryweather will have a great surprise when the ship sails... You'd better go now before it begins to rain. There's that woman."

"Come in, Mrs Chilcott," Mrs Barker sweetly said to Mrs Chilcott who still had money. "How many girls do we have today for the park?"

"There's Sallie, I'm afraid. Just Sallie."

"You can always rely on Sallie."

The placard for Sallie to carry was in the hansom cab waiting at the kerb outside the rented flat. As she got in to be driven to the park, a sharp April shower drummed down on the roof. She was a little frightened at the prospect of leaving England. Familiarity was comfort in itself. Then there was the adventure, and she was only nineteen years old. By the end of supper in the Greek restaurant, the wet dishcloth she had thought of as Mr Merryweather's personality, had not been so wet at all.

When they reached Green Park the rain had stopped drumming on the roof of Mrs Chilcott's hansom cab. Mrs Chilcott, of course, would stay out of the rain and trouble. She was a firm believer in telling other people to do the work. Mrs Chilcott wished to be the first woman member of the House of Commons. She would go down in history. She would be remembered.

Sallie looked around for Mr Merryweather, but he was nowhere to be seen.

ALBERT PRINGLE STOOD outside the tradesman's entrance and pulled the chain for the third time. Inside the kitchen, the bell rang as the long chain jerked it up and down. He was full of one of his mother's plum pies. There was no doubt in his mind. For as long as he might stay in London as a gentleman's gentleman his mother would always be the best cook in the world. The thick pastry covered in nutmeg, held up in the middle of the pie by the upturned old cup with the broken-off handle, was delicious. For a boy to grow up in a house with a mother that could cook was the greatest blessing a boy could ever want. That, and a happy family where everybody laughed. Well, they laughed more in Dorset than all the rich he had seen in London. Most of them did.

The old house was unusually quiet. No one came to the door. Turning back, he looked over the low stone wall into the herb garden that had been laid out in the time of Robert St Clair's great-great-grandfather. The garden was a blessing for the cook and the rest of the village for that matter. When the gardener carefully cut back the plants at the end of the growing season the cuttings were tied with raffia string and hung in the shed next to the kitchen garden to dry. Anyone who did any business with the Manor was allowed to take away bunches of the dried herbs. They only had to ask the head gardener first. The Pringle cottage by the stream had always smelled mysterious for as long as Albert could remember. Big bunches of herbs hung away from the stove in the kitchen, just low enough for Mrs Pringle to reach up. He had eaten stews without herbs away from home. They never had the same taste.

The telegraph boy from the village walked into view. Albert could just see his head over the hedge. The yew hedge around the kitchen garden on the side near the back road to the Manor was not very high. The boy had been walking the most part of the morning. His shoes were very old, having passed down three brothers before they reached him. The boy had not seen Albert though they knew each other. Everyone knew everyone else in Corfe Castle. Albert knew the boy would be hungry and looking forward to a good lunch in the maid's kitchen. All telegraph boys were given a lunch. It was one of the rules at Purbeck Manor. There were two telegraph boys at the village post office, and they fought for the chance of walking to the Manor and Cook's lunch. Not all the mothers were as good cooks as Mrs Pringle or Cook. Many of the houses didn't have enough food to cook because the fathers were lazy. Albert had always been grateful his own father wasn't lazy. He rather thought his mother wouldn't have allowed it, anyway.

The telegraph boy had still not seen Albert standing behind a clump of shrubbery, and almost jumped out of his skin when Albert called his name. Albert liked to play small jokes on people.

"There's nobody in. No lunch for you, young Fred."

The boy was twelve years old and looked crestfallen. The shine of expectation in his eyes had gone out like a light. The small leather pouch hung over his small body by a strap and was buttoned down tight.

"There must be someone. The house is so big." The boy piped the words in the Dorset brogue that was soft on the ears.

"Three times I rang the bell," said Albert.

"Then ring it again. I'm very hungry. There wasn't any breakfast."

Albert rang the bell an extra good ring and felt sorry for the boy. The kitchen door opened in an instant.

"What you want, Albert Pringle? You most in London they say. All posh."

"I've got a telegram," piped the boy.

"Who's it for?"

"Can't read."

"Give it to me... Who's Mr Brigandshaw? Must be that friend of Mister Robert's. Come in, boy. Albert Pringle! Stay where you are. Not a foot over my step."

"I've come to see Mister Robert."

"That might be so but does Mister Robert want to see you?"

Albert smiled to himself. Villagers who left the village were never popular when they came home. Unless they came home from a war. Then they were popular.

With the kitchen door shut in his face, Albert went off to look for himself. The rule was to show yourself to Cook first. Then you could do what you liked. Almost everyone in the village knew their way around the Manor.

HARRY BRIGANDSHAW TOOK the cable from the small boy and gave him a shilling. The boy's face was plastered with food and grubby marks showed where he had wiped his face with the back of his dirty hand. Robert was talking to a man in a town suit who was speaking with a false accent; from Harry's experience, once a man reached eighteen there was no point in trying to change. At Oxford, they had called him the Colonial as much for his nasal accent as where he lived. He was proud of who he was, proud of his upbringing on Elephant Walk and his schooling in Cape Town at Bishops.

Robert was trying to explain to the man from London how to load and fire a Stephen Grant shotgun. There were two barrels and the firing mechanism was free of pull-back hammers. Harry had missed most of the early part of the conversation while he was mucking out the stables. He had been more interested in the long, one-sided conversation Lord St Clair was having with Daisy while the sow ate out of His Lordship's hand.

"Tried it once with Hector," Lord St Clair had said to him happily from the pigsty outside the stable door. "Damn boar wanted my hand as well as the apple. He won't even let me tickle him behind the ear. You don't mind mucking out the stables, young man?"

"Worst thing in life is having nothing to do. No. I love horses."

The telegram had reached him having first gone to Oxford. The rule was always to leave a forwarding address even though he wasn't going back to university. The cable was from his maternal grandfather and had been sent from the Salisbury post office in Southern Rhodesia. The name of the sender 'Sir Henry Manderville Bart' was clearly marked on the top of the telegram. That and where it had been sent from.

Just as Harry read the message, Albert Pringle fired the twelve-bore shotgun, accidentally firing both barrels at the same time.

Lucinda, who was swinging on one half of the stable door trying to show Harry her ankle again, giggled. There was always something impulsively funny about someone else hurting themselves. And with the gun up to his shoulder, hoisting his trouser legs up by the braces, Albert Pringle was wearing red socks for goodness sake. She rather thought her giggle at the red socks had broken his concentration. At least someone was paying her attention. She gave an elaborate back kick to rid herself of the stable door and fell in the dry hay clutching her ankle in what she hoped was a pretty disarray. She waited for Harry to run to her and pick her up off the floor. The seconds ticked and nothing happened. Slyly she turned to him, hooding her eyes. He was standing stock still staring at Fred the telegraph boy from the village. All thought of flirtation left her face, replaced by puzzled concern.

"What is it, Harry?"

"My father's been killed by an elephant. My father! My father could never be killed by an elephant." Then he was crying like a child and Lucinda ran and put her arms around his waist.

Lord St Clair found them clinging together while Fred picked up the fallen telegram, which he gave to Lord St Clair.

"Oh, my God," said Lord St Clair. "Fred, go up to the house and tell my wife to come down here immediately."

Leaving his youngest daughter hugging Harry, he walked out into the spring sun. Life had its habits of moving very fast. Bess would know what to do for the boy. She was good at those things. She was the kind of person who was always a comfort.

# 3

# LATE APRIL 1907

*F*ifteen days later, Harry Brigandshaw stood on the first-class deck of SS *King Emperor* looking down at a tug pulling the liner away from the pier. The powerful boat towed the long steel cable in unison with a second tug pulling the stern. A brass band was playing patriotic music as the ship broke free from the shore. The ship was owned by Colonial Shipping, the company founded by his grandfather, who had first sailed Sir Willoughby Potts to the Pacific. Harry had not paid for his cabin, Uncle James had seen to that; his uncle had taken control of the shipping line after leaving the army at the end of the Boer War after Harry's grandfather died of a heart attack.

Harry had first gone up to London to visit his grandmother in her South Kensington flat. She lived with a companion and a Pekinese dog. He went to his grandmother out of courtesy more than love. They were strangers, a product of his grandfather's vindictiveness. The rumour went that Harry's father had run away to Africa with Harry's mother who, at the time, was married to Harry's uncle. One day soon he would make his mother tell him the whole story. He rather thought his birth had had something to do with it all.

"You're a good friend, Robert," he said to Robert St Clair standing next to him, both leaning on the wide wooden rail. "There are some times in life when a man just doesn't want to be alone."

"Your uncle was generous giving me passage."

"They are all suffering from guilt. Grandfather again. The family skeletons in the cupboard. We'll have to sit at the captain's table. Part of the family rules. Let's hope the Bay of Biscay is not rough. You've never sailed before?"

"My poor sisters. All three of them are in love with you." Down below the three girls were waving madly, faces turned up to the high deck of the big ship. The whole St Clair family had come to see them off at Southampton.

"Don't be so silly, they're your sisters!"

"Lucinda swore to Mother she has a broken heart."

"She's just turned fifteen!... It's my poor mother we have to worry about. And Madge. And George. They are my sister and brother."

"You remember I said I would never leave England."

"This is a holiday, looking after a friend in need. You are not leaving anything. The best bit about going away from home is coming back again. That man down there playing the cornet is dreadfully out of time."

"He is, isn't he? Granny Forrester was rather choked up when I was leaving. Potty slipped me ten quid... I'm hungry."

"Why don't we find a bar and have a drink? There will be snacks at the bar so you won't starve before lunch."

"You think the food will be all right?"

"I'm quite sure." Harry smiled to himself. For a brief moment, he had forgotten his father was dead.


BEING A SENTIMENTAL SOUL, tears ran softly down Lily White's cheeks and disappeared into her ample bosom. The tugs had left the ocean liner and had turned back to port. The coal-fired steam engines vibrated in the soles of her feet and the palms of her hands that were holding the railing in the second-class section of the ship. She had briefly caught Jack Merryweather's eye before boarding. For everyone else on the ship, they did not know each other. Albert Pringle had seen her luggage on board. The lady with whom she was to share the cabin had a London accent that the lady, who was not a lady, tried to hide. Lily, smiling to herself, was sure their predicaments were similar. Good-looking women from the lower classes either became their husband's servants or went adventuring. At the thought, she wiped the last tear from her cheek with a gloved finger and let her excitement rise. Even if she never saw England again, it would mean she had found a future for her life that was not drowned in drudgery: chapped hands from washing, flushed face from cooking over a hot stove, the constant fear of penury for her and her children. With just one life to live, despite the vicar's promises, she wanted more than that.

She turned her back on the sea and spread her arms down the wide wooden rail, looking up at the ship's superstructure, two raked funnels throwing most of the soot over the ship into the Solent as they passed by the Isle of White and headed for the English Channel.

The ship and Lily White alike were free of their umbilical cords.

"There's nothing more exciting than the unknown," said Albert Pringle, as he joined her at the rail. "You ever thought how many Englishmen left these same shores? First America and Canada, now Australia, New Zealand, and South Africa. As a race, seems we're never satisfied... You ever been on a ship before?"

"Never."

"Me neither. One of the seamen says the Biscay's as smooth as a baby's bottom. Be nice not to be seasick. Woman all right in your cabin? Bloke seems okay in mine. Just to sleep, see, so it's not too bad. They try to put the same ages together. Lucky not to be travelling third. Sleep in bunks inside the ship they do. No portholes. Least we both got portholes, though I can't open mine. Too close to the water line. Only the toffs in first can open their windows, like. You ever thought about being rich, Lily?"

"All the time," she said, turning round to look down at the sea. The gulls were flying close to the water, screaming in a long series of plaintiff cries.

"Me too. Just be nice not to have to suck up to people. Never to have to think about money. That must make a man very happy."

Lily began to laugh. She had a good, deep chuckle of a laugh. "I hope we're right," she said. "About the happiness. All Jack moans about is having too much money and not enough to do."

"He can give me some."

"I wonder if we are all destined never to find what we think we are looking for?"

"Cheer up, Lily. Tell you what, Mr Merryweather gave me an allowance to look after you, seeing the circumstances. There's a bar back there I just passed."

"Can ladies drink in public?"

"Who cares? We're on board ship. The rules are different. Don't you feel different now we've left Blighty? Now we's all English away from home. What's your tipple, Lily?"

"Gin. I'll have a gin. Do you despise me, Albert?"

"Course not. Why should I? We both serve his purposes but in different ways... You and I are going to enjoy our first voyage. Come on. They've got a thing called deck quoits. That's after the gin, mark you. We'll get one of them seamen to show us how to play. Deck quoits! Has a nice ring to it don't you think? 'Who's for deck quoits?'" he said in his most lah-di-dah imitation. Then he took his eyes off Lily White's bosom and led her to the small bar next to the second-class swimming pool. There was a strong smell of the wide-open sea.

FROM THE FIRST-CLASS rail that looked down on the second-class swimming pool, Jack Merryweather guardedly tinkled his fingers at Lily White who did not seem to see. The rail ran across the centre of the ship with steep steps from the second class up to a locked gate on the first-class rail. The classes had been separated permanently for the rest of the voyage.

Slightly miffed, Jack turned away as his servant led his mistress under the first-class deck to what Jack suspected was a bar. For a brief moment, he was almost jealous.

"Ah, Mr Merryweather!"

"Ah, Mrs Barker."

"This is a surprise. You do remember my daughter Sallie? We thought you saw us earlier on but were not sure. You remember that delightful restaurant and our cousin Ernest Gilchrist? He waved us goodbye from the dock. Such a well-mannered young man. Do you know anyone on the ship?"

"Not a soul," lied Jack.

"What a coincidence to see you here. Are you going to South Africa?"

"I rather hope so, unless the captain has changed his mind."

"Do you go on business?"

"I do not have a business, Mrs Barker. I am not in trade. Hunting is my predilection at the end of this voyage. But then we are all hunting, Mrs Barker, Miss Barker, I rather think. How long are you staying in the Cape Colony? They say the winter begins quite soon there in the Cape. The Cape of Storms. Well, this is a pleasure. It is so nice to see a familiar face in unfamiliar surroundings. We shall meet again."

"Do you know your table in the dining room?" asked Mrs Barker.

"I shall be dining with the captain."

"How fortunate."

"Depends rather on the captain and his guests."

Behind her mother, Sallie Barker's dark eyes were twinkling at Jack and both of them were trying not to laugh.

"This really is a very enormous coincidence," said Mrs Barker, knowing everyone knew it wasn't. "Until we meet tonight at the captain's welcome glass of sherry. Or do they serve rum on a ship?"

"No, I rather think the rum is reserved for the Royal Navy."

Jack, on his way down to his cabin, had a sneaking suspicion that before the voyage was out he would have an uncontrollable urge to throw Sallie Barker's mother into the sea.

There was a saying in the family, passed down to them from his great-great-grandfather: 'A man with money is easy prey.' But if they wanted to waste their last pennies on a sea voyage, who was he to stop them? They would probably have done better on a fishing trip to India, a pretty girl like Sallie Barker. And she was pretty, he thought, as he let himself into the cabin.

He walked across and closed the porthole. There was a cold wind off the English Channel, even though he loved fresh air. Well, it seemed he wasn't going to be bored. He hoped she was going to show her black ringlets for the captain's party. They were pretty.

CAPTAIN HOSEY, commanding the SS *King Emperor*, felt like a stuffed dummy in his monkey jacket and rued the day he had agreed to captain a passenger ship. To make it worse, he was forced to cut his beard to make himself look more like the philandering king who at last had succeeded his mother, Queen Victoria, to the throne of England. King Edward liked to be photographed in his naval uniform when he wasn't pursuing the wives of his subjects.

Captain Hosey was a Manxman, born and bred on the Isle of Man, and had always lived in sight of the sea. He was a rough seaman and not a man for boosting first-class passengers' egos. And to make it worse tonight, there was going to be a toffee-nosed grandson of The Captain sitting at his table. If there was one thing Captain Hosey hated most it was people spending other people's money. The Captain, founder of the line, had earned his money, even if some people had called him the Pirate.

Not even trying to hide his Manx accent, he greeted his first-class passengers one by one. The ship was neither rolling nor pitching, which was uncommon in the Bay of Biscay for the time of year. Through his feet, he could feel every throb of her engines and knew his old shipmate, Jim Green, was doing his job. The sea was always an enemy, never to be taken for granted.

Personally, before his ship sailed, Captain Hosey had inspected every part of the SS *King Emperor*, even climbing up into a lifeboat to make sure the water cask contained fresh water. He was known as fussy Hosey to his crew and liked the name. The more he fussed, the more he could push the dangers away from everyone on board his ship.

A girl with black ringlets that hung past her ears drew every man's eyes even before she joined the queue to meet the captain. Comfortable in the knowledge of his wife in the small house in Castletown with the last of their brood, young Jim, his only son, he let his eyes rest on the perfection of a beautiful woman.

"This is Mr Harry Brigandshaw, Captain," said the purser.

Harry, having seen Sallie Barker for the first time a fraction earlier, saw the direction of the captain's eyes and smiled as he put out his hand for the man to shake. He was almost sure the captain gave him a wink that had nothing to do with his grandfather. Then the purser was introducing the Honourable Robert St Clair just loud enough for Mrs Barker to prick up her ears.

"Anything is possible," said Mrs Barker, as they lined up to join the queue.

"What is, Mother?"

Putting her mouth close to her daughter's ear she whispered, "Every man in the room is looking at you. That young man shaking the captain's hand is an Honourable. His father has to be a peer of the realm."

Sallie, more interested in the young man in front of what she suspected would be an honourable twit, watched the other man take a glass of sherry from a ship's steward. His skin was somehow dark from living out of doors, but she rather hoped he was an officer in the Royal Navy. With willpower, Sallie concentrated on the back of Harry Brigandshaw's head. Then, just as he turned to take a sip of sherry, he looked up across the twenty yards that separated them, his piercing blue eyes sinking deep into her soul. She was so dumbstruck she was unable to give even a flicker of a smile in return. Then the eyes turned away, leaving her sick in the pit of her stomach.

"So there is such a thing as love at first sight," she said to herself.


THREE CRYSTAL CHANDELIERS hung from the ceiling of the first-class dining room, crowning the flower of England with a celestial light. The heavy silver cutlery shone at their places on the pure white damask tablecloths, eight passengers in evening dress at each table except the captain's, where there were twelve including the captain and the chief purser. There were no flowers on the tables for fear of the ship rolling with the swell; the legs of the tables were clamped to the deck. From a raised platform designed to look like Juliet's balcony, two fiddlers expertly scraped their bows over catgut, making a pleasant sound that lingered with the well-bred genteel conversation and the flow of stewards carrying silver dishes under silver domes to people who had never been hungry in their lives. There was a self-satisfied air of ownership in nearly every face, the face of a race of people who had reached the pinnacle of the greatest empire ever seen on earth, people certain of their heritage who feared no one, with a Royal Navy twice the size of the next four sea powers put together. The Boer War had merely been an irritation, a colonial war, a necessary use for a small portion of the treasure of the British Empire. Maybe if some of them had taken the time to count the number of ships being built by the Kaiser in Germany and the government of the United States, they would not have been so complacent.

The captain had just explained to Lady Worthington-Hall how he had begun his career at sea before the mast as a cabin boy. The lady had deliberately and slowly replaced her soup spoon in the bone china soup bowl from Royal Doulton. Then she stared at the captain for long seconds, saying not a word. The captain slurping his asparagus soup with relish, his head bent to the bowl, was ignorant of the horror in the eyes of the lady who found herself dining with a man who had once been a cabin boy, however long ago.

Harry, stifling a smile, received a glare of his own that told him clearly the lady knew his grandfather had been in trade. From his right, Jack Merryweather gave him a slight dig in his ribs and made him spill the soup from his spoon that was halfway from the bowl to his lips. From his left, Robert St Clair was desperately trying not to giggle. Across the white-clothed table, a man with a monocle, a bald head, and two rows of campaign ribbons stitched to the breast of some kind of colonial uniform, widened his eyes in disapproval at the three reprobates, causing his monocle to drop to his chest, just stopped from the soup by a purple cord that hung around a scrawny neck. The meaning of the look was clear. The three of them should be sent straight back to the nursery where they belonged.

"I sailed twice with your grandfather before he went ashore," Captain Hosey said to Harry across the table. "He was a great man."

"I never knew him despite the fact he died when I was in my teens. Fact is, when my mother and father ran away to Africa he never mentioned my name or that of my father ever again."

The captain had pushed his soup bowl away with satisfaction and was waiting for the fish. If Captain Hosey didn't like passengers on the ship, he appreciated the food, which came with the inconvenience. Then he let his mind go back many years. There had once been a rumour about The

Captain's youngest son running off with the eldest son's wife. Put a ladder up to her bedroom and carried her off with her little son and the boy's nurse. Old Captain Doyle had told the story with too much gin in his belly when both of them were ashore on leave in Liverpool before he had caught the weekly package to Douglas and the Isle of Man. The next day Boyle had told him never to repeat the story.

"I don't know the whole story," the boy was saying to him, "but now my father is dead, I intend asking my mother and my maternal grandfather for the truth."

"Maybe some things are best unanswered," said Captain Hosey. "I didn't know about your father. I'm sorry, son."

"Elephant. An elephant," said Harry, letting it hang in the air as the misery washed over him.

For the rest of the fish course, no one spoke at the captain's table.

With his mind on a problem that had vexed him all his life, Harry ate his way through the poultry, the meat course and a large bowl of ice-cream, letting the prattle of conversation go on around him without joining in. Some of the other passengers, sensing the bad undercurrent, talked polite trivia for the rest of the meal.

Harry was sure he was a bastard. There had been a church wedding of his parents at the end of the Anglo-Boer War, performed by his missionary uncle in his uncle's great new church that was to lighten the darkness of darkest Africa. They had all said the wedding ceremony was a re-avowal of a much earlier civil ceremony as, at that time, there were no Christian churches in Rhodesia. Uncle Tinus and Aunt Alison, who had once been Harry's nurse, had trekked all the way to Cape Town and a Dutch Reformed Church just in time before Barend was born. For a while, he had tried to wheedle out the year of his parent's civil ceremony from his grandmother Brigandshaw, who had finally come on a visit from England, and his Grandfather Manderville, who had lived with them in Elephant Walk for as long as Harry could remember, but to no avail. There was no other question he could ask any of his family that caused such a rapid change in the conversation.

"Am I your son?" he had asked his father before he left for his three years at Oxford University.

"Oh, yes. Don't you worry about that one, Harry. That's one thing you will never have to worry about."

"Then how was it that my mother was married to my Uncle Arthur?"

"Who told you that nonsense, Harry? Arthur was a swine. And that's a fact no one will ever deny. I have to check the gang building the weir down by the river."

"Why won't you tell me the truth?" he had said to his father's receding back. For a moment, his father stopped in his tracks and seemed about to turn round and answer his question. Then he had walked on. And now his father was dead, his grandmother Brigandshaw was living with her paid companion and the Pekinese dog in London, and everyone at the house refused to talk. Maybe someone would tell him the truth in the end.

He rather thought the captain of this ship knew the answer to his conundrum but it was not the right thing to wash the family linen in front of an employee of the family company. And then the thought came to him like a flash of light. If Uncle Arthur was the eldest son of the Pirate, sometimes called The Captain, and he had been born when his mother was married to Uncle Arthur, he was the heir to Colonial Shipping, not his Uncle James. He could still be his father's son and the legal heir to the second largest shipping line in all England. Then his thought of Robert and Jack knowing he was a bastard sent cold shivers down his spine. Then there was Madge and young George if the civil ceremony had never taken place. Being born illegitimately in England was worse than being born with one eye in the centre of the head. No gentleman would dare marry Madge if Barend did not fulfil their childhood pledge. And with Barend run away to where no one, not even his mother knew, that was unlikely. Madge would be a spinster for the rest of her life. As a bastard, the chances of ever being accepted in the first-class section of a ship were less than nothing. Captain Hosey might well be right. 'Some things are best unanswered.' But a man had to know. No man could ever go through life without knowing who he was, where he really came from. It would not be fair to his children or his children's children. And he was going to have children as without a family there did not seem to be very much in this life for Harry to make him content.

They all left the dining room to take their coffee in the lounge. With so much on his mind, he was not looking properly where he was going and would have bumped into the girl with the dark ringlets had not Jack put out a restraining hand. His reverie was rudely interrupted by the grating voice of the ringlet girl's mother.

"Good evening, Mr Merryweather. Why what a nice idea. Let us all take our coffee together. So nice for you to make new friends, and the food was so good. Perfect, some would say. Sallie and I are so impressed you are sitting at the captain's table. You must introduce Sallie to your new friends, Mr Merryweather. Mr Merryweather is an old friend of the family," she finished to no one and everyone.

"Mrs Barker, Miss Barker, may I introduce you to Mr Harry Brigandshaw of Rhodesia and the Honourable Robert St Clair of Corfe Castle. Gentlemen, Mrs Barker and Miss Barker."

"The castle, I am afraid, was knocked down by Oliver Cromwell," said Robert.

"And where then do you live, Mr St Clair?" said Mrs Barker accusingly.

"In Purbeck Manor."

"Sounds complicated to me to come from a castle that doesn't exist."

"Life, Mrs Barker, usually is," said Jack Merryweather, placating her.

'More by far than you can ever know,' thought Harry, smiling politely at the old battle-axe while he touched her outstretched gloved hand, his mind again hearing his father's voice.

'Before you marry, my son, always look at their mothers first; in the end, they all turn out like their mothers. It's the way nature's made.' But when he touched Sallie's ungloved hand he had to pull back quickly, there was so much static electricity.

"I'm so sorry," she said. "I have just removed my gloves."

There was something wrong that Harry was unable to put his finger on. The electricity had repelled him from the girl at first touch.

Then they were all swept along into the lounge, and to what later on became three good rubbers of bridge.

The mother, thought Harry when he had taken himself off to his cabin, was a right pain in the arse, but giving credit where credit was due, he admitted to himself she was a damn good bridge player. Harry, not being very good at cards, had lost one pound seven shillings and thruppence. To make it worse, Harry had had to slip Robert's losses to him under the table. The big winner that night was Mrs Barker.

As Harry went to sleep he sensed a change in the movement of the ship. There was a slight roll, followed by a pitch; the classic corkscrew. He rather suspected the dining room would be a lot less full at breakfast time. Then he fell into a soundless sleep and dreamed all night he was hunting elephant with his father.

Harry woke just before dawn, certain forever that Sebastian Brigandshaw was his father.

The swell had gone. The SS *King Emperor* steamed on majestically towards the coast of North Africa. Everyone was down to breakfast though people came and went as they wished. Jack Merryweather had eaten at the first opportunity and gone on his way. Lady Worthington-Hall replied to his cheery 'Good morning' with barely a nod. And the man who was on his way to administer some obscure African colony had removed his monocle while he ate his scrambled eggs and, to Harry, was probably as blind as a bat as he seemed to see nothing but the contents of his plate. The captain's place had not been set; Harry was to find out later, the captain only faced his passengers at dinner time, eating whatever else he wanted in his cabin or on the bridge. The girl with the ringlets was nowhere to be seen. Taking up a glass full of freshly squeezed orange juice, Harry began his breakfast.

Halfway through the meal, the colonial administrator-to-be put the monocle back in his right eye.

"Yesterday's *Times*, I'm afraid," he said, as Harry looked at the paper thrust at him across the table.

When Harry looked up the man was smiling.

"Found out who your father was, young man. After Selous and Hartley, the greatest white hunter of them all. Pity he never wrote a book like Selous."

"You forget Tinus Oosthuizen."

"He was a traitor. A British citizen who fought for the Boers. He was shot for treason."

"With the greatest respect, sir, General Oosthuizen was a Boer. He was my father's partner and my uncle in every way but blood. My father said to anyone who would listen that Tinus Oosthuizen was the greatest white hunter of them all. He never shot an elephant without measuring the weight of its tusks with his eyes. And he only killed bulls, mostly bulls thrown out of the herd by a younger bull. Uncle Tinus said his heart bled for the old bulls getting thinner and thinner with age, so old they were unable to lift their great tusks to forage for the leaves on the trees. Every one of the tusks he trekked to Cape Town to keep himself alive and have enough money to buy the farm in the Cape, which we then confiscated. And he was hanged, not even shot, sir. My father said he was a true gentleman. The British, sir, were wrong to hang a prisoner of war just because he came from the British Cape, and not the Boer Transvaal, or the Boer Orange Free State. He was a Boer. His family were Boers for generations."

"It does you credit to stand up for your uncle."

Harry made himself calm down. He knew it was imperative for an Englishman to behave himself in society.

"Thank you for the paper, sir." His hand was shaking.

"I was sorry to hear about the death of your father." The man pushed the food around his plate for a moment before going on. "I rather think it was Oliver Cromwell who said 'it was only treason if you lose'. This is my first posting to Africa. I also have a lot to learn. In the years to come when I deal with the Boers, as I am sure I will, your testimony to your uncle will remain fresh in my mind." There was a gentle smile in the older man's eyes.

"We will talk again on this voyage," he said.

"Where are you going, sir?"

"To Bechuanaland."

"Then we shall be neighbours. The railway line of Cecil Rhodes goes through Bechuanaland to reach Rhodesia."

"That much I do know."

"Of course, I'm sorry to be rude."

"Now. If you will all excuse me, I shall take my constitutional. Ten times around the deck. Too much good food and not enough exercise are bad companions."

Harry, looking at the back of the man he had been inclined to despise so short a while ago, was surprised to find how wrong the outward appearance of the man had been. The steward poured him a second cup of coffee. Then he caught the look of disapproval from Lady Worthington-Hall as his elbow searched for a rest on the table.

After a good breakfast, Harry went outside and walked around the first-class deck to where he looked over the rail onto the deserted second-class swimming pool. Then he saw Albert Pringle down below and waved. He would have walked down the steep stairs to have a chat were the gate in the railing unlocked. Having tried the gate he shrugged and waved again at Pringle. Then a group of people joined Pringle and headed under the deck at his feet to what he knew would be a bar. They were all young. When he heard them clink their glasses together and laugh he walked away. For no reason whatsoever he felt a shiver run down his spine.

Robert St Clair had still not come out of their cabin so he went down to find out what his friend was doing. When he opened their cabin door the first thing he smelt was fried bacon and coffee. Sitting up in bed, with the specially made tray that clipped on the side, Robert smiled with a mouthful of breakfast.

"You want a piece of toast, old chap?"

"I rather thought you would find a way not to miss your breakfast."

"I know, jolly good. This is just the jolly old way to live. At least have a cup of coffee. I had the steward bring two cups. You want to open the porthole and breathe the fresh air? Very important to have fresh air. You can pour your own coffee if you wish."

"Thank you, Robert."

"Absolutely my pleasure. Now, what are we going to do today?"

"Lunch is in two and a half hours," said Harry, tongue in cheek.

"This whole thing gets better and better," said Robert, ignoring the barb.

"One day you are going to be fat!"

"Probably. There's a price to pay for everything. The trick is to enjoy as much as you can when you can. They can't take away your memories." Robert buttered another piece of toast and slid it under a fried egg. Then he spread the yolk, a rich yellow to mingle with the butter.

"The steward says we have a perfect weather forecast all the way to the Cape," said Robert.

"Don't speak with your mouth full, Robert."

"That's what my mother says."

"I know."


HARRY FOUND Sallie Barker and Jack Merryweather in adjacent deck chairs. An empty deck chair stood next to Sallie that he thought most likely had seated Mrs Barker. Robert, having eaten everything on his tray, had said he was going to take a nap after such a good meal. Harry thought the fact the man was as thin as a rake went against all the rules of nature.

Harry smiled briefly at both of them and carried on down the deck, his soft tennis shoes squeaking on the wood. He had made it look as if he too was taking a constitutional. Jack, he had found out, was rich; and Harry suspected Mrs Barker had rigged their whole journey to have Jack Merryweather a captive audience for her daughter. Short of being rude or jumping off the rail, there was nothing Jack could do. There was one thing for certain: no lady would marry a prospector or a bush farmer. Ladies required company. Ladies required the trappings of civilisation. No, Jack would be the better bet when Mrs Barker found out Robert was penniless. As she would.

He was watching the bow cut into the green sea and thinking of home. He was glad to be going home to his family, even a family without his father. Oxford had been a way of learning a job and seeing the world of people.

"Ah, there you are, Mr Brigandshaw. What a lovely day."

The woman was everywhere, thought Harry. "Yes, it is Mrs Barker," he replied. He too was a captive.

"So sad to lose a father when you are so young. After you have completed your holiday I presume you will be coming back to London to run your shipping line?"

"Which shipping line, Mrs Barker?"

"Why, this one of course. You are the eldest son of the eldest son of the founder."

"You are mistaken, Mrs Barker."

"I am never mistaken, Mr Brigandshaw."

"My father who died just recently was the youngest son."

"But your father was Arthur Brigandshaw."

"My father was Sebastian Brigandshaw."

"Not according to your birth certificate lodged at Somerset House."

"You will excuse me, Mrs Barker."

"Of course. It really is a lovely day."

Finding the first steward, Harry asked the way to the ship's wireless room and told the man to please show him the way.

The room was small with one seaman on duty.

"Can you send messages to England?" asked Harry.

"We are the first ship of the line to have Mr Marconi's invention."

"And you can receive messages?"

"Yes, we can."

"Did a Mrs Barker send and receive messages?"

"I cannot say."

"According to Mrs Barker, I am the owner of this ship."

"You are Mr Brigandshaw! Well of course."

From surliness to subservience in one second, thought Harry. Well, that was the system whether he liked it or not.

"Did you show the captain her received messages?"

"Not yet."

"Then burn them. That's an order. What is your name?"

"Jenkins."

"You will never repeat the content of Mrs Barker's messages. That's an order. You will never sail on any ship again if you repeat her messages."

"Yes, sir."

"Now, who else was she enquiring about?"

"The Honourable Robert St Clair. So far there is no reply."

"The old bag's trying to find her daughter a husband."

"I don't understand."

"Poor old Jack Merryweather," he went on to himself. "Thank you, Jenkins. We may meet again."

"I hope so, sir."

"To where are your cables despatched?"

"Our London head office."

Why couldn't the old bag mind her own business, he thought, and why didn't my parents tell me the truth? If Mrs Barker could find out so easily, everyone in the family knew his father to be his uncle.

Walking back on deck he made sure Mrs Barker was nowhere to be seen. He found a quiet place between a lifeboat hung from its davits and the sea. Alone, he leaned on the rail and stared at the rushing sea, though the sea did not move, only the illusion caused by the swift passage of the ship. For a moment the idea of being very rich sent a rush of excitement to his brain, followed by the consequence of being responsible for a vast shipping line. Sobered, he felt the grip of fear churn his stomach. The African bush came running into his mind, the great highveld of Central Africa, teaming with its multitude of oh so many different species of game. He saw his house, his dogs, his horse, his family that somehow was not quite his family anymore. He heard the cry of a fish eagle and tears began to flow down his face. He felt alone in a new and horrible world of Mrs Barkers selling their daughters, with no regard for happiness, to the richest man. He saw a stuffy shipping office in London and going to work year after year in the winter dark. Never seeing the winter day, except through a grimy fog-touched window, the river ships mournfully sounding their horns in warning. He saw his freedom consumed by his wealth, gone for his natural life. In desperation, he stared and stared at the sea rushing by the ship's hull and numbed his mind... 'But of course,' he shouted in his mind. 'Uncle Arthur died young and my father married his widow.' Then the excitement receded. Even under that scenario, he was no longer his father's son. Then, in his mind's eye, he saw his father and heard his words. 'Don't you worry about that one, Harry. That's one thing you will never have to worry about.'

As the sun would break through the clouds after the main rains in Rhodesia, the truth came to Harry. His mother and father had known each other for most of their lives, that had been confirmed. The trick was to look at the dates. Three dates. The day his father left for Africa, the day he was born. The day his mother married Uncle Arthur as it now seemed she did. With the desperation brought by hope, Harry was never so glad to be a bastard. He missed his father far too much for him not to be real. Now they would all have to talk when he reached Elephant Walk. His mother, his Grandfather Manderville, his Aunt Alison who had at one time been his nurse.

By his small fob watch, an hour had passed. Feeling light of head and light of spirit, he turned his back on the sea, ducked under the forward davit and headed for the open bar that backdropped the first-class swimming pool. He was going home, free as air.

Harry tossed the first whisky down his throat and ordered another. He was the only person at the bar other than the barman. The bar had just opened. No one was in the pool as it was too cold. Old people in shawls and scarves sat in lounge chairs, staring at the pool, the water moving in the pool with the slight roll of the ship. Harry tossed back the second whisky and ordered a beer. The alcohol had gone straight to his head. Then his fuddled head asked another question as the barman poured the lager into a tall, thin glass. His mother and father had loved each other for all the years of his life. They were all happy together. And if they were all happy together, why had his mother married his uncle in the first place? The fog in his mind choked on what he had found out as the truth. Harry sipped at the beer and sadly wondered where he was going with his life.

"Ah, there you are. Such a nice nap... Isn't it rather early to be drinking, Harry? Before lunch! Well, I suppose I had better join you. I'll have a whisky to start with."

"Robert, I should be very unhappy if you didn't."

"Could you run to two, old chap?" The irony had gone straight over Robert's head.

"Absolutely. And then a beer."

"Am I that predictable? Dear oh dear. If I were rich I would stay on a boat like this for the rest of my life. Going round and round the world. Isn't it a beautiful day? Cheers, old chap. Down the hatch... Oh, there's that nice Mrs Barker who plays such good bridge. Mrs Barker! Please come and join us. You do remember my friend Harry Brigandshaw from last night? He was my bridge partner. Terrible player, but a jolly good chap... What are you going to drink? Why don't we all share a bottle of champagne? There's an hour before lunch... Oh just look! I don't believe it. There's that lovely daughter of yours, Mrs Barker. Come! Over here, Sallie. If you don't mind me calling your daughter Sallie, Mrs Barker... Be a good chap, Harry, and order us a bottle of their best champagne."

'I wonder if he thinks the girl's rich?' thought Harry as he ordered the champagne while hoping the maize crop had not failed again this year. It had been one thing to be given a free passage on the family shipping line and another to drink champagne free. And putting Robert in his cabin, which he would not have shared had he travelled alone, was not breaking the family rules. But what Uncle James had made quite clear was that, like in an officer's mess, members of the family travelling free were expected to pay for their own drinks. Colonel Sir James Brigandshaw Bart, had made that quite clear twice... Then Harry's mind went on a ramble again. If the birth certificate at Somerset House was right, then he, Harry, should have become the new baronet when Harry's grandfather had died. The family couldn't have it both ways. No wonder they were so free with the cabin. They wanted him back in the colonies as soon as possible. Maybe no one had told the college of heralds to check for the birth certificate of a certain Harold Brigandshaw. Maybe Uncle Arthur had disclaimed him. But that was contradicted by the birth certificate at Somerset House. He was thinking in circles.

He forced his mind back to the here and now. Whatever he did, he must not forget to tell Robert the girl was probably penniless. Or would it matter if they fell in love?... Oh dear, he said to himself as he looked up from signing the bar chit for the drinks, and the most expensive bottle of champagne he had ever paid for in his life. I'm the old dragon's prime target. She has that predatory look in her eye.

"Why don't you use your title?" asked Mrs Barker sweetly.

"What title?" asked Robert, surprised.

"The baronetcy your friend inherited when his grandfather died."

"I don't think so, Mrs Barker. Harry is the son of the youngest son. Now, why don't we all ask a steward to bring our champagne to that table over there?"

Robert gave Harry a peculiar look, and marched off with everyone else in tow, leaving Harry to bring up the rear.

Suddenly the champagne was a good investment. Harry watched who he thought of as the old bag, shade her eyes as her mental picture changed. She looked puzzled. Poor old Robert, thought Harry. His friend was so naïve he couldn't see what Mrs Barker was doing. But Robert, like his sisters, had grown up secluded at Purbeck Manor. There had only been Oxford to see the real world. Harry had understood that it was what you appeared to be that counted in society. Robert seemed to believe what he saw.

Right the way through drinking the bottle of champagne, Mrs Barker said not one word, to Harry's amusement. Then they went to lunch. Harry, sitting down at the table, was quite tight.

After a good lunch, he did something he had never done in his life. He took an afternoon nap. By the time he went to sleep Robert was snoring mildly. More like a fluting sound, Harry thought, as he drifted off into a dreamless sleep.

When he woke, Robert had gone, leaving his bed unmade for the steward. Harry made a mental note to tip the man more than was usual. Harry would have been happier giving away his own money rather than money that had been his father's, and the product of everyone's hard work at Elephant Walk. There had been talk in his earlier years of his father and Uncle Tinus owning shares in a shipping line that competed with Colonial Shipping, run by a renegade captain who had been fired by Harry's grandfather. The names African Shipping and Captain Doyle had never been mentioned after his Uncle Tinus was hanged.

There were too many loose ends in his life, Harry decided as he climbed out of bed, causing a slight pain inside his head for his trouble.

WHILE HARRY WAS WONDERING what next was going to come out of the family past, Albert Pringle and Lily White were leaning over the half-moon rail that cut off the second-class passengers from the third. Below the deck at another level was the third-class recreation deck at the stern of the ship. On bad days, when the forward speed of the ship competed with a headwind, black soot rained down on the stern deck above the pounding power of the twin propellers. Ignoring the cramped mass of steerage passengers, Albert watched the fluorescent wake of the ship going away with a landsman's fascination.

"They don't have much room," observed Lily.

"Immigrants, most of them. Pushin' off from mother England. There's all that gold in the Transvaal and diamonds in Kimberley. All British know the Boers are beaten. If you want a piece of the empire, got to get up and get it, Lily. Don't have to be poor or a servant for the rest of your life. Look at them what went to America. Don't fancy Australia. Too far away. In Africa, you are a white man no matter where you come from back home. I'm not coming back, Lily. Did I tell you that?"

"No, you didn't... Neither am I."

"What's Mister Jack going to say about that, Lily?"

"Nothing. He's bored with me already and too nice to say so. Poor man's permanently bored. Too much money and too much time on his hands. Probably change his mind about hunting elephant. Jack Merryweather goes where the whim takes him. He needs a bloody disaster to bring him back to life."

"Would you marry him?"

"Of course. For 'is money. When a girl gets to thirty things change. I don't have the sexual power over men I had ten, even five years ago. Another five years it'll all be gone. Why women 'ave lots of kids when they're young and sexy, so the old man won't be able to run away when her looks run out, and they all do. No getting away from nature. If the husband's rich, their wives turn a blind eye to the mistresses and take comfort in the security of the kids. Poor, they just slave away for 'im and the kids until they die of exhaustion. Money, Albert. We got to 'ave money. Money safely put away is the only security we ever 'ave for when we're old. You can't rely on anyone when you're old and no use. Except for yourself. And what you saved. Some kids look after their mums, but not all. And whoever wants to be dependent on their bloody kids?"

"What you goin' to do to make money, Lily?" asked Albert, trying to hide the clear idea of what was in his mind.

"Not that, Albert. Too old. I've got some saved. But not enough. You see that lot down there? Look at 'em. What strikes you? What's wrong down there?"

"Not enough room and no deck quoits."

"No, silly."

"They're all poor people."

"And nearly all of them are men is what I see. Most of them will get hard jobs down the gold mines. They'll be living alone, or with men, and what money they have they'll want to spend on drink and women. But there aren't jobs for women down gold mines and few jobs on tap. I count five young women down there. Combine booze and women and even a fool could syphon off their money. I'm going to start the biggest bloody whorehouse in Johannesburg and pay back all the men in my past who just wanted to fuck me and feel my boobs. You think any of them ever looked at me? Lily? Don't be daft. They were too busy looking at my cunt and my tits."

"And where are you going to find the women? People out there frown on white men taking up with black women. Call it goin' native. Same in India, I 'eard from a bloke who worked for an Indian army colonel. Nice flat in the west end to himself. Worked six months every two years. We may be servants, but if you get that out of your mind, we live the same as them. Gentlemen's gentlemen are looked after in the wills. Look after 'im proper and he'll give you a pension."

"And what if Jack Merryweather marries? His new wife will throw you in the gutter. The last thing any woman wants in the house is a confidant that knows her new husband better than she does. All the old servants will be out the door. She'll bring her own. She wants to control her man every way she can. It's a war, holding a man... There'll be women in Cape Town ready enough to go north like me. People who don't have real money. Some may have a touch of the 'tarbrush', but that don't matter. Give 'em some Russian name. More exotic the better. Good leather couches you can sink right into. Dim lights and corners where they can get to know each other. Big house. Have to be. Ten girls, maybe fifteen, working the rooms... We'd need a doctor to check 'em out. Big log fires in winter. Cold up there they say in winter. Six thousand feet up. A mining camp. With Kruger out of the way, no one will give a damn. Five years is all we need. Then we go proper. Build a proper hotel. By the time we're fifty, they'll think we come from the landed gentry. What you say, Albert?"

"What about?"

"Helping me run a bloody brothel."

"My mother wouldn't like it."

"Your mother isn't going to get it. Why don't we go down there and mingle with the buggers? Get a feel for what they want. There's a small gate right here. Come on, Albert. A bloody whorehouse isn't a bad way to make a living. Excuse me," she said to a man in a thick blue seaman's sweater. "This gate's locked and I want to go down there."

"Can't do that, miss, that's third class. Can't 'ave the classes mixing. You wouldn't know which passenger belonged to where."

"That's daft."

"If you wanted to travel third class you should have booked third class."

"That's even dafter."

"Please, I 'ave a job to do. And company rules say we're not allowed to talk to female passengers. I'm deck crew, see."

"Everyone in his bloody place."

"That's how it goes, miss. Ta-ta."

The seaman pushed his wide sweeping broom further down the deck. Lily watched him for a moment.

"You think about what I said, young Albert Pringle. Like is you'll never 'ave another chance. And not everyone even gets a chance in this life. You think of it."

ON THE FOURTH day of the voyage, the SS *King Emperor* dropped anchor off Las Palmas in the Spanish Canary Islands, not quite two hundred miles from the North African Coast. The sea was as calm as a millpond and azure blue.

Tourist boats motored out to the ship, and steps were dropped from the side of the liner to the level of the boats, that would one by one tie themselves to the bottom of the steps with the help of two Colonial Shipping seamen. For the first time since the ship sailed from Southampton, the classes mingled, as the younger and braver passengers took the steps one by one to a bench seat on the boat. Women and one old man were helped down by the sailors and when the first boat was full, it cast off and was replaced by a second. At the stern of the ship, rowing boats loaded with tropical fruit were concentrating on the third-class passengers who could not afford to go ashore. Black haired tradesmen, all shouting "One shilling", held up small hands of ripe bananas, still on the green stalks, and baskets of red mangoes. The Spanish boatmen were all dressed the same: black bell-bottomed trousers, dirty black and white ringed shirts and sandals. Sailors from the ship helped the transactions by lowering wicker baskets on lengths of rope, where small groups of third-class passengers found a shilling between them, the money resting hopefully on the bottom of the basket while everyone held their breath. When the three-foot stalk, cluttered with yellow bananas, came up the side and landed on the deck there were squeals of delight. A small boy given a banana took the first bite without peeling off the skin, chewed unhappily and gave it back to his mother; in England where he came from he had never seen a fruit that needed peeling.

Harry heard all the noise and waited like a thief. Mrs Barker had dragooned Robert St Clair before Robert was able to make sure Harry was going to follow the excursion ashore. They were all going to the local hotel for a drink and, Harry surmised, the right to say they had set foot on the Canary Islands, a big tick on the list of people's lives. He waited a full five minutes after the last motor boat left for the shore, then he opened his cabin door and looked both ways down the corridor. Harry smiled with satisfaction before making his way up on deck. The first boats at the stern were being rowed back to shore, and the first-class deck was empty of anyone he knew. His feeling of freedom was overpowering as he looked for a deck chair to sit in and contemplate his luck. Making sure the thing did not collapse he sat down facing the palm-fringed island. It was very beautiful and free of the smells of a closer look.

Watching from his own escape door that ended at the top of the stairs from his luxury cabin, Jack Merryweather had watched Harry's antics with considerable amusement. Then he climbed over the step onto the deck and stood behind Harry smiling. When Harry turned, feeling the presence behind him, Jack gave him a look of sympathy.

"Sanctuary at last," said Jack.

"How long are they staying ashore?"

"You think the boat could sail without them?"

"Oh, no. And the motorboat won't sink. We've got them for the voyage. You'd better pull up a deck chair and sit down. Deck chairs are funny. Your bottom is so close to the deck... Isn't she absolutely terrible?"

They both knew they were talking about Mrs Barker.

"Bloody 'fraid it's my fault. I told them where I was going. You don't think comparative strangers will follow you to Southampton and on board a ship bound for Africa. So I told her the name of the ship. We had sailed from England before the woman became obvious. You know, having money can be a bloody bore, Harry. You think I'll be bored hunting in Africa?" Then he reverted to the problem in mind. "It's all the fault of Ernest Gilchrist but don't let's talk about them. The island looks very pretty."

"Smells when you get ashore. The Spanish out here are not good at sanitation or digging holes to bury their rubbish. Maybe it's too hot to worry about unnecessary work... No, I doubt you'll be bored, Jack. Bitten half to death by tsetse flies at dawn and dusk. Thirsty. Too bloody hot. Frightened out of your wits by a charging elephant, or the surprise look up at a kopje and into the yellow curdled eyes of a leopard. Bored, I don't think so. Had a chap out from England with dhobi itch who scratched his balls all day. Had to send him home. He was on fire down there. Never had that itch before... The word boredom, Jack Merryweather, and the vast, empty expanse of the African bush are not synonymous. My father could have shown you places."

After a moment of silence, Jack turned to look at Harry staring sightlessly at the island. Tears were flowing down his cheeks.

"I'm sorry, Harry."

"When people are dead that's it. Over. Excuse me for a moment."

Harry got up and walked away down the deck. Willing up his self-control, he cut the cancer of loss temporarily from his mind, wiped his face, and went back to his deck chair.

"No, you won't be bored," he said keeping the choke out of his voice.

"Will you take me out? Into the bush?"

"Yes of course. You'll come and stay at Elephant Walk? Make it easier on Mother. Unlike me, she never cries in front of strangers."

"I hope I'm not a stranger to you. And thank you, yes I will."

"No, of course not. I didn't mean it that way. You know what I mean. I won't shoot though. Unless you're in danger or for food. Dad always said."

Jack Merryweather put out his right hand and gripped Harry's left arm for a brief moment. Then they sat in silence. When he thought the time was right, Jack suggested they went to the bar for a drink.

They drifted off down the deck, straw boaters keeping the hot sun from their heads, two young, good-looking men in the prime of life, who to others seemed not to have a care in the world.


The Pimm's No. 1 Cup sloshing around in the ice with pieces of fruit revived Harry's spirits. He was mostly a happy person. He had not reached the age for mood swings and melancholia without good reason.

They were seated at the bar. At the other end, five bar stools away, sat an elderly couple who had not said a word to each other. They had been at the bar when Jack and Harry arrived. The barman had found the furthest distance from his two sets of customers, his back almost touching the rows of half-full bottles on the shelves. The ship was quite still, the engines silent. They were to sail in the morning, at first light. Only the fires were kept alive in the boilers. The tall funnels were just visible to Harry from his seat at the bar, trailing thin streams of smoke. The swimming pool was empty. One old woman, well covered against the now hot rays of the sun, lay out on a lounge chair. Harry thought she might have been dead until she sat up suddenly and called for a steward by raising her hand. The old wrinkled skin of her face changed places to sag from her jaw. Surprisingly, the old woman had bright blue eyes as young as the day she was born. The smell of salt in the air was strong, the sweet smell of the sea.

"You ever been bored, Harry?" asked Jack.

"No. I don't think so. Maybe as a kid. No, I don't think so. On the farm, there was always something to do... Are you going to marry her?"

"Sallie Barker! Of course not."

"You seem to both have an understanding."

"We both know that we both know what her mother's up to if that's what you mean... I have a mistress on board. In second-class, of course."

"I know. Albert told Robert who told me."

"Lily's very nice. You'll meet her in Cape Town. She's going to stay in Cape Town while I'm up north on safari. You'll help me buy the guns, won't you?"

"I'll go along but the gunsmith will know far more than me. My father was the white hunter, remember."

"How big is Elephant Walk?"

"About ten thousand acres. Only the red soil is fertile. Comes in big patches between the great rock outcrops. The rest blows in the wind if you take out the trees and don't plant grass after a crop and there are late rains. We're still farming."

"Don't the Africans farm? The blacks?"

"In patches. Before we got there they were raided every two or three years by Lobengula's impis. In Africa, it has always been a fight for survival. The bush looks harmless, but it isn't. Very beautiful, but not harmless. There are diseases of all kinds. Malaria, sleeping sickness, cholera. There are wild animals and the Matabele, Lobengula's Zulu tribe. The bush is pretty thin on people. A few huts near the rivers. A patch of pumpkins. Mealies. Sorghum to make beer. A short, sweet life. Harsh, very harsh when it goes wrong like a drought. They own a few scrawny cows and goats. Mostly they ask us for work so they don't have to worry about regular food. It's one thing to starve yourself but not much fun to watch your kids die. I speak the local language. Had a friend called Tatenda. Ran away during the rebellion. Taught me Shona. Never found out what happened to Tatenda. His family had been slaughtered by Lobengula. Dad brought him home as an orphan. He told me he would have died. He was the only one left behind when the raiders left with the young women and children. He'd been in the bush tending the village cattle when the Matabele struck. They were an offshoot of Shaka's Zulus from Natal. Mzilikazi, Lobengula's father, raped and pillaged his way northwest, and finally settled down north of the Limpopo River. The tribe they call the Matabele are a hotchpotch of Zulu warriors but most of them have mothers from the tribes raped and pillaged. We British put a stop to it but I wonder if we will ever get any thanks for it? They probably think they've exchanged one master for another but at least we don't rape and kill. The land was empty of farms and mines so maybe pillage doesn't come into it either. It probably all depends on which side of the fence you are looking from, which point of view... If you are so bored, Jack, why don't you cut yourself a farm out of the virgin bush? Keep you going for a lifetime. Generations, in fact. In Rhodesia, everything still has to be done, from more roads and railways, dams so we can water the lands, and avoid the deadly cycle of droughts. Telegraph wires. Sanitation. Hospitals. Churches. Oh, you come and settle with us in Rhodesia and you and your family for generations will never be bored. It's not as safe and cosy as London, but bored, never."

"Someone like Sallie Barker would never want to marry and live in the bush surrounded by savages. They want culture, comfort, and tea parties three times a week with their society friends."

"Then marry your mistress. Marry Lily White if that is her real name."

"Oh, Harry, do you think it might not be?"

"Bloody certain if you ask me."

He had spoken softly but not softly enough. The couple at the end of the bar got up and left.

"Why do people who listen to other people's conversations get so upset when they hear something they don't want to hear?" asked Harry.

"Maybe it serves them right... Steward. Would you be kind enough to make two more Pimm's exactly the same? The last time was perfect. And I rather think the lady in the lounge chair at the pool wants something... Ah, I see the problem. She can't get up from the canvas bed on her own. Make amends for swearing in public, Harry, and go and help the old dear... No. We're all right. She's made it. All the arm waving was to change her point of balance. She's up and leaving. Her hearing must be perfect. Did you see that terrible look she gave you? You could almost hear her say 'damn colonials'."


UNTIL HE MET MRS BARKER, the idea of marrying for money had never entered Robert St Clair's head. Mrs Barker was obsessed with the Honourable Robert St Clair, son of Lord St Clair whose title and lands went back into medieval history, and the romance of chivalry that even Robert's second-class degree in history had warned him was anything but chivalrous. When it came to men with power they usually behaved like thugs when anyone challenged them. Nothing really changed through history, only the weapons of destruction. But Robert was not going to destroy the images in Mrs Barker's head. If what he had by the luck of birth was so important, maybe he could sell it to another Mrs Barker whose family was rich, very rich... The idea of teaching small boys history as it was written paled at the potential of being a rich girl's husband.

They had come ashore and been driven in open carriages to the local hotel, the horses seeming even older than the carriages. An avenue of fluted brass poles held up a yellow awning over a worn strip of red carpet that took them through the hotel's entrance to a lounge where overhead fans were slowly trying to stir the air. The fans were powered by three small boys with little red caps on their heads. Nowhere had Robert been able to see the name of the hotel to tell his parents where he had been.

"You want to marry a rich girl, Robert?" whispered Sallie when her mother went off to powder her nose in the cloakroom. "I don't have a bean and neither does Mother. The truth is father went bankrupt and drowned himself in the Thames. It was so silly. I'd have loved him rich or poor. He was my father. Just don't take any notice of Mother. She has an obsession that if I don't marry a rich man, both of us are going to end up in the poor house."

They waited silently for her mother to return.

Sallie knew for herself she was far too young to settle down with a husband to breed children. She wanted to have some fun before the drudgery began. Before her father's company had got into trouble, being rich had never made her mother happy. There had to be more to life than coming to a full stop at the altar.

She noticed when her mother finally came back, that Robert St Clair ordered tea and not the best bottle of champagne in the hotel.

Having finished her cup of tea, Sallie quickly got up to take a walk through the hotel gardens. The flowers were beautiful and strong with scent.

Most of them she had never seen before. The Honourable Robert St Clair had not even half risen from his seat when she had left.

When she got back her mother was sitting on her own. When the waiter presented the bill, Mrs Barker paid for the tea.

"I think we shall return to the ship, my dear," said Mrs Barker.

"I think we should, Mother."

"This is not going to work."

"No, Mother."

"You had best have a good time as this may be your last chance."

# 4

## MAY TO JUNE 1907

*I*n the cold light of dawn, the rising sun silhouetted Table Mountain as the SS *King Emperor* steamed slowly into Table Bay. Most of the passengers were at the rails. The ship had anchored in the bay at midnight, Captain Hosey waiting for the dawn to dock. There was no wind and only small pockets of dark cloud. Black-backed gulls twisted and screamed in flight behind the stern where the third-class passengers craned their necks for a view of Cape Town and the houses spreading up the lower slopes of the mountain. At the bow of the ship Harry shivered, all his thoughts with his dead father. He had forgotten how cold the Cape winters could be in the dawn and had left his jacket in his cabin. To his surprise, Robert had followed him up on deck to see Cape Town for the first time.

"Sir Francis Drake called it 'the fairest Cape in all the world' in his journals," said Harry. "Luckily there's no wind. Others have called it 'The Cape of Storms'. Our train leaves at three o'clock this afternoon. Are you packed, Robert?"

"Ready to go."

MRS BARKER WATCHED the shore reach out to her with a deep fear. After she had paid the second purser for their incidentals there was one hundred and ten pounds, four shillings and sixpence left in her handbag, all the money they had in the world. She would have to take a cab straight to the relations she had never met, Ernest Gilchrist's letter of introduction being the only thing left of value. Like all small communities, the first-class passengers had found out her pecuniary situation and shunned her. No one liked a poor relation.

When the liner was halfway across the bay, the sky behind the flat mountain began to glow red. Mrs Barker shivered with fear.

Sallie, silently standing next to her, saw the shudder go through her mother's body and thought it the shiver of excitement.

"Isn't it beautiful?" she said.

JACK WATCHED Mrs Barker from a safe distance and pondered the cruelty of life. He knew her predicament. After Las Palmas, everyone had still been polite to the mother and daughter, but there had been no thought of intimacy. There he was, a young, educated man with a large built-up store of energy and too much money. And Mrs Barker, penniless.

Robert had largely shunned the girl soon after he had told Jack in confidence, 'the girl hasn't a penny', and Jack wondered how many other people Robert had taken into his confidence. For Jack, the dark brown eyes that had reached him in the park were just another pair of dark brown eyes in a pretty face. And anyway, he was not looking for a wife, even if he did feel sorry for the girl. He hoped the relations in Cape Town would be kind to them.

Having found Harry Brigandshaw on the boat, he had decided to leave Albert Pringle in Cape Town with Lily White. He and Harry had become easy friends, neither wanting more than good company from the other. They were wealthy young men in their own rights, he suspected. Neither of them talked about money. People with money didn't have to. Whether Harry took him hunting it didn't matter. The man knew everyone in Rhodesia.

"Oh, there are plenty of white hunters making a living. When we get to Elephant Walk we'll work it out from there."

"I need to buy some guns in Cape Town."

"I rather think Elephant Walk has the best collection of hunting guns in Africa. Not only my father's guns but Uncle Tinus's. His widow lives on the farm with her children. The British confiscated his farm in the Cape for going out with the Cape rebels but they do not know my father gave Aunt Alison half the value of his own shares in African Shipping, not Colonial Shipping; there's a long story there too. Tinus had sold his own shares to buy the Cape farm, to go back to his Boer roots. Anyway, you can borrow whatever you need for your safari."

"Do you know how they work?"

"All of them," Harry had said soon after leaving Las Palmas.

The sun began to rise up behind the mountain as the harbour tugs took control of the SS *King Emperor* and began to shepherd her into the dock.

He would tell Lily White to give Mrs Barker the address of the small Cape cottage the shipping line had found for her in central Cape Town. He would give Mrs Barker support if she needed it. Lily could wire the post office in Salisbury. It was the least he could do for Ernest Gilchrist. Of course, the girl should have married Ernest and stayed in England, but the obvious was rarely so apparent to those most involved. Lily would look after them.

Coming out of his hiding place he walked down the deck to join Harry and Robert at the rail.

"You'll catch a cold," he said to Harry.

"Good morning, Jack... Beautiful sight. I always get up in time to watch the ship come into Table Bay. Just forgot how cold it is in May. The first thing you need to do is go to the railway station to book a sleeper on the three o'clock. If there isn't room you'll have to come up later. Takes us two and a half days to get to Salisbury. Now, if you'll excuse me, I'm going below to put on a sweater... They do look rather forlorn." Harry had followed Jack's eyes to Sallie and Mrs Barker. "Is there anything we can do?"

"I'm going to give them Lily's address in Cape Town."

"That makes me feel happier."

LILY WHITE WAS LOOKING FORWARD to the rest of her life. She'd had a good trip. Not all the second-class passengers were new immigrants. Many were people who lived in the mining camp of Johannesburg, surrounded by the shafts and mine dumps of the gold mines that had survived the Boer War without being blown up by the retreating Boers. A good-looking woman like Lily, with the perfect cleavage, had found no difficulty in talking to whichever male she wished. And with Albert as a chaperone, she had not even had to pay a price for the information.

By the time Lily watched the thick ropes being thrown ashore to attach to the iron bollards that dotted Quay Four, she knew as much about Johannesburg as anyone who had not been to the Rand. She could even visualise Commissioner Street and its buildings. After careful planning on a large piece of paper, she knew how large an establishment she could afford with the money she held in Consols, accumulated from the men who had come and gone in her life. She would give Jack Merryweather two weeks to lose himself in the interior, and then she would cut loose, with or without

Albert Pringle, who had received a message from his gentleman to say Albert would be staying in Cape Town. There had been no other explanation for the change of plan but people like Jack Merryweather did not have to give reasons. And one day she was going to be so rich that she would not have to reason with anyone.

Albert rounded up the luggage while the passengers milled around in a vast shed that housed the local officials, some of whom had come aboard with the pilot boat to clear everyone for landing, long before the passengers came ashore. Being a British colony, there were no formalities for British citizens. All they were waiting for was the luggage that was being lifted down the gangplanks into the shed by black porters.

Standing alone next to her trunk she was surprised to see Jack detach himself from two young men, cross to a middle-aged woman and a pretty girl with black ringlets down the side of her face and signal Lily to join them.

"Lily, this is Mrs Barker and her daughter Sallie. I have given them your new address. Should either of them need anything you are to send a telegram to this address in Rhodesia. I will be in contact with Elephant Walk every two or three weeks. Miss White is my private secretary," he said to Mrs Barker, who gave Jack a knowing look and Lily one that said 'private secretary my foot'.

"Miss White, please meet Mrs Barker and Miss Barker... Ah, there's my man Pringle...

Pringle! Have you got everything? My trunks are to be sent straight to the railway station. The train leaves at three o'clock this afternoon. I will see you both when I come back from safari. For now, Pringle, please see Mrs Barker into a cab with her luggage. They have relations in the Cape, I think. My friends over there are going to show me Cape Town before we take the train. Lily, here is a draft on my London bank which will cover all your expenses. It is enough for three months. Don't spend it all at once."

For a moment, Lily thought Jack was going to give her a kiss. She looked at the draft for a thousand pounds made out to herself. With the rent she would recover by taking the cottage for only a month, Jack Merryweather would have furnished her establishment.

When everyone had gone, she turned to Albert Pringle.

"Bert, my boy. That's the kind of looks I want you to find. Ten like that and we'll be rich. I wonder why Jack gave them our address?... And is he going to get a surprise when he comes home from his hunting and finds himself alone! I wonder who he'll miss more? You or me?"

"He can always find another servant."

"And that goes for a mistress. No one is indispensable. A year from now he'll have to search his memory to find my name. He'll remember the tits but not my name. So are you with me, Albert Pringle?"

"For better, and probably for worse. What can a man do if he doesn't take a chance?"

HALF AN HOUR LATER, Albert put the shilling in his pocket, more convinced than ever not to stay a servant for the rest of his life. The cab drove off with the two women inside, blankets wrapped around their knees and feet, the roof and side of the carriage closed against the cold.

"You understand where to go?" he had said to the cabbie, talking up to him on his high seat.

"Yes, baas."

"You are sure?"

"Yes, baas. Constantia Manor."

"Do you know the rest of the address?"

"Constantia Manor, baas." The reins had been shaken over the rump of an old horse that had first defecated before starting the journey. The cabbie sneaked a smile at Albert, satisfied with his horse.

The shilling had come to him from Mrs Barker's gloved hand without a word. The trunks that he had helped load on the back, disappeared from view around the corner of a warehouse, the iron wheels of the cab grating the iron railway lines that ran the length of Quay Four. The girl had smiled at him. She was very pretty.

OUT OF THE DOCKS, the horse picked up speed. The mountain was high on the right of them, the slopes rising to the foot of the steep mountain cliffs.

"Do we have enough money to go on to India?" asked Sallie.

"No, dear."

"Should we not first stay in a hotel and send our cousins a message, asking them to call?"

"We cannot afford a hotel. Where is this driver taking us? We are now going out of the town."

"Mr Pringle asked him twice if he knew the way." There were butterflies in her stomach with the thought of imposing themselves on strangers even if they were cousins.

"How are we related to Mr and Mrs Flugelhorne?" she asked her mother.

"Mrs Flugelhorne is Mrs Gilchrist's cousin."

"But we are related to Ernest's father."

"Then we are all cousins by marriage. What does it matter? Ernest has written to them and I have another letter from him in my handbag! Anyway, they are English."

"With the name Flugelhorne?"

"Then Mrs Flugelhorne is English."

After ten more minutes the trotting horse drew them into the countryside and they could see a line of mountains, peak after peak, going away from the back of Table Mountain. Sallie watched her mother's clenched fists resting on the blanket that covered their knees. After five more minutes, Mrs Barker spoke, still looking out of the window away from Sallie.

"We must rely on the driver. The savages can do nothing to us. This is a British colony. We must remain composed and sure of ourselves. It is the privilege of being English... Why men have to bankrupt their businesses I have no idea. Your father had no right to leave us penniless."

"Why don't we ask the driver if he knows where he is going?" asked Sallie.

"That would only tell him we are lost."

"But we are."

"But he doesn't know that. And Sallie, sit up straight. You are rounding your shoulders. Rounded shoulders are so unattractive."

"Yes, Mother."

Half an hour later when their panic had reached its peak, they turned towards a long, oak-tree lined driveway towards two pillars that rose twenty feet in the air and supported a wrought iron sign, which Mrs Barker leaned out of the cab window to read.

"Constantia Manor," she said with deep satisfaction as she sat back. "My dear, not only are they cousins, they are rich."

On either side through the tall, leafless oak trees, row after row of cultivated vines ran off over fields, the lines coming to a point they were so far away, the vines leafless and perfectly pruned. There were no weeds between the rows of trellises joined by a stiff wire. A Cape Dutch house came into view, and the cabbie swung their vehicle up onto the drive that ran the length of the barn-like building, with its gabled front and many latticed windows. All around the house were flowers, and at one end, an aviary full of singing birds, some gripping the side wire with their small claws. Further along there were duck ponds and big trees, and lawns perfectly cut, dark green at the beginning of winter.

"It's so beautiful," said Sallie. "Look, those must be stables. Oh, Mother, I hope they like us."

"They will."

The cabbie stopped the horse at the great door. He opened the cab door and pulled down the steps. The big house was silent, no one in sight. A large dog watched them from the veranda that swept from both sides of the steps that led up to the front door. The dog rolled on its side and went to sleep. The driver was about to unload the trunks when Mrs Barker stopped him. She walked up the steps and rang the outside bell. Immediately the door swung open to reveal a large black man who blinked at them. He was dressed in some kind of uniform neither Mrs Barker nor Sallie had seen before.

"Mrs Barker of England, calling on Mrs Flugelhorne," she said stentoriously. Mrs Barker was not afraid of servants. The man continued to blink, adding a half-smile. Mrs Barker repeated herself. The black man blinked twice.

"No English," said the cab driver from the gravel driveway. In Afrikaans, he told the man in the fancy suit to call the madam. The women heard him go off into the house. The dog was still asleep on its side. They waited as the tension came back to them.

"We can't stand here forever," said Sallie.

"We must," said her mother.

Finally, a small woman with a beaked nose and eyes close together came down the winding stairs. Sallie thought many years ago she had probably been pretty. Ernest also had eyes close together. The woman saw them standing at the front door and hesitated.

"I'm Ernest Gilchrist's cousin," said Sallie, moving into the house. "You must be Ernest's aunt. The resemblance is quite clear. This is my mother, Mrs Barker. I am Sallie Barker. We have just landed in Cape Town from England."

"We thought to call straight away," said Mrs Barker. "To find from you the name of a good hotel. What a most beautiful home you have."

"You are from England?" said the woman almost hugging herself. "Oh, how wonderful, how wonderful. I never even speak English now. German, yes. My husband is German. The servants only speak in Afrikaans. Dutch really. Oh, please come in. Shall we have some tea? You must stay here, of course. I'm sure my husband won't mind. He's away at the moment. On business. I get very lonely, you must understand. Dear Ernest. He wrote so well of you... From England. That is wonderful. Come along into the sunroom. My servants will pay the cab driver and bring in your trunks. You do have trunks?... Oh, good. From England. This is so wonderful... You see, we don't have any children. Call me Violet please."

"Please call me Doris," said Mrs Barker.

Behind, the dog got up and walked away down the long veranda to plonk itself in the sun at the far end. From the aviary, the birds were singing their hearts out.

With an inward sigh of relief, Sallie moved into the great house.

The conservatory was full of potted plants and smelt of sweet damp earth. Most of the plants were strange to her. From the glassed-in room with its sloping glass roof, Sallie looked out at the buildings: sheds, stables, and servants' quarters. There was another high building that dominated the sheds with a tall 'winery' sign over the front door. People, all black, came and went from the buildings.

The tray of tea was brought to them by a fat black woman with the largest bottom Sallie had ever seen in her life. Her mother and Mrs Flugelhorne were talking nineteen to the dozen, neither listening to the other. Sallie thought Mrs Flugelhorne must have been alone for a long time. On a low, cushioned seat at the foot of the glass window, a large white cat was fast asleep. Sallie got up and went to the cat. After a moment, the cat began to purr. Well, they don't have any sons, she said to herself. Concentrating on stroking the cat, she put all thought of the future out of her mind. Even with all the people outside, the house felt empty. It was very large for two people, and Sallie wondered why people lived in houses that were far too big for them. Then, for some unaccountable reason, she shivered, even though the glassed-in room was warm from the rays of the winter sun.

TEN DAYS LATER, Albert Pringle was walking down Adderley Street in the centre of Cape Town, wearing a small green bowler hat tilted slightly to the right. He was very chipper. Along with his new green hat, he wore a new green suit and twirled a dark cane with a silver handle. All presents from Lily White.

Having come from a family and village that supported its own, Albert had never known how people could find themselves cast off with no one to turn to.

Like so often after a debilitating war, South Africa was in a financial depression, the commerce generated by the war gone with the peace of Vereeniging. Large numbers of blacks and whites were out of jobs, and there was no welfare system in place to provide them with the basics of life. The ones that had left their parishes in England to seek a fortune were not even able to turn to their church for support. In ten days Albert had found five young and pretty girls and moved them into the rented house in lower Strand Street, close to where the harbour joined the city. They were sleeping two to a room, and happy to have a roof over their heads, even though they knew why they were there. None of them had the fare back to Europe.

"Any business has to be honest, especially to its staff," Lily had said the day they moved into the house having told the landlord they only wanted it for a month. Lily had only managed to pry one month's rent back from the pre-paid three. "The girls, right from the start, must know what they are in for. They will have our protection, and will never have to leave the establishment if they fulfil their contracts, but however you look at it, they are whores. They will be poked by fat, old, drunk men, like many a wife, but they will be paid a king's ransom in comparison to what lies ahead of a young woman in a strange country with no money and no support. Stress the support, Albert, but if they don't want to join us let it be. Everyone in my business has to be willing. Also, anytime they wish, they can go."

Walking on the side of the road in the sunshine, his only regret was having to let down Jack Merryweather, who had never treated him like a servant, more like a friend.

Lily had gone on when Albert voiced his worry. "The man doesn't own you anymore than he owns me which he would were I his wife. We are going to give him notice. If he didn't want us he'd give us the same notice. I'm not his first or last mistress. Valets are ten a penny in London."

"But he's a good man."

"Then we'll both write that in the letters telling him so."

As Albert turned up left into Strand Street, he still felt uncomfortable deceiving Jack Merryweather. 'Can't go around letting people down,' he said to himself.

A girl with a small hat and side feather was standing at the steps of the three-storey townhouse. She had her back to Albert, but he knew who she was by the black ringlets that hung down by her ears. She was just standing looking up at the front door. By the time Albert walked the hundred yards up Strand Street to the steps, the girl had still not knocked on the door.

"Miss Barker," he said. "It is Sallie Barker?"

Before he could mount the steps the girl ran down into his arms, sobbing.

"I just didn't know who to turn to," she kept repeating.

One of the new girls answered the door and they went through to the small sitting room with the open fire burning softly in the grate.

"It'll be all right, dearie," said the girl, patting Sallie on the back. "Being a whore is no worse than being a wife, and I know. How about a nice cup of tea?"

After tea, Sallie composed herself and told Albert the story.

FOR THREE DAYS they had been alone in the house. No one came to visit. Only the house servants were allowed in the house and none of them could speak English. Outside the big house, the business of the wine estate went on before her eyes, the comings and goings of drays bringing empty wine barrels two at a time and going back with the new ones full. There were two white overseers who never came to the house or even glanced its way. Ernest Gilchrist's aunt had given her a small, pretty room to herself, with light blue curtains and big windows that felt as if no one had lived in it for years. Even after leaving open the big windows the room was dead and lifeless. Not even the smell of flowers or mown grass penetrated the second-floor room that looked out far to the distant mountains that for Sallie had no name.

There was never the mention of the present, except for the needs of food and sleep. All the two women talked about was England, and England twenty years ago, before she was born. They were fast becoming bosom friends, Mrs Flugelhorne and Mrs Barker. Never once was there a mention of neighbours. Never once was there talk of what was to be done. Both of them, her mother and Mrs Flugelhorne, were reliving their happy childhoods, where Sallie had no part. Finally, for Sallie, there was boredom, mixed with the regret of wasting time. She wanted to be out and doing something, enjoying her life instead of being locked up in the house of strangers.

Then Mr Flugelhorne came home and at the first sight of Sallie, he literally licked his lips.

He was a man of fifty, florid from good food and wine, his body all the time trying to burst out of his clothes, his belly protruding so he could only see his feet with a mirror. The servants were plainly frightened of him, inside and outside the house. Mrs Flugelhorne was petrified of the man and stammered her introductions. To what seemed Mrs Flugelhorne's surprise and greater relief, the master of the house gave his guests a handsome welcome, and listened to every word of Mrs Barker's flattery, the few questions he asked her were pertinent and to the point. By the end of the first evening, he knew their predicament without having to be told, his eyes taking the clothes off Sallie piece by piece. Somewhere she had read the word 'lecher' and the following day, briefly alone with her mother in the garden, she had explained her fears.

"Don't be silly, Sallie. You young girls imagine these things. He's a gentleman, a rich gentleman, and old enough to be your father."

"And a lecher; watch the way he looks at me. Mother, I want to go."

"We can't go, Sallie. This is our opportunity. To find so much wealth in the family when we are so poor. Now, Sallie, don't be silly."

"The way he looks at my bosom says he knows that we are poor as church mice."

"How can he? You are looking a gift horse in the mouth."

"I'm looking at a dirty old man and I certainly have no wish to look in his mouth."

"Sallie! Now you behave yourself. It's difficult enough as it is. He hasn't done anything has he?"

"No, Mother," she had said wearily. Arguing was obviously pointless.

"Then don't be ungrateful."

There was no key to the small room with the blue curtains even if Sallie had wished to lock the door. She avoided the master of the house as best she could, finding a bench among some trees on the far side of the duck pond. Once she heard the white overseer and his white assistant talking to each other. They were speaking in English. The one man spoke with a Worcester accent, the other she rather thought was German. The conversation was brief. She would have liked to know which one of them was English but they were hidden by the trees and shrubbery. When she walked out to catch a glimpse they were gone. Twice Mr Flugelhorne ordered a horse and trap from his stables and was driven into Cape Town. One night he did not come home. Her mother and Mrs Flugelhorne chatted in their element whenever the master was out of the house. Mrs Flugelhorne spoke nothing but trivia and Sallie doubted if the woman had a brain in her head.

Mr Flugelhorne came home drunk late the following afternoon and didn't even bother to hide the way he leered at Sallie. Passing a message through the house servant, she excused herself from supper on the grounds of not feeling well, most of the conversation with the servant conducted in sign language. In the end, when the maid gave a big smile, Sallie was not sure what message would be delivered to Mrs Flugelhorne. Her mother, even though she saw the man was drunk, had not even furrowed her brow.

Sallie leaned the back of the only chair under the doorknob and tried to go to sleep. She had shut the window, even though there was no way a drunk, a fat drunk, could climb up the outside trellis work into her bedroom. She had never felt more alone or vulnerable in her life. She tried praying to God and finally fell asleep.

When Sallie woke, the moon was shining full into her room, the chair was no longer up against the doorknob but lying on the carpet on its back on top of a sheet of plywood that had not been in the room when she went to sleep.

The man was fatter and even more repulsive with his clothes off, and sickly white in the light of the moon, his bald head glowing with its reflection. There was something over her face. She felt the bedclothes being ripped off from on top of her body as her mind drifted. She had felt the nightdress being pulled over her head. The hand that cupped her firm, hard breast was ice-cold. Her legs were forced apart, crushed by the weight of the man on top of her. Mr Flugelhorne farted before entering her, tearing parts of her flesh with the hard rod he thrust into her body. The chloroform had been enough to stop her fight but not enough to stop his pleasure. When she screamed he laughed at her and went about his business with greater pleasure.

In the morning the bed sheets were covered in blood and Sallie could still smell the man. The piece of plywood that had pushed back the legs of the chair was gone.

She had waited in her bedroom all morning, waiting to speak to her mother. There was no sign of the master of the house who had raped her. When she saw her mother in the garden next to the aviary she flew out of the house to hysterically recount what had happened. Her mother coldly refused to believe her and dismissed her hysterics. Sobbing, Sallie returned to her room.

Packing everything she owned into a small suitcase, she had watched and waited, trying all the time to ignore the dull, aching pain between her legs. When the white overseer went to the stables she let herself out of her room and she ran down the wide flight of stairs and out of the house through the sunroom.

She told the overseer that Mr Flugelhorne had told her to take the trap into Cape Town. The man leered as if he understood one way or the other and put the small leather suitcase in the trap. In the Dutch she did not understand, the overseer told the driver something. Then she was in the trap and going down the driveway between the oaks and through the pillars onto the main road. She was relieved when the driver took the road back the way they had come out from Cape Town harbour ten days before.

At that moment she was completely alone in the world. Halfway there she found the card in her purse with Jack Merryweather's name and address in Cape Town. In case the driver reported back to her mother, she got off in the middle of town and stood on the kerb with her small suitcase until the trap was out of sight.

Then she had picked up the case and walked slowly to the house in Strand Street. People were very kind when she asked for directions.


AT THE TIME Sallie was telling her story in the Strand Street house next to the small wood fire crackling in the grate, Jack Merryweather was riding through tall grass that came up to his knees. He was hotter than he had ever been before in his life, and the rifle he had been assured would kill an elephant was banging against his knee in its bucket holster. On either side, thickly wooded msasa trees stopped any vision further than twenty yards. The hat band of his broad-brimmed brown felt hat was soaked with sweat and the tsetse fly was beginning to attack as the sun went down, blood-reddening the western sky, leaving patches of turquoise blue. They had been riding since dawn, the four of them, Jack, Harry Brigandshaw, and two big black men that worked at Elephant Walk.

They had found not a trace of the Great Elephant that had killed Harry's father. They had been riding for a week, searching the vast open bush for one elephant that had last been sighted by Tinus Oosthuizen thirty years before – before, that is, it was wounded by an American hunter and Sebastian Brigandshaw had gone out to put the animal out of its pain. It was thought the elephant was seventy years old, the biggest in Central Africa, and had roamed all its life between the Congo and Limpopo rivers, some said as far as the sea. Before being wounded by the American, the Great Elephant had been a legend that nobody believed.

The train had arrived at Salisbury Station in Southern Rhodesia three days after the SS *King Emperor* had docked in Cape Town harbour. Jack Merryweather had had no problem booking a sleeper for himself, as Harry and Robert St Clair were again sharing together, the three of them eating their meals at the same table in the dining car. The Great Karoo, the semi-desert of Bechuanaland, had been dry, and dotted with patches of mopane forest, tall, thin-trunked trees, some of which had been pushed over by the vast herds of elephant roaming out from the Okavango Delta, the wetland at the heart of the British Protectorate that teemed with every species of game known to Southern and Central Africa. On the third day of their journey north, they crossed the border into Southern Rhodesia and rode the steel rails through the mopane forests of Matabeleland to Bulawayo. Early the next morning they stepped down from the train at Salisbury, the capital of Southern Rhodesia. After a good breakfast at Meikles Hotel, they had taken the hired trap out on the Mazoe Road and arrived at Elephant Walk just before lunch. The eldest son had returned home, this time as head of the family.

Robert St Clair, thinking of a good lunch to follow his good breakfast, had forgotten the reason for Harry's return home.

"Leave them alone, Robert," Jack Merryweather had said after the brief introductions. "This is family. There's a river down past the lawn. Let us leave them to console each other."

Madge and her mother were crying. Young George was hugging his elder brother for comfort. The old man that had been introduced as Harry's maternal grandfather stood back holding what looked like a butterfly net. Aunt Alison and her daughter Katinka were somewhere at a place Jack Merryweather could not pronounce. It was a sad homecoming, and Jack, with Robert in tow, left them alone and waited on the rocks overlooking the river, shaded by a tall acacia tree where Harry found them two hours later.

"Thank you," he had said. "Mother's in a state and young George is hysterical. Not a good thing to lose your father when you are only eleven years old." They stayed silent for a long time looking at the flow of the river.

Harry broke the silence. "There has been a legend in these parts for as long as many black people can remember, an elephant so big they named it the Great Elephant in every language spoken from here to the northern borders of the Belgian Congo. Every white hunter including Uncle Tinus hunted the Great Elephant for the weight of its tusks and the legend that would stay with the man who killed the greatest mammal on earth. Sometimes they saw the huge footpads marked in the dust. Once my Uncle Tinus caught a glimpse when he was descending the escarpment into the Zambezi Valley but by the time he reached the floor of the valley, the Great Elephant had swum the river and headed north at a run. Two years ago a party of Americans on safari found the Great Elephant and one of them put a bullet in its head. The white hunter followed the blood trail all day but never caught up with the elephant. He presumed the animal would die on its own but it didn't. Reports came in of African villages being ransacked by a huge elephant. People were killed. The government sent the police out to track and kill the rogue elephant. Instead, the elephant killed two black policemen, trampling them to death. Ten weeks ago the administrator came himself to Elephant Walk to plead with my father to hunt down the killer elephant. For the first time in twenty years, my father agreed to go out and kill an animal for other than its meat. My Grandfather Manderville tells the story from the report of the serving major who mounted the expedition for my father. Not even seventy miles north of here the Great Elephant charged the camp. My father stood his ground but the bullet was old and when he pulled the trigger at twenty yards the gun did not fire. The major by then was high up a tree, along with the rest of them in their separate trees. The last he saw, the elephant was heading north. My father was dead two seconds after his gun misfired. I'm going after the bloody elephant and I'm going to kill him. If you want to come you are welcome. But it's dangerous. That elephant is in great pain, probably with a lead bullet lodged in its head. It does not like people."

"Not really my bag, Harry," said Robert St Clair. "You know me. Better stay and look after your family. How old is your sister Madge?"

"Don't waste your time. She's been in love with Barend, Uncle Tinus's son, since they were toddlers."

"But he's not here, I understand. Went off no one knows where."

"Doesn't matter to Madge. She'll wait for him." Slightly irritated, Harry had turned to Jack Merryweather... "Jack, it's dangerous but you won't be bored. Hot and bitten to buggery by insects, but not bored. I'm taking two black men from the farm. You're welcome. I'd like the company. I'll teach you how to handle an elephant gun as we look for this elephant. You said you'd come to hunt. You can ride, of course? I want to leave at first light before he kills again. The villagers who are scattered sparsely through the bush don't have elephant guns to protect themselves. We may be gone for weeks."


THE NIGHT SALLIE BARKER spent her first day with Lily White and Albert Pringle, Harry and Jack were camped on the high bank of a small river, the blacks having gathered wood for a fire that would burn all night. An old, hard teak, the tree pushed over long ago by an elephant wanting to eat the green, succulent leaves that grew at the tree top, was burning on the fire, throwing light and shadow into the surrounding msasa trees. Sparks like fireflies were drifting upon the hot air from the fire towards the vast dome of sky, layer upon layer of stars that Jack had never experienced before.

That night, when it was his turn to feed the fire, he stood alone looking up at the stars in awe, with the fire burnt down and glowing red at his feet, and saw the vastness of the universe for the first time. A hyena cackled a laugh from the pitch dark of the woods, sending a cold shiver of primal fear through his body. Quickly he picked up some of the stacked wood and threw the pieces on the fire, sending sparks flying high up into the night. Somewhere further away he heard what he now knew was the roar of a lion. He built up the fire, sending flames twenty feet into the air. There was no wind, the flames tonguing straight up to the heavens. Feeling happier than he had ever been in his life, he crawled back into his sleeping bag as he was, fully clothed, not three feet from the fire. Within seconds he was sound asleep. Around him, in the bitterly cold night air, the rustle of Africa continued. The hyena, frightened of the flames, went off for easier prey. An owl hooted softly from far away.

When Jack woke, the dawn was touching the high leaves of the trees. A black man, kneeling by the burnt-down fire, was putting a pot of coffee on the coals. From everywhere, and slowly, the birds began to sing. Below the opposite riverbank, three impalas were drinking the water, their front feet splayed. Hunched in his sleeping bag, his arms around his knees, Jack watched a baby rhinoceros mock charge an elephant to be hustled away by its mother. The elephant ignored mother and child and went down into the river to wallow in the water, the sound of tumbling water evocative of Africa's emptiness, great size, the extent of nature. None of them spoke. All of them, black and white, listening to the sounds of Africa, part of it, content.


AT ELEVEN-THIRTY that morning the cable arrived in the Salisbury post office. It was to the point, all three of them having worked on it through the early morning before Albert Pringle had gone out and sent it from the Cape Town post office. It was addressed to Jack Merryweather, Elephant Walk, Poste Restante, Salisbury, Southern Rhodesia.

The clerk in Salisbury wrote the address on a brown envelope. The cable had been translated from Morse code by a second clerk. On a separate piece of white paper, which he put into the brown envelope and sealed, he wrote the message:

'Raped by cousin. Desperate for protection. My mother unwilling to believe the rape. Please help me. Sallie Barker.'

There were many people roaming the new country, looking for gold, looking for excitement, and none of them had a fixed address, many only coming into Salisbury every six months, some alone, some in pairs. All received their mail 'Poste Restante', to be collected at the post office by themselves. A seven-tier box of pigeonholes, each claiming a letter of the alphabet was stuffed with mail awaiting collection.

The second clerk had seen the name Elephant Walk and recognised it and the fact that the farm had its own pigeonhole. For a brief moment, he was unsure whether to stuff the envelope into the separate Elephant Walk box or the Ms box. In his confusion, he pushed the brown envelope deep into the pile of Js (J for Jack), the fullest of the pigeonholes with all the English Johnstones, Johnsons, Johns and James. With his hand deep in the pile, the clerk gave it a final push where the small envelope slipped down the back through a crack and stayed lodged half in the back of the Js and half in the back of the Ns, which was also stuffed full with all the Normans, Nairns, Nuttalls and Nollens.

When travellers called for their mail, the clerks stuck their hand into the box that carried the first letter of the traveller's surname. They rarely looked deep inside the long box, only feeling for stray envelopes with their hands. They then thumbed through the envelopes looking for the traveller's name. Then what was left of the pile was pushed back into the pigeonhole. Less than half of the envelopes were ever collected from the Poste Restante. Some of the letters had been thumbed through for years.


IN CAPE TOWN, Sallie Barker waited through the days while Jack rode down into the Zambezi Valley, her call for help stuck, not even thumbed through by the clerks at Salisbury post office. For three weeks she did not go out of the house on Strand Street, convinced her mother and Mr Flugelhorne would be searching for her for different reasons, her mother to retain her place in the rich Flugelhorne household, Mr Flugelhorne to use her at his will with impunity. Twice, the thought of white, fat flesh, the smell of his foul wind, the stench of drunken breath, sent her to the bathroom to be sick. She was a prisoner of her own beauty, her own magnetic draw for men, old and young. The prize even she had thought would save them both from poverty had turned against her. Men took from women what they wanted when there was no protection.


BY THE END OF JUNE, when she understood clearly the reason for so many young girls being in the house, Sallie had given up all hope. People were people. They looked after themselves. The appearance of manners, love and trust was a mockery of the truth. Jack had no wish to have anything to do with her now she was out of his sight. The card had been a gesture, a way of showing himself off in a good light. He probably thought she was chasing him once again, the new plot hatched by her mother. 'Out of sight, out of mind' the old true saying. Anyway, why should he care? Why should anyone care?

Four days before the rest of the household were due to entrain for Johannesburg, Lily having gone north the day after Sallie arrived on her doorstep, Sallie turned twenty. She was not pregnant, of that she was certain, having learned it three days before with an overwhelming sense of relief.

They had given her gin that first night after the tea when she had told her story. Whether through gin or nature, and except for the scar on her body and mind, she was free of Herr Flugelhorne.

"It's not like Mr Merryweather," Albert Pringle said. "He cares about people. Why I worry about dumping him, but a man has to have his own life and opportunity only knocks once."

"Don't rationalise, Albert," said Sallie. "A few weeks ago I would have said you were wrong, loyalty is more important than personal gain. Now I know you are right. All the society, words, the things we should do to be right, even religion, are to keep us in our place, to make us do what others want us to do without being forced, for fear of society ostracising us in this life, or God punishing us in the fire of hell in the next. Men have created a web to ensnare us... You go your own way, Albert. You and Lily are good people. The girls know what they are doing, the alternative is far worse than this reality. Men will use us whatever we do. Maybe a good husband won't, if there is such a thing. There are many more ways of hurting a woman other than raping her... I have grown up, Albert Pringle. Not in the way I expected, with my own family, my own children... Brutally. A man so rich he could do what he wanted. If you and Lily will have me, I'll come to Johannesburg. Fact is, I have no alternative. I won't whore, Albert. I'll keep the books. Do the buying. Run the house Lily has bought. That much I can find from my education. I worry all the time about my mother, but I wonder if she worried so much about me. Can mothers be selfish? It's against nature. Maybe I am wrong. Maybe she will listen to me. But mostly in my short life, I have found people don't hear what they don't want to hear until it's too late. Raped again by that fat slob, I will kill myself. Am I right or wrong?"

"Probably both... Lily said you were welcome from the start. What job you do is your decision. The whole thing is rather new for all of us. Including the girls. I just don't understand Jack Merryweather... You think we should send him another cable?"

"If he doesn't want to answer the first, what's the use of a second?... Once I'm out of this town I'll feel less dirty. And I don't really want to kill myself. Somewhere out there, there's a lot of fun to be had in life... When I'm settled in Johannesburg, and far enough away from the Flugelhornes, I'll write her a letter... Maybe she'll want to join me."

"You do understand we are going to be running a brothel?"

"You're right... And, yes, I do understand. Can you think of another alternative for me? Anywhere else to go?"

"Not at the moment."

"Ernest Gilchrist would have had me before all this but I don't want him.

Not now. Certainly not now. Young men in London don't take too well to their wives being raped before they marry them. He'd run a mile worrying what his employer would do to him if it ever came out. And he needs his employer. Oh, no. They don't want soiled goods themselves."

"Don't hate all men."

"You won't be raped, Albert, so you'll never know. And I'm sick of being cooped up in this house. Then it's settled. The first real job in life for Sallie Barker will be working in a brothel and I suppose like everything else I'll get used to it... And the girls may need a sympathetic shoulder to cry on every now and again... Can I cry on your shoulder, Albert, when I'm lonely?"

# 5

## JUNE, JULY AND AUGUST 1907

*T*here had been a brief electric storm during the night. The sky had rumbled ten miles away, forking streaks of lightning over the dark sky. The bush was tinder-dry and no rain had fallen in the Zambezi Valley since the end of March, ten weeks before.

"The gods are angry," Harry had said to Tembo.

"One of the ancestors turned over in bed."

They both spoke in the language of the Shona.

"Bushfire?"

"Maybe. We shall see."

Then they were asleep again and the night went on.

THEY SADDLED up in the pre-dawn after loading the packhorses. As soon as they could see five yards ahead, they rode out of camp without making breakfast. When the sun came up it would be burning hot in the valley, even in June.

Harry smelt the woodsmoke ten minutes later when the night sky was running away from the dawn. The wind was in Harry's face, coming from the direction of the river. As hard as he and Tembo looked they could not see the glow of a bushfire. They were both puzzled and afraid. When the dawn became day, the soft breeze in their faces could turn into a hot wind that would fan a bushfire towards them faster than the horses could gallop.

Bushfire. The worst fear of the hunter, when the grass was as high as the horses' withers, scorched dry of moisture by the sun.

With the rising sun pushing up bright light from the eastern earth came the full light of a new day that showed them a single, thin spiral of white smoke rising just above the height of the river trees, only to be blown away by the wind. Everyone smiled, including Jack Merryweather. Garth, the youngest of the blacks, who had been brought by his parents to Elephant Walk when he was four years old and christened by Harry's Uncle Nathaniel, smiled a set of pearly white teeth in a face the colour of coal. Harry turned his horse slightly to head for the fire. There were people, the first strangers he had ever seen in the valley.

Riding carefully round the thorn thickets through the tall, brown elephant grass, they came upon the hundred-foot-high trees that lined the bank of the river. It was three hours after the dawn. Not once had they seen a trace of the Great Elephant.

AT THE FIRST sign of danger, the doves in the high trees above the camp had stopped calling to each other. A pair of African fish eagles that had patiently perched on the boughs of a dead tree since early morning, flew off. The big river flowed on, the white clouds mirrored in the dark brown water. On the opposite bank, some hundred yards away, a pair of kudu broke from the cover of a thorn bush and headed away from the river, the females' big, round ears having picked up the sound of danger. A few minutes later they both heard the distinct clink of metal that only came from a ridden horse. Jared Wentworth got up from where he was writing a journal and pulled his hunting rifle out from inside the four-wheeled wagon.

"What is it?" asked his sister.

"People. The doves have stopped calling. I think I heard the clink of a harness."

"No one lives here."

"Get in the wagon and lie down."

"You're frightened of your own shadow. There are no strangers."

"We are the strangers in Africa."

Slipping a bullet into the breech, Jared pulled back the single hammer to the half-cock position and waited where he was, his back to the river, his ears and eyes straining for the danger. His heart, easily excited, pumped in his chest. The horsemen were riding straight at his camp. Moving the gun forward to the sound of danger, Jared slid silently onto his stomach and pulled the hammer back to full cock, the butt comfortably in his shoulder. He waited patiently, mostly hidden by the pile of wood ready for the night's fire, the barrel of the rifle pushed clear of the wood. The worst predator in the bush was man, that much he knew. He wished he had not sent all his blacks downriver to look for a crossing.

They had been following the river for ten days and had still not found a way. With the valley empty of man, there were no makoris (dugout canoes made from a single tree trunk), no boats at all. Jared had wondered if anyone had ever lived in the valley permanently. There had been no trace of man, only the myriad feet of animals.

Whoever it was had stopped. Jared could see the outline of horsemen through the dry, leafless thorn thicket that guarded the way to the river trees. A herd of buffalo could hide in a thorn thicket if they stood still.


"CAN YOU SEE ANYONE?" asked Jack Merryweather.

"Not a soul. To the left through the trees I think is a wagon... Anyone there?" Harry waited a moment before repeating his question in Shona. The horses were difficult to control having long smelt the water of the river.

Jared carefully let the hammer of his rifle back to safety and stood up from behind his pile of wood.

"Who are you?" he called.

"Hunters. What are you doing here?"

"Looking for a way to cross the river."

Four men, two white and two black, rode through the trees to the top of the riverbank and looked down on him where they had made camp on the lower slope.

"Don't you have a guide?" asked Harry, seeing where they were camped.

"Blacks. Four of them, but we can't talk to each other."

"They let you camp down a riverbank! You get a hippo cow on the wrong side of its calf and you'll be dead. Hippo can't run uphill. Always camp at the top, high as you can."

"I'll remember that."

"Where are they?"

Jared looked puzzled for a moment. "The blacks? Sent them downriver to look for a crossing. Presume that's what they're doing... You say the hippopotamus are dangerous?"

"Very. My name's Harry Brigandshaw. My friend Jack Merryweather from England, Tembo and Garth. We're all from Elephant Walk. Now tell me, what on earth are you doing out here on your own, mister?"

"Wentworth. Jared Wentworth. London."

"He's not alone," said Jack.

From the wagon, a girl crawled out from undercover, swung her legs around over the tailboard and dropped to the dry earth. There were elephant droppings either side of her. Long brown hair hung to her waist, and when she moved from the shadow of the covered wagon, the sun shone on her hair and picked out the seams of red. Her cheekbones were one long smooth curve to her ears. Her nose was peeling from the sun. Her legs were long and finished with a small pair of boots above a brown skirt that came down to her ankles. She was smiling at a very good private joke while her eyes moved from Jack to Harry to Jack as she walked up the slope towards them. Tembo and Garth received some of the smile. When she reached Harry, she put up her hand.

"Hello, I'm Sara Wentworth, Jared's sister. I'm also from London."

Harry dismounted and let the reins fall loose. "Watch the horses while they water," he said in Shona to Garth and Tembo. "Watch for crocodiles and don't let them drink too much."

"You must be out of your mind," he said, turning back to Sara.

"Probably. What you don't fear you don't worry about. Can I make you some tea? We always keep a pot of water half in the previous night's fire."

"So you do make a fire at night."

"Oh, yes. It gets cold don't you think?"

"But to keep away the animals."

"That as well. We have been in Africa for three months. Really, quite old African hands by now. You do drink tea, don't you?"

"How did you get into the Zambezi Valley?"

"We wanted to see the river," said Jared. "Livingstone's river, but we can't get across."

"How long do you intend wandering around Africa?" said Harry sarcastically.

"As long as we dare," said Jared.

"Are you running away from something?" asked Jack, who could not take his eyes off the girl.

"Oh, yes," she said. "Aren't we all? What are you running away from, Mr Merryweather? What a lovely surname. Far better than Wentworth."

"Boredom."

"Oh dear oh dear, that is a sin. One life and you are bored already. My grandfather says he is bored but only because he can't do anything anymore. You should be ashamed of yourself at your age... And what are you running away from, Mr Brigandshaw? I'm very good at remembering names by the way. Some people are good at tennis, I'm good at names."

Tembo and Garth had let the horses drink briefly from the river before unloading the packhorses and dropping the heavy saddles to the dry earth. Harry could smell the mud churned up by the horses. The girl irritated him and he didn't know why. He made himself watch the horses to give himself more time to remove the rush of irritation that saturated his mind. If Londoners wished to leave their bones by the big river, who was he to stop them? She was young, younger than her brother. Probably twenty-two, Harry thought, the brother two years older... Then he understood and smiled at the truth. They were intruders in the bush he thought was his and Tembo's and Garth's. Finding strangers in the Zambezi Valley, his valley, had made him jealous. She was still looking at him for a reply. Her expression had softened when she saw his smile.

"We are hunting a big elephant. Have you seen the spoor? They say it's almost twice the size of a normal footpad. It's wounded and dangerous and it killed my father."

"I'm sorry. I'll make the tea. Our blacks may have seen something when they come back. Ten days we've been looking for a way to cross the river. If there was this enormous footprint of an elephant they never got excited... Do you think Dr Livingstone came this way in his travels?"

"Probably not. We are too far east. The Victoria Falls are four hundred miles from here if we followed the river. We are almost in Portuguese territory. The Portuguese have been in these parts of Africa since Bartolomeu Dias and Vasco da Gama. Over four hundred years. They traded this far inland from ports they dotted down the shores of the Indian Ocean. This was then the Kingdom of Monomotapa."

"What happened to it?" asked Jared.

"It came and went like all empires, leaving little trace. They mined gold and copper and traded it for pretty beads. Or that's all we've ever found of the transactions. A pretty coloured bead was worth more than a lump of gold."

"How very sad," she said, though Harry could not see why a coloured bead was prettier than a lump of gold. "Are you going to camp with us tonight?"

"Thank you. But on the high ground."

"You'd better give us all the tips before we do something silly... We don't have any sugar for the tea I'm afraid. Our local helpers have very sweet tooths."

"Jack and I will go after an impala. We can spit the carcass over the fire. If your blacks come back there will still be enough for everyone."

. . .

By the time Sara and Jared's blacks returned from their fruitless search for a crossing it was getting dark. The camp had been moved under a tall acacia tree, with dense thorn thicket protection on one side, and the steep bank of the river on the other. Two fires were burning with the splayed carcass of an impala rammed on a greenwood spit over coals that were replenished from the second fire. The crude spit made by Harry earlier in their hunting trip was turned ten degrees every few minutes. Tembo had rubbed wild sage into the flesh of the carcass as much for the sweet smell as the taste. Two large frying pans were ready for the filleted river bream that Harry had caught on a hand line. Jack, always prepared, had stored a bottle of Cape brandy in his saddle bag. The blacks had gone off to a third fire of their own where they could talk and gossip. Harry wished he could translate their stories that went on for hours in minute detail, but without a knowledge of the blacks and their traditions, the stories would be boring to the other three. Only when the buck was cooked enough for a first carving did the black men come up for their food and stay to eat. None of them had wanted fish, waiting to gorge themselves on a surfeit of meat, the fat dripping down their black faces, shining in the light of the fire, everyone happy. For a while after the second and third carving, they all sat silently digesting their food, looking into the cooking fire, completely satisfied. Then the black men went off to their own fire to continue the same story they had all heard from the first conscious days of their lives, the familiarity giving them peace and the security they craved in their nomadic lives.

Sara had fallen asleep by the side of the fire, her head on the coat her brother had taken off and put under the side of her face.

"She doesn't want to get married," said Jared. "There's nothing really she can do. She calls this her one break in life before the responsibilities of children. I suppose we all have to do our duty in the end. Merryweather, you're nearest the pile of wood. Throw on some more but don't shower Sara with sparks."

Embarrassed by the revelations of another's private life, Jack did what he was told while Harry kept quiet.

"I also hate him," said Sara without opening her eyes.

"Thought you were asleep," said Jared.

"I was for a while… Why do we have to do our duty, big brother?"

Everyone waited for a reply.

"Because if we don't our way of life disintegrates, society falls apart, people start fighting with each other. Without everyone doing their duty the empire would fall apart."

"Does that matter?" asked Sara, her eyes now open.

"People rely on us, Sara. Without our discipline, they'd be at each other's throats. People wouldn't have food. Wouldn't have shelter. With everyone doing their duty everything is stable, everything works."

"You think it works for everyone?" asked Jack. He was thinking of the storytellers round their fire.

"No system in life works for everyone. There are some people in life for which nothing works."

"Do your parents know you are in the middle of Africa?" asked Harry.

"No. I persuaded them to let us do the grand tour of Europe. We kept on going. Through the Suez Canal. Down the east coast of Africa. Got off at Lourenço Marques and took a train to the interior. Hired those blacks in Salisbury with the help of the district commissioner."

"I'm surprised he let you go off on your own."

"I said I was a prospector. Sometimes you have to lie to get what you want."

Jack Merryweather was asleep by the fire, the half-full bottle of brandy next to him. The blacks stopped talking and the night sounds of Africa took control. Harry fed the second fire away from the stark carcass of the impala drying out on the spit over the dying coals. Left where it was, the ants would not get their teeth into what was left of the venison.

No one, not even the blacks who had searched the river for a crossing, had seen any sign of the Great Elephant. As he went to sleep he thought he heard his father's voice telling him to leave the animal alone.

When he woke at dawn, his rage at the animal had gone. At least his father would not have to suffer the pain and indignity of old age.

THE WENTWORTHS HAD PROBABLY NEVER FELT hunger for a thousand years. Their father was a stockbroker. Their grandfather, a country lawyer. The lawyers in the family did the wills and testaments. The stockbrokers invested the clients' money. What they needed to succeed was connections, preferably family connections.

"Oh, Sara, don't be so silly," her mother had said while she sulked. "Love and kisses are so temporary. Money goes on forever. For generations. The need we feel to fall in love is only nature forcing us in the right direction. And when we have fulfilled nature's requirements, love flies out of the window, its passion spent and rightly. And thank goodness. Six children were quite enough."

"Did you never love Father?"

"I respect your father and that is quite enough."

"I hate Mervyn. He's a pompous pig."

"You are a very attractive girl. To throw away the wealth of your children for a brief, fluttering heart is absurd, if not downright criminal. You are being selfish. You must think of your children."

"But I don't have any children."

"But you will. Mervyn will give you a lot of children."

"I don't even want him touching me. When he shakes hands it's like shaking hands with a dead fish, a wet dead fish. Probably cod."

"Your mother and father always know best. Just don't forget that. Life is not easy, Sara. Only money makes it possible. Your father has agreed Jared may take you to the continent. Then you will come home and do as you are told. I don't have time to argue with you... When Jared comes back he will enter the family firm. He will become a stockbroker. You children can't just run around on a whim. You have to be safe. Whatever would children do without their parents? You can help me arrange the flowers for your father's dinner party tonight. Your father has to entertain his clients, remember. That's why we have this big house and all the servants. Go to the greenhouse and ask Bellamy to cut the best flowers he can find... And, Sara, please stop sulking. You will learn to respect Mervyn."

"Respect a wet codfish. I don't think so," she mumbled as she walked away.

"Sara, I heard that. Don't be rude to your mother."

She knew the reason they wanted her to marry Mervyn Braithwaite, whose fishy eyes followed her around whenever they were in the same room.

They wanted to be the family stockbroker. Braithwaite and Penny had started after the Napoleonic wars, selling cotton goods dirt cheap to the Indians, and flimsy Indian cotton goods dirt cheap to the poor in England. How it worked, Sara had not quite understood. If they had each bought their own cheap cotton goods they would not have had to pay for transport half the way around the world. It was, she thought, something to do with trade and the stupidity of people who imagined others had something better. An Indian shawl in Cheapside made an English woman that bit superior to her neighbour. In Bombay, it was the snobby thing to wear a cotton dress made in Birmingham, or wherever they made cheap cotton dresses, of which Sara had no idea.

It was just before Christmas and the greenhouse was warm and full of blooming flowers oblivious of the snow on the paths just outside the glass. Bellamy was nowhere to be seen, so she cut what she could find with a pair of scissors into a long low lattice-woven basket and shivered her way back to the big house despite the long cloak she had thrown over her shoulders. She hoped her father's guests, who were already in their rooms as they had come for the weekend, would appreciate spring flowers in the middle of winter. She thought there might be some parallel with the cheap cotton dresses.

Soon after, she and Jared had hatched their plan to escape to freedom, even if it was only a short period of time... And at Christmas, in a few days, Mervyn and his family were joining the Wentworths for the Yuletide festivities. It was not fair. If she knew a young strong man with dreams she would elope with him tomorrow, but as hard as she racked her brain she could never remember meeting a young strong man with dreams.

LIFE AT ELEPHANT WALK was very good to the Honourable Robert St Clair. The food was plentiful and excellent. He had yet to see a drop of rain.

Harry's grandfather, Sir Henry Manderville, had overseen the building of a rondavel just behind his own house in the family compound for Robert to sleep in and be alone when he wanted his privacy. Made of wattle and daub to fill in the cracks of the bush timber, with a new yellow thatched roof, it was just what he wanted even if the floor was made from polished cow dung. The one window had a lovely view down to the Mazoe River past the stockade built, he was told, by Harry's father and Uncle Tinus in the first Chimurenga when the Shona had risen in rebellion against British rule.

So far as Robert was concerned, Jack and Harry could stay out in the bush hunting elephant as long as they liked, even if Madge made sure they were never in the same room alone. Whoever this Barend Oosthuizen was, apart from being the son of the late Tinus Oosthuizen, he had a strong grip on the young girl's heart and she wasn't letting him let her go. But as Robert said to himself philosophically after a particularly good meal, you can't win them all.

Taking an interest in butterflies and all things collectable that came out of the bush had won over Grandfather Manderville in a week. Robert thought the old man was a bit off his head but even that served his purpose. Being looked after by a pack of servants and fed good food was as far as Robert wanted to see into the future. To make himself useful and not quite so obvious, he took on the idea of teaching young George, eleven years old, history and English. The boy was lonely for his father and reminded Robert of young Barnaby, left so often on his own at Purbeck Manor. Robert understood young George and made a point of keeping the young mind occupied with things to do.

There had always been dogs at Elephant Walk and often they were killed. The last pack of four Alsatians had made the mistake of attacking a leopard and paying for it with their lives, along with the two terriers that had joined in the fight. The six-month-old lion dogs were just at the right age to be trained to do what they were told, and soon after Harry had gone off on his expedition, Robert had concentrated George's young mind on the three dogs and bitch. Training dogs was a favourite pastime of Lord St Clair and he had passed the knowledge down to all his sons.

Ten weeks after Harry had ridden out after his father's killer, Robert was down by the river with George and the dogs trying to teach the boy how to write in a way that others could understand. So far as Robert was concerned, he, Robert, was an indispensable part of the family, which was how he wanted it to stay. Standing up, he and the boy watched the file of horses, pack horses, and a four-wheeled wagon pass through the gate into the stockade. The dogs took off as fast as their young legs would carry them while Robert and the boy walked up over the lawn dotted with tall msasa trees, the dogs barking all the time.

When Robert reached the back gate nearest his rondavel, where he went and left the books he had been using to teach George, he was surprised to see one of the men wore long straight hair down past his shoulders, like a picture he had once seen of Colonel Custer's last stand. One of the horses shielded the dogs before everything came back under control.

Putting on his best smile of welcome, Robert strode across to greet them. Mrs Brigandshaw was hugged by her eldest son.

"My goodness," he said under his breath, seeing the skirt. "That's no man. That's a woman." Peeling off the dirt and dust, he rather thought a good-looking woman after a bath. She had not been riding side-saddle which was unusual for a girl. Robert, with even more reason to enjoy his African stay, concentrated his mind on the girl, hoping this time there would be some money. He also thought a little competition for young Madge would do her good. And do Robert some good as well.

There were dogs and horses and people all over the place. Ducks that roamed the lawns took off for the river. The old man got into the act by shaking his grandson's hand more than was necessary.

Tea was brought out onto the lawn and placed on tables under a large msasa tree. Biscuits were served, the newcomers properly introduced.

"Oh," said Robert to Sara's question, "I was up at Oxford with Harry. He was staying with us in the old place in Dorset when the call came that his father had been killed. He asked me to go with him before I start a career."

"Do you have any idea what you want to do?" she asked.

"I have so many dreams but I think I will be a writer." The idea had come out of the top of his head.

"What college were you at?"

"New College."

Hearing the name of the place where he had spent three years studying geology, Harry broke off listening to George and turned to Sara and Robert.

"Did either of you know Mervyn Braithwaite?" asked Sara.

"Fishy Braithwaite," they both said together in chorus.

"He's my fiancé," she said.

Mrs Brigandshaw, Harry's mother, seeing the debacle, smiled. "I'm sure he's very nice," she said.

"His father was very rich," said Robert, his normal flair for saying the right thing at a loss.

"I wish he wasn't," said Sara.

"But why?" said Robert with genuine astonishment.

"Because then I would not have to marry him."

THE DAY after the hunting party returned empty-handed, Elephant Walk became almost crowded. For months, especially during the rains when the roads were often impassable, the family lived alone, going about their daily routine without a visitor.

Peregrine the Ninth arrived in his old wagon and was taken away by Henry Manderville for a hot bath before he was invited to sit down even for a cup of tea. And, as usual, he smelt like a herd of buffalo. Henry had the water in the bath changed twice before he offered the old man a clean towel with which to dry himself.

The smell of paraffin drifted from the house to the lawn and Madge, reading a book under a tree. She wrinkled her nose. Madge had known Peregrine the Ninth all her life. She put down the book, smiling to herself. The paraffin her grandfather administered to the old man's nest of hair was meant to kill off any parasites that lived in the thick growth of white facial hair and beard, or the long head hair that dropped down his back. Few in the family had any faith in the remedy. Peregrine the Ninth had never, to her knowledge, been offered a bed in one of the family compound houses. The old man, older than Methuselah, retreated at night to his four-wheeled wagon that everyone thought was crawling in vermin waiting their turn to get into the old man's nest of hair.

An hour after being escorted from his wagon to the bathtub, the old man reappeared in an old shirt and an old pair of trousers that belonged to her grandfather. One of the servants was feeding the clothes the old man had arrived in, into the furnace that heated a drum that fed hot water into her grandfather's bathroom. It was said that outside of the capital Salisbury, her grandfather was the only man in Rhodesia who boasted hot and cold running water plus a pull-and-let-go on the design invented by Mister Crapper. People had come from far and wide just to look at the system that started with metal windmills down at the river and ended with the water pumped up the long slope to a holding tank the size of a swimming pool. Another windmill pump pushed water up into a header tank high behind her grandfather's house that produced the water pressure to flush the toilet and run water into the house and feed the outside boiler under which were burning the old man's clothes.

The most remarkable of remarkable things for Madge about Peregrine the Ninth was the very plumby, upper-class British accent that emanated from the small, round, fleshy mouth exactly the size of a small ripe plum.

No one had ever heard the old man's last name, though many had asked, to be told one name was good enough for anyone. And no one had any idea how long the old man had been in Africa or whether he was ever going home.

Peregrine the Ninth was an itinerant storyteller, a modern-day minstrel without his lute, who went from a lonely farm to lonely mine bringing news and the only entertainment anywhere to be found in the bush. He was fond of modern gossip mixed with the tales of years gone by, and no one ever knew how much was true and how much the old man's imagination. So far as Madge knew, it was the way the old man made his living. The two old donkeys, long immune to the bite of the tsetse fly, were the same two she always remembered. The one was Clary, and the other was Jeff, though no one was ever told which was which. How the lions hadn't eaten the lot of them had been a mystery to Madge most of her life.

Going to his wagon in his fresh shirt and trousers, barefoot, as usual, he came back with the family's mail that he had picked up in Salisbury the day before. Even the post office knew enough to release the Elephant Walk mail if the old man said he was going that way.

With a flourish and a bow, he presented the small pile of tied up envelopes to Madge under her tree.

"You bloom more beautiful every time we meet."

"Thank you, Uncle Peregrine." The small blue eyes twinkled at her out of the sprouting face hair, both eyebrows going high in tangles, the only dark colour in the whole of the old man's face. At that point, he gave her a kiss. Surprisingly, his breath was always sweet, his kiss light as a feather.

The piece of string around the letters was tight. Her fingers tried to loosen the knot where the string had furred. Her grandfather leaned over with his small red penknife and cut the string. Quickly, she searched the pile for Barend's handwriting and came up empty-handed. As the next best thing there was a letter from Aunty Alison addressed to her mother. She gave the rest of the pile to her grandfather as most were addressed to Sir Henry Manderville Bart. To everyone's surprise on Elephant Walk, there were people all over the world who collected dead butterflies and dead bugs. And they all seemed to write to Grandfather Manderville in search of more bugs and butterflies. And he was writing a book that would be very nice if he could find an illustrator, someone who could accurately draw the poor things stuck forever through the back in glass-topped boxes, the produce of grandfather's years of tramping through the bush. Madge also thought it surprising a lion or a leopard had not eaten her grandfather. On his hunt for bugs in the bush, he was oblivious to everything other than his quest. Madge thought maybe the lions felt sorry for him searching for so small a prey. There had to be some honour among predators.

She took the letter into the main house, as the servant, dressed in a starched white long shirt and shorts to his knobbly knees, put a large tea tray down on the table under the msasa tree. Lucky for Uncle Peregrine there was a large chocolate cake she had baked that morning. She left her grandfather and Peregrine talking nineteen to the dozen between messy bites of chocolate cake.


HER MOTHER PUT the letter aside unopened while they both watched the cake demolition from the veranda that ran the length of the house. Madge was itching for her mother to open the letter but knew from experience that nagging would prolong the agony. She had not heard one word from Barend since he left Elephant Walk, having long refused to speak English to anyone. The grief for his father had turned to a bitter hatred of the British.

"But your mother is English. I am English," she had pleaded with him.

"Then I shall go."

Why Uncle Tinus being hanged by the British for treason should have ruined her life and Barend's, made no sense whatsoever. She was equally and hysterically furious with the British but, as her father had said, no war had ever been petty, that in the stupidity of war people killed each other, even friends killed each other.

When she looked up her mother was crying again, tears silently falling down her face, her eyes not even seeing the two old men crouched around the chocolate cake. For a moment, she forgot her own pain and went to give her mother a hug. There was so much more to learn of life and none of the new experiences was proving pleasant.

The world of Madge Brigandshaw had been turned upside down.


THE OTHERS CAME BACK from their ride around the farm as the sun was going down behind the small hill on the other side of the Mazoe River. Peregrine the Ninth and Grandfather Manderville had moved onto the veranda, where the servants were putting the fly screens in place, before lighting the four lamps that hung along the back wall between the heads and antlers of long-dead animals.

The tea tray had gone back into the kitchen with the cake dish cleared of every morsel of chocolate cake.

A servant was putting glasses on the sideboard at the far end of the veranda that Tinus Oosthuizen would have called the stoep. There were sherry glasses, glasses for the bottles of beer that were protruding from a large zinc bucket, and small, fluted wine glasses. Separate were two cut crystal whisky glasses. Comfortable chairs and low tables littered the length of the veranda. The daily ritual of sundowners was about to begin.

Jared Wentworth, always curious, looked in the zinc bucket and was astonished to see large chunks of ice floating on water in between the bottles of beer. There was a separate bucket full of ice chunks.

"My grandfather," said Harry, seeing what Jared was looking at. "He gets magazines from all over the world. Says just because we live in the bush doesn't mean we can't be civilised. Had the paraffin-fired refrigerator imported from America. There's a new type that works from electricity but it will be a long, long time before Elephant Walk has electric lights... Fresh clean water from the Mazoe River and a chunk of ice in your whisky. Or a cold beer in the heat of the day. Now that's civilisation. That's living. Help yourself to a beer. One of the rules in this house. We don't like the servants kept up just to serve us food and drinks after six o'clock at night. They need their time to relax as much as we do. Sara, what are you going to drink? Jared, please take a glass of sherry to my mother. That bottle over there. Jack, after that ride I expect you'll go for a beer. Help yourself... Oh dear, Uncle Peregrine has filled his whisky glass to the top so if we want the best of his stories we had better gather round him now."

"You would never think we are in the middle of nowhere," said Sara.

"We're not," said Madge, taking a small glass of sherry. "We're on Elephant Walk. That's not nowhere."

"To Sara and Jared Wentworth and Uncle Peregrine," said Harry. "Welcome to Elephant Walk."

BY THE END of the second tumbler of whisky, Peregrine the Ninth was in full flight about a cave to the north he had heard about that had once been inhabited by the most powerful witch of the nineteenth century. He even claimed the woman had instigated the Shona uprising in 1896. Peregrine told the story second-hand, only saying what he had heard from an old Shona he had befriended years ago on his travels. In the witch's cave was a beam of light that shone into the bowels of the earth and anyone who found the beam of light would find the hidden hoard of gold, the gold of Lobengula, King of the Matabele. Whoever found the gold would rule Rhodesia.

Harry was half listening, more interested in the light falling from the nearest paraffin lamp on Sara Wentworth's long hair, bringing out the lovely streaks of red. The dogs, exhausted by following the horses all day, were spread out around the reed mat-covered floor, flat on their sides and fast asleep. He was coming to terms with being on Elephant Walk without the sound of his father's voice. He was gone, Harry thought, but would live on in the minds of his friends and family. The elephant had gone too. Maybe one day someone would find the great tusks. Uncle Peregrine had said, before launching into his story of the witch, that some in the villages doubted the reports of the Great Elephant. That the isolated attacks on villagers by elephants had been going on for as long as anyone could remember. That evoking of the Great Elephant had brought the white men to chase away the elephants that were eating the villagers' crops of maize. The old people were saying the Great Elephant was dead, dead of its terrible wound.

Then Harry heard Uncle Peregrine talk about a man who had helped the witch and the uprising. For some unknown reason, this great right hand of the witch could speak the language of the conquerors, the only black man in the north of the country who could speak English.

"What was his name?" asked Harry, humouring Uncle Peregrine and to keep the story flowing. The guests were enjoying their first taste of the myths and legends of Africa.

"Tatenda."

"What did you say, Uncle Peregrine?" asked Harry, every one of his senses brought into focus.

"His name was Tatenda. And he hated the English."

"Is he alive?"

"Probably. Why?"

"Because I think we know him, we taught him English, we saved his life from the Matabele. Elephant Walk was his home until he ran away. And soon after that, we had the rebellion. Uncle Peregrine, could you take me to your friend who knows Tatenda?"

"Probably. Can I have another whisky?"

So far as Peregrine the Ninth was concerned, a good story deserved its reward. He kept his gnarled fist firmly around the cut crystal glass, holding it out to Harry to fill from the bottle. Only when the glass was full to the brim did he go on with the story. The old man had never been a one for ice or water in his whisky; there was only so much room in a glass.

He made them all wait while he took a long, welcome sip. Then, with everyone still hanging on his words, he continued the story. And like all good actors, he played to the audience. Using his imagination to brighten the brief facts he had heard about the young man they had called Tatenda, he made him the centre of the story. The evil witch took a step backwards. If young Harry wanted to find his old friend Tatenda, he could lead him around the bush for weeks drinking whisky every night. With a smile of deep satisfaction, he went on and on with the story, stopping twice for a refill until he lost his train of thought in the whisky.

By the time everyone went in for supper, the temperature had dropped near to freezing. The sky above Elephant Walk was crystal clear, the night sky littered with millions of twinkling stars, layer after layer going back into the black void of the universe.

A big log fire had been lit in the lounge where they carried their plates of cold supper from the dining room.

From the grip of cold and silence of the bush outside came the snores of Peregrine the Ninth. Without his supper, but with half a bottle of whisky in his stomach, Harry and Jack had carried the old man to his covered wagon. They had got him up on the tailgate where he had stood for a moment before crumbling forward on his face.

Before opening the whisky bottle, Grandfather Manderville had gone across to make sure the mattress was in its place. It was part of the myth of the man that required him to fall flat on his face when sufficiently drunk. Somewhere behind the old man's wagon, probably a mile away, Harry thought a lion roared as he covered the old man with the patchwork of skins that made do for a blanket.

As will happen after a long day in Africa, soon after they had eaten their fork supper the eyelids began to droop.

The double front gates and the two back gates to the stockade had been closed by the servants when they had gone off duty in the quickly falling dusk. The dogs had found a better place around the fire as it glowed less and less into the beginning of the night. Once more the lion roared and one of the half-tame ducks quacked in its sleep. In all directions, a man could have walked all night without likely seeing another human being.

When the moon rose at two in the morning it threw a colourless light through the stark bows of the msasa trees and shadowed the slopes of the houses across the lawn.

By the time they woke in the morning, the moon had gone. Only the big stars, the planets, could be seen in the chill clear air of morning. Peregrine the Ninth was still sleeping face down on his mattress. The dogs were the first to get up and look at the dawn, sending the geese into cackling flight up and over the stockade and down to the river. They were the first to splash the water, and then the buck and a wild pig came down to drink and the new day began, the cycle of life. Somewhere further downriver, a blood-curdling scream rent the dawn. For one life, the day would never be again.

By the time Harry got out of bed, the dawn was blood-reddening the sky and when he looked out of the window he was glad to be home. He hoped he would marry and have a son of his own to one day look out of the same window. Then he smelt the richness of cooking bacon and put on his clothes to hurry through for his breakfast. Robert St Clair was already seated at the breakfast table the servants had set up on the veranda. The screens had been taken away and the sun was licking through the trees. Even though the air was cold, the rays of the sun were warm and full of colour. Jack Merryweather came in next, rubbing his hands against the cold and wrinkling his nose with pleasure at the coffee pot. Within a minute of sitting down at the table, a plate of hot bacon, eggs, tomatoes, and sausage was put in front of him. Even the toast was warm from the open fire in the kitchen.

Sir Henry Manderville preferred his breakfast alone in the privacy of his home.

A metal plough disc was being hit continuously in the native compound, bringing the farm workers out for their day. The ducks flew back over the stockade into the compound. Doves and pigeons called from the trees, sweet in their sounds. A grey heron landed slowly on the lawn on long gangly legs.

"I have never slept so well in my life," said Sara, coming in for breakfast. She and Jared were staying in Alison Oosthuizen's house while she was away looking for her son Barend. "A good bed beats the hell out of my bunk in the wagon. Where's Madge?"

"She has something about her weight," said Harry. "She'll be over at grandfather's later having her coffee. Mother has a little veranda off her bedroom where she likes to eat her breakfast alone and plan her day. It was a way for my father to have some peace in the morning without us children."

"Where's young George?" asked Robert. "Not like him to miss his breakfast."

"He's eating with Uncle Peregrine in the wagon I expect," said Harry. "They kind of like each other. Mother will dunk him later in the bathtub and delouse his clothes. Now, who wants another cup of coffee?... Today, I have to plan this year's ploughing for the maize and then we will be dipping the cattle. We should have ploughed at the end of the rainy season, the moisture would have stayed in the ground. But Father was dead and I was in England. Without careful management and pre-thought, farming in Africa quickly becomes a disaster. I wish my grandfather would take more interest in the farming aspect of Elephant Walk but he says it's not his business. Can you all look after yourselves? I'll take my lunch in the lands... It's going to be another beautiful day."

"So you're going to be a farmer and not a geologist?" said Robert, still pleased that Sara had sat down next to him for her breakfast.

"It rather looks that way," said Harry. "Jared, you and Sara can stay as long as you like. Aunt Alison is not coming back to Elephant Walk. She is going to stay in Cape Town hoping Barend will contact friends he knew when they farmed in Franschhoek. No one has heard of him. Poor Aunt Alison. After three years and no trace, he's likely dead. Running away from home at the age of fourteen to disappear into the African bush on your own is not the most sensible start to life. Hatred does terrible things to people, even young boys. Hatred and love. My poor sister. Madge has been set on spending her life with Barend since they could first talk to each other. Mother says the letter was terribly sad but there is nothing more she can do for Aunt Alison and Katinka. Katinka's twelve. Well, there we are. Make yourself comfortable in their house."

# BOOK 2 – JOURNEYS OF DISCOVERY

# 1

## DECEMBER 1912

*A*fter Madge had given up hope of receiving a letter, it had taken Barend Oosthuizen another five years to find what he wanted, and he had found it twice in one day.

With the consummate charm of a man who knows he is good-looking but doesn't have to use it to get his own way, the eight-year odyssey since leaving Elephant Walk at fourteen had been surprisingly easy. Wherever he had found himself people had wanted to do him only good. They wanted to give him things. They liked him. And most of all they only wanted him to like them in return. And it did not matter whether they were old or young, male or female. Everyone wanted to do Barend a favour and many of them did.

Not long after crossing the Limpopo River into South Africa at the beginning of his journey, he had found a solitary farmhouse in the lonely scrub and ridden his horse for three hours before coming up on the homestead he had first seen from the hill that overlooked the flatland of the veld. No one, especially Marie Putter, who had been widowed in the Boer War when she was twenty-seven, childless, would have taken the good-looking man for fourteen years old. When they met in the chicken run at the back of the house he received from a woman the first carnal look of many to come. When he asked her for a job on the farm she was so excited she left the door to the hen house open along with the gate to the run. With squawking chickens running in all directions they were soon laughing happily together. That night, Barend lost his virginity.

That one had lasted a month. When they parted it was as friends, and the saddle bags of the packhorse he led on a long rein behind the one that he rode, was full of dried meat that would see him, if necessary, as far as Cape Town.

Long before he reached Cape Town, a journey of twelve interesting months, he had forgotten about his mother, sister, and Madge. The only thing that had travelled with him from Elephant Walk and stayed was his hatred of the English who had killed his father. And he always felt at home on the Boer farms as most of the farms nursed the same hatred of the British.

Even when in 1910 the two Boer republics and the two British colonies became the Union of South Africa under General Louis Botha, a Boer, some Boers were still looking for revenge.

At the age of seventeen, he stood on a kopje overlooking the battlefield at Paardeberg where many of his relations had fallen and swore his oath to the Brotherhood of Hate.

"I, Barend Oosthuizen, in the name of my father General Tinus Oosthuizen and the Oosthuizens that fell at Paardeberg, do hereby swear I will do all in my power for the rest of my life to revenge the Boer republics and restore the Boer nation to its rightful position in Africa, so help me God."

On the same day Barend climbed down from the kopje to wash his face in the Modder River that seven years before had flowed with so much Boer blood, Harry Brigandshaw was setting out from Elephant Walk, hundreds of miles to the north, to be led a dance by Peregrine the Ninth in Harry's abortive quest to find out what had happened to his childhood friend Tatenda.

When Barend turned eighteen a year later, in 1908, he was six feet tall and worked in a gold mine, chipping gold-bearing rock in a tunnel that made him lie on his side to swing his pick. The mineworkers union demanded the good jobs for whites and higher pay than the blacks, but they all died together when the tunnels collapsed. It was the hardest work he had ever endured in his life but the money was better than odd jobs on the farms. With very little education except what he had learned from his mother, Barend had few skills that would pay him money. His charm went only so far and the thought, at eighteen, of marrying a farmer's daughter had never entered his mind. To work for twenty years waiting for an old man to die to inherit the farm was not his style. After months at the rock face his arms and shoulders were taut with muscles, his skin smooth, washed by the daily sweat and the fine dust from the bowels of the mother earth.

After a shower above ground at the end of his night shift, he liked to wear a clean shirt every day and walk the new streets of Johannesburg. There were so many people, so many horses and noise from the motor cars of the rand barons, so many women dressed in expensive clothes, so many shop windows to look into, so many dreams of wealth and power to be dreamed about. His blond hair kept short and his face clean-shaven, the slate-green eyes smiled at everything he saw. Without the hatred that permanently knotted the pit of his stomach, he could have been a happy man.

On the surface, he looked like the man Madge had loved from the age of six, but hidden behind the good-looking man with the gorgeous smile was a man with a tormented soul. If there was ever a case for not judging a man by his appearance, Barend was the perfect example. Fortunately for them, no man or woman could look into the recesses of his mind, to what he was thinking in his head. Some of his brothers in the Brotherhood of Hate had some idea but even they would have run from the truth. If there was the devil in the form of a Greek god, Barend Oosthuizen was that devil, brooding, hating, planning revenge, and all the time smiling the outward smile of loving his neighbours more than he loved himself.

Over the years it had not once crossed his thoughts that his mother was in daily agony for not knowing where he was in the world. And only in his dreams did Madge come to him, and these brief dreams he put from his mind in the light of morning.

On the day the British had hanged his father they had warped the inside of his son's brain.


SALLIE BARKER HAD SEEN the clean-shaven man with the short blond hair and slate-green eyes sitting alone at the bar, the smiling eyes watching her going about her business. She never spoke to him but every time the slate-green eyes smiled in her direction she felt a shiver run through her body.

The Mansion House, though it had another name at the time and several afterwards, had been built on the corner of Rissik Street and Plein Street by Barnet Isaacs, or Barney Barnato as he was better known by his stage and pugilist name, soon after he had merged his diamond interests with Cecil John Rhodes, for money but, more importantly, for a membership of the Kimberley Club, the first Jew to be accepted by the largely British institution. His grand house in Johannesburg, a monument to his foray into the goldfields of the Witwatersrand after enriching himself in Kimberley, had been placed on the market soon after Barney Barnato drowned from a ship taking him to England. To Sallie, whether Barney Barnato had jumped or was pushed made no difference, but the five owners after Barnato drowned were convinced the house was haunted.

By the time Lily White bought the great house she picked it up for a song, which is what she had in mind anyway.

Barney Barnato was an East End Jew from the slums of London, a situation close to the heart of what once had been Lily Ramsbottom, the bastard child born in the industrial north of England near Wigan. To honour the name of a man who had worked his way up from the slums to be one of the richest men in the empire, Lily had called her house of fun the Mansion House, after the home of the Lord Mayor of London. Whether this put away the ghost of Barney Barnato or not, from the day the house was grandly renamed after all the refurbishing paid for without his knowledge by Jack Merryweather, with Sallie and the girls who had come up from Cape Town looking on with a certain sense of pride, nary a ghost was ever seen again. A year after opening the best brothel in Johannesburg, Lily was rich. And with Sallie applying her new-found accounting skills, there was a pile of money in the bank. Good strong drinks and good-looking whores, women paid for handsomely, but only in the time of passion, was a combination that never failed to make money throughout the indulgent history of man.

There were four bars in the Mansion House and each charged a different price.

"You can't just cater to the very rich or the poor sod with a quid to spend on a Saturday night," Lily White had said during the grand refurbishing. "You have to cater for the lot but keep them apart, see. Man being so bloody conscious of his status, the rich will pay five times more for something to prove they're rich. Even the poor bloody miners will save up for a whore they really fancy and meantime we take their quids for booze. The girls charge rich and poor the same, only the drinks change price. In the top-class lounge, we have an orchestra, in the cheapest a girl, if we can find her, on a piano. And you never know, a poor man today is a rich man tomorrow, isn't that right, Albert Pringle?... You got to use your brains in business."

The four lounges were equally sumptuous, with soft plush leather couches that oozed sex by just sitting in them and feeling the squirm. In a corner of each was a well-stocked bar, and a barman to listen to anyone's woes, dim chandeliers hung from the ceilings, red carpets, thick with pile, covered the floors. For summer there were overhead fans, for the ice-cold highveld winters there were two fires to each lounge, and a fire in each of the twelve bedrooms that led off the corridors on the first floor up the broad stairs from the ground-floor hall.

The old kitchen Barnato had designed to cook food to impress his new friends was put to good use in the downstairs dining room and the two private eating rooms for guests who did not wish to be seen. There was even a lift from the ground floor to the whores' bedrooms, operated by a power plant imported from England by the previous owner, that only got stuck once in a while when the power plant failed. Most of the regulars preferred to walk up the stairs, some not even bothering with the bars and dining rooms, too impatient to get on with the job, remove their sexual frustration and get back to the more important job of making more and more obscene quantities of money.

Johannesburg, the most exciting mining town in the world, was booming for the rich. And so was the business of Lily White. As Albert Pringle was inclined to say when the three of them were alone after a busy day, "Landed with our bums in the butter, what we did. Bums in the butter."

The fact that the operation was quite illegal had never crossed anyone's minds.


THERE IS a quirk in some good-looking men that makes them like to pay for their women. In the more lavish spenders, the dripping diamonds on their wives, mistresses and whores are often in direct proportion to their ability to satisfy a woman sexually. Albert Pringle thought of them as 'wham-bam, thank you ma'am' and there were many of them at the Mansion House who liked to pay out money after their failure, as if to say 'I may be no good to you in your bed but I can still spit in your eye by paying for it.'

Others, like Barend Oosthuizen, liked whores for the simple reason there was no repercussion, nobody wanting your body and mind for the rest of your life after you had taken them to bed. It was probably a way of confronting his subconscious for running away from Madge, but this was so far back it never came into his conscious mind. One by one, when he managed to save his money, Barend had paid for every one of Lily White's girls.

Sallie had watched the young man come and go through the months, had even seen the desolation in his eyes while he drank a pot of coffee in the corner of their cheapest lounge while he waited for the girl of his choice. Always the slate-green eyes tried to search for contact with her own, but always she slid hers away. Some men, she had learned, she just did not look at or it gave them ideas. Being naïve back in Cape Town she had not known that rule with Herr Flugelhorne. She had foolishly thought you could look straight in the eye with a smile at an elderly cousin by marriage.

The word had soon spread that Miss Sallie was part of the management, that she had no price. The word had gone out in the mining town with the psyche of a mining camp that one of the rand barons had offered Sallie Barker ten thousand pounds for one full night. The girl had politely laughed, so they said, patted the fat old bastard's cheek, and asked him what he thought she was, putting a finger to her lips. The two had even laughed together. There were many such stories in Johannesburg of the rich and the poor but this one was true.

"You're a fool," Lily had told her. "He was drunk. Silly old fart would have given you twenty thousand."

"Then I'd have been a whore," Sallie had said sweetly.

"One day, Sallie Barker, you might just grow up to the facts of life, how women survive in a world full of nasty men. Never look a gift horse in the mouth, young lady. That kind of money don't come around too often."

The Mansion House had been in full swing for a year and ten days when the club, as they liked to call it, was visited by a group of young toffs from England, out of Daddy's way and out to have a good time at anyone else's expense. They spoke loudly in patrician accents. Not knowing their way around, they stumbled late at night into the miners' lounge and proceeded to make fools of themselves. They were all drunk. One of them climbed up on the bar and crawled along on his hands and knees barking like a dog, with the barman moving the glasses in front of him to stop them being broken. To begin with, it was quite funny and everyone laughed. Being overbred and underworked, as none of them had ever had a job in their lives, they had no concern who they upset.

All might have been well if Barend Oosthuizen had not woken from a nightmare in the middle of the night. He had dreamed of Madge, a Madge floating away into the clouds of death calling him to join her in the afterlife. With the sweat of fear damp on his chest, he had got up from his bed in his cheap lodgings in search of a woman to overcome his pain.

The coffee had been put at his small table when the barking dog fell off the end of the bar, cracking his head so hard on the floor everyone in the room stopped talking to look. With everyone's attention, the toffs wanted more drinks. Sallie, having made sure the one on the floor was all right even if his eyes were glazed, told the barman not to serve them any more drinks. Albert Pringle was out of the room and the barman unable to jump quickly enough over the bar. Whether it was the shock of being spoken to by an educated English woman in their own patrician accent or the thought that their upper-class accent was being mimicked, no one ever found out. The leader of the pack threw his full glass of wine in Sallie's face.

"You're a whore. Who the hell do you think you're talking to?" he slurred.

The speed with which Barend left his small table brought him up to the toff before the toff could haughtily turn and walk out of the club.

"You, sir, are a pig," he said. Which were the first words in English anyone had heard Barend speak.

Sallie turned in surprise by the words spoken in upper-class English, the red wine dripping down her face, her dark brown eyes looking briefly into the slate-green eyes full of hatred.

The fight was no contest and neither was the repercussion. The next day the Mansion House was closed for business and Barend Oosthuizen left Johannesburg for good, feeling well pleased with himself. Smashing up five English faces had given him the best feeling of his life. It was the start of his revenge.

The closure lasted a week. Like anything in life that is popular, legality never had the last word. With the mollified toffs on the train down to Cape Town and the boat back to England where it was hoped they would behave themselves, the Mansion House re-opened for business. It turned out the rand baron had not been so drunk after all. He was proud of Sallie and not only for not taking his money. And if money cannot buy influence, whatever can, they said in the streets of Johannesburg.

On the re-opening night, the rand baron invited Sallie out to dinner as his formal guest, treating her like any other woman of class. Sallie smiled sweetly and turned him down, memories of Herr Flugelhorne too vivid to trust any man.

Lily White heard the story of the invitation the following morning.

"Darling Sallie, you are beyond redemption. You will die poor but please remember another piece of my advice. Not every man is a horse's arse."

"But how do you tell one from the other?"

"That is the trick. Woman's instinct."

"But when he tried to buy me for ten thousand pounds you called him an old fart."

"That was before he convinced the police we are a legitimate business."

"Who was the man who saved my honour? He'd always spoken Afrikaans before so I never understood a word."

"There's a strange story there. The police did find out. His name is Barend Oosthuizen, the son of General Tinus Oosthuizen, who was hanged by the British during the war for leading a Boer rebellion out of the British Cape Colony."

"Then how does he speak such good English?"

"His mother is English."

"Where can I thank him?"

"You can't, he left town."

"Why? They let us re-open."

"No one forced him to leave. They come and go in a mining town... My goodness, business is good tonight. There's nothing like publicity. We'll catch up on last week's losses by the end of the night. I had to send out for more champagne. Albert really is a darling. I've hired him an assistant. A rather large young man with big hands. A bit stupid but very strong. And he has a friend if we need any more muscle."

WHEN BAREND WAS twenty-two years old the odyssey had lasted five years and the fight in the Mansion House four years earlier was long forgotten. There had been many more fights after the English toffs had their faces bloodied, and fights being mostly the same for Barend, like getting drunk, they had the habit of blending in with each other, their individuality lost. In many of the bar fights, very largely fights with Englishmen that he picked whenever he found the smallest opportunity, Barend was drunk and remembered nothing of the details, except the feeling of satisfaction.

The road to what he wanted had taken many paths after the policeman suggested he left Johannesburg before the English toffs laid a charge of assault. The two policemen that had visited his room were Afrikaners like himself and brought with them ten pounds they had raised among themselves in the Johannesburg police station. Being a badly paid and dangerous job, few of the British immigrants, even if they had fought in the British Army, sought a job in the South African police force. When the complaints had been lodged that General Oosthuizen's son had beaten up five Englishmen in a high-class whorehouse, jubilation had run through his fellow Afrikaners on the force.

To the Englishman with the swollen face, who had first complained to the British consul in Johannesburg, the police gave the assurance the criminality of the assault would be carefully pursued; to Barend they brought the ten pounds, a glow of admiration in their eyes and the suggestion he leave town for a while.

Even without the rand baron who fancied Sallie, Lily White would have been allowed to re-open the Mansion House soon after the toffs' train left Johannesburg central railway station.

For the first time in his life, Barend found himself a hero. Ten pounds plus small change was a lot of money, more than he could have saved in a year, and he decided to take advantage of his windfall. The thought of leaving Johannesburg and the lying all day on his side with a pick cutting out a seam of gold-bearing rock was not hard. He decided to look around the country they were shortly going to call the Union of South Africa. By the time the Union was declared with General Louis Botha its first prime minister in 1910, Barend had reached the port of Cape Town and was eyeing the ships and wondering where they were going.

Though he did not know it, as his mother had long ago stopped talking about her family to her son, his maternal grandfather had been a sea captain in the British Merchant Navy, travelling to all corners of the world for more than thirty years. The sight of all the ships in the harbour brought out the sailor hidden in Barend's genes. After four weeks of brawling around the dockside bars, he took ship as an ordinary seaman on a boat bound for the Dutch East Indies.

Though he had thought of the home he had last lived in with his father, he had not visited Kleinfontein, his father's farm confiscated by the British for his treason. He had not even visited the Franschhoek Valley or the people who had rebelled with his father to join the Boer army and fight the British, many of whom had gone home after the war. Only the general, Barend's father, had been tried for treason.

The ship was the MV *Orange*, flying the Dutch flag.

The next time Barend saw Africa it was then 1912, and the ship he had sailed on for six months, an old rust bucket of a coaster, called at the port of Walvis Bay in German South West Africa where the captain signed him off with residual pay of two pounds, ten shillings and sixpence. The ship was British as mostly ships calling around the coast of Africa sailed under the British flag. For the whole of the six-month voyage, no one on board knew he spoke English. Most of the crew were lascars from the East Indies where Dutch was the common language, a sister language to Afrikaans.

Barend Oosthuizen was twenty-two years old and as tough as teak, his handsome face burnt to the colour of light mahogany, only the slate-green eyes testimony to his Caucasian ancestry. It is doubtful whether Madge or his mother would have recognised him.

With the remnants of his ten pounds, hoarded against the inevitable catastrophe which had yet to come, and the proceeds of his last voyage, Barend bought two good salted horses, horses that had been bitten by the tsetse fly and had survived the sleeping sickness. Both animals were used to the shaft of the small covered wagon but only one pulled at a time, the other following behind on a long rein. Barend was going back into the African bush but first, he was going up the coast to the Portuguese territory from where he had the idea of following a great river into the hinterland. From his father, the white hunter, he had inherited the gene that pulled him back into the bush. In the wagon, with a good supply of ammunition, he carried three guns; two rifles and a twelve-bore shotgun. He was going to live off the land. Unlike his father, there was not a book to be found in the wagon, not even a Bible.

With no great purpose in mind, he began his journey up the Skeleton Coast.

FOR THE FIRST FEW DAYS, he was unable to explain his euphoria. It was June and the nights were cold, with squalls of rain dashing his clean-shaven face during the day, pouring water off the rim of his big black hat with the wide brim and the pointed dome. The smell of the salt sea air was fresh but the smell of the sea had been in his nostrils for three years. The West Coast black mussels were huge, and some as wide as the palm of his hand, and cooked in their shells full of seawater sucked in by the live mollusc were delicious to eat. There were rock lobsters crawling out of the cold Atlantic to be picked up on the beach without even getting his hands wet. There were so many giant slipper oysters on the rocks at low tide he grew sick of eating them, he ate so many. And when he felt like meat, he saddled up the horse that was out of shaft that day and rode not a mile into the scrub desert to shoot a springbok, the buck so remote they had never seen a horse or a predator man with his deadly gun and had no knowledge to run away. The heart, liver and kidneys went straight on the fire, the rest of the animal, except one front leg, was cut into strips and hung along the side of the wagon to dry in the sun, soak in the salty sea mist or wash clean in the squalls of rain. There was fresh water with which to fill his water barrels when he needed it, the water springs easily found by following the tracks of the jackals that preyed on the seals that honked and swarmed on the smooth black rocks, after filling their bellies with fish from the sea. There were gulls and eagles to sound music in his ears.

On the morning of the tenth day, within a short ride of the cross placed by Bartolomeu Dias in the fifteenth century, he woke up to find what it was. He was happy to be home. Happy to be back in Africa. With the understanding of his euphoria coursing through his mind, he twirled a dance up the sandy beach, scattering the black-backed gulls and chasing a jackal from its hunt. The big black cape that kept off the rain twirled from his body making a skirt. The black hat was thrown at a gull high in the air.

"I'm happy," he shouted. "I'm happy."

· · ·

WHEN THE WINTER sun came out from above the mist from the sea, there was mile after mile of straight sandy beach stretching in both directions. On the day that changed his life, the Atlantic was so flat, the sea washed up the beach as if a giant had sloshed a large bucket of water up the white sand. As the slosh of water retreated it left a series of high water lines with pieces of seaweed, dead crayfish shells, mussels torn by an earlier storm from the rocks and now washed ashore, and pieces of wood, many fashioned by the hand of man, mostly long-dead men as the skeletons along the rugged coast were those of ships sailed by men, ancient and modern, Portuguese caravels to the new iron ships powered by steam generated by coal. The flotsam and jetsam fascinated Barend and many a day was spent walking the soft beach looking at what the sea had brought him ashore.

Very often he was not conscious of seeing what he saw, discarding the obvious and ordinary like a good tracker looking for animal spoor. Sometimes he thought of Madge but mostly of the time when they were very young and innocent of life's pain. He laughed out loud at their old jokes and remembered how happy they had been. For hours he lived again as a child as he walked the long beach, the horses left behind with the covered wagon, only the dried meat hanging from the roof vulnerable to predators.

He had grown so used to his own company since leaving Elephant Walk eight long years ago when he was fourteen years old, he had no conscious idea of his loneliness. Loneliness was what he was, what he had become, and he hugged the feeling of self-satisfaction he had brought about without another person's help. He was content to leave behind the baggage of other people's minds, other people's wars, and for a while, he forgot his hatred of the English. There was a whole week on the Skeleton Coast when he did not once take out the revenge in his mind and have another look at it. With the sea and the beach, and so much easy food and water, Barend delayed, again and again, his trek inland, the journey that would take him back deep into the African bush.

From force of habit, which went back to when he was nine years old, Barend carried a gun over his shoulder. The .375 was powerful enough to kill an elephant at one hundred yards if the shot was put through the heart. There had been rumours in Walvis Bay of desert elephant that came right down to the sea, though what they would eat was a mystery to Barend, as tufts of scrub bush that could keep a springbok alive were nothing for an elephant that needed food in tons. He had once seen a pair of lynx hunting the beach for seals with the jackals, but the cats had run away. Only once, in the dark of night, he thought he heard a lion far away in the desert but he was not sure, and the wind had been blowing from the sea taking the sound.

Sometimes he carried the rifle at the trail to relieve the ache in his shoulder. Over his chest were two crossed straps that held the leather bags resting on his hips. Attached to the back of his belt was a metal water bottle covered in strips of khaki cloth he had bought in Walvis Bay. Had he known the bottle was British Army surplus from the Anglo-Boer War he would have died of thirst before taking a drink. In the soft leather bags at his hips was enough food for a day in case he was caught in a storm and forced to take shelter among the rocks and burrows out by the sea. The food was mostly cooked tails of rock lobster and strips of dried venison.

The crystal rock was the size of a chicken's egg. It sparkled in the sun and brought him back from his reverie to bend down and pick it up. It was far too heavy to have been washed in by the torpid sea where, in the shallows, the kelp was barely moving to the swell. The crystal was washed clean. The edges were flat and disappeared into each other like a deck of cards, only solid and strangely transparent. When the sun caught a flat surface as he turned the rock on the flat of his hand, the stone came alive with an inner fire. His rock was sparkling in the sun and Barend scratched his head with his free hand, wondering what had come to him out of the sea.

He looked around the beach for something similar and picked up three more rocks of the same type, two of them smaller and one larger than the first he had found. All four of them were washed clean by the waters of the sea and sparkled in the winter sun. Barend decided they were pretty and put them in one of his bags as a keepsake.

Checking the sun for the time, he began to retrace his steps back to the horses, his wagon, and a good night's sleep. It had been a long day's walk along the beach. He was tired but content in himself and by the time he heard his horses' neigh he had forgotten the four rocks in the small leather bag on his right hip. With the wind at his back, he knew the horses had smelt him and were calling to him with anticipated pleasure. It made him smile, quicken his pace, and begin to whistle. Tomorrow he was going to trek north until he found the first river to lead him inland across the scrub. He was hoping to find the Kunene River his father had talked to him about when he was a child sitting around the campfire in the Rhodesian bush.

There were three men in uniform sitting against the wheel of his wagon. They were chewing dried venison they had taken from the side of his wagon and all of them were smiling. Barend lowered the rifle that could kill an elephant at one hundred yards that he had pointed at the belly of the man in the middle. His horses were eating fodder laid on the sand and ignored him, the neighing coming from a culvert in the rocks where two more horses were hitched to an army wagon. Barend's horses had never eaten such good fodder since leaving Walvis Bay. The man in the middle got up, put out his hand, and spoke in a language Barend thought to be German but which he did not understand.

"Who are you?" Barend asked him in Afrikaans.

"You don't by any chance speak English?" said the German. The man's uniform was different from the other two and Barend correctly surmised he was an officer.

"Have I done something wrong?" asked Barend.

"Of course not... Your horses smelt the fodder we carry in our wagon. We gave them some. I hope you don't mind us eating your dried meat. Very good it is. I went to Oxford for a year after university in Berlin. Father wanted me to speak English so when we win the war I can be a military administrator in England. You are Afrikaner, I presume, and you don't like the English, which is good. We must be friends. With the help of the German army, you will restore your Boer republics. My name is von Stratten, Lieutenant von Stratten, Imperial German Army. At your service."

"My name is Barend."

"You don't have another name? Is Barend a Christian name or a surname?"

"It is both." For some reason, he did not wish to tell anyone who he was. The rest of him was part of his other life.

The two soldiers kept their crouched seats against the wagon and chewed the dried meat in their mouths like cows chewing the cud. The light had begun to go as the sun sank into the South Atlantic. It would be gone with minimum fuss in a matter of minutes. From out to sea, fifty feet above the ice-cold surface of the sea, the mist, a great roll of cotton wool, was rolling into the shore. Barend went to his wagon, pulled out a sheepskin jacket and put it on. The temperature was dropping one degree Fahrenheit every thirty seconds. The white, oily fur of the sheep was warm against his skin. He had walked the beach barefoot. Barend pulled on his sheepskin boots before the blanket of fog rolled in over them, cutting their world to a few yards around the wagon. The lieutenant's wagon and horses had disappeared in the fog. Barend's two horses were still eating the German fodder, oblivious to fog and cold.

"Best we make camp together," said von Stratten. "Even an Afrikaner can get lost in the fog. I have some good German wine."

The idea of a good German wine banished Barend's feeling of intrusion. He had not been drunk for a very long time. What the man meant about war and the Boer republics had roused his interest. The thought of revenge was again vivid in his mind.

"I have a leg of springbok I shot three days ago hanging in my wagon. If you tell your men to light a fire I can make a spit. It will take some time to cook, but it will be worth the waiting."

"How is it you speak such good English without a Dutch accent?"

"My mother was English."

"Do you like the English?" said von Stratten in alarm, annoyed he had already spoken too much.

"I hate them."

"Why do you hate them, Barend?"

"They hanged my father for treason."

"What did he do to make them do that?"

"He went out with the Cape rebels during the Anglo-Boer War."

"And who was your father, if you do not mind me asking?"

"General Tinus Oosthuizen."

"Was he?" said von Stratten. He was smiling with his lips but not with his eyes. "Then you will join me in a glass of hock and drink to a brave soldier. Your father is one of my heroes. Soon we will crush the arrogance of the English and their empire."

There was plenty of driftwood for the big fire between the tall rocks and the sand was dry to a depth of six inches. Only the infrequent great winter storms burst that far up the shore. The men took their lower rank to the other side of the fire to Barend and von Stratten. All of them had pulled on heavy clothing. There was no wind and the smoke from the fire rose into the fog that wrapped them in its cocoon.

There was no sound from the outside world, only the crackle of the big fire that warmed them on one side and cooked the meat on the other. The venison was placed alongside the fire on a crude spit made from pieces of metal Barend had welded together in Walvis Bay. There was a handle that turned the thin rod and the leg of venison had the habit of staying in the same position. They regularly turned the spit round for the fire to cook the other side of the meat. When the top and bottom were to be cooked, they propped a forked stick under the leg of springbok. There was little or no fat and Barend had not bothered with a drip tray.

After an hour and a half of juggling the meat against the heat of the fire, Barend carved the top slices and handed them round on the end of his long hunting knife. They ate with their fingers, the red juices flowed down their chins, and everyone was smiling. The meat, sprinkled with sea salt Barend had collected from dried-up rock pools over his long journey up the beach, was better than anything any of them could remember. Watching the meat cook and smelling its flavour had made them ravenously hungry.

Barend let the meat cook another ten minutes before he sliced again and handed round slivers of meat. They had just finished the first bottle of hock. The men were drinking schnapps out of the bottle, and one of them was drunk, dropping his slice of meat in the sand that was now damp from the fog. The man wiped off the sand as best he could and ate the meat. They all laughed, von Stratten opened another bottle of hock. They said 'cheers' in German and Afrikaans.

Barend sparingly sprinkled sea salt where he had carved the last slices and put the spit right over the open coals and let the meat drip for a moment into the fire before it sealed again and began to cook. The cut crystal glass, which the German had produced from a conical container with the opening of the first bottle of hock, had been placed on a flat piece of rock where it was safe. He placed small pieces of driftwood on either side of the fire to give them warmth and light, picked up his glass from the rock and sat down on his buckskin mat that stopped the water rising through the six inches of dry sand. With his arms around his knees, and his chin resting on his knees close to where he could take a sip from the ready glass, he looked into the red coals of the fire and for a moment forgot that he was not alone. He was mellow, though far from drunk on half a bottle of good wine the German had left in a rock pool during the day to keep it cool. Even in the middle of nowhere, the man seemed to know how to look after himself, his men and his horses.

When he turned his head, von Stratten was looking straight into his eyes, and to stop the man seeing what he was thinking, he smiled. Apart from his father, there had been no one in his life he had been able to trust. People generally were after something, emotional like Madge, or material like the German. There was no doubt in Barend's mind the man wanted something. He let his booted feet run out to within three feet of the fire, and leaned his left elbow on the sand, leaving his right hand with the wine glass free to find his mouth. A small drop of fat fell from the diminished leg of venison and sizzled in the fire. The men on the other side of the fire were lying on their backs as close to the fire as possible. Barend rather thought one of them was asleep.

"And what brings the German army into this desolate spot?" he asked into the fog-shrouded night. Their meeting, he was sure, had been an accident. How could there be premeditation when no one knew where he was or who he was? He had spoken to no one for weeks.

"Can I ask you the same?"

"I am going north to follow the Kunene River into Central Africa. If I can find it. Or, more importantly, I can recognise the right river."

"Won't the Ovambo tell you?"

"They may. They may also cut my throat. No one likes strangers. After strangers come invaders. The black man found that out to his detriment when he made the missionaries welcome. There is an old joke in Rhodesia: when the missionaries told the blacks to kneel down, shut their eyes and pray to God, they did. When they opened their eyes the Union Jack was flying over their heads."

"You were once strangers in Africa. Your people."

They both lapsed into silence without the German answering his first question. Barend sat up straight. His left arm was going to sleep. One of the Germans began to snore. He turned the meat using the forked stick to prop the carcass where he wanted it to cook.

After a minute of silence, the German spoke again. He had taken something from his pocket and was offering it to Barend on the palm of his hand.

"You walked the beach, you say. Ever seen anything like this washed up on the shore?"

The small rock was the size of a pea, about a tenth of the size of the largest rock in the leather bag he had pushed under the fodder in his wagon the moment he thought no one was looking, at the same time he had put on his sheepskin coat. The German had his palm stretched taught, pushing the stone up on his pink skin. The stone was between Barend's eyes and the light of the fire. The stone burnt with an inner fire as hot as the coals of the fire only more beautiful. Quickly hooding his eyes he hoped the German had not seen his instant recognition.

"What is it?" he asked innocently. "I've never seen anything like it before," he lied. The lie was instinctive, as was the choking of his words when he saw again what he had found only hours before on the beach. Even before the German spoke the word diamond, Barend knew what he had in his bag and his stomach lurched at the realisation and its implications.

"It's a pure white gem diamond. If there are more than this one in German South West Africa the Kaiser will be pleased. Very pleased. He will make me a captain, I think. But one swallow does not make a summer, as they say."

"Did you find it yourself?"

"Yes, I did. This morning along this stretch of the beach. You were further north. Do you comb the beach with your eyes?"

"Always. Like walking in the bush. Even if my mind is not consciously looking, it will jolt my thoughts if something is unusual on the ground or in the surrounds. Is your diamond worth anything?"

"I think so."

"Are you sure it is a diamond? I know there is fool's gold. Maybe there are fool's diamonds, stones that sparkle in the fire but fall to pieces with the slightest tap. Have you tried tapping your find?"

"I have. Hard. Many times."

"And it did not shatter?"

"No, and nothing chipped either. I made a cut down the side of the glass wine bottles. It's a diamond."

"Lucky you. Why not make it into a ring for your wife? A lucky omen. Finding something of value. Picking it up off the beach. I can't believe the Kaiser would be interested in one diamond the size of a garden pea. I rather think he has many more, and much bigger. Are your men asleep?"

"They are drunk. Drunks sleep when they have had enough. It is another way of leaving their world."

"Let us have one more cut at the meat and then I will retire to my wagon."

"We will finish the wine."

"If you insist. It is very good."

"So is the meat."

"Then we are not obliged to each other."

Von Stratten had closed the palm of his hand and put the diamond in his pocket.

Barend's mind was screaming. 'If he's so excited by one the size of a pea, what must the ones in his wagon be worth?' he thought.

When he went to sleep that night he had the long leather strap of the bag wrapped around his right arm. In his excitement, he had forgotten to ask the German what he had meant by going to war with the English.

When he woke in the morning the fog had rolled far out to sea and the sun was sparkling on the calm water. It reminded him of the diamond on the man's hand as the firelight had brought it alive. Quickly he felt in the soft leather bag. They were there, all four of them. His stomach was so tight it made him feel sick.

With a sigh of relief, the bag in his hand, and his stomach still churning, he climbed out of his wagon and looked around. The Germans, their horses, and their wagon had gone. Barend shivered in the cold light of the morning. Down the beach ten yards away a black-backed gull put its head forward and squawked at him, its beak wide open as it screamed. His horses had eaten all the German fodder and were looking at him with large brown liquid accusing eyes.

"I'm not the German army," he said to them in Afrikaans.

His first instinct was to flee the place in case they came back and took away the rocks in his bag. Greed overcame the first instinct; caution then greed. Carefully he checked the direction of the Germans' wagon wheels for more than a mile on foot. It seemed they were going back to the German port of Swakopmund. The enclave of Walvis Bay next door belonged to South Africa. He would have to watch the Germans did not circle round and come back at him. If von Stratten had seen his flash of recognition he could be setting him a trap, sending him out to find more of the stones, and confiscating them in the name of the Kaiser. His hope was the three glasses of good German wine had dulled the man's wits. Had von Stratten been looking at the diamond on the palm of his hand or Barend's eyes when he asked the question? As hard as he replayed the scene in his mind, Barend was not sure. To look as innocent as possible in case he was being watched somewhere from the rolling dunes that flowed on into the Namib Desert from the coastal rock line, he went fishing, throwing his line with great expertise over the kelp and into the calm, grey-blue water beyond the coastal reef with its mussels and oysters. He fished all day long, looking for the tell-tale glint of sun on binocular lenses, chewing at the leftover cold venison that tasted just as good cold as hot. During the day the sun was warm. He caught two large fish but his mind was elsewhere, up the beach, combing the sand and rock pools for diamonds the size of pigeon eggs.

He waited a week, curbing his impatience. Then he went north up the beach, on foot, leading the one horse in the shaft, the other following behind on the long rein. All the time his trained eyes were glued to the sand. The first morning he found three more stones and then nothing. He surmised correctly there was a diamond pipe out to sea in front of where he camped and met the Germans. He rather thought if he was going to find any more of the stones he would have to dig; he would have to dig up the whole beach and sift through the sand.

THREE WEEKS after Christmas in the new year of 1913, he struck the Kunene River where it flowed into the sea. The one thing he had done was take a careful compass bearing of the beach where he had picked up his diamonds. If, as he told himself, they really were diamonds. Maybe one day he would come back and make himself rich, should someone buy the seven stones now in his soft leather bag. To be certain he found the right place again he had chiselled his initials in the black rock that had protected them and their fire on the night he had cooked them the leg of venison. He had done this after the fishing when it was dark.

.  .  .

DURING HIS SLOW trek north through German South West Africa, Barend's ignorance proved his greatest protection. A man frightened by a lion is liable to be eaten by the lion unless he kills the lion first.

Barend's only schooling had been at the hands of his mother. She had taught her son to read and write, to add, subtract and multiply, but his mother, who had once been Harry Brigandshaw's nurse in the house of his grandfather, the Pirate, in England, knew nothing of African history. The only history Barend had learned was from the evenings around the campfire with his father when he was not yet ten years old. He knew about the Voortrekkers fleeing the rules, regulations and taxes of the British. He knew about the battles the Afrikaners fought with the black tribes of Africa, but no one had known to tell him the German army had massacred the Herero people eleven years before he found his stones and not many miles away. The Herero, despite all the potential benefits of European civilisation, had rebelled against German rule. And no one had told him the Germans had never confronted the Ovambo because they were frightened of the warlike tribe that straddled the Kunene River that cut through German and Portuguese West Africa. And it was just as well as when, on the rare occasion he came across the indigenous people, he was not afraid and, like the lion, when a man is not afraid of them, they feared the man was powerful, would do them harm, and in their own fear they gave him a wide berth.

At the mouth of the big river there was not even a footprint left by man, and by then he had given up looking for diamonds on the beach. The desert had turned to scrub right up to the river and the Portuguese border, where he turned inland to follow the life-giving water. His father had talked about the great swamps far inland that were more beautiful than anything his father had seen, and what his father had seen and cherished, the son wished to experience to feel the presence of his dead father. In the Okavango swamps, he told himself he would be nearer to his father.

Some two hundred miles from the Atlantic coast the land became fertile, and the first strands of maize struggled out of the poor soil to give the Ovambo a permanence, a place where they could stay year after year without searching for grazing. Not till then was he sure the river he followed was the right river. A small boy herding cattle with his brother, nodded his head when Barend said 'Kunene' and pointed at the river, not knowing Kunene was an Ovambo word and head nodding as universal as the life of man. Without fear or thought of fear, he rode on through Ovamboland, passing village and tilled field, smiling and waving at the people who, dumbstruck, had never in their lives seen anything like the combination of a wagon, horse, and white man. It was beautiful country, even if the mosquitoes were deadly to most white men who had not built up an immunity to malaria. Barend did sleep under a net at night in his wagon but round the campfire at night, he was constantly bitten by mosquitoes. If he had known, he would have thanked generations of Oosthuizens who had gone before him in Africa as, even when he reached the great delta of the Okavango River, he had not once come down with the fever, nor had his horses gone sick from the bite of the tsetse fly and the sleeping sickness that killed unsalted animals.

The gods were good to him. Except for one thing: by the time he reached the magnificent beauty of the Okavango Delta, where the great African river, instead of flowing into the sea, disappeared into the desert creating an animal kingdom unsurpassed on earth, Barend had convinced himself the seven stones were not diamonds but pretty rocks he had picked up on the beach.

# 2

## APRIL 1913

For Harry Brigandshaw, the best period in his life was when nothing really happened. He got up in the morning after a good night's sleep, looked out of the window at the beautiful African morning with the sun shining, went down to breakfast where the smell of bacon, toast and coffee mingled, and everyone in the family was pleased to be part of the new day.

He then went out to work in the lands wearing a wide-brimmed hat to keep off the sun and did the jobs on the farm that were mostly a pleasure. At lunchtime, the houseboy on a bicycle found him in the lands and brought his lunch as Harry had no wish to waste time going back to the family compound in the middle of the day. The labourers went off at three o'clock most afternoons when they had finished their set tasks. The ones who worked at a fever pitch went back to their own compound at one o'clock. Each family had half an acre of ground next to the Mazoe River to grow what they wanted, which was where the energetic worked in the afternoons, alongside their wives and the older children.

Half an hour before the sun went down, Harry began his ride home, his horse having grazed all day on a long lead. He took a shower and a shave, and dumped his khaki in the wash basket, soiled with the day's sweat. The drinks tray was set out on the veranda, fly screens slotted into place by a servant. Putting ice in crystal glasses, he poured his mother and Madge the evening drink and sat down in a wicker chair. His grandfather most evenings stayed in his own house, where he liked to be alone but still able to hear their voices. Those were the rules, and Harry, five years after coming back from England and Oxford, had found them pleasant to live with.

George was at school at Bishops in the Cape, where Harry had spent his secondary school years before going up to Oxford. Everyone thought George would do the same. He would most probably take a degree in English literature.

Madge spent her days thinking about the wonderful life she would have been having with Barend and did very little; in a house with servants, there wasn't very much to do anyway. She and her mother produced tapestries that were dutifully placed over the seats of the dining room chairs, so the family could sit on colourful birds in flight when they were taking their meals. No one in the house brought up the Oosthuizen family, though everyone was aware of the unspoken presence. Madge was twenty years old without a suitor insight: everyone, including Madge, had long discounted Robert St Clair as a delightful man but one who took more than he would ever be able to give, a financial tax on everyone who took an interest in his welfare. Madge was convinced that being the son of Lord St Clair of ancient lineage, Robert thought the world owed him a living. The fact that he was empty-headed with no aptitude for work never crossed her mind.

"Charming but expensive," she said after his second uninvited visit. "He should find a rich girl in England, marry and settle down."

Twice he had invited Madge to Purbeck Manor in England and twice she had declined. She had the crazy notion that the moment she left Elephant Walk, Barend would arrive looking for her and if she weren't there waiting he would never come back for her again.

The one thing Harry wanted to ask his mother he kept to himself, as each time the opportunity seemed to arrive his mother got up and left the room, using an excuse. Grandfather Manderville was no better.

"Ask your mother," he said when Harry was only halfway to asking the question about his parents' marriage.

After the short reply Grandfather Manderville was usually grumpy for the rest of the day.

On the surface, everything looked very nearly perfect. They were all very good at keeping up appearances.


IN LONDON, Jack Merryweather had long since replaced Albert Pringle with another impeccable manservant so that life at 27 Baker Street had returned to normal. Jack got up, ate his breakfast downstairs, went for his constitutional if weather permitted, ate his lunch in the Pall Mall Club after reading the newspapers, took a snooze in one of the large, black leather club chairs and, after a cup of tea, thought about what he was going to do for the evening. He was thirty-two years old and past the stage of boredom, having sunk into a rut so deep there was no way on his own he could climb from the hole. He had not bothered to look for another mistress. It was too much trouble. If he ever admitted anything to himself, he would have said his pride had been hurt, Lily walking out on him, vanishing. There were strangers in the house he had rented when he called, full of expectation after his hunting trip that had seen him shoot a number of big-tusked wild pigs and deer with sweeping horns that would have been far better left on their own. The bright idea of farming in Africa had come and gone with the dying animals. If London was boring, he concluded, it was better than going off thousands of miles to tramp through long dry grass and the heat of the day to shoot poor, unsuspecting animals. Jack rather thought that Africa would be better off as it was, without sending proselytes from a dozen different churches to save the black man from damnation: the few black villages Jack saw on the banks of rivers were happy enough without a new God to worry their heads about; talking to heaven through the medium of their ancestors had a logic of its own if there was any truth in a life after death, something Jack found frightening to talk about.

Having heard not a word from Lily White and Albert Pringle in more than five years he had put them from his mind; there was no point in thinking about something to which he would likely never know the answer.

The showgirls were quite fun to take out to supper, and sometimes, even shower with gifts. And when they went their own way it was little or no pain. Ships in the night. Many of them. Blurring into one another in his mind... And the idea of getting married and having children had never entered his thoughts.

On an afternoon when Harry Brigandshaw was visiting the family grave on Elephant Walk to put flowers on his father's grave, Jack, walking down Pall Mall from his club, was accosted in the street by a well-dressed man in a business suit, high stiff collar and the new fashion must, a bowler hat.

"I say, aren't you Jack Merryweather? Must be years, old boy. Ernest Gilchrist. Don't you remember? I've been away. Ceylon. Colombo more precise. For the old company. We are in tea, lots of tea." And he laughed.

Jack looked at his watch on its chain, snapped it shut and looked again at the newly prosperous Ernest Gilchrist.

"Do you have time for a drink?" he asked Ernest Gilchrist.

"I've always had time for a drink."

"Good," he said. "We'll go back to my club. There's something I've been wanting to ask you, for about five years."

"Sounds serious."

"Not really, old chap. Just curiosity. I like my ends to be tied up."

Just before they reached the entrance to the club, a short sharp April shower made them both wet before they could put up their brollies in the gusting wind. Inside the club, a fire was burning, as it did most of the year. They stood in front of the fire waiting for their drinks. There was no one else in the room, with its big, black leather chairs. The hot fire was gently steaming out the rainwater from their suits, giving off a musty sweet smell.

Jack looked at the man who had introduced him to Sallie Barker and her abominable mother. The eyes were somehow too close together. The man was sharp rather than intelligent.

"Do you have a club in London?" asked Jack, having decided to have a drink before assuaging his curiosity.

"No," said Ernest Gilchrist too quickly. "We only get home leave once every two years. Doesn't seem worth it."

"What you do in tea?"

"I'm a buyer."

The steward brought in the drinks and saved the foundering conversation. Jack decided the appearance of wealth only went as far as the suit and the bowler hat. The man was probably a big shot in the colonies but not very big in London. They both drank deeply from the drinks, having turned their backs on the fire to steam the other side.

"Do you ever hear from Sallie Barker, your cousin, I think?" asked Jack.

"Didn't you hear?"

"No I didn't or I would not be asking you... Would you like another drink? That rain made us rather wet. Another ten minutes of this fire and we'll be dry. Steward! Be a good chap. Same as last time. Thank you."

Jack waited for the new drinks and when the steward had left the room he smiled at an agitated Ernest Gilchrist. "Now, Ernest. What didn't I hear?"

"My cousin, Mrs Flugelhorne of Cape Town, was hanged for a murderess."

"Good God, Ernest. What does that have to do with the beautiful Sallie?"

"Everything, Jack."

"Did your cousin kill Sallie? Why?"

"No. She killed her husband, Mr Flugelhorne. Sallie ran away from Constantia Manor, that's my cousin's home near Cape Town, soon after they arrived off the SS *King Emperor*. But you, of course, were on the boat. She had told her mother Mr Flugelhorne had raped her but her mother didn't want to believe her daughter. After days of searching Cape Town for Sallie, Mrs Barker told my cousin Mrs Flugelhorne what had happened. Next time her husband was drunk, she shot him with an old gun that hung over the fireplace. It was one of those guns you had to load with gunpowder. She was such a small little woman. Devoted to her husband. But you never can tell. She filled up the barrel of the old gun with small nails she found in the winery that was used to close the wooden cases of wine. She fired at just below his belly. Emasculated him. Took Flugelhorne four days to die in terrible pain. I had to scrape up the money to bring Mrs Barker back to England third class. She was destitute."

"But what happened to Sallie? She must have seen the newspapers."

"Not a word. She just disappeared. After her mother left South Africa no one bothered to inquire. She is an orphan in a kind of way. Sallie, I don't think, ever came back to England. Before I went to Ceylon on my first tour, I found Mrs Barker a job in the country as a housekeeper. I believe she periodically put advertisements in the London papers. She has promised to tell me if Sallie sends her a reply. Then I will ask Sallie to marry me. She'll have a good life in Colombo. Poor, poor Sallie. It's all her father's fault."

"I doubt it, Ernest... She's probably dead, poor girl. She would have run away to England. Contacted you."

"Yes, she would, if she came home."

"Why don't you go and look for her in Africa?" asked Jack Merryweather.

"I don't have the money. My salary gives me a good living in Colombo where everything is cheap and they give me a company house."

"So no one's been looking for her?"

"Only the London advertisements."

"What a strange story... I think we are dried out now, Ernest. Nice seeing you again. When are you going back to Ceylon?"

"Tomorrow."

"Have a good voyage. You go through the Mediterranean and the Suez Canal, I presume. Very nice." The man looked crestfallen. "Don't worry about something you can do nothing about."

"I don't think she'd have married me even if I'd asked," said Ernest Gilchrist, and for a moment Jack thought he was going to cry.

Outside in the street, they went their separate ways.

"If she was in trouble, why didn't she cable me in Rhodesia?" he asked himself out loud when he was back in 27 Baker Street.

"Did you say something, sir?" asked Cox, his manservant.

"Not really, Pringle."

"My name is Cox, sir."

"Of course, Cox."

"Are you going out tonight, sir?"

"I'm not sure."

Jack Merryweather, even the next morning, was unable to get Sallie Barker out of his mind. All he could see were the dark ringlets and dark brown eyes. He could see her quite clearly in Green Park all those years ago with a suffragist sign. Strangely, he was quite certain she was still alive. He remembered their dinner together, their unspoken understanding. The girl had been far too smart to get herself killed, even in darkest Africa.

At lunchtime, it came to him all of a rush. He would himself go to Africa and look for Sallie Barker. It would be a worthwhile venture. Only this time he would leave his manservant at 27 Baker Street.

Leaving the soup untouched he quit the dining room and walked quickly to the offices of Colonial Shipping. He was smiling broadly and his mind was rushing on a very fast track. They all knew each other, and they had all vanished from the face of the earth round about the same time. If you found Sallie Barker, he rather thought you would find Lily White and Albert Pringle. He could tie together two lots of loose ends at the same time.

Then he laughed out loud in the shipping office and smiled at the ticket clerk.

"Every time I meet Ernest Gilchrist I end up going off to Africa."

"What was that, sir?"

"Nothing, dear boy."

The elderly ticket clerk smiled back. He had not been called a dear boy for a very long time.

THE SAME DAY Jack was finally interviewing the owner of the Strand Street townhouse he had hired six years earlier for Lily White, Harry Brigandshaw was reading another cable from Robert St Clair, his Oxford day's friend who was fast becoming a burden. Without saying a word Harry gave the cable to his sister to read: Madge's stomach had taken a sharp turn at the sight of the man on his bicycle from the faraway Salisbury post office, thinking Barend, at last, was sending her a word. Harry told the houseboy, Garth, to take the hungry-looking telegraph boy to the kitchen and give him some food. Harry also gave him sixpence for bicycling the twenty miles.

"Beats me how they don't get eaten by lion on the way," said Madge, handing back the cable. "How long do you think he will stay this time?"

"If you went to England he wouldn't come here. You'd love Purbeck Manor. The family are delightful... And who is going to be eaten by a lion?"

"One of those telegraph boys one of these days. And what's the surprise he's bringing with him? Dear old Robert. In many ways, I'm rather fond of him but he does go on a bit... It must be over twenty miles on a bicycle and the road is a cart track full of ruts."

"I'm sorry it wasn't Barend," said Harry, sympathising with his sister.

"So am I. Where the hell is the damn man?"

"Don't swear, sis, or Uncle Nat will come back from England to read one of his homilies. And that we can do without. Isn't it funny how people are so much part of your life for such a long time and then they're gone? All we have left is poor little Christo in the graveyard, all that's left of the Oosthuizens."

Madge Brigandshaw ran back into the house crying, leaving Harry with the cable from Robert St Clair.

"My poor sister," he said, shaking his head.

Then he put the cable in the pocket of his khaki shorts and walked through the gate of the balustrade, meeting Garth back from his errand in the kitchen. The black man was grinning, showing rows of perfectly white teeth.

"That boy was hungry... You want your horse, baas?"

"Thank you, Garth. Mister Robert is coming to stay with us again."

"One day we build him a house and have done with it."


THE ONE THING Robert St Clair had learnt in his life was to never spend money until it was necessary. Using the minimum number of words, he had sent his cable and watched a black man go off with it on a bicycle. It was nine o'clock in the morning. The man would rest four or five times but by Robert's estimate, a man on a bicycle was likely to reach Elephant Walk in four hours and have time to cycle back to Salisbury before it was dark. There were some hills but the downhill bits compensated for the climb. Robert thought the post office would have been better off giving the man a horse but then again you did not have to feed a bicycle.

Before sending the cable, Robert had hired a horse and trap with a driver who would have to return that day, leaving Robert and his sister nicely stranded at Elephant Walk. At two o'clock that afternoon, having foregone the cost of a lunch in expectation of the Brigandshaw supper being the main meal of the day, Robert waved with great satisfaction at the telegraph boy pedalling furiously on his way home. He rather hoped the lad would reach Salisbury before dark as the surrounding bush was full of night-prowling predators.

By his calculation, they should arrive at the farm just in time for sundowners, a civilised habit which he fully approved of.

LUCINDA HAD BEEN GIVEN the trip to Africa by her maternal grandmother, Granny Forrester, a twenty-first birthday present, Robert having told the family he had once again been invited to stay with the Brigandshaws at Elephant Walk. With one lie in the bag, as Robert had a habit of saying, he had included Lucinda in the invitation, remembering Harry had once, when she was fifteen years old, extended her an invitation. After teaching snotty-nosed prep school boys the rudiments of history he had resigned his teacher's job, having saved sufficient of his salary to buy a return ticket to Africa and not a single: Robert, being sensible, always had his bolthole if something went wrong with his schemes. It was not only Madge that drew him to Elephant Walk, he told himself, but the pleasant colonial style of living that suited his temperament down to the ground.

Lucinda, having watched only one of her sisters getting married, and Annabel's marriage had taken place in a hurry, was desperate and if it took going out to Africa to find a husband, it was better than sinking back into spinsterhood and genteel poverty at Purbeck Manor where her father's finances were nothing short of critical. Sir Willoughby Potts had died and with him his government pension. And anyway, like all the sisters, she had had a crush on Harry when he had stayed with them after coming down from Oxford, a crush she had told herself was love. Maybe girls were in short supply in Africa, which was why he had included her in his invitation. She knew for certain that at twenty-seven, Harry Brigandshaw was not yet married.

"How much further do we have to go?" she asked her brother. "This place is wild. Where does everyone live?"

"We'll be there before the sun goes down."

"Can the driver go back in the dark?"

"He'd have to. And there is something else I better tell you before we reach Elephant Walk. They don't know you're coming."

"But I was invited!"

"Neither of us were."

"Robert, you're quite impossible."

"Desperate situations require desperate solutions. There was no way I could have spent another term at that damn school."

"How are you going to earn a living?"

"I'll cross that bridge when I get to it."

"What am I going to say to them?"

"I said in my cable I had a surprise for them. It's too far to go back now," said Robert, giving out a nervous giggle. Robert worked on the principle that people living in the sticks were pleased to see anyone, invited or otherwise. And even if he had to say so himself, Lucinda was certainly a sight for sore eyes… He was so hungry he could hear his own stomach rumbling over the clip-clop of the horse's hooves on the dirt track; even though it had rained two days earlier, the track was as hard as nails.

The sunlight was yellow when the driver took the trap through the main gate of the balustrade into the Elephant Walk compound, where they were promptly met by a pack of excited, yapping dogs that set the tame wild geese into flight up and over the balustrade and down through the msasa trees to sanctuary on the water of the Mazoe River.

Emily, Harry's mother, was the first to greet the uninvited guests as if they were long-lost and precious relatives. It was the way it was done in Rhodesia. It was the way it was done in Africa. Any traveller passing through a village was given food and a hut to sleep in, no matter who they were.

A WEEK of polite animated conversation passed without any of them saying what they were thinking. They all looked to be having a good time.

Harry found Robert alone by the river. It had not rained and most likely would not rain again for six months. The cool morning was full of birdsong. The river ran smooth and dark. Robert was sitting on the dry bank with his legs pulled up, his arms hugging his knees. He had not heard Harry.

"Mind the crocodiles, old chap," Harry said softly to announce his presence. He was standing ten yards behind Robert, higher up the bank.

"To hell with the bloody crocodiles," said Robert without moving. "Do you really know why I came this time?"

"Robert, please, you don't have to explain. We love to have you at Elephant Walk."

"You don't, so stop pretending. Even the first time I outstayed my welcome. I'm a parasite abusing your hospitality. The St Clairs are broke, Harry. All those years and now we are broke. I saved up a year's puny salary to buy the ticket. Granny Forrester gave her last money to Lucinda thinking you had sent her an invitation. Granny doesn't want anything now Potts is dead. I do hope they were lovers. To hell with grandfather. Good old Potts and his government pension. Stopped dead like someone had slammed the door shut when he died. Now, what kind of life was that? A governor, for God's sake, and the door slammed in Granny Forrester's face. Well, it's going to slam in all our faces soon. I came out here to say goodbye... I was happy here."

"You can always come back. You will always be welcome. You are good company."

"Ah, there we have it. Sing for my supper... There's going to be a war."

"There are always people at war somewhere. Rather sadly, men seem to take to fighting with each other."

"You haven't heard?"

"Nothing much reaches Elephant Walk. The local *Rhodesia Herald* is four pages and thankfully local chatter." They were silent for a while. "Madge is another story. You can't compete with a man who is only in her mind."

"Oh, I know Madge wouldn't marry me in a fit. I've known that since the time we first met. With or without Barend, there would have been no difference in the end. You can tell... You're not going to marry Cinda, are you?"

"She's a very nice girl."

"Don't give me that, Harry. This is Robert."

"No, Robert. I have no plans to marry your sister and even if I had, it would not be fair. You can't bring someone from England and dump them in the bush. My father did just that to my mother but they were so in love they could have lived on the moon. There has to be that kind of love to compensate for the loneliness and lack of social life, any kind of life for that matter, other than farm life, the bush, the animals. Cinda would be bored to distraction inside a year and all the children in the world would not make her satisfied. I'll find a local girl if I'm lucky. Or I'll stay as I am. Being a bachelor is all right if you don't think about it."

Quietly, Harry sat down next to Robert on the riverbank, pulled up his knees, put his arms around his legs, his head on his knees and turned to look at Robert. A piece of dead tree floated by in midstream. A red cormorant was standing on the log, its black wings held out wide to the morning sun to dry. Harry watched the bird float by out of the corner of his eye.

"The one thing we St Clairs are good at, is wars," said Robert, ignoring the bird. "We've been there for England for hundreds of years. All we are good at, probably. To fight for King and country. The only time we pay for our privilege. Might be the end of us this time. Evolution is wonderful. We were left behind unwarranted guardians of a now irrelevant piece of coast. Keep the peace and the enemy at bay no longer applies to Dorset... You don't know what I'm talking about, do you Harry?"

"Not really."

"Germany. There's going to be a war with Germany. They're building dreadnoughts bigger than ours. Battleships to challenge the Royal Navy and British trade."

"Don't be silly. The Kaiser's Queen Victoria's grandson."

"They're all Germans. They want to challenge the empire. It's going to be a terrible war, Harry, and I'm going to die. We won't be fighting each other like gentlemen with swords on horseback. We'll kill each other with machine guns from one thousand yards. Not seeing who we kill. Aeroplanes will drop bombs on people. If it isn't over quickly we'll wipe each other out. We're all going to die, Harry. They'll even take poor Richard. Put him in an officer's uniform. He won't know what's going on but that won't matter. He thinks like a child you know, and he's so beautiful! Barnaby, Frederick, Merlin. The lot of us. If it goes on long enough they'll soon kill young Barnaby. Then the fact we don't have any money won't matter anymore."

"Snap out of it, Robert. You're hysterical. None of this is going to happen. Being a schoolmaster isn't all that bad. And you used to love history at Oxford."

"Well, I don't anymore. And I'm not hysterical. There's going to be a war. You better believe it. They might even make you come home to fight for England. Without England, Rhodesia wouldn't be much good. You'd be swallowed up by a new Shaka. A new Mzilikazi. You would last till the ammunition ran out with no king to ride for help from England. Okay, I even know your history, whatever use it is to me. You mark my words, Harry Brigandshaw. This may be the last year of the empire. The Americans won't do anything to help. They don't like the empire as they were once a colony themselves. Makes them feel inferior. They'll enjoy watching the British Empire go down the drain. And we can be high and mighty, so I don't blame them. Unless the Royal Navy can stop them they'll sell guns to the Kaiser... All you have to do is read history. People and nations do what is most profitable for themselves whatever they might say. And once they see a chink in the British armour they'll all be at our throats. Ever since the Battle of Waterloo they've been too damn scared of us, but not anymore. And you can blame the time it took us to win the Boer War for their new smirks and confidence. Oh, what the hell. I read too much. I understand too much. Never be a historian. You can too easily see what's coming next. Europe's been in turmoil ever since the Romans lost their grip. And now we're losing our grip... You mind if Cinda and I stay another week? Then we'll be on our way. The proud St Clairs going home to face their final duty."

"Robert, don't be so bloody dramatic. And you can both stay as long as you like."

. . .

AFTER A WEEK HARRY had to smile to himself. There was not even the first sign of his friend's departure and there probably would not be any time soon. The veneer of civilisation had returned to everyone's composure. Europe was forgotten. Trivia was spoken. Everyone, on the surface, was happy and the only noise came from the dogs.

Sir Henry Manderville arrived back with the horse and trap from Salisbury with the mailbag and the stores that were needed on the farm. It was the job he did once a month to pay his way. Careful buying at the right price was a key ingredient for keeping the farm profitable.

Along with the bag of mail at the post office came a small, brown paper-wrapped box with his name and address written in his cousin's handwriting. The postage stamps were American. The return address Salem, Virginia. The Canadian cousin, the heir to Sir Henry's baronetcy, Sir Henry having no son, had given up being a lumberjack and gone down south to a warmer climate, having somehow made himself some money. George Manderville had bought himself a small farm in Virginia and had written to his cousin to give him his new address. By some miracle of the British postal system, or the more likely help of Harry's uncle, James Brigandshaw, the current owner of Hastings Court, the letter had been redirected and had arrived at Elephant Walk just before the rains. Sir Henry surmised the Americans were more impressed with British titles than the Canadians; his second cousin did not wish to miss out in the social swirl of Virginia; maybe had his eye on some rich planter's daughter.

For the first time in their lives they were in correspondence, and since the cousin was trying to use him, he had also thought it in order to use his cousin. His cousin had told him rather too grandly in the first letter that had sailed around the world, that he was now a tobacco planter, which had set Sir Henry Manderville to thinking.

In his botanical quests and forays he had come across a wild tobacco plant used by the Shona for generations. They dried the leaves in the sun and smoked them wrapped up in one of the leaves, apparently achieving some degree of satisfaction. So Henry had cut himself some stalks that grew down by the river and taken the green plants home where he had hung them in the sun to dry. The first few pipes had half choked him but in the end, he only smoked his own home-cured tobacco, knowing to use the middle leaves of the plant, which was when the letter from his cousin gave him the idea. All the cigarettes and most of the pipe tobacco he had smoked in his life came from America, and most of the packets claimed somewhere in the writing that the tobacco had been grown in Virginia. If wild tobacco grew, why not the good stuff the Americans exported around the world, making the farmers, he was sure, a fortune?

When he got back to his house, having given the mailbag to his daughter, Emily, he opened the brown paper parcel to find inside small bags of tiny black seed. With the bags came growing instructions. The ex-lumberjack was no longer a fool. Tucking the seeds away out of sight, Henry determined to plant them in a small seedbed at the back of his house at the beginning of spring, just before the rainy season. What he was going to do about a curing barn he would worry about when the time came. First, he would see if he could grow himself some Virginia tobacco in the wilds of Africa.

With a feeling of intense satisfaction, he poured himself a large glass of whisky and drank a toast to his new venture.

HARRY RUMMAGED through the mailbag when he came back from the lands at the end of his day's work. He was sitting on the veranda with his first sundowner, the taste of the whisky sweet in his mouth. To Harry's surprise, his grandfather, for a change, was already sitting drinking whisky, with a big smirk on his face. Harry rather thought his grandfather was happily drunk.

He looked at his grandfather with a question mark, received a sweet smile in return and went on rummaging in the mailbag. Most of the letters were farm business and most of those were bills. He would take them to his small office next to the packing shed in the morning. When he found Jared Westwood's letter from England he smiled, followed by an instant picture in his mind of Jared's sister Sara, who had still not married the man she was meant to marry last time he heard. Neither Jared nor his sister had been back to Africa for six years after their one and only venture into the wild. Jared now worked in the City and was miserable.

Robert walked across the lawn from the house that had belonged to the Oosthuizen family and closed the fly screen door behind him. Lucinda was still enjoying her evening bath.

"Help yourself," said Harry. "Letter from Jared Wentworth. You remember him. His sister was meant to marry Mervyn Braithwaite."

"He really did have a face like a wet codfish," said Robert, helping himself to a whisky from the sideboard, sloshing in a shot of soda water from the syphon. "What's Jared got to say? What's he doing now?"

"Let me read first, Robert."

"Evening, Sir Henry."

Harry's grandfather kept on grinning but said not a word. The three of them drank in silence while Harry read the letter from England.

DEAR OLD FRIEND,

*I sometimes find it much easier to write down what I want to say rather than bring the subject up in conversation. Anyway, most people never want to hear bad news or talk about it. If you're coming over to England as you have been saying for years in your letters I think you had better do it fast. Or as fast as it takes the horse to get to Salisbury, the train down Africa to Cape Town, and one of your family ships to England (I still have a good memory of Robert St Clair extolling the virtues of the 'SS King Emperor' – did you ever hear of him? – if you do, give him my best regards). Strange how you sometimes get to know people so well over a short time and never hear from them again. Which is why I so much value our correspondence.*

*Harry there's going to be a terrible war in Europe any time soon. The balance of power that has kept us away from each other's throats is crumbling. Germany is becoming far too powerful, and when a country has more military power than it needs to defend itself it becomes a predator, coveting its neighbour's property. And there are so many alliances between so many countries that if two go to war the rest will be dragged in by treaty. Did you know we have a treaty with the Serbs, for goodness sake? Even Russia will be pulled head first into the fire.*

*The Americans I rather think will sit and watch and keep out of it. They don't have any pacts with Europe. They'll probably wait to see who's winning and come in at the end to share the spoils. People in the City are taking precautions, moving money to America, buying shares in American and British armament firms, trying to calculate who will win and who will lose in a great war. You have to wonder sometimes, seeing them burrowing away for their blood money. Quite disgusting. Why I will never do well as a stockbroker. I don't have the killer instinct, though if there is going to be a war, and everyone with brains in the City is certain there will be one, I'd better find one soon or at least the instinct to survive.*

*Now let me tell you about Sara, which is why you must come over to England as soon as possible. Don't you get a free ticket or something, being family? That damn Braithwaite man and his money are still breathing down her neck. Persistence can sometimes be a deadly force. If you see each other again I'm sure you'll want to rescue her from hell.*

MADGE HAD COME onto the fly screened veranda from inside the house and poured herself a gin and tonic before picking up the mailbag. She plucked the tabby cat off her chair and sat down. Outside, the dogs were still chasing each other around the flowerbeds, regularly changing who was chased and who was chasing. The sky was blood-red behind the msasa trees, the colour of the sinking sun. A pair of Egyptian geese were flying around honking at each other and Madge did not even think it was the mating season. Her grandfather was giving her a queer look. 'Oh, well, we'll probably all end up a bunch of drunks,' she said to herself, taking a swig from her drink. Satisfied she had put enough gin in the tonic, she began rummaging around in the mailbag for something interesting. 'There's nothing else to do but drink when the sun goes down,' she said to herself, sighing. Rationalising with herself was a trait she had learned early on in childhood. There was nothing in the mailbag for her.

The sister, Lucinda, came in smelling rather sweet.

"Help yourself," said Harry, not looking up from his letter.

The rule of pouring each other's drinks had been stopped a long time ago.

One of the dogs barged in through the fly screen door, which banged behind her. The succession of clangs brought in the rest of the dogs that then lay down on the mat-covered floor and slobbered.

BEHIND, through the window into the dining room, the houseboy was laying out the cold food. All the food platters were covered with a muslin cloth, the pile of empty plates and cutlery standing either end of the food line on the sideboard. Madge's mother counted the plates to make sure there were enough, including her father. It seemed he was set on spending the evening with them. Looking through the drawing-room window onto the veranda she wondered what her father was up to. It was obviously quite something as the old man was almost hugging himself with glee. They would all find out soon enough. Her son had finished his letter and was staring into space and she wondered what that was all about. The girl with the two names, sometimes Lucinda, sometimes Cinda, was trying to catch Harry's eye. The girl had groomed herself carefully. If nothing else, Emily was glad she did not have to go through all that again.

THE TABBY CAT had got back on the chair by sitting on Madge's lap and Madge had not noticed even though she was gently stroking the cat's fur. She was again rummaging one-handed in the mailbag and picked out a brown envelope in which the post office sent out cables. Someone had written on the outside of the envelope in pencil.

'This was found when we moved to our new premises. It was tucked down the back of your letterbox. The Post Office apologises,' said the unknown hand.

"Look at this," said Madge, her eyes widening. "It's a cable for Jack Merryweather. Wasn't he the bloke who came out with you on the SS *King Emperor* in '07? Why would anyone want to cable him here? What's the matter, Harry? You look as if you had seen a ghost."

"You remember Jared Wentworth, Robert," said Harry. "I think he was here during your first visit. I must have talked about him. He also thinks there's going to be a war."

"What war?" said his mother, now pouring her first drink. She sipped the drink, topped it up with gin, and turned from the sideboard to her son. "What war, Harry? No one's told me about a war."

"Robert here, and my friend Jared in England think there's going to be a terrible war in Europe."

"Whatever for? We're civilised. Civilised people don't have wars with each other. What absolute nonsense. And Father, what have you been up to today?"

"Nothing, Em, nothing."

"I don't believe you."

"Good Lord," said Madge. "This cable was sent in 1907, six years ago. It's from someone called Sallie Barker. Says she's in trouble and wants Jack Merryweather to give her some help. She says something terrible has happened to her."

# 3
___

# APRIL 1913

*T*here had been other moments in Jack Merryweather's life that he would have liked to wipe clean, expunge, take out of his life so they had never existed.

The same evening Madge was reading the belated cable from Sallie Barker, Jack walked into the Mansion House only half suspecting what he would find. Having come so far, he overruled his better instinct that he had known from experience was better not done. The landlord in Cape Town had started the rot.

"Had to give her back one month's rent. Not that I mind. There was something fishy going on in that house. Soon as you left to go up north to go hunting elephant, young girls started to arrive. All pretty, they were. And they stayed. Now, my house in Strand Street don't need no reputation. No men came, I'll give 'er that, but all them young girls in one house? One of 'em was coloured, I can tell you that. Pretty. Very pretty. But coloured, if you see what I mean. They all went together."

"Where did they go?"

"Johannesburg."

"Are you sure?"

"She gave me an address in the end. Case of letters for 'er from England."

"Did one of the girls have black ringlets past her ears and dark brown eyes?"

"She was the prettiest of the lot."

"Did she go with them?"

"Did you hear what I said? They all went together. When renting property, you got to know what's going on."

"Can you give me that address in Johannesburg?"

"If I can find it. Years ago it was. Grand name, remember that. Something to do with the Lord Mayor of London. The Mansion House. That's it. And I should know. I'm a cockney, see."

At the reception desk of the Langham Hotel, Jack had asked, strangely expecting a positive answer, if the man knew a house in Johannesburg called the Mansion House. The man had not even bothered to turn from the row of keys in their pigeonholes to give him the address, which came with directions, and a street address. "Any one of the taxi drivers will take you there, sir. Would you like tea or coffee in the morning?"

It would have been better to have a good night's sleep, drink the tea in the morning, go back to the Johannesburg railway station, and start the journey home to England. But he had come this far. And Mrs Flugelhorne had been hanged for murdering her husband. And Ernest Gilchrist had said it had everything to do with Sallie Barker. The ends were still untied. It would nag his mind for ages if he did not find out once and for all. 'And frankly,' he told himself, 'I don't have much else to do with my life,' even though he knew that curiosity killed the cat, and usually, in life, it was better to mind one's own damn business.

It was past midnight, the train having only arrived in Johannesburg at eight o'clock that evening. The cab driver had needed neither directions nor the street address. The Mansion House, when he walked in, having given his hat and cane to a pretty hat-check girl, the same cane with the hidden sword inside, was packed with people. They had first made him sign a register to become a club member, whatever that was. He had given a false name and a false address in London. They had explained the three bars in a way that let him choose his class. He would not be drinking with the gold miners.

A small string quartet was playing in what the man at reception called the most exclusive lounge even if it was a little expensive! The quartet was remarkably good. Jack recognised a Beethoven late quartet. He made his way across to the bar and there holding court was his one-time gentleman's gentleman, Albert Pringle. The young man looked disgustingly prosperous, though for Jack's taste a little too flashy. Like magnets, their eyes drew together despite the years and the crowded room. Jack thought afterwards it was probably due to a bad conscience. Jack also suspected he was the last person Albert Pringle expected to see across the crowded room, or wanted to see for that matter. Well, that untied string was about to be tied.

· · ·

ALBERT PRINGLE'S whole stomach flipped over in one sickening heave. In a moment, he went from being a man about town, a man of property, to being a manservant for Jack Merryweather, the man he had run away from and his job. It was not a pleasant feeling.

"GOT TO GO," he said to no one and everyone as the crowd briefly obscured Jack Merryweather of 27 Baker Street. "Got to go."

Albert ducked under the service counter of the bar, and without standing up straight pushed open the service door at the back corner of the bar, and escaped into the kitchen that served the four small dining rooms. Moving with the speed of a small boy caught in a terrible act, he ran through the kitchen and up the back stairs that led to the private suite on the top floor, away from the well-used bedrooms on the floor below.

Remembering to knock properly, so Lily would know without asking who was at the door, he banged the hardwood and hurt his knuckles. Lily herself opened the door still fully dressed. At midnight, it was her habit to take a nap before cashing up at three in the morning, after which they would all drive home to their respective houses.

"You look as if you've seen a ghost, Albert Pringle."

"I only wish he was a ghost. Lily, downstairs, right now, is my gentleman and your ex-lover, the one what paid our passage to Africa. He's after us, I tell you. Saw me 'e did. Got a right turn. He didn't look happy."

"What the hell you talking about?"

"Jack Merryweather. In person. Downstairs. Truth. Cross my heart. Looked right through my black soul, he did, and it wasn't nice, Lily. What are we going to do?"

"Buy him a drink, silly. He won't bite. Attack is the best form of defence. Where's Sallie?"

"Somewhere in the club. I don't know."

"We're all in the same boat, silly. The card he gave her. The cable she sent. His conscience has pricked at last. He's not come after you or me. It's poor Sallie. Pull yourself together and remember what we are, now. Not what we were then. You can say you came straight up here to tell me. He doesn't have to know you ran away like a scared rat. Money levels everything in life. We are rich, remember? You ask 'im how his grandfather made his money and it won't be no different to how we made ours. A good product and hard work. You mark my words, Albert. Your grandchildren will look just like Jack Merryweather if we carry on as we are. And a lot of thanks to Sallie Barker. Now pull yourself together and we'll both go downstairs together. I don't really know what the bloody hell he's here for so let's go and find out."


SALLIE BARKER SAW the man who ignored her cable for help without being seen herself. He was sitting at the bar by himself looking miserable, not even trying to engage the barman in conversation. Maybe the man had had better things to do than help a nineteen-year-old girl in distress, but then why had he given her his card? There had been something between them she was certain. From the meeting of the eyes in Green Park while she had help up the suffragette banner for her mother, to the dinner he had taken them to, to the days and evenings on the boat out from England. Or had it all been polite flirtation to pass the time for a man who did not have to work for a living, who had too much money and too much time on his hands?

She had written three unanswered letters to her mother at the Flugelhorne house in Constantia and then given up. She had done her best. She had explained. She had not even blamed her mother for not believing she had been raped. She imagined her mother ensconced in luxury and too busy with her social life to worry about a daughter who had run away to start a whorehouse with friends. Sallie rather thought her mother could have found out that she worked at the Mansion House. The world was small. Everyone liked to tell tales. There were often men in the club with businesses in Cape Town. She had never changed her name like Lily White. If she had made a mistake, it was too late to change anything now. She was what she was. Sallie Barker, financial manager of the Mansion House. They could all take her or leave her, including her mother if that was what they thought of her precious reputation.

Oh, what the hell, she thought. She had a top salary and a share in the business, same as Albert Pringle. She had a house of her own with servants. She was rich in a comparative sort of way. And she had not stolen one cent. Neither had Albert. Lily White might not have been able to manage her own money, but she knew how to manage people. She knew how their dirty little minds worked, or so she said.

"Give an employee too much and he'll think you a fool, which you are. Give him too little and he'll steal. That's your job, Sallie. Give me the right balance. And that goes for you and Albert. Strike the right balance and we'll all strike it rich. The rest goes without saying. I don't want no one stealing from me, barmen, waiters, or whores."

.   .   .

SIX YEARS IS a long time if you have not seen a woman, especially if you liked what you saw the first time, and kept the picture clearly in the memory, thought Jack Merryweather.

Jack watched the woman in the mirror behind the rows of bottles, the face just above the Booth's London Dry Gin; he had his profile to the girl. He looked down the bar at the door beside the service hatch, through which he was sure Albert Pringle had escaped on his hands and knees. He had seen the door obviously open and shut without the visible sign of human hand.

The lovely black ringlets had gone and the soft brown eyes were now as hard as coal and as dark. There were no smile lines around her eyes or mouth. The hair was cut short for convenience with a sharp fringe along the forehead. The dark tailored suit she wore was well cut but severe. Every ounce of femininity that had been Sallie Barker at nineteen years old had blown away in the six years; Jack Merryweather was glad Mrs Flugelhorne had killed her husband who had chased the life out of the face he was studying above the Booth's gin bottle. The woman Mrs Flugelhorne should have been a hero, and not hanged for her pains. Once again, Jack wondered if he would ever understand the human condition. He decided he would not like to find out what had gone through the girl's head in the past six years and looked away.

With luck, he had changed considerably himself. He looked again in the mirror. What a way to find out about life. Someone, other than Mrs Flugelhorne, was going to pay. The circle of hate would go on round, recreating itself. She had not moved or stopped staring at his profile. He knew that if he turned and looked directly into the dark eyes some of the hatred would be directed at him and he wondered why. As far as he knew, Jack Merryweather had never done anyone a bad turn.

He was concentrating so hard on the face in the mirror, willing it to stay where it was and not come forward that he did not notice two people sit down beside him at the bar.

"Hello, Jack. How've you been?"

Between the time it took for Jack to turn around at the bar, Sallie Barker had vanished. He even took a quick look again in the mirror. She was gone.

"Can I buy you a drink, since I own the place? You remember Albert Pringle? Well, here we are. What do you want, other than a drink and a good old chat with old friends? Used to belong to Barney Barnato, if you ever heard of 'im. Built solid as I like it."

Jack turned and looked at her. "Thank you, Lily. I'll have some of that nice Booth's gin with some French vermouth. I can't say you haven't changed because you have. Nice suit, Albert. For my taste a bit flash. The landlord in

Strand Street told me what happened, so we don't have to go down that road, now or ever."

"What brings you here?" asked Lily, feigning indifference. She even tried to look at her fingernails.

"I met an old friend of mine in London and one thing led to another. He told me a very strange story about his cousin, Mrs Flugelhorne. There was a lot about Sallie Barker. For some reason of impulse, I took the first boat to Africa. I must be sentimental or romantic. I'm not sure which."

"You didn't get a cable?"

"What cable?"

"The one she sent to Elephant Walk. Did you shoot an elephant?"

"No, I didn't. Neither did I receive a cable and I stayed for two months. Neither did anyone else on Elephant Walk so far as I know. All you owe me is two months' rent for the Strand Street house. No, on second thoughts, you don't. Have it as a house-warming gift. Funny enough, there's nothing better than ex-employees doing well for themselves. I rather feel I had a part in your education."

"I was an employee. That how you think of me, Jack?"

"Lily. Please. How else would you like me to put it?... Thank you, Mister Barman. A very dry martini, with Booth's gin and Noilly Prat vermouth. Cut a piece of lemon rind, hold it over the full glass, break the lemon peel, and as the juice spurts, burn the juice with a match. And Miss White is paying. I rather think it is the least she could do for an old friend... Now you had better tell me about this Barney Barnato. Who was he?"

Jack let the woman who had once been his mistress prattle on while he tried to take stock of the situation. By looking at her he would never guess her age at thirty-six, which, on casting back his mind, he knew to be correct. The large bosom that had been the cause of her becoming his mistress was now all one of a piece with the rest of her body. The hips had risen up to match the stomach, and the stomach had happily merged with the girl's large bust, which joined with the wobbly flesh that hung from her arms and chin. Her chin had largely given up the ghost and lost itself in the flesh. What had once been a good-looking buxom wench was now a fat, square woman, with legs that matched the size of the legs of the grand piano being played by a young girl rather well, the quartet having gone off for their late supper. Without hearing Lily's voice he would have sworn under oath in a court that he had never before seen the woman in his life. Sadly, Jack thought, there is always a price to pay for everything.

Albert Pringle had not said a word, he was so full of guilt. Jack tried unsuccessfully to give him an understanding look while he listened to Lily in full flight. There was one thing he knew about people. Get them talking about themselves and they will love you all night. Having let his mind fall out of the conversation, he jolted it back to say the right thing to appreciate Lily White's great success by nodding his head with approval. If money was the currency of happiness, the once upon a time Lily Ramsbottom had to be a very happy girl. He finished the dry martini and ordered another one. He had the feeling it was going to be a long night. By the end of his fifth cocktail, he didn't care. That was the wonderful thing about alcohol, he told himself. It took care of things. Blanked the mind. Made ugly situations comfortable.

When Sallie Barker sat down next to him he was drunk. He did not even remember taking a taxi back to the Langham Hotel.

She thought to ring him the next day to remind him of his invitation to lunch.

Jack had tried every trick he knew to bring down his hangover but nothing had worked. The front of his head had the wish to split open. His hands were visibly shaking. He rather thought that after the dry martinis he had drunk a bottle of red wine. He certainly had a red wine hangover.

He told the head waiter to find him in the ladies' cocktail bar when his guest arrived and sat down on a finely made upright wooden chair at the bar, a similar barstool to the one that had started the rot the night before. It was twelve noon and the bar had just opened. Sunlight was streaming through the open window searing his eyes. He had forgotten how bright the light was in Africa. The barman put down a gin and tonic, quinine tonic, ducked from behind the bar under the service hatch and covered the offending window with a heavy lace curtain. The first gin tasted terrible. The second not so bad. The man down the end of the bar looked as miserable as Jack felt. Together with the barman, they had the place to themselves. No one spoke. They drank in complete silence.

"Probably the best thing to do," she said from his left elbow.

"Was I very drunk last night?"

"Yes, you were. I'd have let you go back to England without seeing me if you did not think it so important. You don't remember asking me to lunch?"

"Not really." Jack stood up. The movement jolted the pain in his head.

"That bad?"

"Did I drink red wine?"

"Yes, you did."

"You don't believe the cable never reached me?"

"Lily doesn't. Neither does Albert. They said at the time you'd do nothing."

"I'd have come... It's pretty primitive up there in Rhodesia. Probably the telegraph boy was eaten by a lion along with your cable. I'm sorry, do you want a drink?"

"Can you face lunch?"

"Not really."

"Can you tell me everything you know?"

"You didn't read about Mrs Flugelhorne in the papers?"

"The Mansion House is a whorehouse, not a library. People don't talk about middle-aged women. All I want is the truth, warts and all."

Sallie sat down next to him with a glass of perfectly crushed orange juice. The other man down the bar was set for the day. The third stiff gin had steadied Jack's hands. He told her everything he had heard from Ernest Gilchrist.

"Do you know what happened to my mother?"

"She took a job in the country as a housekeeper."

"Poor Mother... Do you have her address?"

"No I don't but I'll find out for you."

"Can you watch me eat lunch? I'm starving."

"Funnily enough, I feel much better. Hair of the dog. Let's go and have lunch, and you can tell me all over again what you've been doing. After drinking the gin last night I don't remember very much."

"The irony of life. Father goes bust and kills himself. Mother becomes a servant. I get rich."

"There always was something to be said for a whorehouse." Jack was smiling. He was trying to lighten the mood.

"I was never a whore. They tried. If the rich want you they'll offer a fortune. I was pretty then."

"You are now," lied Jack, finishing his third drink, which he decided was enough.

"You do believe I never whored?"

"Yes. Yes, I do. It was never in your nature. I knew your mother was shopping for a husband for you. When you are a rich bachelor it happens often. We understood each other, you and I, that first dinner with your mother and Ernest Gilchrist. I knew you weren't a gold-digger. Your mother was digging for the gold. Not you."


THE ROAST BEEF in the Langham's restaurant was as good as anything Jack had eaten in Europe. They both ate hungrily at a bay window table. Some of the men looked Sallie's way and pretended not to recognise her.

"None of them can believe I'm just the accountant. The one with his wife two tables away offered me ten thousand pounds. He even tried the legitimate route before he married that girl. He's what they call here a rand baron. What in England you would call a rich crook. They say he salted three gold mines with gold from elsewhere. Word got out. Shares went up. Friend over there dumped his shares. Gold seam ran out. What's better, that or whoring? We look after the girls. I invest their savings and they trust me. Lily would have lost the lot years ago. Any good-looking man with a dream can make her invest her money. I vet everything. She can't even write the cheques without my signature."

"How did you learn all this? Accounting? Finance?"

"I may not read the scandal sheets, but I do read all the financial papers. And I took a three-year correspondence course. We both did, Albert and I."

"Are you two?..."

"Not like that. Neither of us ever wish to rely on anyone except ourselves. Not my father. Not my mother. Flugelhorne. Lily. You, Jack. We want our own money so we can tell the rest of you to go to hell. Independence. Personal security. Money. To have money. I wanted to have money, real money. I will soon. I found a buyer for the Mansion House. Like my friend over there everyone will have forgotten the foundation of my wealth in five years. No one worries about his salted gold mines. I'll be able to tell the lie that Daddy left it to me. Society will accept me because I'm rich and educated. The men who know my past will keep quiet. Education, Jack. Run a whorehouse for six years and you will be amazed. The University of Life. It gives you the sixth sense in business. Did Albert tell you he is going up to Oxford?"

"Don't be silly. He only went to school for a few years. Can barely write properly."

"Well, he can now. Our Albert's going a long way. Mark my words. He sent his mother money, which is why I want my mother's address. I don't want to see her. She could have found me easily enough. You did. I want to send her money. Lots of it. Rather like mud in your eye."

"You really think Albert will get into Oxford?"

"Cecil Rhodes did as an adult scholar."

"But he was Cecil Rhodes. The empire. Some say the richest man in an empire he dreamed of extending from Cape to Cairo."

"Albert may not get to Oxford for other reasons. Rhodes found it difficult to run a financial empire and go across to university. Albert now has the same standard of education as my own. There's a lot of spare time running our business. For the non-participants. Until there's trouble. So we have to be on the premises all the time. On immediate call. We have lots of time to read and study. To talk. Did you know he read many of the books in your library? You thought he was just sitting around when you went to the club or went to see Lily. He was always waiting up for you, wasn't he? To keep himself from going out of his mind with boredom, he began reading your books. You are right, his handwriting was terrible and his reading not much better when he became your valet. But he went on for nothing better to do. Slowly, he understood what he was reading and after that, his reading became a compulsion. He wanted to know it all."

"We never even talked about books."

"Most people leave school and never read another book. Their education stops dead when they walk out of the classroom. For Albert Pringle, he only began to use his brain when he found your library of books."

"Will Lily want to sell the Mansion House?"

"She does what I say when it comes to money. She's going to buy a top hotel. Or build one. She's good at looking after guests and very good at running a restaurant as you could see. 'Got to try everything, Sallie,' is her motto. And she means only the food."

"May I ask you something very personal? Please don't take it as being male. Why did you cut off the ringlets? Fringe your hair? Wear severely cut suits?"

"But you said I was still pretty, Jack."

"I was lying. Sorry. The truth is best left unsaid. You were one of the prettiest girls I ever saw in my life."

"Thank you, Jack. That was very sweet of you. And you didn't mention the glasses. Would you like to have a look through them?"

Guiltily, Jack took the pair of spectacles and half propped them on his nose.

"They're plain glass!" he exclaimed.

"Exactly. In a whorehouse, it's better not to look too pretty."

"I wish you would stop calling it a whorehouse."

"And who was the one for telling me the truth?"

"And what are you going to do with your money? The way you just said it, Lily is going into the hotel business, not you."

"No, we're not. Albert and I are going into the mining business. To compete with the man two tables away who thought he could buy my body for ten thousand pounds."

"Wow, that really is a lot of money now I think of it."

"How much would you pay, Jack? Or rather how much would you have paid those six years ago when I was nineteen?"

"Not a penny."

"Why?" she said, looking annoyed.

"Because you are not a whore. Do you hate the rand baron?"

"Not at all. I envy him. And when I envy I don't want to destroy the other person. Most people are just jealous of the wealthy. Want to see them lose their money so they can all be poor together. I want to be as rich. I want to be a rand baroness, Jack. Only, of course, I can't. Albert will be the front."

"But you said he's very clever. Going a long way."

"Some people are marvellous employees and lousy employers. They have to be directed. They don't have the new ideas. They are not creators. Albert is like that."

"And you are a creator?"

"Haven't done too badly so far as a runaway." The eyes were still hard but the smile was soft.


ALL THE WAY back on the boat to England, Jack toyed with the idea of visiting Mrs Barker rather than writing Sallie her mother's address. Waiting for the ship to sail from Cape Town, he had stayed at the Mount Nelson Hotel and used his time to put a long-distance phone call through to Ernest Gilchrist in Colombo, having remembered the name of the tea merchant. The telephone company had found the telephone number but in the end, and despite a person-to-person call, Jack sent a wire asking Ernest to cable Mrs Barker's address to the Mount Nelson Hotel; Jack had grown bored sitting in the manager's office waiting for the connection that never came. The day before the boat sailed, he had his information.

Jack had caught the train the day after the lunch in the Langham Hotel. There was no point in staying any longer. The untied strings were tied. Lily repulsed him covered in fat. Albert had not said a word, tongue-tied despite his new-found education. Sallie was as hard as nails. And none of them needed his help. The last thing would have been to cable the mother's address to the Mansion House and leave it at that.

The boat arrived at Southampton. The address in his pocket was Plaitford, only a few miles from where his ship had docked which made up his mind for him. Having nothing much better to do, Jack hired a taxi and gave the man the address.

Spring was in full bloom, the trees bursting their buds and flowers in the hedgerows. Jack enjoyed the drive and the English countryside. His trunk had been sent up to London by goods train. The small grip next to him on the back seat carried his shaving tackle and what he would need for a night in a hotel if the task he had set himself took longer than expected. The train to London left at three in the afternoon. His hope was to reconcile mother and daughter. He rather liked doing what he supposed were good deeds.

The address led them to a small mansion hidden from the road by tall trees.

"I want the tradesman's entrance," said Jack to the driver.

"Are you sure, guv?"

"I'm sure, thank you."

The tradesman's sign pointing off the main driveway was quite clear soon after they entered the grounds. When they stopped, there was a butchery van unloading an order. Mrs Barker was supervising the packets with great authority, ticking them off against a list in her capable hands. Jack rather thought the business sense of the daughter had come from the mother; no tradesman was going to under-deliver to this mansion, he thought with a nervous chuckle; the woman intimidated him for some reason.

"I may be here for some time," he said to the driver. "Please wait. That will be your tip." He gave the driver a five-pound note, which was far too much but he didn't want the man driving back to Southampton if he thought his fare had run off without paying.

"I don't understand the tradesman's entrance, guv," the man said, licking his lips at the large white folded banknote.

"There are lots of things we don't understand in life. You can keep the meter running. I don't wish to be stranded."

Jack got out of the taxi and walked towards Mrs Barker, who ignored him. He waited for the order to be checked, feeling sorry for the butcher. The butcher was obviously below Mrs Barker in the pecking order of things. Then she looked up at Jack where he stood five yards away, waiting patiently. If there was any recognition in her mind it did not show on her face.

"What do you want?" she asked rudely, and Jack wondered if he would have received the same reception had he come through the front door of the mansion. Probably not, he guessed rightly. She might have even claimed to recognise him after all her hard work on the SS *King Emperor* trying to marry off her daughter to a rich man.

"To speak to Mrs Barker." She looked at him sharply, having recognised the well-educated accent of the upper class. "We have met before. Fact is, I once bought you supper with Ernest Gilchrist and your daughter. Ernest kindly gave me your address. My name is Jack Merryweather."

"He's in Ceylon."

"So I discovered when he led me in a roundabout way to your daughter's address in Johannesburg. Fact is, I lunched with your daughter last month and she asked me to find out your address."

"Why does she wish to know my address?"

"To send you money."

"She enticed that poor man. He was a good man. Mrs Flugelhorne got what she deserved."

The back door was open and Mrs Barker marched off into her domain, slamming the door in Jack's face.

"You earned an easy fiver," he said to the driver when he got back into the car. "With a bit of luck, I can still catch the three o'clock to London."

"What was all that about, guv?"

"Just about everything. Murder. Retribution."

"Cor blimey."

"Exactly."


WHEN JACK GOT BACK to 27 Baker Street, the letter from Rhodesia was waiting for him on the silver tray where it had been placed by his manservant. The bills and commercial correspondence were left in the study. Visiting cards and personal letters were to be placed on the silver tray in the small entrance hall of the house. Jack was still annoyed at having called on Mrs Barker rather than writing her Sallie's address. Never before in his life had anyone slammed a door in his face. But then again, he told himself, it was the first time he had visited a house through the tradesman's entrance. Jack could still be amazed by people who refused to believe what did not suit them. He rather thought Mr Barker had done the right thing by killing himself whether or not his business had gone bust. Consoling himself with the fact that people still had to live with themselves despite what they did wrong in life, he put the Barker family out of his mind once and for all. He had done his best. It was not good enough. But he had done his best.

"At least I wasn't bored," he said picking up the letter, not recognising Harry Brigandshaw's writing. The note was brief, the old cable to the point.

"It seems those two women wish to haunt me," he said out loud. "Stuck in the mailbox for those years. Poor Sallie. The gods were not with you." Then he shook his head, walked into his sitting room and poured a large amount of whisky into the waiting crystal glass. This time, he did not even bother squirting a slosh of soda from the syphon into the glass.

For no reason whatsoever, a cold shiver ran through his body, as if someone had walked over his grave.

·  ·  ·

THE SALE of the Mansion House went through quickly. Sallie had discreetly put the business on the market as she concluded everyone with money thought they could run a restaurant, a bar and a whorehouse. She rather thought most men were familiar with all three of them, which made them feel comfortable and competent; all they had to do was pay their money and reap the profit. Sallie wished the buyer the best of luck. She had her money in the bank. The first big gamble had paid off. Never again would a business of hers be illegitimate.

Lily had gone off on a world cruise before deciding what to buy with her money. They both waved her goodbye at the railway station.

"Do you think we will ever see her again?" asked Albert.

"No. Some man will have that money off her before she reaches New York."

"What will she do then?"

"Who knows? People find a place somewhere or they die. Always other people have made Lily her money. Men. Jack Merryweather. You and me. None of us owes each other anything. It was a business partnership. Who the hell knows, Albert? Maybe she'll meet a man on the boat who likes fat women. I believe the Turks are like that."

"I hope you're wrong about losing her money."

"So do I... We will both have to sell our houses."

"Whatever for? I like my house."

"We need the money. There's going to be one hell of a war in Europe. Everyone at each other's throats. The Americans, the Germans, the French; they have all envied the British Empire for too long. The Americans talk about freeing our colonies for egalitarian reasons but the real reason is they can only do business with them without British interference. Kick out imperial Britain, bring in the imperial dollar. The Germans covet our possessions. The French and English have hated each other for centuries, though this time for fun we are going to be on the French side. Balance of power to stop Germany. They need us, we need them. The Germans made a mess of everything in 1870... The Americans will try and trade with everyone. There's going to be one big world war, according to the financial papers I read. Despite the Boer War, I think here the generals, Louis Botha and Jan Smuts, will side with the British Empire. They have found which side their bread's buttered. Smuts, in particular, has been so feted by the English he's besotted with the attention of so many royals. Flattery. Nothing like a bit of flattery. He's joined the big club... Now, Albert Pringle: it's time we went for lunch. We will each pay half of the bill which is the way I want it for the rest of our partnership."

The train carrying Lily had run out of the station leaving the platform empty. Sallie took off her glasses and tossed them in the first dustbin.

"Why did you do that, Sallie? You always say never waste money."

"I don't need them anymore."

"You can see properly now!"

"I always could. Before lunch, I'm going to the hairdresser and then I'm going to buy myself some clothes. Oh, and there is something else I never told you. There are two sets of books."

"You've been stealing!"

"In a kind of way. Hiding would be the better word. It cost something when I sold the business, as the second set of accounts show a higher profit and would have valued the business for more than we got. Lily is her own worst enemy. I have created a legal trust for Lily Ramsbottom from which she can only draw the interest. Your share of the skim is in a separate bank account that can only be drawn upon with your signature. You will see for the last five years there are only credits, including half-annual interest on the balance. It represents your twenty per cent of the skim. Lily's sixty per cent is in the trust. Lily will never go hungry. She was more than good to us... Do you think I did the right thing?"

"You said she would have to settle for a Turk."

"I wanted you to understand why I hid the trust from Lily. She may not come back to Johannesburg. But one day she'll be asking us for money. She'll say we owe her one, which we do."

"You think of everything."

"Over lunch, I want to tell you about our dynamite factory. There are two shareholders at present. One is an industrial chemist and knows how to blow things up; the other is a fool. Inherited his money. Couldn't run a brewery selling free beer. He is the one you and I are going to buy out and then refinance the company."

"I thought we were going into mining?"

"We are. The factory sells explosives mainly to the mining industry. When the war comes they'll want a lot of explosives to blow up people instead of rocks. I want a new factory ready within the year. Why we have to use all our money now."

"What happens if it doesn't work? If the other man wasn't such a fool?"

"Then we go broke. Where we started, Albert. What's the difference?"

"Can't I keep my house?"

"No. And we're not going to go broke. You just start reading everything you can find on dynamite. Detonator caps. Safety precautions at explosive factories, if you can find such literature, which I can't. Every piece of knowledge in the world is in between the covers of books. Someone said that years ago."

By THE TIME Sallie joined Albert at the restaurant in the Langham Hotel, there was no resemblance to the girl who had run the accounts at the Mansion House. The very pit of his stomach ached for what he knew he would never have. They were business partners. She had made that quite plain.

"There is always a snag in all good things," he said, getting up from his chair as she sat down.

"What are you talking about?"

"You, Sallie."

"You can stop that right there," she snapped. "I may not have told you in as many words but after that fat, farting German raped me, men and sex frighten me. Don't even let your mind think down that road or our partnership stops right now."

"Then why the clothes? The new hairstyle?"

"It will give me power. Power over men, and I like that."

Like Jack Merryweather had done early in the day, Albert Pringle shivered as if someone had walked over his grave.

"Did you ever hear from Jack about your mother's address?" he said after a moment.

"Not a word."

# 4

## JULY 1913

The Ninth Earl of Pembridgemoor, Peregrine Alexander Cholmondeley Kenrick, woke from his dream under the wild fig tree on a tiny island in the Okavango Delta. For a moment he was not sure where he lay, while the tears rolled down the deep crow's feet from his eyes into the grey-white bush of his unkempt beard. Above in the tree, the birds were singing, strange birds for the first moments from his dream, and then he remembered and tears followed tears from the small blue eyes. The fleshy mouth was open, caught by a ray of the African sun through the tangled branches.

The tree was full of birds and all of them were singing their separate songs, the sound of different calls mingling in a symphony of sound. By the shallow water, the two donkeys grazed the lush grass that, without the thousands of rivulets sinking into the Kalahari sands, would be gone, left to die in the dry red dust of the desert. The swamps, Peregrine called them, rioted throughout this lost Garden of Eden, the Okavango the only river in Africa he knew to flow inland and disappear into the sand; other rivers, like the Nile, meandered into the sea giving their pure sweet waters to the fish; Peregrine the Ninth thought that was rather a pity.

The rivulets, five feet deep at the worst, surrounded his island with a tree topping the central mound, the water so pure and clear, so good to drink, he could see every detail on the bottom; the reeds, tall at the water's edge, were to the height of a man's shoulder; the thicker forest was across the thirty feet of water, where a tall island dominated the great river on its last flow as the waters dispersed over mile after mile into the thankful desert that drank and drank. Peregrine could hear the elephant moving on the big island, the tall, tangled trees keeping them from his blurred vision. His small leathery hand came up and wiped away his tears. He had dreamed of his long ago.

He had first run away to France, the rough rude winter channel testimony to his father's wrath. He was twenty years old, and educated to tell others what to do in far-flung colonies or, when his time came, to inherit the great estate that had belonged to his family for centuries. For all intents and purposes, he was penniless with not even the skill to steal. None of them had been on his side, not even his mother. They – and that meant all of them, his brother, his sisters, both families, and with some help from his father's purse – had conspired to send her away, out of his reach, out of his life, and when she was gone he was meant to do what he was told. Looking back he wondered if the whole performance, the pride, the pain, the sheer longing, had been, along with his wandering life, fruitless, wasted, sometimes mellow, sometimes sad, mostly alone. Well, he had told himself a thousand times, he had burnt his boats, and there was no going back, not even when he read in the paper his father was dead.

The family had put notices in many newspapers around the world. The estate was entailed, and despite his father's better wishes, would always belong to the eldest son, the head of the family, the holder of the title. While leading Harry Brigandshaw on a wild-goose chase looking for the last gold of King Lobengula, he had chanced to read a piece of old newspaper used to wrap the crystal glasses they drank from when the sun went down. His father was dead at the age of ninety-five. He no longer needed guile to drink good whisky. He burnt the piece of paper on their fire that night. Going back was out of the question. It was far too late, he told himself.

She had seduced him, a virgin. There had been no wicked uncle to take him south to London, to pay an older woman. No older brothers, he was the eldest. And she had probably known exactly what she was doing. Having caught his eye, she called his body in the woods. From then on Peregrine was besotted with the girl. Still was, with her memory. His father, he suspected, like many fathers before him, had been right. There had even been some patience in the beginning.

"Perry, my boy," he said. His father had always called him 'Perry, my boy'. Never plain 'Perry'. "We all fall in lust when we are young. That is primal nature calling. Probably way back then, when land and money had not come into the equation, we procreated with whoever came along, fighting for the survival of our species. I don't even think man and woman are meant to be monogamous. In the beginning, there was no need to take a lifetime partner to protect our property and our children. Everything and everyone belonged to everybody. I rather think the tribes in darkest Africa and Borneo are the same today. Most likely they have a short sweet life, the fittest surviving the weak by killing them. Mr Darwin has some interesting theories which if they get out all over the place will change the way we think of ourselves, even the way we are told on pain of fiery hell the way we were created. Fact is, I rather agree with his logic that comes back to you, my son, and our ancestors. We have been on this land for a long time but to survive we have had to be the best, the strongest, the richest. We have to dominate as the empire dominates or we will be knocked off our perch. Do you really think I married your mother for love, though you might think so after eleven children? There was a girl in my day, I forget her name deliberately. Like your girl, she was poor. No dowry. Probably after me for my potential money and title as much as anything, though we both swore to each other money had nothing to do with it. My father took away my horse. Told the stable boys on pain of dismissal not to saddle me a horse. They locked the stables at night. He took away all my money and anything else I could turn into money. He knew I would not steal what was not mine and there he was right. We all so hate being told we are wrong. I had met your mother a few times socially. We had not even glanced at each other. And then it was arranged. You see, Perry, my boy, your mother had the right breeding and half a million pounds. So they married us. The other girl married into her own class. I heard she was happy. And I ask you, my son, is this a happy house? Don't you love your mother? Doesn't your mother love you? Are we not a close family in harmony with each other and our surroundings?"

"Yes, Father."

"Then do as you're told. If we have to have this discussion again I will not be so pleasant. With wealth comes responsibility. You will have a great weight on your shoulders when I die. Mary's not a bad girl. You have the same background, the two of you. In the end, you will find that more conducive to harmony than primal lust. You will be able to trust each other. The families will be marrying each other. If she were to seduce you in the bushes, how many others might she seduce, and then where would you be?"

"How do you know?"

"I have my spies."

And all the logic in the world had been to no avail. He was in love, not in lust. He was incapable of other thought. The arguments with his father grew violent. The happy family began to disintegrate and they told him it was all his fault. Then the girl had gone and in this temper and frustration, he had run away. Put his back to them. And still, in his dreams, she came to him and made him cry. They were sweet moments in his life.

Peregrine rather thought to himself, as he looked back on his lonely life, that we want what we can't have, and curse a moment when we have what we want and it is taken away from us. He knew, in his heart, if the affair had been allowed to follow its natural path it would have petered out like the others. His love, his lust, his passion would have waned. He would have satiated himself. But all the daylight logic churning in his mind had never stopped the night-time dreams. Somewhere, back then, there had been perfection in his life. The cold hard reality he had faced since then was, to him, an indictment on life itself. Without that sweet, brief perfection in his mind, he rather thought he would not survive. She never changed. Never grew old. Was always perfect in his thoughts.

The journey through his life had gone on and on, place to place, people to people, country after country and little had stuck in his memory. He had soon found a way to make a living, a transient living but mostly it had worked. When he wished to be, he could be the most charming man in the room. Educated, well spoken. Good at talking. Good at listening. And he had a courtesy title, Lord Peregrine Kenrick, which he used sparingly, only letting out the surprising news when he had found himself a mark. And they had never been difficult to find throughout his wandering, especially in America, when hostesses would have killed to lay their hands on a young handsome genuine English lord. In many ways, it had all been too easy. Like the lady he wanted in his dreams, they always wanted what they could never have. No matter how much money they had, no one would ever call an American the Right Honourable, the Earl of Pembridgemoor. They had fought a war of independence to make sure it never happened, that they were all a happy, egalitarian commonality. But if by chance their daughter married an English earl... It was all rather pointless, Peregrine had thought. But then, so was the variety of certain men and women. And he had to have a living, and in a roundabout way, he was selling them a product, their ability to refer to their good friend Lord Peregrine Kenrick for the rest of their natural lives. He was a celebrity in America, and celebrities cost money, 'that's Lord Peregrine, you know'. The fact that Lord Peregrine was a bum never entered their heads.

Like with any job, he grew tired of the constant need to keep on his toes to stop the lie being understood by his benefactors. To give them their money's worth. He hoped it was the way of people to create a façade that gave them the most from life. And society and business, because of all the falsity, were riddled with the fear of being found out.

After thirty years of drifting and ignoring letters from his family as they followed his career in the American social papers, he had come to Africa. He had never married one of the daughters, as none of them compared to the lady in his dreams. And then he had disappeared from sight. And in Africa he called himself Peregrine the Ninth just in case: it was his own private joke.

There were moments when his lack of family responsibility involuntarily turned his stomach. Someone, one of his youngest brothers, would be running the estate. Maybe they had proclaimed him dead. Maybe he was not the ninth Earl of Pembridgemoor. But whichever way he looked at it all, it was too late now, in the swamps of Africa, six years after reading about his father's death. He would be a ghost from the past, a past best left to get on with itself. Even friendly ghosts were rarely welcome, he argued. He had a letter for them in the wagon should there be someone around to give it to when he was dying. And then again someone might find the wagon and his corpse. And then again he would just turn to dust and sink into the soil of Africa, Clary and Jeff, his donkeys, himself, and an abandoned wagon.

He was hungry. Reminiscing in his mind always made him hungry. A nice piece of dried venison was exactly what he fancied for his breakfast. Getting up with surprising ease for a man of seventy, he walked across to his wagon in the beautiful yellow light of early sunrise. A heron rose above the reeds, long-legged from the river, and somewhere deep in the swamps an African fish eagle called its lonely cry.

"My, it's grand to be alive," he said to the donkeys as he passed.


ON THE BIG island across the thirty feet of clear river water, Barend Oosthuizen was preparing the morning shoot for his German clients, among them Lieutenant von Stratten of the Imperial German Army, the man who had met Barend on the Skeleton Coast and been gone in the morning without saying goodbye. The smell of coffee, that surprisingly would shortly find its way into the nostrils of the ninth Earl of Pembridgemoor causing him concern about his mind, was strong. There were ten of them camped on the island, four white men and six black men, the blacks having carried the guns and equipment for so many miles in the heat. The bearers were huddled together ten yards away from the white men's camp, and to Barend's trained eye they were more excited than they should be, talking in a language Barend suspected was spoken by less than ten thousand people in the world. Barend had been unable to draw from them their tribe name or the name of their language. One of them, the leader, who had worked in the mines in

Johannesburg, spoke enough Afrikaans to take and relay orders to the rest of them. Barend had found him at the small trading post at Maun where the swamps began and the stray tourists looked for guides to take them hunting in the great Okavango Delta. The surprise had been meeting von Stratten again, which had been little surprise to the German. Having put up his shingle as a white hunter, the word had spread quicker than Barend could ever have imagined. From Portuguese West Africa to Portuguese East Africa, through all the British colonies of Central Africa, wherever the business of hunting animals was done for the white man's pleasure, many of the white hunters and their trackers heard that Tinus Oosthuizen's son had become a hunter like his father. At night around the campfires, there was little to talk about but shooting elephant or lion and retelling the legends of the old white hunters, blown out of all proportion by so much repetition over so many years.

Unlike Peregrine, who had walked his donkeys along the old hunters' paths and through the drifts that sank his big iron wheels underwater, flooding the bottom of the wagon and drowning some of the bugs, the Germans' party, having hired Barend in Maun, had driven as far into the delta as possible, before leaving the big army trucks with their drivers to be fetched on the way back.

Barend had noticed the excited chattering among the black men soon after he had hired six makoris with local oarsmen to take them up the reed-lined rivers that marked the swamps to look for elephant. The locals, the previous night, had made camp next to the river and their canoes, not wishing to join the hunting party. Barend was certain the blacks were not telling him something and he wanted to know what it was. With a mug of hot coffee wrapped inside the palm of his big right hand, he went down to join his employees by the river. When they saw him coming the blacks stopped talking immediately, every one of them looking sheepish. In all of their eyes, Barend saw the signs of fear, causing his hackles to rise at the hidden danger. He stood for a long time looking down at them crouched on their haunches, silent, averting their eyes. To them, he was a huge, blond, hairy, slate-green-eyed monster drinking a strange-smelling liquid, the name of which they were unable to pronounce.

Having finished his coffee slowly, to maximise the intimidation, Barend, with the tin mug now in his left hand, walked slowly to the group, and one-handed gripped the one-time gold miner by his shirt front and jerked him to his feet. Behind, the Germans looked up to see what was happening. Barend stared into the eyes of the frightened black man for a long minute before he spoke to him in Afrikaans, a language none of the others understood.

Barend smiled sweetly and waited, having asked his question.

"They frightened of ghosts," said the black man. "The people in the makoris say since you arrived at Maun the Great Elephant seen many times. They think dead father sent you the Great Elephant to kill but they say the Great Elephant kill you way it killed Baas Brigandshaw."

"And where is this Great Elephant?" asked Barend mockingly, inwardly surprised at the accuracy and travelling distance of the bush telegraph which had spread the death of Sebastian Brigandshaw.

"On island, baas. It was last seen two days ago on island."

"Then that's good. My clients will be pleased. We will kill the Great Elephant and my German friends will become part of the great legend. Don't be afraid. It is only an elephant."

"Those men in the makoris say elephant kill all of us."

"But I will shoot the Great Elephant if my clients fail."

"But you can't kill the Great Elephant. No one can. It is a spirit."

"Then if it is only a ghost it can't kill any of us."

"That is not true, baas. A ghost can kill who it likes."

"Then why do you stay with me?"

"We more frightened of being left alone in the swamps."

"But you all know the swamps."

"No, baas."

"But you said they all knew the swamps better than their mothers."

"I lied, baas. We were hungry. We want a job. Now we say the Great Elephant ghost kill us or the lions eat us. We think elephant kill us more quickly. We stay with you."

"So you've never been in the swamps before?"

"No, baas. I come from Johannesburg."

"Why did you leave Johannesburg?"

"That is a long story."

"Yes, I'm sure it is. Did you kill another man or steal his wife?" he said sarcastically.

"Both, baas. But the man, he was going to kill me."

"Have any of the others been in the swamps before?"

"No, baas. They too come from Johannesburg. They are my brothers."

"You have the same mothers and fathers?"

"No, baas. We are brothers."

"If you knew the Great Elephant was on this island, why did you let the oarsmen bring us here?"

"The Great Elephant is on all the islands."

The belly laugh, made first by tension, swelled up in Barend and burst in loud guffaws. Shaking his head he walked back to the Germans.

"What was all that about?" asked von Stratten in English.

"He was telling me a joke."

"It must have been a good one. This island is thick with bush and trees. You think we'll see anything to shoot? My colonel wants to take home to Frankfurt a big pair of elephant tusks. And tonight, when we come back to camp with our trophy, he wants to talk to you."

"I can't speak German."

"My colonel speaks English."

THERE WAS no shoreline to most of the island, the trees growing out over the water in tangled roots thicker than Barend's arm. Like his father before him, Barend never believed in coincidence. When the man he had met on the Skeleton Coast appeared at Maun, Barend was sure the man had a reason other than killing wild animals. The man was too smug. Too sure of himself. A man on the brink of great things justly deserved. Barend would have turned down the client had he any nerve. Despite the shingle on the front of his small hut on the side of the only dusty road in Maun, he had not received a commission and was about to go on his endless wagon journey. He had the idea to go to Kimberley and the big diamond mine to find out if the seven stones hidden in the soft leather belt strapped around his stomach were really diamonds. Some of the hatred for the English had seeped out of his mind. All the wandering had been pointless. He was getting nowhere going around in circles. The German money, despite the prospect of an ulterior motive, would take him to Kimberley, and if the diamonds were real he would sell them on the illicit market and go home. He was not as tough as he thought he was. He had never before experienced the strange feeling that lately kept returning to his mind, a feeling that spread to a physical sickness in his stomach, and that only went away when he allowed himself to think of his mother, Madge, Katinka, and Elephant Walk. After nine years alone, Barend was finally homesick.

Thinking it better to leave the bearers in the small clearing where they had camped for the night, Barend led the Germans down the one path between hundred-foot high trees in search of an elephant, trying to remember all the knowledge his father had taught him when he was a boy. Within two hundred yards they were swallowed by the trees, Barend consciously taking the sight of the sun so he could lead them back to camp.

He would not have been the first white hunter to go into the swamps and never come out again.

PEREGRINE THE NINTH had been worried all morning. Smelling freshly made coffee in the swamps was a sure sign of dementia. Instead of his body giving out at seventy years of age, his heart stopping, his kidneys gracefully giving up after the years of abuse in his youth, his mind was going. He told himself in quiet despair, 'I'm going crackers'. And when Clary looked up from chewing the grass, he knew he had spoken out loud. The possibilities he decided were twofold: if he was going crackers, he would lose himself in the bush; but if his mind went he would not know what was happening so it wouldn't matter. Not sure there wasn't a fallacy in his thinking, he had eaten his stick of dried venison, congratulating his teeth on their ability to still chew the biltong, as it was called by the Afrikaners he sometimes met on his travels, and made himself a rare pipe from his limited supply of tobacco. If he was going crackers he had better enjoy the smoke before he had no idea what he was doing. Back under the fig tree, and with the taste of tobacco deep in his lungs, he began to enjoy his morning. The idea of eating a nice large river bream appealed to him. He never ate lunch. Two meals were enough for an old man. He would find a spot between the tall reeds from where he could cast his line in the water and still keep an eye out for crocodiles. Crocodiles and snakes were still his pet aversions, even after so many years in the bush. The bugs in his bedclothes worried him not at all, they were part of life, but he always checked his bedding for snakes when he went to bed, especially in winter when they had a bad habit of climbing straight away into the warm spot when he got up in the morning and spending the rest of the day. Once one had got in with him when he was asleep which caused a ruckus in the middle of the night that had the donkeys bolting into the bush.

With the pipe finished and propped against a root of the fig tree, his mind pleasantly thinking of fish for supper, the donkeys happy on their own grazing next to the wagon, Peregrine the Ninth fell asleep.

THE SUN WAS VERTICALLY above them when they came out of the trees into tall grass as high as their armpits. The Germans were sweating in the heat, their guns heavy on their shoulders. Thirty yards through the elephant grass, brown at the top despite so much water underground, the river circled the mile-long island, the stretch in front of them blocked at the back and both sides by the giant trees of the forest. The open land was sprinkled with small, flat-topped trees. They could all hear a wallowing noise coming from a patch of trees next to the river. The wallowing and slosh of water went on for some time while they waited motionlessly, their guns, .37 Mausers, off their shoulders, with a bullet pushed into every breech, the safety catches pushed forward, ready for whatever it was wallowing in the water. Barend recognised the ears above the height of the trees and watched the trunk ride up and curl to spurt water on the back of the elephant hidden by the trees; its feet still in the river. Barend shivered with fear; for the first time in his life the ghost of the Great Elephant was eighty yards in front of him, and from the sound of the cascading water falling into the water, the animal was coming out of the river. First, the top of the great head and tusks appeared above the trees at treetop height. Then the elephant rested them on the earth while it took in the heads and shoulders of the five men looking at him in awe. The ears flapped once, slowly, and then again fast. The tusks came off the ground. The ears flapped with claps of thunderous sound and the trunk went up in the air, showing the red, gaping mouth.

"He's going to charge," said Barend quickly. "On the count of three we all fire at the heart at the same time; the colonel wins the trophy."

Four trained soldiers and Barend brought their guns to their shoulders as the elephant charged, the animal quickly picking up speed, trumpeting, great ears flapping, the ground shaking under the platter-sized pads of the feet.

"One. Two. Three. Fire!" called Barend and four heavy calibre bullets hit the elephant, not even changing the animal's stride.

Barend had deliberately not fired, to give his clients the kill. The raging, wounded beast was charging straight for the German colonel. Barend, his brain cold as ice, took aim for the brain, the more difficult shot, and fired, dropping the animal dead in its tracks, ten yards in front of the German, breaking one of the tusks as it fell. The colonel was swearing profusely in German as the old elephant looked at Barend through dead eyes. He turned away from his clients, bent below the height of the elephant grass and retched and retched, tearing at the innards of his stomach. When he stood up again he was crying and the colonel was standing on top of the dead elephant, von Stratten taking his picture.

"We'll send the bearers for the tusks when we reach the makoris," said Barend. "This hunt is over."

No one was taking any notice of him.

. . .

PEREGRINE HAD WOKEN with the volley of four shots, certain he had not been dreaming. The donkeys had taken no notice. Birds were arising from the canopy of the dense forest and the black-headed heron was making slow haste with heavy wings. Then came the lone shot and Peregrine felt a flood of relief that started in his stomach and dissipated in his brain.

"You silly old bug. It was coffee." Then he scowled. Once again the world of people had caught up with him. The idea of the fish on the fire for supper was no longer attractive. The gunshots, the coffee smells were intrusions. The afternoon found him irritated. He liked it better when his hermit's world was left alone.

The next day with the dawn he packed a few things in the wagon and this time remembered to hang his bedding and mattress from the roof of the wagon. With the donkeys in harness and a piece of biltong in the cheek of his mouth, he headed out of the swamps across the shallow river. The heron watched him without taking to flight. Even in a few days, they had grown used to each other.


THE COLONEL HAD COME to the point the following afternoon. The elephant tusks, including the one with the broken tip, were safely in the German military truck after the bearers had hacked them out of the carcass of the dead elephant. The oarsmen had been paid, the new bush story was already going from mouth to mouth, spreading like the ripples from a stone thrown into a silent pond. The Great Elephant was dead. Whether it was the one spoken of so many years before by his father was a point in question to Barend. If it was not the one that had killed Uncle Sebastian it did not matter either. All the hatred had drained out of him. Never again would he shoot an elephant unless to protect himself. His days as a hunter finished in the dead eyes of the biggest animal he had ever seen, dead at his feet for no reason Barend could understand.

The colonel had gone on about a great war the Germans were going to bring on the English. But all Barend could see was a great elephant dead, the ears not moving, the trumpet silent, the years of life shot out of him for man's sport. The colonel was talking about meetings with the old Boer generals that had fought the British with his father and now wanted to fight them again. De Wet, Beyers, Kemp, Maritz; how old man de la Rey would have joined the rebellion if he had not been accidentally shot dead. But all the anger had gone out of him and he listened with half his mind.

"When the time comes you will join us, Oosthuizen?"

"Join us?"

"Against the British. When we invade South Africa and make it a republic again."

"With allegiance to Germany?"

"Of course."

"What will be the difference?"

"You will have your republic again."

"But under German hegemony."

"Germany will then lead the world. You will join us, no?"

"Of course, Colonel."

"The young Afrikaners will follow the son of General Oosthuizen." The colonel was pleased. "I'm glad. Good. Very good... It was good hunting. We shall meet again."

"I hope so," said Barend, wishing the opposite.

When the two German trucks drove out of Maun the following day Barend smiled at the irony of life. Satisfied he had enough money to reach Kimberley he went inside his small rented hut and began the preparations for his departure the next day. The bearers had said they wanted to stay in Maun now they were local heroes. They had been part of the killing of the spirit of the Great Elephant. Everyone was safe again.

PEREGRINE HAD the beginnings of a whisky thirst and wondered who he could prevail upon to buy him a drink. It was early in the following morning, Peregrine having travelled through the night, finding it easier to navigate his way around the bush by reading the stars; the moon had been good but not too bright to dull the pointer star of the Southern Cross. With the sound of waking birds and the slow clop of the donkeys' hooves, he made his way towards the small cluster of dust-covered buildings that was Maun.

The Duck Inn was on the far side of the only street, and one of Peregrine's favourite places in the world, though the word 'inn' was a misnomer, as all old Dawie had put up was a shed open on three sides, with a small room attached to the only wall with its back to the road, so he could lock up his stash of booze. During the rains, it became rather muddy but no one seemed to care. Dawie opened for business with the first customer and closed for business when the last went home. No one had ever seen him sober and no one had ever seen him drunk.

As the donkeys drew Peregrine's wagon towards the first of what might be called a building, the whisky thirst grew stronger and by the time the wagon with Peregrine on the box drew alongside Barend's small hut with the new shingle that was about to be taken down, the thirst was raging.

He had heard the name Barend Oosthuizen over the years, especially from young Madge Brigandshaw, and clutching at any straw that might bring him a drink, Peregrine stopped Clary and Jess right outside the hut and studied the shingle further. The donkeys were quite happy to stand still in the middle of the road. Far down the dirt track, Peregrine could clearly see the object of his desire, the sign 'Duck Inn' being the biggest sign in Maun.

A big blond man with slate-green eyes surveyed him from just inside the open door and quickly lost interest, turning his back.

"Excuse me. Are you Barend Oosthuizen from Elephant Walk?"

Involuntarily, Barend spun around and gave himself away, wondering how on earth this decrepit old man knew where he came from.

"Were you making coffee in the swamps the day before yesterday?" asked Peregrine. His desperation to hold the man where he was focusing all his guile.

"Probably."

"And you shot something?"

"Yes, we did."

"I was glad of that. Not for the animal, of course. Thought I was going crackers smelling fresh coffee coming out of the bush. Then I fell asleep and woke to gunshot and birds rising from the canopy. Then another shot, which made me happy as it obviously told me I was not out of my mind after all. That I thought was rather pleasing for an old man."

"How do you know where I come from?"

"It was just a good guess." Trying one of his best tricks (he rather thought he had the man's individual attention), Peregrine slapped Clary with a stick and told the donkeys to 'loop'. As expected, both donkeys failed to move. Peregrine looked at Barend through small blue twinkling eyes and prepared his long stick for a second mild blow.

"Won't you join me for coffee?" said Barend, homesickness overcoming his caution.

"Do you know Dawie?"

"Ah," said Barend smiling. "You would like a drink."

"Specifically, a large whisky. And then I'll tell you where I was when last I was drunk."

"At Elephant Walk?"

Peregrine stayed silent.

"You do have some money?" Peregrine asked as an afterthought.

"Well, well, well. Fact is, I haven't been drunk a while myself. Do you know the Duck Inn well?" asked Barend.

"Oh yes I do," said Peregrine all in one piece.


DAWIE HAD BEEN WATCHING the whole performance, as he did not sleep well when he was sober, and drinking alone in Dawie's mind was only for drunks. Fact was, he had not seen a customer for two days and his whisky thirst was also raging. The two donkeys, Clary and Jeff, and the wagon were recognisable, as everyone else used salted horses to pull their wagons, or in the case of big wagons with big loads they used oxen. No one used donkeys except the black men with small carts they used for collecting firewood. Dawie licked his lips and had even made up his mind to allow Peregrine to drink on the house. The stop outside the white hunter's hut was a surprise. And a further surprise when the big man climbed up onto the box bench next to Peregrine, almost upsetting the wagon. Dawie felt immediate panic. His only chance of a drinking companion was driving away. Using all the mental telepathy that he knew about, he willed the wagon to stop, all the time pretending he had not seen the wagon despite all the squeaking and grinding noises. It would never do for the landlord of the Duck Inn to solicit business. In agony he waited, looking the wrong way. When the squeaking and rattling stopped almost next to him he froze.

"Morning, Dawie," said Peregrine softly, leaning out of his wagon to within a yard of Dawie's ear; they were both on the same level as the back of the inn was raised to keep the very limited stock of food dry in the lock-up. There were wooden steps from the room down to the open bar that looked across the start of the swamps, a view so beautiful it usually made Peregrine cry when he had drunk enough whisky.

"Why it's Peregrine the Ninth, isn't it?" he said, having turned around. Speaking in English, his accent was thick but understandable. He was an Afrikaner, who managed to overcome his dislike of the British when in pursuit of his favourite pastime, which was drinking whisky. He had been heard to say many times, 'the British can make whisky, there is room for forgiveness'. Usually, and always with Barend, he spoke Afrikaans.

"Are you open, Dawie?" asked Peregrine, knowing exactly what was going on.

"Well, I suppose we could be, Uncle." It was a habit of Dawie Lamprecht to call anyone a lot older than himself 'uncle'. Peregrine rather liked the habit. A drinking friend with a good respect was essential in his life.

"This is Mr Barend Oosthuizen," he said.

"I know."

Without any more ceremony, Peregrine climbed down from the box and walked across into the bar, leaving the donkeys in the middle of the road. Dawie, always thoughtful, and mindful of not wishing to be interrupted when he was drinking, gave them each a bucket of water. Barend, seeing no one else was going to help, relieved them of their harnesses, dropping the shaft in the middle of the road. When he went inside Peregrine was already seated at the bar filling his long pipe with tobacco. When he lit the pipe with a match from Dawie Lamprecht it gave off a smell like an old rope, which overpowered most of the old clothes smell emanating from Peregrine.

"Let's get started," said Dawie, lining up the glasses.

Barend, bursting with curiosity, picked up his first shot of whisky and tossed it back. No one said a word until the shot glasses were filled again.

"Now let's get started," said Peregrine.

"How do you know about Elephant Walk?" asked Barend, unable to contain himself.

"Oh that comes much later," said Peregrine, his small blue eyes twinkling. "Just lucky I had a good bath yesterday in the river. Must have known I was going to be in good company. I'll make a toast: to the man who invented whisky."

"I'll drink to that," said Dawie.

There were a few tables and chairs behind Barend and Peregrine. They sat at the wooden bar that Dawie had laboriously cut from a mukwa tree, ruining three bandsaws in the process, the wood was so harsh. Polished by many elbows and washed with spilt alcohol, the surface of the bar top was a mahogany blood red. The stools were made of stout bamboo from the delta, and between the tables on the floor were scattered zebra, kudu, and leopard skins, that Dawie washed and shook clean after every rain. Nailed to the uprights and crossbeams were many species of animals, just the heads trying to still look alive, with their tails hanging down the uprights, the bodies having probably been eaten. The view of the delta down the slope of the cleared bush, over a river to primal forest, went on and on, alive with birds circling the treetops. A pair of crocodiles were taking the morning sun on a sandbank in the river close by, the eyes and guarded heads of hippo were watching from just above the surface of the river. Three warthogs were rooting halfway up the cleared bush that gave the Duck Inn a good firebreak, and circling high in the sky far, far away, the scavengers of Africa, the vultures, were going round and round, lower and lower, still afraid to land and tear the last flesh from the Great Elephant.

Barend watched them with remorse, knowing the jackals and hyenas would be waiting, hidden in the bush and long grass, waiting for the old lions, too old to make a kill themselves, to finish what was left of the bloated carcass of the old elephant. Last would come the black ants, leaving huge bones to bleach white in the African sun forever.

After two quick shots of whisky, the drinking had become more patient, the glasses bigger and topped up with river water. The heat of the day began to rise but no one noticed. Peregrine went out to feed his donkeys from the fodder still in the wagon but they had wandered off the road, grazing quietly under the canopy of acacia trees. The wagon was still where it had been left in the middle of the road. After giving himself a good scratch all over, he went back into the bar, glad to be alive.

Very quietly he took Barend by the arm, first smiling to Dawie to convey the need for confidentiality. Just inside the shade from the roof, seated at a wooden table, the breeze still cooling slightly from the river, he talked to Barend about Barend's mother, his sister, his dead father. He even mentioned little Christo Oosthuizen, Barend's only brother, buried next to little James Brigandshaw in the family plot on Elephant Walk, dead so long from heatstroke. Only last did he mention Madge.

"She's waiting for you," he said smiling sadly with his own memories. "Every day, I think. Time you went home, my boy." They sat in silence for a long time... "Now. Let's go and join Dawie. He hates drinking on his own."

"Who are you really?" asked Barend.

"That's my business." It was the first and only time Barend ever heard the old man being rude to anyone.

With the knowledge that life was a lot more simple with its repetition than people understood, Peregrine sat quietly at the bar. He was still quite sure in his belief that each person had the destiny to marry only one person, that one person who could make the other content with the vagaries of life. He rather thought Madge and Barend were two of those people destined for each other. When he had lost the love of his own life as a young man, he had hoped it was only the first love experience he would have, and another person was waiting for him down the road. But he was wrong. There had been many more women in his life but none that he could look back on and say he missed. Some of them would have stayed friends but none he had loved, and being a sentimental old goat he let a tear drain into his grey-white beard, not for himself, but for two other people who could well go through their lives alone having missed their boat together.

"The whisky and the purity of the view," he said to hide his melancholy. "And a bit of old age." He was wondering again how different his life might have been. Not the money, that had never bothered him one way or the

174

other. The lifelong love of fellowship is what he had missed. He was also sure of one other thing in life that he had seen too many times. Bad marriages. It was better to live alone than live in a bad marriage. Yes, he was certain of that.

Then he broke into a passable rendering of 'Greensleeves' to change his mood.

The stones came out of the pouch onto the blood-red bar when the sun was directly over the Duck Inn. No one else had come or gone. The faraway vultures had sunk out of sight. The crocodiles had gone into the water. Even the birds had stopped singing. Dawie had produced a brace of cold roast guinea fowl on a large platter, which they had pulled apart with their fingers. A loaf of bread was torn apart in the same way. The three of them were drunk but still coherent; no one was slurring their words, and to Peregrine's surprise, he had not once wobbled on his bar stool perch. They had all three given out variations of their lives that bore very little resemblance to the truth, happily knowing that none of them would remember what had been said. They had all enjoyed themselves immensely.

The glittering stones on the bar brought a moment of silence.

"What are they?" asked Barend. "You're the first to see my stones. Friends, what are they?"

"Where'd you get 'em?" asked Dawie, his eyes popping.

"On the beach."

"What beach?"

"No, no, no. That's the bit I'm going to keep to myself." If he had been sober he would have left the stones in the pouch tied around his waist. "Like our wise old drinking companion here who will not even tell me who he is... What are they, friends?" One of the stones was knocked to the floor and picked up by Barend with difficulty. Peregrine had picked up the largest of the stones. He was quite sure they were diamonds but his old mind was pleasantly thinking in circles.

"Well, I'm not sure," he lied, "they look like diamonds but who knows? Only an expert will tell you for certain. I believe at Elephant Walk there is a young man with a degree in geology from Oxford. Likelihood is, he would know for certain."

"What's this Elephant Walk?" asked Dawie more interested in the stones, his mind-boggling at the possible wealth in front of him.

"You were going to Kimberley to find out. Now I know why you are asking me to go to Kimberley. Instead, I'll make you a bargain, I'm sure Clary and Jeff can walk back to Rhodesia if we take it slowly."

"You think Harry will know for certain?"

"They don't give degrees at Oxford for nothing, I think. I rather hope you have to know something... Did you really find them on a beach?"

"Yes."

"But you never found the source of the diamonds, if indeed they are diamonds. Harry's knowledge might make you rather rich... There was a rumour a few years back. 1908, I think. A railway worker found diamonds south of Lüderitz near the Orange River, the Germans proclaimed the area around Kolmanskop a no-go area. You were not in the wrong place at the right time, young Barend Oosthuizen?" He gave the lad a wink.

"It was much further north," blurted Barend.

"That's good. Now put them back in your belt. There's probably nothing in all this. Personally, I don't think they are diamonds. But just in case they are, you can carry on buying me drinks."

In Peregrine's life, he had found it wise never to be too careful.

# 5

## NOVEMBER 1913

*S*ir Henry Manderville had sown the tiny oblong black seeds in shallow wooden boxes where they rested on waist-high wooden benches; the sun reached them through the window in the morning. After three weeks, the specially prepared soil from the Mazoe River silt, black as the seedlings, sprouted tiny feathers of green all over the place, sending Henry into raptures of excitement. There was nothing more exciting in his life than a quest. The idea of seeds collected in America and sent around the world to grow in his seed boxes without the slightest fuss or surprise, gave him pleasure out of all proportion to the achievement. The shed he had built for the experiment was always locked. Henry kept the only key. Everyone on Elephant Walk was aware of the new shed at the back of the house but no one said a word. It was not his first experiment, and not all of them had worked out as well as the pull-and-let-go, and the system of pipes and pulleys, chains and cogs that drew the water from the river to the header tank outside his bathroom with a series of windmills that gave the cistern water to flush Mister Crapper's toilet. For all he knew, the seeds could have been sterile or his cousin in Virginia had sent him some obnoxious local grass seed to keep the supply of Virginia tobacco in America.

After two weeks of the seedlings bolting out of the ground, there was no doubt. They were plants, not grass, not weeds. They were all exactly the same.

"You'd better come and see what I've been up to," he said to Harry Brigandshaw, his grandson. The rains had yet to break properly, but the lands planted to corn were sprouting maize spikes in straight lines, row after row, land after land, the red soil rich from the meandering river that had cut out their valley. How the rich red soil had come from black silt was a mystery to Henry. He left that part to the gods to worry about.

He let himself into the shed with the big, long key and stood back.

"What is it?" asked Harry.

"Tobacco. Not only tobacco, American tobacco from Virginia. Cousin George. He is farming now... I want to plant some of the seedlings in the lands."

"And what do you do with it when it's grown?"

"You put it in tall barns and light a fire to dry up the moisture in the leaves. I questioned that and Cousin George sent me all the plans. Takes a fortnight... You're right. The curing, as they call it, is the tricky part. We probably won't get it right the first time."

"Who's going to buy it?"

"The British cigarette manufacturers."

"Are you sure?"

"Not yet. I have to grow the damn stuff first. Humour me, Harry. Humour me. I'm old enough to be your grandfather."

"But you are my grandfather." Harry was convinced long ago his grandfather was potty.

"That's the point. Now, can I have an acre of ploughed land to plant in?"

"You can have as many as you like. Tobacco. Who would have thought of it? There's tea in British India and Ceylon. Rubber in Malaya. Nowhere in the empire are we commercially growing tobacco. But you'd better stop these damn dogs getting into your boxes. Down, my dog. Down. Fletcher, you are a right royal pain in the arse. How many boys do you need?"

"Six."

"You can have them tomorrow morning... The rains are going to be good this year. Come on Fletcher... That damn dog's got too much energy."

Harry walked out of the shed followed by Fletcher, the dog, and the three bitches. They were Rhodesian ridgebacks. Lion dogs. They were seven years old and had not left any of their curiosity with their puppyhood. Madge was feeding the wild geese, Egyptian geese, with handfuls of yellow corn. The geese were too busy gobbling up the corn kernels to worry about the dogs. The dogs looked at them hopefully and wandered off. One of the cats got through a window into Sir Henry's house straight away. The other cats lived high off the ground, only coming down to earth at feeding time. The dogs never chased them when there was food in their bowls.

"What was it?" asked Madge.

"Tobacco seedlings. Cousin George, the Canadian lumberjack, is now an American farmer in Virginia. Where the seed came from. Funny thing is, it might work. A lightweight high-value crop we can send to England at a profit. I saw a picture once. On a pouch of pipe tobacco. They compress the dried leaves into square bales and cover them with hessian... He's as happy as a sandboy."

"I heard that," came from his grandfather in the shed.

The dogs had begun chasing each other in and around the flowerbeds, in and around the msasa trees within the stockade that protected the houses.

Robert St Clair was sitting in a deck chair under one of the trees. His sister Lucinda was sitting next to him watching the dogs.

The St Clairs had been on the farm seven months and Harry wondered if they had cashed in the return half of their tickets back to England. But maybe it was his own fault. For months he rather hoped he would fall in love with Lucinda. His mother hoped so too. Robert hoped so. Probably his grandfather as well. But as hard as he tried, Harry could not find anything other than friendship for Lucinda, which Madge told him was a perfect shame. And at least Robert had stopped following Madge around... There was also no doubt the brother and sister were good company. And Elephant Walk was far from the nearest crowd. The farm was self-supporting in food. And who was Harry to deny an old friend a few drinks at sundowner time? It was the highlight of everyone's day.

THERE WERE times in Robert St Clair's life when he wished he were rich. The thought of going back to an English winter, jobless and poor, to the cold of Purbeck Manor, was horrible. After sitting in the shade of the sun for month after month, the idea of a log fire burning the front of his body while his back froze from the draught coming through under the door was appalling. If he had money he would buy himself an African farm. There was plenty of labour. There was plenty of sun, and the rain came when it was needed to grow a crop, leaving the winter six months crisp at night, warm in the day and not a drop of rain to be seen. Provided the river kept flowing, which it did, Rhodesia to Robert was paradise. There was no way he could ever again face being cooped up in the family mansion or an old English school with even gas heating. And he hated small boys asking stupid questions.

The idea of marrying Madge was not the answer as the Brigandshaw farm belonged to Harry Brigandshaw. There would always be a good home for mother, grandfather and sister but the farm would always belong to the son. Not that he had got anywhere trying to compete with a ghost whose only fault was not being where he was meant to be. He rather thought she despised him sponging off his friend but was too polite to come right out and say so. Harry seemed friendly enough. Living alone in a house with his sister was perfect. They could keep out of other people's way. Once he had overheard Madge suggest he had pawned his return ticket that was valid on any Colonial Shipping liner out of Cape Town. But that was one thing he never did. He never burnt his boats. He always had an escape route even if the destination was no longer to his liking.

Everyone thought he did not have a care in the world, which is how he tried to portray himself, but under the smooth façade, he was scared. He was twenty-eight years old, with no idea what he was going to do with the rest of his life. The idea of war with Germany was his only glimmer of hope. If war broke out he would go off like all the other surplus St Clairs before him and die for a good cause. Then it would be over. Even with glory, though how getting killed was glorious, he rather thought was owed to politicians who required willing cannon fodder to take politics into their next dimension of war. He would not have to grow old. He would not have to be a burden on other people. He would be dead. And in Robert's mind, dead was dead.

Discreetly he looked at his watch. Always the last half hour before six was the longest half hour of the day. He had only been pretending to read a book. He wondered what his sister was thinking as she watched the dogs. If Harry did not propose soon it would be too late. She was twenty-two in April. Girls had such a short time to secure the long years of their lives. And if they failed to find a husband there wasn't much left for them to do. He felt sorry for her. He rather thought the life of a penniless spinster was worse than a penniless bachelor. At least he could go to war. Anyway, he told himself, he had done his best. You could only bait the hook. The fish had to come up and swallow the worm.

"Feel like a drink, old chap?" he heard Harry calling.

"Splendid idea."

He jumped up, the unread book falling on the grass. It was six o'clock at last.

"Drinking time, sis. Are you coming?"

"Why not?" And almost under her breath so only her Robert would hear, "There's nothing else to do."

Now a little irritated, Robert walked across to Harry's veranda where the servants were slotting the fly screens into place. An animal some way over in the bush made a horrible noise, which he ignored. His sister shuddered.

"What's that?" she asked.

"I have absolutely no idea," said Robert.

"A lion," said Madge. "There he goes again."

This time, Robert shuddered. He did not like the idea of lions out on the loose. He really needed his drink.

EMILY LOOKED at her two children and her father on the veranda and rather thought they all drank too much in Africa. Since her husband had died she really did not care. Everyone was able to look after themselves. She was forty-two years old and withering up. Her time of usefulness had gone. The thought of marrying again had never entered her head. There had never been any other man for Emily Manderville ever since she was a child. She had decided to marry Sebastian Brigandshaw when she was ten years old. The fact she fell pregnant with Harry before she was married had everything to do with their love of each other. And if the Pirate, Captain Brigandshaw, Sebastian's father, had not banished Sebastian to the colonies! And if her father, who was up to something in his new potting shed, had not made a pact with the devil! If she had not been forced to marry the heir to the Brigandshaw fortune so Arthur's father, the Pirate, could lay his hands on the ancient estate of Hastings Court and mix his blood with old family! If! Too many ifs. Too many people wanting what they wanted with little thought for others. She and her father had never yet had it out but now it did not matter. They had talked. He had said he was sorry. But they had never had it out. Arranged marriages were common in her father's day. She looked at her older son and thought one day she should tell him the truth. They had made her marry Arthur. They had paid and received what was tantamount to blood money. But they had never been able to force her into Arthur's bed. And as Arthur had only wanted money from his father and his cheap whores, that part worked out well. She lived as mistress of Hastings Court but she never consummated the marriage. And then Seb had got back, somehow, from Africa. Put a ladder up to her bedroom window, and with the help of Alison Ford, Harry's nurse and Barend's mother, they had all run away to Africa and left their old lives behind to live only in memory.

Emily poured herself a stiff gin. Even George, her youngest son, was away at boarding school. No one needed her now. And she missed Seb so much it physically hurt every time she thought of him. Which was far too often for her sanity. Maybe she thought the truth got muddled up too much as it went along. So long as Harry knew Seb was his father, the rest might best be left alone. There are some truths in life we are best not knowing, she tried to tell herself, as she procrastinated yet again from telling Harry the truth. She was only a woman. People told her she was tough living on a bush farm without a husband. But she wasn't.

One of the other dogs clanged through the screen door that automatically crashed closed behind it. The big dogs flopped on the big reed mat that covered most of the veranda floor. Madge was lighting the paraffin lamps. She half listened to her father going on about growing tobacco. Her drink was empty sooner than she thought it should have been. Then she got up to stand at the sideboard and poured herself another drink. Through the window into the dining room, she could see the houseboy laying out the cold fork supper on the dining table. Not for the first time she asked herself what she would do without her routine. On Elephant Walk, nothing changed. And nothing would. Even if they all went to war with each other in England, nothing would change in the African bush. They were too far away. Cut off from everything.

The second gin and quinine tonic tasted better than the first. Without anyone really noticing she sat down again where she had been. Harry gave her a smile, which was comforting. She had children. Yes, she had her children.

Her father gave her that funny look again, and she wondered if he had been reading her mind.

HENRY MANDERVILLE COULD READ his daughter's mind with the greatest of ease. He had watched her thinking as he talked about the future of flue-cured tobacco in Africa.

He had sold the only two items left in the Manderville fortune. Over the generations, the money had shrunk to the old house and a few acres, the title and his daughter, the daughter who would have been penniless had he died like her mother at an early age. To the right buyer, the history of Hastings Court was worth more than the house itself. To the right father, a daughter-in-law with an ancient pedigree was worth more than the money with which it could be bought. He had known his daughter loved the youngest of the Brigandshaw boys but he had not known then how much. Puppy love. Kids thrown together by the loneliness of childhood. All had rationalised in his brain. Love came and went, he had told himself. Life can be lived without consuming love. Consuming love rarely lasted, except in the memory. Money! It was always money that stayed forever. Money could be passed from one generation to another and another. Mostly love died in life. It always died once both of the lovers were dead.

Why a man with money was so concerned with so-called pedigree, breeding, Henry found difficult to understand. 'What's the difference?' he asked himself. 'What is so important?' Most old families started with rape and pillage. Thugs stealing what they wanted. Forcing their will. Yet he knew the likes of Captain Brigandshaw were obsessed with titles. Obsessed with buying their way from humble roots. They wanted respect. A daughter-in-law from an old family would, to that man's way of thinking, give his grandchildren respect. And if by political pandering the man could buy himself a hereditary title, which Captain Brigandshaw from the profits of Colonial Shipping had finally done, in three generations his family would go from ordinary seaman to titled gentry. And if their mother's family was hundreds of years old in the collective memory, no one would question their worth. The fact that everyone's family was hundreds of years old, or otherwise they themselves would not be alive, made the whole thing to Henry's mind a lot of nonsense. But there it was. He had the old house, an old title and a marriageable daughter. Brigandshaw had the money. He made a pact with the devil to protect his own descendants, though he never saw the irony of the situation until many years later. He had done his best. And he had not known his daughter was already pregnant by the young scallywag she had been, he thought, innocently playing with since she was a child.

Like his daughter, who he knew had not told Harry she was only married to his father years after the children were born, he thought it better to keep his reasons to himself, to not bring out the story that now had a very different view. In hindsight, he rather thought, most things were easier to understand. If he had sold Hastings Court on the open market, the proceeds would not have covered the mortgage. He had done his best. Well, maybe he had been thinking of himself just a little. In the end, he smiled to himself, we all just think of ourselves a little. It's the nature of man. Then he caught his daughter's eye and looked away. There was only so much rationalisation but even that could never assuage a man's guilt.

Quietly, he got up and went to the sideboard and poured himself another drink. The roar of the lion, he thought, was a little nearer.

THE LION ROAR was two hundred yards from Barend's camp. Peregrine had hoped they would reach Elephant Walk before sundown, whisky on the veranda vivid in his mind. It was pitch dark, the light having dissipated completely in less than an hour. Only the planets could be seen in the night sky. The fire Barend was nursing, bending down on his knees, blowing the embers of leaves that were still damp, refused to burst into flame. Barend shivered. A thin lacework of cloud added to the dark. The moon would not rise for three hours. Barend's horse whinnied with fright. He could hear the donkeys pulling against their tethers to the old wagon in which the old man was sleeping. During their four-month odyssey, Peregrine had turned seventy-one. For a man of his age, he was still remarkably fit, but it wasn't right. For Barend, old men should have a place in the sun, a chair, grandchildren to look after them, memories to mull.

"Wasn't that a bloody lion?" came from the direction of the covered wagon. "Bloody thing woke me up... Can't see the fire."

"Leaves are wet."

"I'd better come and help. Always said the only way to get anything done was to do it myself... So near to a bottle of whisky and yet so far. It's dark, my word it's dark. I rather think only leopards can see at night."

"Lions can smell."

"Well, my gun's loaded. Fear not, Peregrine is nigh."

The fire caught and burst into bright flames, bringing the campsite into view. The lion roared again, further away. Twigs caught and burnt, and when Peregrine put a pile of precious dry fodder on the flames he could see the slate-green colour of Barend's eyes. The donkeys had stopped pulling at their tethers and Barend went across in the new light of the fire, a big man with wide, powerful shoulders, to stroke the ears of his horse. The stallion showed him its teeth. On the other side of the wagon, something small was moving in the thick bush.

He had changed his mind the day they left Maun four months earlier. A man, he told himself, could not walk back into people's lives like nothing had happened. Even without his hatred, he was not the same person who had run away from Elephant Walk more than nine years earlier. They would all be different.

He and Peregrine had come out of the swamps and gone south, Peregrine not greatly minding, rationalising there was always time in Africa to talk, to reason. Life was to be lived as pleasantly as possible for the moment. The flight of a bird. The call of frogs that started and stopped abruptly altogether. A thin sickle moon in a star-studded sky. The evening echo of falling water from drinking game, the only sound in the universe. Peregrine was not in a hurry. He had the rest of his life to spend getting nowhere. For him, the only important place in time was the present moment.

They had first trekked week after week to the diamond town of Kimberley, where illicit diamond buying was punishable by life in prison. The mining people did not like anyone stealing their diamonds. Diamond buying was a closed shop. A monopoly of the De Beers Diamond Corporation. Without careful control of the supply, the prices would fall, some said to nothing. A stone was only valuable when it was rare. They spent an unsuccessful month in Kimberley looking for a buyer and then moved through to Johannesburg, certain at least the seven stones were gem quality diamonds. Selling rocks found on a far-off beach was more difficult than either of them had thought.

Barend had been away from the gold mining town since his fight in the Mansion House. All his old acquaintances had moved on. Everyone was new, expectant, waiting to get rich in a hurry, or waiting with dull eyes to go away. Only a very few grew rich. He had walked into the Mansion House but with no money, they had turned him away. New, meaner-looking people were running the whorehouse and he was glad not to have any money. They turned him away at the door. Inside it was empty of customers where he could see into the cheap bar. The girls looked worn out and uninterested. The band he could hear would have sent him to sleep. Going back anywhere was a failure. Nothing was ever the same. Sadder than he knew why, he had found Peregrine and the wagon with his horse, and though it was night they had gone out of town, moving slowly forward throughout the night. When the dawn came they were safe in the bush and had made camp.

"Why are we going north?" Barend had asked Peregrine.

"You're going home."

"I don't have a home."

"Oh yes, you do. She's waiting for you. Now, humour an old man. It's a long time since I drank Brigandshaw whisky. Hopefully, Harry will have forgiven me for leading him a dance in pursuit of Lobengula's gold. Which, by the way, I don't think exists; money gets spent if it's left lying around. We had a nice time looking. There was no trace of his boyhood black friend, Tatenda. No one had heard of him for years. An old witch gave me the evil eye. I think she knew. Even Harry's fluent Shona couldn't get it out of her. The old hag gave me the shivers. Bloody ventriloquist. Could throw her voice up into the trees. The villagers were petrified of her... I need a good bottle of whisky to drink."

"It'll take a month or more."

"So what? Young man, do you have a better idea? If it doesn't work you can go on your way. You won't look back and not know. Face life, don't run away."

"I'll go north on one condition. You tell me why you ran away. Why you ran away from your family and hid in the African bush. I'll go to Elephant

Walk only if you tell me who you are. After so many months you owe me that much."

"If I tell you a very long story. And there are rivers to cross and this is the rainy season, early but here. We may spend days waiting for the river to go down so we can cross over. It may take us many weeks... I want you to be the custodian of a letter I have written to my family. I have lived a long time. At my age death can strike quickly and I'm not talking about the lions. All those bits inside us that keep us going year after year. Only one has to pack up. Poor old Clary and Jeff. They worry me the most. No one else will look after them. Maybe they will carry me to Valhalla but I don't think so. But my family should know about my death. You see, this wreck of an old man with not a penny in his pocket for all these many years, is Peregrine Alexander Cholmondeley Kenrick, Ninth Earl of Pembridgemoor. Our greatest estate became my property in trust when my father died. Luck was, I saw his death in the paper, a piece of old newspaper young Harry Brigandshaw had used to wrap his crystal glasses. The trust will have taken care of everything, that much I knew when I read the notice, in 1907 I think it was. I had then been away over forty years, so it was far too late for me... Her name was Patricia. A very ordinary name. She was Irish. She was, I still tell myself, the other half of myself. Maybe she was or maybe she wasn't as I was never allowed to find out. She was the first girl I ever knew, the only one who could look through my eyes into my being, that individual, us, without which the universe does not exist. Maybe it was an illusion. Maybe she was built by my mind as a lifelong companion. Maybe I am a romantic old fool and now it doesn't matter except for you. If I can do one last thing in my life, it is to bring you back to your Madge, to find out. To not have a demon, a lonely demon to rule you the rest of your life. Looking back I can see my life was pointless. I did nothing with it. Not even one child. Not a painting. Not a book. Not one poem. I did nothing with my gift of life and that was wrong. Don't you, Barend Oosthuizen, make the same mistake. You have been like a son to me these many weeks. My first companion since leaving America. I don't want you to lose your life. So bear with an old man and take this letter to post when you hear I'm dead. Let an old man go and find what I hope will not be my last bottle of whisky... Now, that's enough about me. I've always found it boring talking about myself."

"What happened to her?"

"I have absolutely no idea. In life, we never find out what happens."


THE REST of Peregrine's life flooded out in the next three weeks. Barend thought he was hearing a man's confession, and without the knowledge of a priest, he kept quiet and innocent. At first, he thought the story had been for his benefit only, a way of making him go home by example. By the time the lion roared, heard by both Madge and Barend, Madge from the Brigandshaw veranda, Barend from his camp just short of Elephant Walk, he knew Patricia as well as any other person in his life. Twice, alone in the dark, he had found himself crying at the pointlessness of life. The old man's story made him think in ways he had never thought before. To him at twenty-three, life was endless, and here he had been listening to another life from its beginning to almost its end.

The next day, Peregrine fiddled around, seemingly unwilling to journey the last part of his endless journey.

"Why don't we go?" Barend said impatiently.

"Manners, my boy. Always arrive at the right time of day. Sundowners are the answer. When the sun goes down. Then we shall join them. Joyous, oh joy, a cut crystal glass full of whisky. Now there is something to look forward to in Africa. Funny, isn't it, how the last minutes are always the longest? We will do one last hunt, you and I. Our gift of food to the family. Then Clary and Jeff shall take me in state. Your steed below you. Knights of old, back from the Crusades. We will be welcome. Joy will flow. Be patient, Barend. You are almost home."

THEY RODE through the open gate of the stockade that had been built by Barend's father during the Shona rebellion of 1896, not long after Tatenda had disappeared from Elephant Walk. The two donkeys led the way, with the old wagon and Peregrine seated on the wooden bench, and Barend riding in behind on his horse. The dogs pelted across the well-kept lawns between the msasa trees, ready for whatever fight or fun befell them. Egyptian geese took off in honking fury for the river, up and over the other side of the wooden stockade. The sinking sun was only just beginning to redden in the western sky. It had rained shortly before, and the bush green and the russet foliage of the msasa trees were still dripping water onto the round flowerbeds below.

Sir Henry Manderville heard the commotion from his potting shed, where he was inspecting the small, green seedlings that had not yet been planted out into the land. Not being a man to waste time when he was onto a good idea, Henry had been standing in the lands all day watching a gang of shirtless blacks in three groups, the first with Dutch hoes ridging the ploughed land, that otherwise would have been planted with maize corn, the second with hand trowels and green plants, the trowels opening the head of the ridge at intervals, so when the soil filled in again the roots were standing up untangled. The third group came along with buckets of water and sloshed each plant despite the probability of rain. There were enough seedlings to plant out two acres and Henry was well satisfied with his work and the planting instructions from Cousin George in Virginia. The barking dogs reminded Henry it was almost time for his well-deserved drink. He went into the house to wash his hands before joining his family on the veranda of Emily, Madge and Harry's house; the guests, Robert and Lucinda, would come across from the house that had been built by Tinus Oosthuizen, Barend's father, and left vacant when Alison and Katinka went south to search for the son who had run away in 1904.

When Henry had washed his hands in the bathroom that boasted hot and cold running water, and one of Mister Crapper's flushing toilets, he moved into the only bedroom in his small house to change his shirt. Outside, his granddaughter Madge was picking flowers for the main house where he was about to enjoy his drink when she dropped the cut flowers and the scissors on the grass and began to run. All Henry could hear was the dogs' commotion, his view of the matter plain to Madge but blocked to him by the wall of his bedroom. Going to the window, he leaned out as far as he could to see Madge running past Clary and Jeff with old Peregrine waving his hat in the air while standing up precariously on the box section of the wagon. Then a good-looking horse walked into view with a broad-shouldered blond stranger sitting high on its back who was leaning down to hoist his granddaughter up behind onto the horse's rump.

"Hey," he shouted in desperation, thinking the man was snatching his granddaughter, and about to turn the horse's tail and bolt out of the compound through the open gate.

Ducking back into his bedroom, he ran through the house and out of the front door, to find Madge clinging to the back of the stranger who was riding forward with a big, somehow familiar grin on his face. Everyone else was coming out of the houses including the house servants, grinning from ear to ear.

"What's going on?" he demanded.

"It's Barend," shouted Madge. "Barend's come home."


THE FESTIVITIES CARRIED on well into the night. Peregrine the Ninth had been taken off by Henry Manderville for delousing which Peregrine thought quite unnecessary; anyone who lived with him was quite welcome; he had never once seen a bedbug Henry was so determined to exterminate. But like any good guest singing for supper, he went through his paraffin-laced bath, and appeared fresh and scrubbed in a smart white shirt and khaki shorts that only hid his old, knobbly knees when he stood up. It was too hot for the long socks, so there he was on the veranda in his old, faithful sandals with an endless glass of whisky. To keep up the charade, he allowed himself to totter to the back of his wagon when the grandfather clock in the dining room, which he could see through the veranda window, struck one o'clock in the morning. He even did his head-first dive onto the prepared mattress and snored immediately to get rid of Henry who was just as drunk. Peeping through a tear in the canvas, Peregrine watched him walk into one of the msasa trees, swearing profusely, and reach the safety of his one-bedroom house by the light of the moon, followed by a loud crash from inside that Peregrine wondered about. Satisfied by one of the better whisky drinks in his life, lying on his back and listening to all the night sounds of Africa, he drifted off into a dreamless sleep.

Emily, Harry's mother, had been the first to go to bed, determined herself to ride into Salisbury the next day to send a cable to Alison, Barend's mother, her heart soft with the pleasure she knew her words would bring.

Alone in the house they would now share with Barend, Lucinda convinced Robert St Clair there was no point in her brother staying longer at Elephant Walk. She had never seen anyone shine with so much happiness, and hoped it would last for Madge, but she wondered. Nine years away was a long time. They were both grown up, no longer children, even if she herself still remembered the crush she had had on Harry Brigandshaw when he first arrived with her brother at Purbeck Manor in Dorset. She was now going to be a spinster for the rest of her life. There were no more feminine tricks she knew to play on Harry to draw his attention.

Barend had basked in the centre of attention all night and told them selected stories from his travels, forgetting the oath of vengeance he had taken on the kopje overlooking the old Anglo-Boer War battleground at Paardeberg. There was no mention of Marie Putter, the first of many women who had shared his bed. No mention of the many men who had shared with him his hatred of the English. No mention of the Mansion House in Johannesburg, or his fight with the English men that had given him so much satisfaction and sent him running out of Johannesburg. After months with Peregrine, his English had returned to full fluency and he was the man they wanted him to be. The prodigal son who had come back to them. Twice he retold the death of the Great Elephant that Harry had once hunted and how it had stopped his wish to hunt big game forever. They drank and ate and talked and laughed. On the surface, all was well and the drinks helped. Madge had changed from the girl in his dreams to a woman, twenty-one years old. They tried all night to remind each other of their childhood together and kept up the smiles. Madge was the last before Harry to go to bed. Barend was even a little relieved to be left alone on the veranda with Harry, the pretence left alone for the night. They took their drinks out into the night where clouds were scurrying across the moon. Peregrine was snoring from his wagon, Harry's grandfather from his house.

"They are both going to have sore throats in the morning," said Harry.

"Yes, they are."

For a long while they were silent, each with their thoughts.

"You'll have to start all over," said Harry at last. He had drunk himself sober but knew he was going to have a hangover in the morning. "She was a kid. Now she's a woman. Give her time... We can either split the farm or farm Elephant Walk together... You think grandfather's tobacco might work?"

"You'll have to build a curing barn to find out. Before the plants mature. I'll look at Cousin George's plans tomorrow."

"It's already tomorrow."

"I've something to show you that might change all this and I need your help. We'll have to go back inside."

"I'm a bit older than you, Barend." He spoke softly so no one in the house could hear what he was saying. There were often people lying awake, thinking. "You can't make life do what you want it to do. I won't ask you why you came home. Those years are your business. Glad enough to have you back. Hard as I've tried, I can't imagine myself married to Lucinda, pretty as she is. I saw my parents as you did. Your father and mother to begin with. That was love. My mother's and father's would have lasted forever. Maybe it will. You don't have to do anything you don't want to do, is all I'm saying. Now, show me what you've got."

"Do the dogs always follow you?" asked Barend.

"Even in their sleep."

They were still talking diamonds when the sun came up in the morning and the new day began.

"Do you hate us very much?" asked Harry.

"What on earth are you talking about?"

"The English. The people who hanged your father."

"How do you know?"

"We grew up together. Men hate for good reasons. I rather think I would have hated the same as you."

"It's not as bad as it was."

"I'm glad of that. The human race has made a bloody mess of it ever since we can remember. And I rather think it's going to do it again, only worse. There's going to be a terrible war in Europe. A world war, I think, because everyone on earth is going to be affected."

"Yes, I know."

"The Germans you hunted with?"

"They are very confident they can destroy the British Empire. Create their own. They are jealous of you. And if they can't have it themselves, they'll destroy what you have built, and enjoy your destruction. People don't like other people to be richer than themselves. Or other nations. The powerful stay rich or the new lords become powerful. Your Mr Darwin. The evolution of man. Both of us are products of the fittest surviving, or we would not be sitting here looking at seven rough diamonds I have been unable to sell... Old friend, it's time I found a bed before the rest wake up."

"I'll show you the way."

"It was my house, you know."

"There's a spare bed in my room for George when he's back from school. You don't snore, do you?"

"Not that I know."

"The bed's made up. Hell, it's good to see you again."

"Madge said we were going to marry each other when she turned sixteen."

"Maybe you should have done."

"Would it have worked?"

"Everything works to some extent... Take a tall glass of water for your hangover. There's a jug in my room... Stop speculating. No one knows what's going to happen in this life which is often just as well."


NEITHER OF THEM mentioned the diamonds the next day as both were feeling sorry for themselves, swearing they would never drink alcohol again in their lives, knowing they would both break the oath when the sun went down which they did. Robert thanked Barend for the use of his house for so many months and said it was now time to go back to England and teach small boys the vagaries of history. Emily made the perfunctory effort to change his mind but when she left in the trap for Salisbury to send her cable, Robert came along to book a passage for himself and Lucinda and use the return half of their tickets. Tembo, who had been at Elephant Walk most of his life, took the reins. Behind him, the passengers were quiet all the way to the new capital of Southern Rhodesia. Emily had finally told Barend she was sending a cable to his mother and sister.

"They'll be coming back," she said to him.

"We all have to start again somewhere. Just please tell my mother, when she does arrive, some things I can't explain. Or more correctly, I don't wish to explain."

"Harry says he understood. So did my husband. We all lost part of ourselves when your father was hanged. Just don't please take it out on your mother, Barend. We are your friends, not your enemies."

WHEN HER BROTHER left in the trap, Lucinda had gone off down to the river on her own, where she had a good cry and felt better. She even saw how silly it was to wallow in self-pity. Life for her in Africa was not meant to be. She was going home. That was it. The years ahead looked long and dreary but they still had to be lived. "I should be thankful for what I have," she told herself, wiping her eyes. She thought of her home that had been her family's for hundreds of years; she thought of her family. For the first time in months, she was homesick. When she came through the back gate into the stockade she was smiling. Three of the Egyptian geese waddled in behind her. She could smell meat cooking over the open fire. Having missed their breakfasts, Harry and Barend were cooking chops over a fire in a large metal drum that had been cut in half and partially covered with a wire mesh. If nothing else from Africa, she told herself, she would remember that smell for the rest of her life. She waved at them and crossed to the main house to look for Madge, not wanting to catch Barend looking at her again. Robert was right. It was time they went home before truly outstaying their welcome.

ACROSS THE GRASS, some hundred yards from the cooking chops, in his small cottage, Henry Manderville was drinking tea with Peregrine the Ninth. The last of the tobacco seedlings had been planted out in the lands, and Peregrine had been taken to look at the hapless plants, the six-inch leaves flopped over in the sun. To his surprise, some of yesterday's plantings were perking up at the centre. He had made all the right noises about a splendid idea and a splendid opportunity, secretly thinking the baronet was wasting his time. Under his breath he had said, 'nothing ventured, nothing gained', and wished him luck.

"You'd better stay here," said Henry Manderville.

"What d'you mean, old chap?"

"What I said. You can't roam around anymore. You're too old."

"I'm only seventy-one."

"That's my point. I'll build you a rondavel next to the potting shed with an attached bathroom. If you're very good I'll put in a flushing toilet. Clary and Jeff can go out to pasture."

"I haven't a bean."

"Oh yes, you have."

There was a long silence while they slurped at their tea, something they would never have done in front of the ladies.

"Do you know? How long have you known?" asked Peregrine.

"Quite a few years. Your business is your business. When your father died they must have sent investigators to every English-speaking country. You'd been gone into the bush for months. I heard about it shopping in Salisbury. They had a missing persons poster up in the post office. Did you know your father was dead?"

"Yes. I read a piece of old newspaper. Strange coincidence. Harry had the paper wrapped around his glassware to stop it breaking when we went on our wild-goose chase... Do you think I should have gone home?"

"You're probably better out of the way. Why you should stay here. I can keep an eye on you. You might write and tell them."

"No, Henry. I've done that in a way. Gave Barend a letter to post to the family solicitors when he hears I'm dead, or after two years, whichever comes first... If I'm to stay here I'd better get some money from them," he said as an afterthought.

"Don't be silly."

"I'll leave a bit to Em in my will. You can keep the second letter for the solicitors... You think those two will get married?"

"No, I don't. But you never know... So that's settled."

"Thank you, Sir Henry."

"You are very welcome, Lord Pembridgemoor. You see, there's method in my madness. Over our drinks at night, you can tell me your life story. What you got up to. Why you ran away. Should keep us amused for months."

"Her name was Patricia."

"Good. I only ever loved one woman. Emily's mother, who died so young. Did she die, Perry?"

"I don't know."

"That makes it worse in some ways. Not knowing. What might have been."

"What was that crash last night?"

"Didn't you pass out on the mattress?"

"No, I didn't."

"I fell over the bloody cat... And don't laugh."


THE NEXT DAY, while the old were putting their lives into perspective, Peregrine exhausted from all his years, the young were planning a future. Harry and Barend had taken with them shotguns for protection but more as an excuse to get out of the house and talk about what was on both their minds.

"If Father had not been killed I would have used my geology degree," said Harry, when they were alone in the bush still wet with another short shower of rain. The main rains from Mozambique had yet to break. "I had the romantic idea as a kid to go off with a pick and shovel and find my fortune in them yonder hills. Why most prospectors find nothing. You have to use science. You have to have a method. Know where you are going for a reason. As Uncle Peregrine rightly told you, a railway worker found gem diamonds at Kolmanskop in 1908, and the Germans locked up the area under tight security, having worked out the gems had come down the Orange River, probably from the Kimberley pipe exploited by Cecil Rhodes three hundred odd miles from the mouth of the Orange. We even know the diamonds are three million years old. I keep up with geology. My prof sends me papers from Oxford he thinks will interest me. Everything that's written about Africa. So I know as much as anyone about the diamonds on the coast of German South West Africa."

"I found my stones hundreds of miles to the north of the Orange."

"That's where science comes in. We are talking millions of years to shift the stones from the Kimberley pipe. Over millions of years, the rivers change their course."

"But not by hundreds of miles."

"Oh yes, they do. Especially through desert where they can wander around without impediment. There may have been a tributary to the Orange taking the diamonds so far north. You found them, Barend. You know where they were. No one dropped them on purpose. And your seven stones are diamonds. When we find you a legitimate buyer you will have a small fortune. You may not even want to farm. A 'rich life' in one of the world capitals."

"There won't be that much from seven stones."

"There will be if we find the old river bed and dig up the rest of them."

"You want to come and help me?"

"We can't go now. Anyway, any find belongs to the German Kaiser.

Maybe this war will change things to your advantage. If the Germans go to war with the British and lose, they will lose their few colonies to the British. Or even the South Africans. Generals Botha and Smuts have not joined the other Bittereinders as reported."

"What do you know about that? I didn't say anything."

"But others have. They call it a chance for revenge. Botha, the South African Prime Minister, thinks he's better off staying in the empire. He's probably already got his eye on those German diamonds scattered up the Skeleton Coast. Let's wait and see what happens. You can find your way back?"

"I cut my initials in a rock."

"Oh, that's wonderful. Now, all we got to do is find a bloody rock."

"I can find it again. I'm a Boer. We don't forget a place we have been to in the bush or a rock on one of the aridest coastlines in the world. I know exactly how many miles I was north of Cape Cross, where Diogo Cão first planted the cross of Christ. I also cut the Kunene two weeks after finding the diamonds. There was a sand dune I will never forget."

"Sand dunes can come and go in a week."

"Then I will find my initials on the rock if I have to inspect every one on the coast for miles."

# BOOK 3 – FAMILY, WAR AND BUSINESS

# 1

## DECEMBER 1913 TO JANUARY 1914

*T*he SS *King Emperor* docked at Southampton three days before Christmas. Even the seagulls were quiet, blanketed by falling snow on the docks, where workers were ready for the big ship. There was black slush in high ridges between wet roads. There was no one to meet them. No band playing. No coloured streamers from ship to shore, friends and relations at either end. There was no excitement.

"I don't care it is snowing," said Lucinda St Clair. "I don't care no one came to take us home."

She was dressed in a heavy black woollen skirt and matching top that had lain in the bottom of the trunk for seven months on Elephant Walk. The hood that came out from the back was tied under her chin with a green velvet ribbon, and only eyes, nose and chin, glowing with youth and health, were visible.

"I told them not to meet us," said Robert St Clair. "Didn't expect them to take us seriously. Looks like the all-stations train to Wareham and then change for Corfe Castle. Hope old Pringle is there. Might have to spend the night in the waiting room. He always has a good fire. Can't walk the seven miles from the station in this weather. Oh well, the ship's a day late so that explains it... So... That was it, sis. The excitement is over. Reality returns. Pity. I love England but I hate its weather. There goes the passenger gangplank. Come on. We have to wait for the trunks. Good thing about leaving from a British colony is not having to go through customs. Better snag a porter as soon as we can."

"Africa seems far away."

"It is, Cinda. It is. Hey! Look at that. Isn't that young Barnaby? Eight months is a long time for a growing kid... Wondered why that man was waving. Come on. Oh, now that is nice. I just hate being abandoned. Maybe they'll buy us lunch. I'm starving."

"You think the others are inside?"

"Merlin would never stand on a cold dockside when he could sit around the fire. He'll be in the waiting room. All we need now are the trunks and the hand luggage. He really has grown. Didn't recognise my own brother."

"Seems like a foot taller."

"Can a boy grow that much in a year?... Look, there's Mother standing in the doorway to the big warehouse. This is going to be the best Christmas ever. Do you remember which trunk we packed the presents?"

"There's Father!"

"You're right. There's Father... You know, I sometimes expect one of his prize pigs to be here as well."

"You're silly! Oh, I'm so excited... And there's Granny Forrester. They must have brought all the horses and the big old coach that was grandfather's pride and joy. Oh, isn't this all exciting? The best bit about going away is coming home."

BY THE TIME they reached Purbeck Manor, the temperature had dropped six degrees and the fields were covered in a thick blanket of snow. The sturdy stone walls on either side of the lane were piled two feet high with it. The light was going. Inside the old coach, with the arms of St Clair emblazoned on both sides, it was warm from the bodies of the family pressed together. Twice Merlin had swapped with the old coachman who drove the four horses, Jug Ears, named by Barnaby when a small boy, the lead horse on the right. Wet from melted snow, the man was crammed into the coach and covered in a thick blanket to get his blood circulating again. As a boy, the coachman had been Lord St Clair's constant companion, fishing the river and hunting the fields for hare and rabbits. Lord St Clair had each time given him a nip of brandy from his silver hip flask.

"Cold enough to freeze the balls off a brass monkey," the coachman had said both times.

"Well, yes."

"Them old cannons were no good in a freeze. Cannonballs dropped right through the barrel. Them was good days in navy."

Granny Forrester thought it quite unnecessary to satirize the brass monkey's balls, balls that had nothing to do with primates. Old Potts would have had a retort and she smiled to herself at his memory. She missed him... She felt the iron wheels crush the gravel driveway through the snow and knew she was home. She wondered why Lucinda and Robert had been so quiet after the first excitement was over. They all had things to think about, things the others did not know about. Only she would be thinking of Potts. She'd get it out of them, all this Africa, in the days to come, a glad change from constantly thinking back on her past. She counted up to seven on her way to ten before her son-in-law said, as he always said when coming home, 'well, here we are'. As if there was anywhere else in the world. Barnaby helped her out of the coach, for which she was grateful. Climbing around without a thought was long past in her life.

Robert had been first off the coach on the side away from the house.

"It's so wonderful to be home... Ah, there's old James... Familiar faces. Come on, everyone. Out you get. I'm starving."

"There's been a sheep on the spit since lunchtime," said his mother.

"I didn't have lunch. Never mind. A good plate of roast mutton will suffice. It's going to be a white Christmas. When did Dorset last have a white Christmas?... Come on, everybody."

"How d'you find the cold?" asked Merlin.

"I don't know. I can't feel a thing. I'll thaw myself out in front of the fire. Thanks for meeting us, Merlin. What time did you leave this morning?"

"With the first crow of the cock. It was still pitch dark. We all need a stiff drink... Barnaby, come and help us rub down the horses. This time you are let off the hook, Robert. I rather think I would have liked it here years ago when there were plenty of servants."

"You drove the team well."

"It's fun, up high alone on the box in the snow. I have missed that chance. There are always compensations, according to Granny Forrester."

The rest of them filed through the small door to the left in the massive Gothic front door, the whole of which was rarely opened, the central point of the arch rising twenty feet above their heads. Inside it was all gloom. None of the gaslights was aflame. Robert wondered if the family finances had sunk to a new low. Even last year they would have stopped for lunch on the way from Southampton. They must be all near to fainting from hunger having left the Manor before breakfast. The entrance hall was damp and cold, and James, another old servant too old to find a paying job, was just visible in the gloom. The hall, with high ceilings and the stone walls, hand cut centuries before, was cold and damp to the touch. Following his mother and father, Robert went through the doorway to the left of the hall into the big sitting room.

The warmth of the fires at either end of the long room enfolded Robert and Lucinda in the warm history of their family. Lucinda gave a small cry of pleasure. The log fires in the huge grates were banked high and the leaping flames bathed the room in a warm yellow glow. All the heavy curtains had been drawn and the drinks trolley near one of the fires was aglow with twinkling crystal glasses. In the centre of the room, with its back to the long inside wall, there was something neither Lucinda nor Robert had seen before; a dark shape that tapered up to the ceiling.

"Before we have a drink to welcome you home," said Lord St Clair positioning himself between Robert and what looked to Lucinda like an old tree, "we are going to sing a Christmas carol. The old house is as quiet as a mouse and I wanted us to sing 'Silent Night', even if it was first sung in German."

To Lucinda, the old tree, if it was a tree, had an inner life of its own, as if something was trying to shine. It was pitch dark in the middle away from the fires that burnt at each end of the long room. Holding hands, the family stood just inside the closed door and sang. Even Granny Forrester felt tears falling down her face.

"Now," said Lord St Clair, feeling very pleased with himself. "The big surprise." Putting his left hand up to the new switch on the wall, he pushed down the small knob handle, which turned the lights on, on the fully decorated Christmas tree. For a full ten seconds no one said a word, dumbfounded, even though all but the travellers knew what to expect, it was the first time the fairy lights had been switched on in the dark.

"Old Potty was quite specific in his will," said Lord St Clair. "Electricity. That was how he put it. 'My last few pennies shall light up Purbeck Manor.' And there we are. The old house has at last been wired with electricity... Now, who is going to have a glass of sherry so we can raise our glasses to Sir Willoughby Potts, gentleman and friend to all of us?"

"It's so beautiful," said Lucinda.

"Must have cost a pretty penny," said Robert.

"Aunt Nut would have loved the Christmas tree all lit up," said Granny Forrester.

"Then we'll drink to both of them. Sir Willoughby Potts and my late Aunt Nut, who was as sweet as a nut," said Lord St Clair... "Robert. Lucinda. Welcome home."

.  .  .

ROBERT WOKE the next morning in his old room. Everything was familiar, permanent. He had left one window slightly open to breathe fresh air snuggled deep into the blankets and soft eiderdown. There was snow on the outside of the window in a small ridge on the other side of the wooden sill. The world was quiet, at peace with itself. Not a single sound came through the tiny gap left by the open window. From inside the house, there was nothing, not a blemish on the silence. Putting thick socks on under the bedclothes, Robert made himself ready for the plunge into his clothes that he knew were ice-cold. His feet warmed and gave him a feeling of false security, the thought of breakfast making him brave. Someone, somewhere in the house, banged a door.

He made himself not think of the cold until he was fully dressed. Then he looked out of the window two storeys high, down over the white fields blanketed in snow. It was very beautiful.

All through last night, his eldest brother Richard had not appeared. Annabel was away but no one had said where. Genevieve was married, the only one of the girls to marry. Frederick was due home on furlough with his new wife that day if the trains ran from London in the snow. He had left the Indian civil service to work for his father-in-law, even though the man was in some kind of trade Robert had not heard of before. Frederick had gone to London for a week to show his wife the sights. Robert's mother had said the girl was fluffy which was probably not a good start. Lady St Clair had thought her second son would have done better coming home to England to find a wife, instead of competing with all the other bachelors in India for the 'fishing fleet girls'. The subject had been closed, the way the subject had been closed when Robert asked about Richard.

Over three helpings of roast mutton and all the trimmings, as Robert liked to think of the roast potatoes, four root vegetables and last year's blackcurrant jelly, he had told them bits and pieces about Africa, giving them all Harry Brigandshaw's best regards, and avoided the question of what he was going to do with himself now that he was back in England. Apart from the bit about 'Silent Night' being first sung in German, no one mentioned the looming war that had been a constant topic on the SS *King Emperor* all the way from Cape Town to Southampton. He rather hoped the war was going to happen soon before he found some country prep school in which to bury himself. He was going to join the Territorial Army right after Christmas, that much he had made up his mind. He rather thought it a good idea to learn how to kill other soldiers before they killed him. He hadn't told anyone about that, not even Lucinda, who had grown quieter and quieter as the evening went on. He rather thought she was missing Harry Brigandshaw. They had all spent a lot of time together, day and evening.

It was all now so far away. In years to come most of what happened in Africa would slip from his memory. In his mind, he tried to wish Madge and Barend a happy life together but knew he was not being honest with himself. Maybe the memories of Africa would not fade as fast as he would have liked them to do. Everything looked so different from a distance, so final. He wished he was a better man. Stronger. Able to get a job on an African farm. To learn the business. Save some money. Borrow money to buy a small farm. But he knew he was no good. Too soft. Too inclined to enjoy the good things without working for them. He was a failure. They probably wouldn't want him in the TA. Even the Territorial Army were choosy when it came to picking their officers.


BY LUNCHTIME, there was still no sign of Richard and Robert feared there was something seriously wrong. It was as if the rest of the family, other than Robert and Lucinda, were expecting something to happen. And whatever was going to happen was not going to be pleasant.

All the servants left at Purbeck Manor were part of the conspiracy, and when Robert asked the cook what was going on, he was sharply told to go and ask his mother, and that family matters had nothing to do with the staff. It was the first time the cook had ever been sharp with him, as buttering up the cook had been part of his life for as long as he could remember. Robert, from the age of five, had found that even cooks succumb to the art of flattery.

Cook watched Robert going off in a huff and felt sorry for the whole family. For twenty years she had been wondering why Master Robert was not as round as a barrel, the amount of food he put into one stomach. She called it 'one of life's little mysteries' of which there were many in her way. But when she had been slaving in the kitchen all day, it had been nice of one of the children to come back and say the food was wonderful, even if she did know what the scallywag was after. There was nothing worse in her life than serving up good food and seeing it picked over. What she and the rest of the servants were going to do when the family finally disintegrated, she had no idea. She had been born in the servants' quarters and hoped to die there. If any one of the children had married a lot of money, she and James would not be in a constant state of worry. And neither of them had children to fall back on either. And with this war just around the corner, she was at the end of her wits. The last thing she needed was questions about Master Richard, who as far as she could see had now gone stark raving mad, foaming at the mouth and rolling on the floor. If she had had her way they would have called the parish priest to cast out the devil, not that old fool Reichwald, who didn't even have a cure for her piles. She watched Robert's receding back, wondering what the world had finally come to. She would have a good moan with James when he came off duty for his first cup of tea.

By three o'clock, Robert and Barnaby were off to Corfe Castle station in the trap to meet his sister-in-law. Along with the electricity had come a telephone as father had said something about 'in for a penny, in for a pound'. Frederick had phoned in the time of his arrival from London.

"What's she like?" he asked Barnaby as they drove through the pure white landscape.

"Fluffy."

"Mother always was rather good at picking one word... You'd better tell me about Richard. Why am I not allowed to see him, Barnaby?"

"He's been having fits. Seizures, according to Doctor Reichwald. The slightest bit of excitement and he drops on the floor, foaming at the mouth. We all have to make sure he doesn't swallow his tongue. Father said he wanted you and Cinda to enjoy your homecoming first. It's quite a worry for all of us. It just happens. Look, he's always been a bit simple, like a kid really, but there was nothing outwardly wrong with him. Nothing you could see."

"My poor brother."

"There's nothing we can do. To get better, I mean... I think he's going to die and then Frederick will be the heir."

"Has she got any money?"

"Yes. A lot. Granny Forrester found out somehow. You know how she is. But keep it secret. I don't think Granny's told Mother."

"Why did she tell you?"

"Because I'm her favourite."

"I can tell you Cook doesn't know," said Robert.

"Then it's you, me and Granny... Why didn't you marry the sister?... What was her name?"

"For sixteen you shouldn't even know about such things. Straight answer? She wouldn't have me. I'm not good enough."

"Don't talk rubbish, Robert. You're the cleverest one of all of us. The only one to go to Oxford."

"But as Father says: What are the three most stupid things in the world? A degree in history. A man's tits. And the Pope's balls."

"I have never understood that one."

"Thank goodness for small mercies... You'd better jiggle Jug Ears along or we'll be late. By the way, where's the cat?"

"Which one?"

"Tiddles."

"She's dead."

After a long time, and with the ruins of Corfe Castle now coming into view, Robert said quietly, "I loved that cat."

"She was very old. Mother said she must have been twenty. Do cats live to twenty?"

"I don't know... What's Frederick's wife's name?"

"Penelope. Not Pen. Not Penny. Penelope. Very fluffy."

"You don't like her?"

"I never said that. You can't dislike a person you don't know."

They drove on for a while.

"What are you going to do with your life, Barnaby?"

"I'm going into the army. All youngest sons go into the army. I take the Sandhurst exams next year."


INWARDLY, Penelope St Clair was shaking like a leaf as the train drew in at Corfe Castle station. Old man Pringle shuffled forward with a trolley and Frederick helped him load the two small cases.

"How's Mrs Pringle?" he asked.

"Arthritis. Same as me. Cottage too close to river. Damp. You've got surprise. Mister Robert's in trap with Master Barnaby. Merry Christmas."

"And Merry Christmas to you and yours, Pringle."

"I'll tell Albert."

"Albert! I thought he went off to Africa."

"Our Albert's rich. Owns shares in a gold mine. And mining supply company. Dynamite. Says 'e's going to be millionaire."

"Where's he staying?"

"In cottage. Same as usual. Says he can't beat his mother's cookin' no matter how much money he got. Our Tina thinks he's wonderful."

"Dynamite, you say? Fuses. All that sort of thing. How very interesting."

It was as if she did not exist. People talked around her. Over her. Never included her in their conversations. And now she had to meet another St Clair. They all frightened her to death and Lady St Clair left her quite tongue-tied. The only one who had given her even a smile was Granny Forrester. The family and people around them were all so close. She even knew they were poor. Father had found that out, but he said they were honest. Which is probably why they were poor, he'd said. Why being honest made a family poor she didn't understand.

Three years before, her father had endowed her with exactly half a million pounds. Put in three per cent Consols it had grown, as she spent very little, and in the six months that they had been married, Frederick had not asked her for a penny. She had told him about the money and he had just smiled... The strangest thing in all of it was he loved her. She didn't love him yet. Maybe she never would. Her father had done everything for her as usual. He knew about Richard and the fact he would never marry.

"Have a son or two, luv. That way my grandson will be Lord St Clair. When you got my kind of money you got to think up things to spend it on. Owning mines in India and halfway around the world is one thing. Owning the Nineteenth Baron St Clair is something else."

"I don't love him."

"What the 'ell has that got to do with the price of cheese?"

They went through the rigmarole of being introduced. Robert seemed far away, as if he had not yet fully returned from Africa. Barnaby, the youngest son, was more interested in talking to the man called Pringle about a girl called Tina. No one had introduced her to Pringle, but then he was a servant and not even a St Clair retainer. Robert was talking to Pringle about thick sandwiches and pickles. It was all over her head. Then they squeezed everyone into the trap for the seven-mile ride to Purbeck Manor on a road that had probably been laid during the last Crusade. Even the soft layer of snow failed to stop the road jangling her bones. Her teeth snapped shut frequently. She bit her tongue once and tasted blood. Going away to London for a week had been worth it but this time coming back to Purbeck Manor she knew what to expect. Maybe when she had the baby she would become part of the family. If she survived the road. The doctor in London had confirmed her pregnancy when she had gone to him on an excuse. She thought it would be better to tell Frederick when they left Purbeck Manor after Christmas. They were going back to India, which was good. Anywhere was good where she was not excluded. The boy and the two men chatted all the way back to the manor house, without once bringing her into the conversation. And she felt sick. She had heard of morning sickness during pregnancy but not feeling sick half of the day. She missed her mother. Without them even noticing her she began to silently cry.

FREDERICK WONDERED why his wife was crying but was too embarrassed to bring up the subject in front of his brothers. He went on talking as if nothing had happened. He thought of holding her hand but he had never done that before. Apart from his mother, Aunt Nut and Granny Forrester, he had never known a woman in his life. Sisters were different. They were sisters. He had lived in bachelor quarters in India for more than ten years. This being married to a woman he knew nothing about was difficult. What did women think? What did they want to do? The only time you ever touched each other was under the sheets when the lights were out and the black night had fallen. Then a world opened he did not admit to in the morning. What he did in the night could have nothing to do with the demure young woman who greeted him politely at breakfast as if nothing had happened. After the first time, he tried to look into her eyes the next morning but she wouldn't look back at him. He rather thought she was ashamed. He knew he was.

Annabel had been thirteen when he left home to join the Indian civil service. She had been a giggly schoolgirl as far away from what he did at night with Penelope as the moon. Until his marriage and joining the Anglo-Indian mining company he had never had enough money to go home to England on leave. He sold his leave passage and sent the money to his mother every three years, went up into the hills of Kashmir and told his bachelor friends what a good time he had had in England. None of them questioned him and he rather thought the others did the same thing. If their families were rich they would not be in the Indian civil service in the first place.

When he resigned to join his father-in-law's company, that many referred to as an empire within an empire, he was thirty years old, tall, thin, with dark brown hair and wore a military moustache, perfectly cut and tinged with grey. He was a junior magistrate, having taken his law degree at night by correspondence. He could only practise in India, and some would have called it a second-class degree of limited use, which it was. Everything in India needed someone up the ladder to die so everyone could shift up a rung. Progress was made by someone stepping into a dead man's shoes. The trappings of colonial life made the monotony and low salaries worthwhile. In India, every Englishman was a sahib, a gentleman, and when in India they lived as gentlemen would live, with servants and housing that fitted their rank. Part of the system was to make sure the Europeans appeared above the Indians. They lived in married quarters or exclusive men's clubs founded on the same principles as an officers' mess or a top West End club that carefully selected its members. Never, ever, were the British allowed to fraternise socially with the natives except on specific, laid down occasions when everyone was very polite to each other. Apart from the Indian Mutiny, it had worked surprisingly well for two hundred years; something like twenty thousand Britons running the entire subcontinent, with Indians to serve below the British in the civil service. Backed by regiments of the British Army, and regiments of the Indian Army officered by Britons, the rule of law prevailed, and everyone got on with the daily business without, for the most part, trying to kill each other. Frederick thought it was probably the only way to stop the multitude of states, factions, castes and religions squabbling with each other. The only way to trade profitably was under the rule of law. The British maintained the peace, provided an unbreakable legal system, and made a fortune at the same time, and Frederick rather thought he had paid his dues. After years of doing the hard work, it was his turn to make a fortune. He was going to be worth his father-in-law's while. Penelope's money belonged to her. Maybe their children. He himself would never touch a penny. By the time they reached Purbeck Manor, the girl he had married and only knew in the dark of the night had stopped crying. It was snowing hard.

Barnaby, thinking of his girlfriend Tina Pringle, helped Penelope from the trap. Either snow was melting on her face or the girl had been crying. Halfway to the big front door with its side door entrance, the girl clutching his arm stopped and was sick into the snow. Embarrassed, he waited for his brother Frederick to do something. All of them instead made it look as though nothing was happening.

Through into the sitting room with a Christmas tree, Penelope found a chair near the log fire and sat herself down. Someone gave her a cup of tea, which she drank gratefully. Never in her life had she wanted her mother more. The rest of the family were talking nineteen to the dozen, and Lord St Clair was repeating a story about Daisy, his prize sow. Every mouth she looked at was open and talking. No one was listening to a word. They were all having a thoroughly good time.

Lucinda was wondering what it was going to be like for the rest of her life, an old maid with nothing to look forward to but the second-hand happiness of other people. She had seen her new sister-in-law was feeling out of it but was not in the mood to be friendly. If anything, she was jealous of the girl, though what the poor thing would find worthwhile in being the wife of ramrod stiff Frederick she had no idea. She thought her second eldest brother was as cold as a fish. He looked ten years older than she knew him to be. She had never known him. As a child, she remembered this man that went away to some place called India... She tried to join in the happy family conversation but her mind was still at Elephant Walk with all its possibilities that had turned to nothing. And now they said there was going to be a full-scale war and all the joining men would be killed. She was firmly on the shelf, where she would stay. At Purbeck Manor, her father allowed her one small glass of sherry the whole evening. She missed the three stiff gins before supper and most nights feeling slightly tiddly. She missed the dogs. She missed the damn geese, she told herself. A good lion roar from right next to the window would send her into ecstasy. Above all, she would like to be warm right through to the marrow of her bones. She was sick of standing in front of roaring fires, toasting her front to perfection while her bottom froze from the draught coming in under the doors and sending freezing winds whistling round every room in the old house. Even in bed, her feet had not been warm since she came home. And as for poor Robert with that damn prep school of his, she did not wish to think. Inside the masters' common rooms she had heard they only put three lumps of coal on the fire in the depth of winter. The poor brass monkeys wouldn't stand a damn chance. And that was something else, she told herself. Now she was home she must stop swearing, even to herself. Or God would punish her. It was all her fault why God punished her anyway. She was a bad girl from all that drinking and mental swearing in Africa. And then she had a clear picture of Harry's face in her mind and she wanted to cry. Well, she wasn't going to cry. She was going to grin and bear it. Seeing Robert standing back from her father's story about his pigs she walked across to him. They had Africa in common. They would always be close.

"Have you found out what happened to Annabel?" she asked. No one seemed to want to talk about her eldest sister and she wanted to know why. Richard had been left in his room with the young male nurse their father had employed to look after him. The fire in the room was guarded by a strong wire fence and the young man had a cord to pull that rang a bell in the servants' quarters if Richard threw another fit. What they would do if the young man was called off to war she had no idea. Not having heard Robert's answer she repeated the question.

"You don't listen, sis. She's run off with somebody."

"Oh, for goodness sake don't be silly. Annabel would never run off. Where has she run off to?"

"That's the bit I can't find out. Have you met Penelope?"

"No one has thought of introducing me. What's wrong with her?"

"Granny Forrester think she's pregnant."

"How does Granny Forrester know all these things? I know absolutely nothing about being pregnant."

"I know, sis. That's your problem. You should have seduced Harry and have done with it. A few good rolls in the hay and he'd have been head over heels in love with you."

"How can you say such things? I hope your next school will be horrible."

"It will be. Come on. She looks out of it. Do your family duty. How would you like to be dumped into a strange family? Forget about her being pregnant."

"You don't know for certain."

"Ask Granny Forrester."

GRANNY FORRESTER HAD DECIDED years ago she would stop interfering in other people's lives. She was pleased when her granddaughter went across to talk to the poor thing that was sitting ignored by the fire and trying not to cry. She had watched them arrive through a parted curtain in the sitting room and though it was snowing hard she had watched the girl being sick. She saw the girl was probably not more than nineteen, had not told Frederick she was pregnant. She had watched her grandson turn away so as not to notice his wife being sick. Men were impossible! She knew Frederick better than Frederick knew himself. Under all the stiff upper lip nonsense he was as soft as butter. No, she was not going to interfere. They could all fight their own battles. Maybe her daughter would do the right thing and go to the girl. Then she caught Lady St Clair's eye, which told her in a nice way to mind her own business. Mother and daughter smiled at each other. For years they had been able to communicate without using words. At least she knew. That was good news. Smiling to herself this time she thought her grandson would be the last to find out his wife was pregnant.

THE SUPPER that night was a stew rich in herbs and garlic. The herbs from the kitchen garden were dried each year and hung around the kitchen for Cook to take as she needed. Robert ate three full plates and even said to Merlin, who was sitting next to him at the old long dining table, that the last plate was sheer piggery. Which it was. As Merlin pointed out, the base of the stew was pork. They had then gone into a long conversation about their father loving his pigs but eating them just the same.

Merlin was twenty-eight years old and had a job in the City, where he lived most of the time and was reported to live with his mistress, a one-time barmaid who no one in the family had ever met. The job in the City had something to do with Lloyd's of London. He told everyone he was a marine broker, whatever that was. Few people asked further questions. Some of his friends from school with influence in their fathers' businesses had passed him some business and his salary had gone up as a reward. Merlin had rather hoped Harry Brigandshaw would become his brother-in-law but by the way Robert and Lucinda had stopped talking about him, there was no chance of getting his claws on the Colonial Shipping account, the company he all too well knew was owned by the Brigandshaw family. There was a sister out there he thought was called Madge that Robert had talked about but nothing had come of that either. If he had landed the Colonial Shipping account they would have made him a senior broker with a seat on the board before he was forty. And with all the rumours of war with Germany, the war premiums were rising every day along with his firm's brokerage. There was always a chance, as Harry had once stayed with them at Purbeck Manor, and was said to be Robert's best friend. Insurance broking was all about connections.

There had been a flap about Richard during the pudding course but when his mother came back she said he was all right and had merely fallen against the fireguard and banged his head... Poor Richard.

Merlin looked down the long dining-room table that went back so far in the family no one had been able to put a date to it. The spit had been moved to the side of the walk-in fireplace. On its own legs in the front of the fire stood the ten-gallon iron pot that had also been passed down the generations. It was pitch black. The men helped themselves to the stew, but also served the ladies in the family. Even before the servants had become scarce at Purbeck Manor the tradition of self-help had prevailed. Probably, Merlin thought, from the days of marching armies and campfires during a long campaign. The second fire at the other end of the long, vaulted dining hall was just burning wood and had nothing to do with the cooking. Surprisingly, the hall, which was in the centre of the house with no outside walls, was warm, though Lucinda was still complaining of the cold. When he had a moment alone he would talk to her about Harry Brigandshaw and find out if he had any real influence over the family shipping company. He liked being a man of business. There was so much money to be made by a broker who took twenty per cent of the premiums and none of the risk. When he had built up a sizeable account at Cornell, Brooke and Bradley he would demand a high salary, a share in the firm, and then go out and look for a wife. Poor Esther would be upset but even she understood there was no chance of them ever being married. They just did not come from the same class. He would have to think of something to do with Esther when he got married. Maybe he could find her a husband in her own class and buy them a small house in the East End where she came from. She could say she had won the money on the horses or something like that. Wasn't there a saying you should never look a gift horse in the mouth?... Poor Esther. They had had a lot of fun. He would probably miss her but there was a price you had to pay for everything. He would find a wife whose father controlled a large insurance account. Someone in trade. The aristocracy, the landed gentry were on their way out. The future was making money in business. And it was fun making lots of money.

With luck, they would think him too old to go into the army if war broke out. And it would be soon if the way the war premiums were going up was any indication. To hedge against the downside of war, he had bought himself a nice block of Vickers-Armstrong shares. They made machine guns and the new-fangled warplanes that were somehow flying platforms for Vickers machine guns... What next would man think up as a way to better kill his fellow man, for goodness sake? And the kind of war they were talking about would need a lot of machine guns. He had borrowed some money from his bank manager, so he hoped the Germans would not let him down.

Annabel was the one who amused him. She had run off with a man who was penniless. No job. Not a penny. Said she was in love with him and would go to the ends of the earth. They had both come to his small flat in the Barbican, which was all he could afford. Not a fashionable address but close enough to walk to the office when the sun was shining. His umbrella had saved him from a dousing more than once: a bright, clear sky one minute, and then it was raining.

The man she had run off with came from the right stable but when he left home they had bolted the door behind him. The reason he had put them up for a week and told no one was, Merlin told himself, you just never knew in life. The black sheep of the family sometimes turned white, and the man's family owned one of the big pottery companies in the north, even supplying the royal family with their dinner plates, which had impressed Merlin. They sent their dinnerware all over the world and everything had to be insured. At the end of the week he had given them ten pounds he could not afford, and they had gone off to Brighton, where they said they were going to get married. That had been at the end of the summer. He hoped one day his ten pounds investment would pay off. And she was his sister. Geoffrey Winckle said he was going to be a great painter one day. Merlin wished him luck. Most painters he had heard of were very dead before they were very famous. And none of them made any money when they were alive unless they painted flattering portraits of rich men's wives. Geoffrey Winckle said he was an impressionist, whatever that was. Merlin had not asked to see his paintings. There was no point in getting involved in a subject he knew nothing about.

He had toyed with telling his mother ever since he had come home for Christmas. He was probably only the second person in the family to know what had happened to Annabel. It went without saying that she had told Granny Forrester before running away. Where she got the train fare from more likely... It was going to be a boring Christmas but every son had to do his family duty once in a while. Poor Esther. She would spend Christmas all on her own. When he had put up the runaways, he had sent Esther home to her mother for the week. Poor Esther. In a strange way, he missed her. She was comfortable. Never demanded much. She thought he was wonderful. Poor Esther. If only she knew.

When he woke in the night there was more clattering from Richard's room but he rolled over and tried to go back to sleep. There was no point in having a look... He wondered if it was still snowing outside now it was Christmas Eve.

During the night there was a choking scream and then silence.


THE DOCTOR CERTIFIED Richard dead in the morning. Everybody in the family cried as everyone cried when there was a death close to them. Close death was a nudge at their own mortality. Some even cried with relief. It had never been much of a life for Richard St Clair despite how beautiful he looked. They left him in his room covered with a white sheet. The parish church was all ready for Christmas, with a big cut-out story of the nativity in the entrance that had taken the children of the village a long time to build. Richard would have to take his turn. This was Christmas. With the windows left wide open to the fields covered in snow, there was no chance of him going off. The male nurse had cleaned him up nicely, taken a month's pay, and gone off to join his family for Christmas. He did not seem sad to lose his job. Barnaby drove him to the railway station at Corfe Castle in the trap and said the man had caught his train to Swanage. Jug Ears appeared to enjoy the trot as standing still in the stables with the roof covered in cold snow was not pleasant. No one spoke of Richard. Penelope thought it was not the time to tell the family she was pregnant, even if the child inside of her would inherit the title if it was a boy. She had a quiet word with the family doctor after he had seen to Richard.

"God moves in strange and beautiful ways," said Doctor Reichwald. "He takes and he gives. Yes, Mrs St Clair. You are indeed pregnant. Five months I should think."

"Please don't tell the family."

"You haven't told anyone?"

"Not yet."

Doctor Reichwald smiled. The girl was probably not more than nineteen.

Then he forgot the family and went home to his wife and children. He had his own worries. With a German name and a German war looming, he and his family were in trouble. It was too late to change their name now. Even if they did, people would still know them for who they were. German immigrants. Their name change should have been done by his grandfather when he became a naturalised Englishman. But in those days the royal family were more German than English so it did not seem to matter... Wasn't Kaiser Wilhelm of Germany Queen Victoria's grandson? He was very cold when he got home to a warm hearth and a hot cup of tea. Goodness, he was more English than the English. At least the poor boy was out of agony, which he would have been in, could he understand. Doctor Reichwald knew very little about mental illness. He had delivered the boy. Lady St Clair had been so happy. They had rung the bells in the parish church of Corfe Castle as they had done for centuries when an heir was born to the barony. Now they would do it again. Despite all the terrible things, life went on. When the reverend had time from celebrating Christmas, he would be there to give the family comfort. The Reverend Reichwald was the doctor's brother. After the second cup of tea, he would go over to the vicarage and suggest to his brother they change their name. They could do it by deed poll. Three of their boys were old enough to go into the army so they had best hurry up about things. There was no time to waste. It was never too late to solve a problem, even if the words in his head had a hollow ring.

THEY HAD BOUGHT the small gold mine the week before Albert Pringle set sail for England. Sallie Barker had conducted the negotiations, even going down the mineshaft to look at the thin seam of gold she hoped went on far back from the exposed surface. Gold seams had a way of their own. The selling consortium wanted to get out while they were ahead. Sallie had mortgaged the explosives factory to buy the gold mine, and though Albert told everyone at home he was rich, he was not so sure. Sallie had said that if they had lost everything it didn't matter as they had had nothing in the first place.

"Dear Albert. We either get rich and have some fun or go back to England with our tails between our legs. Where's your sense of adventure? Old Bradshaw has lost his nerve. It's why he wants to sell. That seam is going to get wider and wider, richer and richer, and go on for a mile."

"How can you be so sure?"

"Woman's intuition."

"Oh, my God."

The news of Richard St Clair's death had reached the small cottage that had once belonged to the railway company sometime after lunch on Christmas Eve. Barnaby had ridden over to wish Tina, Albert's younger sister, a happy Christmas and bring her a small present. Tina was fifteen. Edward the fisherman was back from Swanage for Christmas and the rest of the Pringle family was scattered to all corners of the empire.

At Sallie's insistence, Albert had travelled first class even though it had made him feel uncomfortable. She had taken him to an Indian tailor who ran him up some evening clothes in a day.

"You have to look rich even if you're not. People don't know we borrowed from the bank to buy Serendipity Mine. Funny how Bradshaw had tried to sink a borehole for water and drilled straight into a gold seam. You go first class, Bert. Tell them who you are. How rich a seam of gold we found. I want to sell some of our shares on the stock exchange and buy another mine."

"Please, Sallie, you frighten the shit out of me."

"And don't use that kind of language in first class."

The food on board had been opulent but none of it tasted as good as his mother's cooking. With all the fancy clothes packed away in a trunk and left with the shipping company in Southampton, he was plain Bert, home with his family. All the money in the world would never make him feel happier than being home in the family cottage, eating rabbit pie and sipping his mother's home-made parsley wine.

Tina and Barnaby went off somewhere. They held hands when they thought they were out of sight. It was easier to see out through the curtains than in.

"That's not good," said Albert's father. "Try to stop 'em. Better someone tells Lady St Clair. Mixing class makes bad 'appiness. Barnaby can't live like us and Tina can't live up at the Manor." He let the corner of the curtain drop back into place. "When you go back, Bert? Back to Africa?"

"Six days."

"Take our Tina with you. She was sixteen last month. Before we 'ave trouble. Never been trouble between us Pringles and St Clairs. Don't want none. Can't mix classes. You got to marry somethin' similar. Don't forget. This Sallie Barker sounds way over your head."

"Oh, she is, Dad. Believe me. Right over my head."

"Do you love 'er?"

"Oh, yes. But she doesn't love me. Don't think she'll ever love anyone now."

"Why not?"

"A long story. She got raped by a fat old German fart."

"I don't want Tina gettin' it off with Barnaby. Once they done that we'll never break 'em apart. Then she'll be miserable trying to be what she isn't. You can give 'er some of this education you talk about. That never hurt... By the way, son, I'm proud of you. Never say that again, most probable. But I am. I'm proud of all my kids. Take 'er with you to Africa. Swap that first-class ticket for two in the third... Now, who the hell's this? Long thin piece of wind with a moustache. You expecting someone?"

LADY ST CLAIR was equally worried about Barnaby and had sent Frederick to bring him home. Merlin had first been asked but Frederick had said he needed the exercise. Bored with doing nothing, and not wishing to think about his new position in the family, he thought he would ride over and hope Albert Pringle was still at home. Maybe the visit home could be made profitable. Buying equipment and stores for the mines was part of his new job. Any cut in the price of goods increased the profit for his father-in-law. It was a chance to do some business as he liked to call it. His wife seemed out of sorts and he put it down to poor Richard dying. Poor Richard. And that was something else he did not wish to think about.

THEY BOTH KNEW what they were going to do but neither of them had said a word. For Barnaby, the primal instinct to reproduce after a death in the family was working in Tina's favour. She had known Barnaby as her best friend ever since she could remember. In those days she was a tomboy. Only when her tits began to grow did she think of him as a man. She was thirteen years old then and their game together had changed forever. Prior to that, it was curiosity. Having a look. Wondering why they peed differently. Their relationship grew from mucking around together as kids trying to fight the boredom of childhood into a first-class lust. For six months she had wet her pants at the sight of Barnaby and the wetness had nothing to do with a pee. The placid object of her childhood curiosity stood upthrust from the inside of his pants sending another flood of moisture down her thighs. No one had to tell them what sex was about.

She had her pants down. The thing out of his pants was jerking so much it was difficult to get under control. Then it spat across the stable just missing her right tit. Her right hand was moist from taking off her panties. The thing in her hand was rock hard again in seconds but wet to hold. She couldn't bring it down without him bending over but with her pants down and legs open, all he could do was stare at the thing jerking away in her sticky wet hand. The second time it happened the white stuff went all over her face. When the thing went limp she had it more under control and on its way to the point between her legs where she wanted it. Barnaby let out a final groan of ecstasy and fell on top of her and she lost the thing just as a male voice called their names from somewhere out in the snow. They scrambled to try to get back into their clothes.

"Tina, that was wonderful. The most wonderful thing I have ever done," said Barnaby.

"Well, it weren't no good for me... You got an 'ankerchief?"

"Why do you want a handkerchief? You're not going to cry are you?"

"You'd spat it all over my face. First shot missed my right tit by an inch."

The humour of it all began to boil, bursting into peals of laughter as they rolled around in the hay, which was how Frederick found them when he opened the top of the stable door. It was dark inside. From the glare of the snow Frederick's eye took a moment to adjust.

"What are you doing in there?" asked Frederick sternly.

"Feeding the horse... Do I know you?" called Tina pulling on her panties and pulling down her dress.

"It's Frederick. My brother. From India," said Barnaby lamely.

"Well, what's 'e doing 'ere?"

"Barnaby's mother wishes to see him," said Frederick.

"Does she now?... Well, go on, Barnaby. Run along. Your mum wants you."

"What are you two grinning about?" asked the ex-junior magistrate from the state of Kashmir.

"Nothing, see."

Frederick, not wishing to confirm his brother's fly buttons were undone turned his back on the stable. He just hoped he had arrived in time. There was something gleaming wet on the girl's face that he did not wish to think about either. The worst part was the smell. It was quite distinct. Like under the sheets in the dark of the night with Penelope. What his family would do if the girl fell pregnant he had no idea. There was no way they could marry.

The girl could barely speak English. She was pretty enough. A wicked little smile. What a pity life was so complicated, he said to himself. He walked away from them back to the cottage. At least he had done a little business. Albert Pringle was going to send him a price list and a box of fuse samples. Dynamite did not travel but the fuses and percussion caps were the keys to successful rock blasting. The kids were still giggling to each other behind him. He felt old, full of responsibility, and envied them their childhood. What a shame all good things came to an end as this one certainly was going to come to an end right now. He would have a word with Granny Forrester. She would know what to do. Suddenly he was happy to remember what he had seen on the girl's face. Luck was with him. He had called out just in time. He hoped. Anyway, girls found it difficult to become pregnant. Look at Penelope after all those nights under the sheets. The idea made him tremble.

They rode back together, the oldest and the youngest of the brothers. Neither said a word but both were thinking similar thoughts. Sex, however much civilisation tried to make it look dirty, was the driving force of life. Without it, nothing ever would have happened. They reached home and went their separate ways, Barnaby to have a good bath. He had never felt better in his life. Next time he would let Tina do what she had been trying so hard to do. He was in a corridor when the thought came to him. He would have to be careful not to think of Tina when the others were around. Unless he was sitting down with his legs crossed... He was going to marry her of course. There had never been much doubt of that and now there was none. When they were married they would do it three times a day. When Frederick had walked away he had made a time to see her on Boxing Day. He hoped his brother had not seen his fly buttons were undone.

THE PHONE CALL had come in soon after Frederick left to haul in young Barnaby. Annabel and her new husband were at the railway station. Merlin had volunteered to pick them up in the trap, as he wanted to make sure his family knew nothing about their stay at his flat in the Barbican. It was going to be dark when he got home but the snow had stopped and Jug Ears knew his way in the dark. There was a small lantern to light and one of them would have to walk with the horse. The white snow would help. His sister was not going to stay in the waiting room. Annabel had said on the phone Pringle had gone home for Christmas and not waited for the last train. The young boy who swept the platform and weeded the garden was the only sign of life and the fire had gone cold. She and Geoffrey Winckle were the only passengers from Wareham off the train. They had got off the Brighton line train and changed at Wareham. They had planned for weeks to throw themselves on the family's mercy as they were completely out of money. Merlin's ten pounds had only gone so far. They had tried phoning Geoffrey's father who had told him to go to hell. 'You made your bed and now you can lie in it.' Geoffrey had the idea his father enjoyed the imagery. When Merlin walked down the deserted platform at Corfe Castle station they had never been more pleased to see anyone in their lives. Even the idea of driving the last part of the journey in the dark was not daunting.

"Is Mother mad at me?" she asked.

"Richard is dead, Annabel."

"When?"

"Last night. We bury him the day after Boxing Day. He is still in his room with the window open. Our brother swallowed his tongue and choked to death. Fred's here with his rich wife. Granny Forrester thinks she's pregnant. Barnaby's being told right now not to see Tina Pringle again. Father's taken Richard badly. Added to that, the family is just about broke. Welcome home."

"And Genevieve?"

"They are spending Christmas with his parents in Norfolk. Other than them we are all together and probably for the last time if you include Richard and a looming war. I like the idea he'll still be at home for Christmas even if he is dead... Don't cry, Anna. It's better for Richard. Living in one room with the male nurse! Even Richard couldn't live that way. You couldn't have timed coming home better. For the first time since Richard died, Mother gave a brief smile. No parent should have to bury their child."

"We may all die young," said Geoffrey Winckle, nervously. As they drove along the top road, the ruins of Corfe Castle were lit up by shafts of winter sunlight that sprang through the cloud. The sun went out as quickly as it came, sending a shiver of premonition down Merlin's spine.

They reached the sanctuary of home without needing to light the lamp. Barnaby brushed down Jug Ears and covered the horse in a thick blanket. On the gravel driveway in front of the tall Gothic door to the Manor, carol singers from the village were singing their last song.

When Barnaby got back from the stable, holding the lantern to see his way, the children of the choir were inside with the Reverend Reichwald, eating Cook's homemade mince pies. The presents were already under the big tree twinkling with its new fairy lights, the presents tightly wrapped and ribboned, each with a small card. Barnaby had the certain premonition it was his last Christmas as a boy. Both fires were burning brightly at either end of the sitting room. Through the undrawn curtains, Barnaby could see the shape of the big car borrowed by the reverend to do his rounds.

Everyone was trying to be cheerful but everyone knew Richard was lying dead upstairs in his room. Barnaby knew it was not going to be a good Christmas after all. Taking a hot mince pie from the silver tray on the sideboard, he wandered across the room to meet his new brother-in-law, the enigmatic painter. The poor fellow was looking petrified.


ROBERT WATCHED his youngest brother across the room and wondered what he was smirking about. The boy had the look of the cat that had licked the cream. Granny Forrester was beckoning to him. When he stood in front of her she just smiled and kissed him on both cheeks.

## 2
-----

# JUNE TO DECEMBER 1914

*J*ack Merryweather rarely looked at the financial pages of the newspaper. He knew his income was grossly in excess of his expenditure and saw no point in watching what other people had done for him. When he was sick he went to a doctor. A legal problem found him with his solicitor. Pick a man in his profession and trust him and mostly it had worked. His money was entrusted to five stockbrokers and one of them was Jared Wentworth. Jack had concluded a man who hated his job could still be good at it. The man was honest, the most precious ingredient for Jack in a money manager. The connection with Elephant Walk helped. Mostly when he visited Jared's office in the City they talked of Harry and Elephant Walk. Sometimes the portfolio of shares was worth more than the last time. Sometimes less. Over the years the profile had made a steady six per cent rise which among the five stockbrokers was the best return on his money.

"Do you feel like a gamble?" said Jared, taking a prospectus from his desk drawer.

"You've never suggested one before," said Jack.

They had talked about the looming war and the dead archduke in Bosnia. He had been pleased to hear Sara Wentworth had still not married Fishy Braithwaite and would relay the information to Harry Brigandshaw in his next letter. They had both agreed long ago Sara would make the perfect colonial wife for Harry. Jack had been about to stand up in preparation to leaving Jared's office when the surprising question was asked. Jack raised a quizzical eyebrow and kept his seat. He was thirty-three years old and had mastered the art of raising a quizzical eyebrow.

"Don't look so shocked. I have not gone off at a tangent." Flicking the prospectus so it landed on the desk facing Jack, Jared leaned back in his chair and smiled.

Jack was forced to read the heading. "Serendipity Mining and Explosives Company! This must be a joke."

Jared was amused to watch Jack climb up on his high horse, his own smile making Jack climb a little higher.

"Blue chips, Jared. Don't you remember my first instructions? Those South African mining companies have been known to float and sink on the same day. They salt the mines, damn it. In a proper world, they would lock up people who float these companies."

"People did well enough out of Cecil Rhodes and Barney Barnato." Jared was openly smiling.

"Take that grin off your face," said Jack.

"Have a look at the names of the directors."

Jack did and looked up sharply. "Lord Kenrick, Earl of Pembridgemoor, is a professional company director. He'd go on any board for five thousand a year provided he doesn't have to attend a board meeting. The college of heralds has not confirmed his inheritance. There have been rumours for years his elder brother is still alive. I wouldn't put a penny anywhere near Rowland Kenrick despite the fact that he's a member of my club. Someone tried to shoot him in a duel for cheating at cards. Dreadful man. Years ago, of course."

"Look at the names of the two executive directors."

"Why?"

"Because you'll recognise them."

"Well, I'll be blowed," said Jack.

"I propose you buy five thousand pounds' worth."

"There's no mention of Lily White on the board. Albert Pringle, yes. But who's S J Barker?"

"Sallie Barker. Used her initials to hide she's a woman. She's the brains, Jack. Take the prospectus home. Read it."

"Why do you want me to invest?"

"To have some fun. He was your valet, for God's sake. Now he's floating gold mines on the London Stock Exchange. Where's your sense of adventure? The gold mine may be a gamble. They always are. But the explosives factory with a war around the corner? They'll be making artillery shots before you can turn round. Mines for the navy. The offer will be five times oversubscribed. When these shares reach the exchange they'll be twice the listing price. Perfect timing. Your valet is going to be a rich man."

"Better make it fifty thousand pounds."

"You haven't read the prospectus."

"You have."

"So you do have a soft spot for Sallie Barker!"

"I'm a confirmed bachelor. You know that. No, I'd like to see Sallie put two fingers in her mother's eyes. If the shares list well it will be my pleasure to point out S J Barker to her mother."

"Fifty thousand pounds is a lot of money to gamble."

"You said to have some fun. Let's have some fun. If you're wrong I'll fire you as my broker... Buy the shares in a nominee. Keep quiet until we know what happens. I wonder what they did with Lily White? Shows what can be made in life from rough beginnings. The three of them were running a whorehouse in Johannesburg." Jack was now smiling.

"It doesn't say that in the prospectus," said Jared, worried for his biggest account.

"If they can run a whorehouse successfully, this will be a piece of cake. Thank you, Jared. I am having fun. And I will read the prospectus when I get home. But put in for fifty thousand quids' worth to the offer broker. If you're right we'll only get ten thousand... Sallie Barker. She had the most perfect dark eyes and long black ringlets past her ears. That was the first time I saw her. Well, I'll be blowed."

Outside on the pavement, Jack felt happier than he had done for a long time. And there was no sign of boredom nagging at the back of his mind... He had even forgotten the pending war.

Lifting his rolled umbrella, he pointed it imperiously at a roving taxi, one of the new ones propelled by an internal combustion engine. The contraption stopped and he got in. It was five o'clock in the evening. He should have asked Jared to come over for a drink at the club. Instead, he gave the driver the address of his new mistress. She was eighteen years old. At that age, he had found, they were not so cynical of life. She did not have the size of the bosom of Lily White but she did have a more pleasant disposition. She was more fun. She made him feel younger. By the time he reached her small flat in Sutherland Avenue, Paddington, he had forgotten all about Lily White and Sallie Barker. He would phone his new valet from the girl's flat and tell him he would not be home for supper. With everything in perfect order in his life, he began to climb a flight of wooden stairs to the small door with a small brass knocker. He gave one wallop on the knocker and the door flew open and the pretty little thing ran straight into his arms.

"Oh, Jack! Now I'm happy." She gave him a big kiss. "What have you been doing?"

"Buying gold shares."

"Come in and tell me all about it and then we can drive to Regent's Park and go for a walk. It's such a lovely afternoon. Oh, I'm so happy."


IT WAS like eating a soufflé when he wanted a proper meal; all fluff and no substance. It wasn't good enough. She tried so hard to amuse him and he tried so hard to be amused. Trivia. Trivia... And more trivia. The pretty little girl parroted bits of the books he had given her to read, moving her eyes round his face to see if what she said was the right thing for the moment. Everything she did centred around keeping her job as his mistress, the void outside the comfort of the small flat he paid for always in her mind, the terrible alternative. There was fear in the chatter, that found him wishing he had gone to the club. She tried too hard and all Jack could see were dark, almost black eyes and black bouncing ringlets in his mind. It made him feel lonely and bored at the same time but he had no heart to hurt the girl prattling at his side. Would she really want to hear about another woman six thousand miles away? Could he talk about the emptiness in his life that had gone so long from one indulgence to the other? That nothing lasted. That there was no real importance in chit-chat or grand meals or plays in vogue; some new singer everyone told him had to be heard; some new amusement to counter his boredom. How lucky Sallie Barker had been when her telegram lay stuck at the back of the Elephant Walk mailbox in the Salisbury post office. He would have paid of course. They might even have started an affair. Whatever they had done, he doubted if it would have compared to a public share listing on the London Stock Exchange. She had been doing something while all the time he had drifted through his life of luxury to the echoing beat of boredom. He envied her. She had something to think about other than satisfying the bodily whims.

They went back to the Paddington flat after an expensive dinner in a favourite restaurant, where he drank enough to bring his mind down to the present. They had gone home after their walk in the park so she could change. Because she so wished to please him they made love in the big double bed. She would have been mortified had he left without taking what he had paid for. It would have been like beating a dog that wanted to play.

She wanted him to stay but he went home. His new valet, the fourth since Albert Pringle, was asleep in the chair in the hall. The man was obsequiously subservient.

"I said to go to bed if it was after ten," said Jack, standing at the front door.

"Oh, sir. It's my duty. I must be ready whenever you come home. Is there anything you require, sir?"

"No, Bradford. Go to bed."

"The whisky decanter is in the lounge."

"It always is at this time of night, Bradford."

"As you say, sir."

"And good night."

"A very good night to you, sir. And may it not be too presumptuous of me to wish you pleasant dreams... Pleasant dreams, sir."

"Thank you, Bradford."

"It is always my pleasure."

In the lounge behind the closed door, he poured himself a whisky and went to his writing desk which he opened, having pulled out the wooden arms that supported the mahogany lid that came down to a table, tooled green leather making a pleasant writing surface where it was smooth in the centre. Jack took a clean sheet of paper from a small drawer and took up his pen. He thought for a while, removing the irritation of Bradford from his mind. Then he forgot his mistress. For a moment before he began to compose the first verse of a new poem he thought of the looming war and wondered if he would be too old to join the army. He hoped not. Even though he knew the piece of paper would end up in the wastepaper basket to the right of his bureau, he began to write. It was his only therapy. The one time he was not bored with his life.

THE MOST STUPID thing a whore could ever do was fall in love with the patron. He had made love to her that night because he felt sorry for her and no other reason. Feeling even sorrier for herself at the thought, she went back to having a good cry. Then she blew her nose and made herself a cup of tea. It was a very nice flat. She worried too much. She was still young.

THE DAY before war broke out between Germany and England, Serendipity was oversubscribed five and a half times when it floated on the London Stock Exchange. Jared phoned Jack the news.

"One pound, eleven and sixpence for a share you paid one pound for. How many do we sell?" Jared was very cheerful and very relieved. He had told the senior partner about his predicament some days before.

.   .   .

"GOODNESS, Wentworth! Why jeopardise the account of Merryweather? You'll be fired if you lose him, of course. South African mining shares! Were you out of your mind? You should leave the company now, of course. We can't change your mistake but we would have a defence. Merryweather might just stay with us."

"He won't. He said so. May we wait to see what happens?"

"Very well. Don't do it again. We are here to make a commission when we buy and sell shares. We don't make an extra penny if Merryweather makes a bundle."

"We both know the executive directors."

"Why didn't you tell me? You know something! Buy me a thousand shares. You have to have inside information to make money."

"Neither of us knows anything. All I have is the prospectus."

"Now I see it. Tell the floor to make it two thousand shares. My private account. Only a fool would jeopardise his job. Well done, Wentworth. No, make it five thousand. I see what you're up to. 'Methinks the lady protesteth too much,' to make a hash of Shakespeare."

"But, sir..."

"Out. Wentworth! Five thousand shares."


THE PHONE HAD GONE QUIET. "Are you there, Jack?"

"I'm here. Just the world's gone mad. How many shares did I get if it's oversubscribed?"

"Eight to ten thousand I should think. It's up to the directors' discretion but they usually allocate in proportion to the oversubscription. How many do I sell?"

"None of course. Let me know the allocation. We'll also be at war by tomorrow."

"Looks like it. Don't you want to sell the few to cover your bet?"

"No. And if it's any help for your sleep, whatever they do now is my fault, not yours... Are you going to join the army?"

"The navy, I think. I've been playing around in small boats all my life. And you, Jack? You don't have to go."

"Too old, haha! My foot. I'll lie. Say I'm twenty-five."

"They won't believe you."

"They will when they get desperate."

"It'll all be over in six months."

Jack was not so optimistic. Austria had declared war on little Serbia for shooting its archduke. The man who had shot him, Gavrilo Princip, was a fanatic. Russia mobilised in support of Serbia so Germany declared war on Russia and France. The rest of the world was waiting for its turn. All the pieces of Europe were being thrown into the air, and everyone who was anyone was getting into position, so when the pieces came down again they could grab as much as possible for themselves. The spoils of war. Jack wondered if there would be any if all the pieces going up in the air were shot to pieces before they hit the ground; war was part of man; nothing had changed; they were all taking sides, hoping they'd chosen the right one. Jack doubted if anyone in power or on the streets had given a thought to the real right or wrong of anything. Once in a regular while, the world wanted blood. Charles Darwin would have understood, Jack thought, walking from his house in Baker Street to his club in Pall Mall. Evolution. Survival of the fittest. He had seen it so often in Africa. All the male animals fought with each other to see who would mate with the female. Only the best strain survived. Man was an animal. They just dressed up better. Or so they thought.

In the club, the Earl of Pembridgemoor was buying everyone a drink.


THE NEXT DAY, after Germany invaded little Belgium, England declared war on Germany. Japan declared war on Germany. Britain's colonies stood ready to join the war. Jack, in his club on Pall Mall, where he had been all day with the excitement building by the moment, put a phone call through to Jared Wentworth. He wanted to try to make the day as normal as possible, but like everyone else, he wondered if anything would ever be the same again.

"What's the share price, Jared?"

"One pound, seventeen shillings and sixpence. On the floor they think they'll go to two pounds by the close. Gold as a monetary hedge. Explosives to blow up the Hun. What a combination! I've been trying to reach you at your home since one o'clock. Had a wire from the company's Johannesburg office. Rather unusual, I'd say. The directors have given you what you asked for. Fifty thousand shares. You own five per cent of the company and will double your money within a week."

"Was there a personal note to the telegram?"

"No."

"I'll be damned. That lunch I paid for with Ernest Gilchrist was the best investment I ever made in my life."

"You'll have to find yourself another broker."

"Whatever for, Jared?"

"I go down to Dartmouth on tomorrow's train. I've joined the Royal Navy Volunteer Reserve... There's a war on," he said into the silence.

THERE'S nothing worse than a guilty conscience that won't go away. Albert Pringle and Sallie Barker had argued for a week, ever since the closing date, when all the application forms had been received in London with bank guaranteed cheques pinned to the forms. All share requests for one hundred or less shares were to be filled in full. Details of share applications for more than one per cent of the company had been telegraphed to the Serendipity office in Johannesburg for review; which had started the row.

It was Albert Pringle's chance to make up for running away without even speaking to Jack Merryweather. He had not even written him a letter.

"Don't be bloody stupid, Albert, he'll think it's me," said Sallie Barker, the day before the shares were due to float on the London Stock Exchange. "He'll think I'm after him again. The shares can still flop and then he won't thank us."

"You forget. Without Jack Merryweather, none of this would have happened. Your mother had her eye on Jack for you. He paid my passage to Africa and I left him in the lurch."

"You're being sentimental."

"He's our talisman."

"Now you are being superstitious."

"Please, Sallie. I've never asked for much. You know the shares are going to open higher than a quid. We know how much we're oversubscribed. Please. I'll go on my knees. Someone's going to make the money. Why not Jack?"

There had been more to Albert's relationship with Jack. Without the master-servant impediment, and coming from a different class, he fancied they would have been friends. Good friends. They understood each other. Talked to each other about their families and, in the end, he had let him down. Taken the boat trip and thrown it in his face. This would make them even.

So much loyalty, thought Sallie, and smiled.

"Thanks," said Albert, without her having to speak. The smile was enough. "But we keep quiet. Let him think it's normal company policy to have large shareholders. You think he'll want to come on the board?"

.   .   .

THE DAY the shares were listed in London should have been the best day of their lives in Johannesburg. They were two hours ahead of London. When the closing price was telegraphed they were all still in the office, all with mixed feelings. People were talking about a world war, not just a war. South Africa was going to be drawn into the fray. Only the salaried young men from the mine and explosives company, who had been invited to head office to celebrate the flotation, were excited. The older men who had been through the Anglo-Boer War were quiet. At the end of the trading day, their shares were trading at a thirty per cent premium. Everybody clapped at the news.

"Now all we have to do is make sure Serendipity makes a profit," said Sallie, bringing them down to earth.

"But it's a start. A good start. We now have the capital. The rest is up to the lot of us in this room and the men at the mine and the factory. Every hourly paid employee will receive a bonus of five pounds whatever the colour of their skin. The rest of you will have to wait for year-end profit when five per cent will be set aside for salaried staff in proportion to your pay. Now just get me the job done... Someone had better start opening the champagne. Mr Pringle will pop the first cork."

THE DAY JARED WENTWORTH arrived at the Royal Naval College, Dartmouth, to start his naval training, Serendipity shares broke through the two-pound level. No one told him. He was too busy collecting his kit. The petty officer in charge of recruits was foul-mouthed and abusive. The way he said 'welcome to the Royal Navy' was a cross between a threat and a sneer. Jared's basic training had begun, and though he did not know it at the time, like a lot of other people in England and around the world, his life had changed forever. The pampered life of an English gentleman was to be lost in the horror of war.

IN LONDON, Jack was sick to his stomach. It was as if the nation had smelled blood. Patriotism. Honour. Duty. Words on everyone's lips. Union Jacks everywhere as if waving the flag would frighten the Germans... What frightened Jack most was everyone seemed to want the war. Eyes gleamed with fervour. Blood rushed to the head. Young men mobbed the recruitment centres. There was no shortage of volunteers. Young men bubbling with excitement of war giving each other false courage. 'We are all together now', as if before the war they had nothing to do with each other. No doubt, Jack thought, in Germany they were waving German flags with equal excitement. Neither side mentioned the stomach flutters to each other. The apprehension. The fear. Jack thought that will come later, with realism.

WITH SOBER MIND and an inkling of what was to come, Jack took himself off to his nearest recruitment centre. The war was a month old. In a business suit and a top hat, he looked incongruous next to men wearing rough clothes and cloth hats. Two of them slapped Jack, a tall thin man with broad shoulders, on his back in the excitement. His hair was prematurely grey under the silk hat. He smiled at the man, for no reason appalled at being touched by a stranger. 'There'll be more of that' he said to himself ruefully. The papers talked of Germany invading France and Belgium. One had said that morning that British troops of one of the Highland regiments had made contact with the Germans. No one was really sure. The truth had already been lost to the censors. What had once been news he could trust was now propaganda. Between the lines, and cross-referencing more than one of the London newspapers, Jack thought some of the regular army had crossed the channel. The Highland regiment in question was famous and the paper had reeled off its glorious history.

When he reached the end of the line he faced a low table. Two bareheaded soldiers with their hats on the table were seated behind it on wooden chairs. One was a corporal, one was a sergeant. That much Jack knew about the ranks of the army. At St Paul's he had been in the Combined Cadet Force, the CCF. He had twice fired a rifle. In badly fitting uniforms they had marched up and down a road at the back of the quadrangle. Then the sergeant who drilled them had been called back into the real army and gone off to South Africa. The school never saw him again. A year after leaving St Paul's, Jack learned Sergeant Small had been killed at the Battle of Colenso. Jack was pleased he had died a soldier's death. Some years later in his club, an old boy who had been a senior when Jack was in his first term, told him Small had died of fever in Bloemfontein without hearing a shot fired in anger. Jack remembered he had disliked the senior when he was at school.

The corporal was having trouble writing with an indelible pencil, licking the blue end of the stump to make it write better. He was filling in forms in triplicate, the carbon paper cramping out of line between the forms, each set pinned together. There was a pile of pinned forms in front of each soldier. He took a fresh set without looking up and poised the stump of the pencil.

"Name!"

"Jack Merryweather. Or rather, John Claud Percival Merryweather."

"Blimey! Where you from?"

"27 Baker Street. About a mile from here."

"Age?"

"Twenty-five."

The corporal looked up at the immaculately dressed Jack standing in front of him.

"Shit, Sarge. 'Ave a look at this... What you doin' 'ere?"

"Offering my services to the King."

They both looked at him, the sergeant and the corporal, and giggled.

"How old you say?" said the sergeant.

"Twenty-five."

"Not in this century. Take off your 'at."

Jack obliged and stood bareheaded while everyone had a look at him.

"Look, sir. We like the idea, don't we, lads?" the sergeant said to the young men in the queue behind him. "You won't see forty again. This is a war. Crawling around on our bellies, see. Put your 'at back on and go 'ome."

"I'm thirty-three."

"And I'm the Pope. Go 'ome. Next!"

As Jack turned around and walked away he had never felt a bigger fool in his life. A taxi driver answered the call of his raised rolled umbrella.

"Three cheers for the toff," someone called.

Jack gave the driver the address of his club. They were raising their cloth hats on the third cheer when the cab drove away. It was all done with good humour but it made Jack feel miserable. The only time he had looked for a job in his life he had been told to go home.


THE CLUB WAS EMPTY. It was three o'clock in the afternoon. Jack did something he had never done before in his life and sat at the bar alone.

"You all right, sir?"

When in company, he had always jollied along with the barman. He rather thought they liked each other... He felt like he had felt as a junior at St Paul's. Insignificant. Totally insignificant.

"Give me a large pink gin."

The barman looked hurt.

"I'm sorry, Jim. I'm not all right. Just been tossed out of the King's army before I got a foot in the door. Said I was too old."

"You've got to lie."

"Said I was twenty-five. Stood there like a twerp with my hat off. Whole bloody lot laughed at me. Called for three cheers for the toff."

"They meant it nicely."

"That made it worse."

Jack took his club card, signed for his drink, and looked up. Jim was openly laughing.

"Don't you start."

"Quite frankly, sir, I wasn't sure whether to laugh or cry. Why do men rush off so quickly to get themselves killed? Why does everyone suddenly in the world want to rip each other's throats?... Why on earth did you volunteer in the first place?"

"It's weird. I can't quite answer that. I was drawn to it. As if going would be important. Didn't want to be left out. I don't think it was anything to do with wanting a fight. Or being called a coward. I didn't want to be left out of the herd for the first time in my life. All that I have I owed to other people. This was my turn to do something for what I have. Maybe I just felt needed until they told me to piss off. And if anyone asks, Jim, I'll always deny I ever spoke those words in the club. Have a drink with me. There are going to be a lot of rules broken in this war. If a member comes, shove it under the bar. And give me another one of those pink gins. I'm glad you laughed. Better to laugh than cry."

WHEN HE LEFT the club he was a little drunk. It had had nothing to do with the club rules. Or the war. He needed someone to drink with. He was lonely.

The taxi, when it came, had to stop quickly as Jack lurched off the pavement into the road. It was seven o'clock in the evening. After three stiff pink gins with Jim the barman, the usual five o'clock old soaks had come into the club. By then Jack was drunk enough to greet them as old friends. In the middle stages of getting drunk, everyone was his friend.

When Fay opened the door it was the first time she had seen him drunk.

"The army wouldn't have me, Fay," he said like a small boy.

"You poor darling. Come in. Your Fay will have you. Your Fay will always have you. I'll make you some supper. We don't have to go out. I'll make us a nice fluffy omelette."

When she came back from the kitchen with the cooked omelettes he was sound asleep in the armchair. She thought of waking him and then sat down and ate both omelettes. When she went to bed much later she left him in the chair. He was too heavy to lift.

When she woke in the morning he was gone.

At lunchtime, there was a knock on the door and she flew to open it. Outside was an old man with an armful of flowers. He said he was from the local florist. And no, there was no note.

'Men,' she said to herself, 'have a strange way of apologising.' She gave the old man half a crown for his troubles, which was far too much. But an apology was an apology. The flowers flowed into three vases. When she finished her arrangements she was perfectly content. There were advantages in having an old man as a lover, she told herself. They may not make love so often but they were too old to go to war. She didn't have to worry about her Jack getting himself blown to pieces.

Not being a man to take no for an answer, Jack had got on the phone. One of his friends from school had joined the regular army and had been sent to South Africa. He had led a small unit of colonials around the bush chasing Boers for nearly two years. Wounded twice, the army had given him a Queen's South Africa Medal. At the end of the Anglo-Boer War, Jeremy Flagstaff came back to England a hero. When war broke out with Germany, the medal on his tunic stood out. When Jack's phone call caught up with him at Aldershot, he was the youngest captain in the British Army, which at thirty-four didn't say much for the peacetime army. Jack told him of his rejection, but not the three cheers for the toff.

"And I don't want a staff job. Or be a clerk in a uniform. How do I get a military training, Jeremy? I want to fight this war and not be a spectator. For once I have something important to me."

"Go back to St Paul's and apply through the CCF. They'll send you to an officer cadet training unit. I can probably wangle you a posting to Aldershot. We're the largest OCTU in the country. St Paul's will lie for you about your age. Get yourself fit, Jack. Don't walk around the park, run. Do physical exercises."

"I'm prematurely grey."

"Then dye your bloody hair. Good luck. You'll make a good officer, Jack. That much I do know. You'll feel like mincemeat at the end of the officer training course, but you'll also feel ten years younger. I probably won't be here. I'm going to France next week. I can't wait to see some action again. Peacetime soldiering is a bore."

THE HUTS WERE ROOFED with tin and had been built during the Crimean War. The heat in summer was intolerable. The parade ground at Aldershot was hard, dusty and large, the days the longest Jack had ever known. The pain was more than his worst imagination. He could have run around every park in London every day, done 'physical jokes' till his head spun. He could have been eighteen years old. Nothing, nothing, he told his tortured mind and body, could have prepared him for the three-month officer cadet training course at Aldershot barracks. They were shouted at from the moment they woke. They ran everywhere. They spent hours at a time on the parade ground, until they wheeled and turned like puppets on the sergeant major's string. They were run through gyms, vaulted over horses, sent up ropes, swung their arms from rafters and verbally abused for twenty-four hours every day, seven days a week, with Sunday's only pleasure a visit to the church for church parade where their buttons and boots shone from their own spit and polish. The worst for Jack was the four hours' sleep.

Slowly his body went from a sea of pain to something close to feeling strong. But lack of sleep was Jack's torture. Not the map-reading; machine gun drill; stripping the guns; putting them back together; firing them, running like hell in between; the lectures; the desperate need to concentrate. All Jack wanted to do as the days went on and on into one long nightmare, was sleep. Four hours a day. It was torture. His previous life, all of it, had vanished from his mind.

WHEN JACK PASSED out as an acting second lieutenant, in front of some major general he was never again to see in his life, Fay would not have recognised her lover. The eyes, dulled from good food and good wine, were alive and bright. His hair was cut so short it had not been necessary to hide his grey hairs. The pip on either shoulder denoting his new rank was the greatest achievement in his life. Out of a course of one hundred and thirty-seven men, Jack was fifteenth in the class. Most of the men were ten or more years his junior. Best of all, he had made more good friends in three months than in the previous years of his life. And his old schoolfriend Jeremy Flagstaff had been right: he felt and looked ten years younger.

On the noticeboard at the drinks party to celebrate their new commissions were their postings. All of them had been given seven days' leave. Jack had been posted to the East Surrey Regiment, somewhere in Belgium. In a week's time, he would be told exactly where he was to go.

From Aldershot, Jack took the train up to London. Instead of going home he went straight to Paddington. They had not seen each other since the night he had fallen asleep in the chair. His solicitor took care of the bills. As required by regimental standing orders, Jack was in uniform, the same shabby uniform he had worn as an officer cadet, with the rank and badge insignia changed. He was looking forward to visiting his tailor. Then he would appear in full rig, keeping his battledress for the rigours of war. He thought he deserved something for all the pain they had inflicted on his body.

Only when he rang the doorbell to Fay's small flat did he realise he had not been bored once in all the three months. Not having any time to waste, he took his mistress straight to bed. She was prettier than he had ever imagined.

"Oh, Jack, what have you been doing?" she screamed with pleasure.

THEY SPENT the whole week together, not even going out to a restaurant. Jack had his cook from Baker Street bring over the food and leave it in the kitchen, having cleaned up the mess from the previous day. They both called at his tailor for his new uniform, holding hands all the way in the taxi. Everywhere they looked men were in uniform. The Union Jacks of summer were nowhere to be seen. Once they went to a music hall at the Windmill Theatre, the day Jack walked down Savile Row in his going out uniform, his number one. In addition, he had had a monkey jacket made for the formal mess evenings, the equivalent of civilian evening dress. He looked like a new pin, brushed and scrubbed. Jack smiled at everyone to hide the turmoil building in his stomach as the week reached its conclusion. Then he was at Paddington station, full of soldiers, and saluted. The engine belched white smoke under the great canopy of the railway station and he was waving her goodbye.

FAY WENT BACK to the flat and the mess in the kitchen she would have to clean up herself. She couldn't imagine the snooty cook bringing her anything. He had gone.

Under the high double bed with the side drapes down to the floor was the old trunk from another life. It was all she had left of her family. All the things that had belonged to her mother. She pulled out the wooden trunk with the old iron hoops and studs and brought it through to the sitting room. Fay was frightened of the trunk. With the big iron key she had hidden beneath her clothes in the cupboard she turned the old lock and heard it snap open. Then she lifted up the heavy lid and looked inside, picking up some of the pieces and dropping them back into the trunk, conjuring the picture of her mother into her mind. For a long ten minutes, she knelt beside the open trunk with her eyes closed. When she opened them, her small, dark eyes were looking inwards. Her sharp almost beaked nose was thinner than usual, the nostrils dilated. Then, long and practised fingers moved inside the old trunk and took out the items of the trade. First, she wound her mother's blue scarf, almost transparent, around the top of her head and tied it at the back, a line of swirling material falling down her back. Then she put on the silk gown that fell to the floor and tied a belt around her waist. Then the pointed shoes. Long earrings for her ears. A small black patch for the height of her left cheek. Bracelets of brass and silver up her sleeves. Then the solemn blue band around her forehead.

She walked quietly through to the full-length mirror in the bedroom.

"Hello, Mother," she said softly, and not even Jack Merryweather would have recognised her voice.

Their name had not been Wheels. That had come from the wagon, and the constantly turning wheels that by the law of the land sent them round and round England, winter and summer, sunshine and snow. They were Romany. Gipsies. Not allowed to stay anywhere longer than a week.

Back in the early part of the previous century, their ancestors had travelled from central Europe to find a place that would let them live in peace. Some said they came from the plains of Asia, others that they were Russian. Others said a mix of many cultures. Whatever they were, they had been chased from pillar to post for as long as the collective memory could remember.

If anyone found out Fay was a gipsy, they would chase her out into the cold street and tell her to keep moving. She had told Jack when he found her wandering the streets around Baker Street. She was then just seventeen, alone in the world, cast out by her own people after the fight that had killed her family. She had run away to London, frightened for her life.

They had followed the circus the length and breadth of England, the gipsies keeping to themselves, their ornate wooden caravans pulled by big carthorses that were fussed over as much as the children. The circus went from county fair to county fair. There was work for tinkers, fixing the pots and pans of the rural villages, sharpening knives. And telling fortunes. Fay thought her mother's act was a way of making pennies. The gipsies were thieves and under their strange clothes was hiding all manner of vile disease. You only had to look into the eyes of a gipsy and see the dark side of life, the evil haunted spirit of the damned, unbelievers, cursed by God to wander for the unnatural span of their lives, feared by honest, God-loving folk. Even Fay as a child had learned never to look into a villager's eyes. In the winters, they camped in barren fields beneath the leafless trees, always on the move. Shunned. Always shunned.

In a family feud, they killed everyone in the other family to stop the retribution. She had run, picking up her skirt, her mother's savings clutched in her mother's purse. She thought she was going to die of the cold. She expected the farmer to throw her back into the sleet and mud. Instead, they had put her into a hot bath and a warm bed and let her sleep.

They gave her clothes, took her to the railway station, and waited to see her safely on the train to London. Someone of her people must have seen her. A week after Jack had moved her into the flat, the doorbell had rung and outside was her family trunk. No message. No person. Just the trunk. She had hauled the thing inside and shoved it under the bed. It was weeks before she relaxed. She had a friend in the world after all... The key had been pushed under the door.

Sitting alone on the carpet in the sitting room, dressed in her mother's clothes, Fay tried to look into the future, bringing the seventh sense, the one of foresight, into her mind. After half an hour she fell back on the carpet exhausted. All she had seen was mud, holes in the ground and barbed wire. And heard the noise. She also knew she was carrying Jack Merryweather's child, and the child was a girl. There were going to be two of them out on the street if Jack was killed.

# 3

# DECEMBER 1914

"*I* thought it might be you," said Robert St Clair. "Can't be many chaps with the surname of Merryweather. Make yourself at home, Jack. What a pity. Those nice new uniforms don't last long out here. We're in reserve for another three days. Then we go up. This dugout is luxury. Even has a roof. Well, we'd better have a drink. You did bring a drink? Long way from Africa. Have you heard from Harry Brigandshaw? Been here since it started. Stopped the Hun getting to Paris, then we all dug like beavers. Front line's three hundred yards from here. Rather higgledy-piggledy. Chaps jumped into shell holes at first. Then dug communication trenches. Linked us all up. Jerry did the same. Mostly we're separated by a couple of hundred yards. Lots of barbed wire, then shell holes and mud. Then the Huns' barbed wire. Funny thing about barbed wire. You can blow it to heaven but it comes down again, more tangled and twisted. I'm the longest-surviving lieutenant. The rest are dead. Jerry doesn't like officers. Sometimes we get a hate on the reserve trench. We'll be in the front line for Christmas. Now, bring out that bottle you're hiding and give me all the news. You look fit, Jack. Dirty from mud but fit. And please don't walk around with that hat on in the trenches. We always wear tin hats. Gives the men a feeling of security. Doesn't make any bloody difference really... Sallie. That was her name. Sallie Barker. Has she sent you any more wires?"

"Nice to see you, Robert, if I'm allowed a word in edgeways. Where do I put my gear?"

"Over on that duckboard."

"How's Lucinda?"

"Miserable."

"Bit of a coincidence isn't this?"

"Not really, Jack. They circulate a list of new officers and we pick and choose. Pretty random. I was an orderly officer when the list came through. They send us a list a month before the new chaps finish training."

"And if I'd failed the course?"

"You wouldn't be here, would you? Now, what have you got in your kitbag, 'officers for the use of'?"

"A bottle of brandy."

"Good. Jolly good. Let's drink it."

"All of it?"

"Of course. Nothing keeps around here. Unless Jerry puts in a push, we won't be disturbed much for three days. Our chaps usually know in advance when Jerry is going to come in force. Tell-tale signs. Big guns start blazing. Big movements behind the lines. Our chaps can see from the balloons when Jerry doesn't shoot them down. Then our chaps shoot down Jerry. Pretty much tit for tat. Jolly nice to see you."

"Do you always talk so fast?"

"Did you notice? The more I talk the less I think and you don't want to think around here. I was one of the first territorials. Joined the TA when I came back from Africa. Madge didn't want to marry and then this bloke Barend pitched up and that was it. Turns out Lucinda and I had been staying in his house for months, the one you stayed in I think. The TA unit was next to the bloody school I taught in. Snotty little kids don't like history, mark my words. There are usually four of us in a dugout. CO likes to spread his officers around a bit. I was the duty officer when the shell hit the other one. Couple of months ago. Short of officers since. Anyway, now you're here Jack, which is good. There's another bloke here tomorrow. You don't have any food in that kitbag, do you?"

"No, Robert."

"When I'm really scared shitless, which is most of the time, I think of Elephant Walk. Or Purbeck Manor. And all the food. Strangely it helps. Look, I tell you what. We'll go show ourselves to the men and then come back for a drink."

Jack followed him out of the dugout cut into the earth from the reserve trench, which traversed on both sides of them, slightly zigzagged so no one could get into the trench from the other side and shoot everyone in line. His feet sank into the mud and his greatcoat pulled along around his feet. He kept his officer's hat on his head. Robert had crammed on a tin hat with the thick band that let it rest on the cranium. The man was a wreck. High overhead he heard a whistling noise and stopped.

"Ours, old chap. Jerry's getting a hate. In ten minutes Jerry will start shelling us. How it works. Sort of tit for tat. No one getting anywhere in the mud. They say it goes right to the coast, so Jerry can't outflank us... Sometimes I hear the African lions at night but that's only when I am asleep."

The cold had reached into the marrow of his bones as Jack followed. It was getting dark, so the men all looked the same. They seemed pleased to see Robert St Clair. Jack wondered how long he was going to live. All that money and nothing to show for it. No one of his own to spend it when he was dead... Overhead the scream of shells was now continuous.


FOR ALBERT PRINGLE, six thousand miles away in the Rand Club, life could not have been better. The Union government under Louis Botha had known which side their bread was buttered and had declared war on Germany. Put down a rebellion by Bittereinders left over and revived from the Anglo-Boer War and, for all intents and purposes, added German South West Africa to the Union of South Africa, all under Boer control but British hegemony, a satisfactory diplomatic alternative to everyone trying to kill each other. Further north the South Africans were trying to kick the Germans out of Tanganyika, German East Africa; Albert thought he and his new country were doing very well, though he had to smile. Despite Sallie Barker being the brains of the company, she was not a member of the Rand Club. Women were not even allowed in the club, let alone to become members. But Albert, Jack Merryweather's gentleman's gentleman, had been proposed, sponsored, and elected all within a week. The only thing that spoke in Johannesburg was money, which was how Albert thought it should be. If anyone knew he had been a valet they said nothing. The past was the past.

Sitting with men twenty years his senior who treated him as an equal was one part of his satisfaction. The other part was keeping out of the war but doing as much business with the British War Office as possible. If other people wanted to use his explosives to kill people, that was their business. He was getting rich, and he wanted a long life to enjoy his wealth; heroes' memories lasted a very short time after they were dead. Anyway, he told himself to placate the niggling feeling he was rationalising, he was too important to the British war effort to be sent to the trenches like his brother. Walter had rushed back to England from Australia to join the same regiment he had fought with in the Anglo-Boer War. What was it about men who always wanted to fight! Now his children were fatherless and Albert was sending Walter's wife money, a woman he had never met, and never intended to meet if he could help it. What did they think life was all about? Poor Walter. His wife now suffered. Not Walter. Heroes! Bloody stupid... Then he brought his mind back to the long bar at the most exclusive club in Johannesburg and tried to put the war out of his mind. Poor Walter would never drink another glass of beer.

IT WAS the speed of the change that made Tina Pringle smile. She had turned seventeen on Guy Fawkes Night the month before. A year before that she had been helping her mother around the small house and wondering what would come of her life. Barnaby, she knew, was beyond her reach, however much fun they had had together as kids. She had left the board school at fourteen without much listening to what the teachers had to say. With a little stretch of her imagination, she said she could read and write but had never read a word since leaving school. Adding and subtracting left her flummoxed.

Barnaby had not been her first, not that he had done it in the end, which she thought was rather a shame. Once a year the fair came to Swanage. The bloke that ran the horse rides for the kids in town had been in her mind since she was ten. He had done her down behind the horsebox when she was thirteen. He was lovely. A big bloke. Everything was big. Dark too. Probably a gipsy but who cared. He was lovely, lovely. She knew she had something all the boys wanted, but she teased more than she shared. Flashing her big tits, giving 'em a smile. It was all fun. She was sexy, not pretty, and that was going to be her ticket into the real world. But like most of her bright ideas, nothing had come of it until Albert came home, brother Fred caught them in the act, and Albert bought her ticket to Africa on a big boat.

She and Albert told everyone she was nineteen. The old housekeeper had been given the sack, poor dear, and Tina was running the house with eleven servants. The house in Parktown on the ridge looked out to the distant bush and had been bought for a song by Albert when the mine owners ran out of gold. She, Tina Pringle, was mistress of the great house, and if one thing was clear, she was not going back to England. In her new clothes and hair dressed in the fashion, young Barnaby was the last thing on her mind. She was going to make something of herself and marry a rich man. Tantalising sex appeal and youth were all she had but in a mining town with little competition, it was enough. No one questioned her Dorset brogue or asked her to spout off about politics or the war. The men had their eyes fixed on her bosom, not her brain. In a crowd of newly rich, the English language was mangled more often than not. She was at home. Powerful. In possession of something all of them wanted.

When Albert came back from the Rand Club, there were already six men paying court to his sister and it made him bloody laugh. With Tina running his new house, Albert was suddenly the most popular man in town. As he walked into the room to greet his guests, the German artillery found the range of the British reserve trench, and Jack Merryweather, without any control, voided his bowels.

THE COMBINATION of Tina Pringle and free drinks was irresistible. Within three minutes of Albert being home, the doorbell rang from the marble hall and a young man strode into the sitting room. Albert had never set eyes on him before. Within thirty seconds he had a drink in his hand and a position to the left of Tina. This stranger had poured his own drink with familiar ease. Before Albert could find his wits the same doorbell rang again. A man of about fifty strode into the room and poured himself a drink. The man had just joined the crowd around Tina when it happened again. Mostly Albert was in his office or the club at sundowner time. Drinking alone, he found himself an outcast in his own home. The man of fifty, having had a good look down the front of Tina's dress pulled away from the crowd.

"Your first time?" he asked Albert.

"In a way, I suppose it is... Who are you, if I may ask?"

"Lightfoot. Benny Lightfoot. I'm an American. And who are you? Do you know anyone here?"

"Just Tina."

"That's right. We all are here to visit with Tina."

"Isn't she a bit young for you?"

"Who cares?... Excuse me. That's a friend of mine just come in... You want me to fill your glass? That first one hit the spot."

Albert was not sure whether to laugh or throw the man out on his neck. He chose to laugh. His sister was having a good time. Maybe one of the men in the room was rich. He liked the idea of a rich brother-in-law. Booze was cheap, so the money did not bother him. Working on the principle that if you can't beat them, join them, Albert refilled his drink, took a swig, and joined the circle clustered around his sister. She was as cool as a cucumber. The clothes he had bought made her look the nineteen she said she was.

Albert doubted if their mother and father would recognise the youngest of their children.

"Oh, it's Albert. Home early, love. Some of my friends come to visit. Everyone say a big hello to Albert. He is my brother. He's the one what owns this 'ouse. Say cheers! It's 'is booze too. He is a bloody darlin', isn't he? Cheers, Albert."

Only the fifty-year-old had the decency to look embarrassed. Then the one-way conversation picked up and everyone turned their attention back to Tina. Albert was again left on his own. The fifty-year-old put his glass down on the grand piano and slunk out into the hall. Albert heard the front door open and close. They knew their way out as well as in. The price of being rich, he tried to tell himself. If there was one thing he had found out in life, the moment a man had money, everyone was trying to get it off him. And rich men were popular so long as they stayed rich. On that note he was confident. As fast as Serendipity Mining and Explosives made artillery shells, they were being blown to pieces in France. The ammunition trucks left his factory for Durban every day. Then the Royal Navy escorted them all the way to France. Only one of the ammunition ships had been sunk by German torpedoes before it arrived. The explosion had sunk a Royal Navy frigate riding alongside. They were working three shifts at the factory. What was the cost of a few bottles of Scotch, he asked himself? Without being noticed, he went outside through the small doors onto the long veranda that looked down from Parktown Ridge. What the hell! Tina was enjoying herself. Maybe even some of the men in the room were going to join the war. By the time the sun began to sink into the African bush, Albert was halfway to being drunk. And it was a Friday. When he went back into the room to refill his glass and join the trivial conversation surrounding his sister, there was another woman standing halfway into the room. She was enormous. Fatter than anyone Albert had seen. The chin was completely lost in the rolls of fat around her face. Even her feet were swollen in her shoes.

The apparition saw him, broke into a broad smile and waddled towards him across the big room.

"Darling. How wonderful to see you. Give your Lily a big hug."

THE CRUISE for Lily White had been a disaster. She had booked and paid to go around the world first class. It took just one day to know she had made a mistake, even with the fancy clothes she had bought in Cape Town to help disguise who she was. The accent she had tried to cultivate so hard let her down with a thud. The looks that had kept the men on her side for so long were gone. The bosom that Jack Merryweather had liked to wallow in was all of a piece. Chin. Stomach. Bosom. All the same thing. So she ate. Morning, noon and night. For three months she ate. Helping after helping. Breakfast. Lunch. Tea. Supper. She waddled up from her cabin four times a day. By the time the ship brought her back to Cape Town, she had doubled her weight. Largely, for the whole journey, no one had spoken to her. She was the largest invisible being on board ship. The worst thing was that when she thought through her problem, she knew any alternative would not be any better. She had had her life. Not even one man tried to get to know her money. She was just too fat to even get a peck on the cheek.

At the end of the voyage, she had sat around in Cape Town doing nothing other than eating. Sometimes she read the papers. She even watched the share price of Serendipity. At the end of her tether, and fearing for her life, she had finally taken the train to Johannesburg. Even walking ten yards was a strain on her heart.

THE FIRST WORD that came to Albert Pringle's mind was 'Shit!' Instead, he put on a big smile and tried unsuccessfully to give Lily a hug. She had obviously run out of money in a year and had come begging. Sallie once again had been right. The trust for Lily set up in 1913 for just this eventuality would solve their problem. Lily would always have an income and not be dependent on their charity. They would be rid of her.

"How did you find out my address?" he asked having floundered in the fat.

"From the prospectus," smiled Lily, feeling better for the first time in months.

"What prospectus?" said Albert, with a sinking feeling in his stomach.

"Serendipity Mining and Explosives. I put my money from the Mansion House into your company. I still have all the shares."

"We didn't see your name as a shareholder. How many shares do you have?"

"Ten thousand. One per cent of your equity. I put it through with my bank as nominee."

"Jack Merryweather did the same thing but we found out the real owner of the shares. Anything one per cent or over we wanted to know who we were dealing with. Our chaps in London were very good."

"My real name's Lily Ramsbottom. Now you recognise my shareholding. Give us a drink, love. A stiff one! I really need a drink! Nice house. Nice view."

"Of course. Of course. What would you like? Well, I should know. Scotch. Yes. A Scotch."

"Don't look so bloody relieved, Albert. Sallie was right to put my money from the sale of the Mansion House in a trust. She may have been a damn good bookkeeper stopping others stealing my money. But she weren't a patch on Lil. I had to put up a cheque for twenty thousand pounds to get my shares remember. How do you think I got that? From the whorehouse! Just in case, so to speak. Don't look so aggrieved. You did all right. Blimey, anyone would think I was a thief. Sallie could stop the others stealing but not me, see." Then she began to laugh, making the fat roll around her body. "I may be big but I'm not stupid. Whatever you two thought."

"Where are you staying, Lil?"

"Right here. My bags are in the hall. The trunk's at the station. Who's the centre of attention? Now that one would have made us money."

"She's my sister, Lil."

"Sorry, Albert. It's just me. Always had a good eye for a whore. Which reminds me. Where's Sallie?"

"At home. We work together but don't live together."

"Sounds like you don't like that, Bert my boy. She is class, our Sallie. Man who marries her will be real lucky."

'I know,' thought Albert and went off to pour Lily a Scotch. "There's no pleasure without pain," he said quietly. Poor Lil.


BEING MORE SHREWD THAN CLEVER, Tina had watched the altercation and read the picture right. The madam had come back into their lives. She got up and walked away from her entourage. She never listened to what they said anyway. She just liked being the centre of attention. The crowd of men fluttered and followed in her wake.

"My guess is you's Lily White. I'm Tina. Bert's sister. The men can introduce themselves. I'm no good at names. Now, why don't you and I go out on the veranda for a natter? You are staying with us? Good. There are more bedrooms in this house than the whole of Corfe Castle, the bloody village, not the bloody ruins."

Lily looked back, checked the line of vision from where Tina had been sitting to the hallway. Then she smiled. The girl had seen the bags. She was good. Better to join a potential enemy at the start.

Left on their own, within a minute, all the men were talking about the war.

. . .

SALLIE BARKER PUT the telephone back on the hook feeling sad. Friends, like husbands and wives, so often outgrew each other. One went ahead, one went behind. Poor Lily. What were they going to do with her? They were the last of her friends, she was sure of that. By the sound of it, no one had thought it worth their while to take her for a ride for her money. The idea of Lily White now transformed back into Lily Ramsbottom and twice the size she had been at the start of her world cruise was frightening. Could a body sustain so much fat and not break in the middle? The woman was still rich but even that did not seem to have helped. And having once been able to flick a finger and any man would have come running! Did the woman have herself to blame? Or had life left her in the lurch with only food for comfort? And then Sallie remembered again being taken in by this woman when she herself had been at the end of her tether. Sometimes owing friendship was the most expensive debt in life.

The house was run by a manservant and his wife. The man, that others in Europe would call a butler, gave her the power to eject any man who thought they could take advantage of a woman who lived on her own. Bill Hardcastle had been a boxer. His nose was fat and flat on his face and the hands that so delicately opened her front door were the size of hams. She paid him handsomely and he looked after her well. A bodyguard would have been a better description of his job. Molly, his wife, was the cook. The rest of the servants were black. When she went out at night, Bill drove the Bentley that Sallie had bought soon after the outbreak of war. The car was her only toy, her only extravagance other than the house. Both were designed to tell the male world she was rich in own right, the house and car visible signs of success. They were the solid face of wealth that every business needed as a façade. People liked doing business with the rich. They felt financially comfortable with the rich. It was all a lot of show-off nonsense so far as Sallie could see but she knew it was essential if they were to continue to succeed. And the car, yes, it did give her a nice feeling.

"Mr Hardcastle! We're going out. There's a crisis at the Pringle household. Put the roof down on the car. I wish the rains would break. It's so stuffy."

The reality was far worse than the phone call. Lily was obese. Hard to look at as human. A freak that spoke from a mound of flesh, blotched red skin, eyes sinking into oblivion, arms the size of a big man's thighs, hair listless. And when she sat down she took up most of the sofa.

"How are you, Lily?"

The good-looking woman, Jack Merryweather's mistress, who had taken her into the Strand Street house when she was desperate, did not reply.

Sallie's attempt to kiss Lily on the cheek had been thwarted by the woman's belly. Lily had flopped back on the sofa and both Sallie and Albert wondered how she was going to get up again. Sallie was glad Bill Hardcastle was sitting in the car outside. The eyes, half submerged in the flesh, began to ooze tears. Tina had gone off with some of the men for dinner at the Grand Hotel. They were alone, the three of them who together had made the first fortune from a whorehouse. There was no longer any point in pretending. Sallie found the tears flowing down her own face. Unless something was done quickly, Lily was better off dead. There was only one way to save the woman crying silently on the sofa, Sallie told herself. Love and care. Lots of love and lots of care.

She walked across the room through the hall and called up Bill Hardcastle.

"This time it's my turn," she said going back to Lily. "You're going home with me... This is Bill Hardcastle. He'll help you into the car. It's food, Lily. We are going to stop the food. None of the Boers who came out of the British concentration camps at the end of the Anglo-Boer War was fat. You're going on a diet after I've spoken to a doctor."

"You're a true friend, Sal."

"Will you do what I tell you?"

"I'll try."

The sofa lurched back as they brought Lily to her feet. Bill Hardcastle had her firmly under the left elbow.

Lily had stopped crying. With Bill on her left and Albert on her right, with Sallie coming up behind, she hoped no one had seen the small sign of triumph in her eyes. People, she thought with satisfaction, were so easy to manipulate. If she had been an actress they would have made her a star. And losing some of the weight was not such a bad idea anyway. She was going to enjoy herself being looked after. She hated being alone. She would persuade the trustees so carefully put together by Sallie to sell the safe investments. She would buy as many of Serendipity shares as possible. She would tell them it was her way of reciprocating, of showing her faith in their ability. Then she would ask for a seat on the board of directors. Everything was going to be all right.

By the time Lily was fitted into the open tourer, she was thoroughly enjoying herself. She wondered if the doctor would have some pills to stop her feeling hungry. Then she went to sleep, with the cool breeze playing on her face.

· · ·

THE SUITCASES WERE STRAPPED to the back of the car on the rack. Over in the bush, it was thundering. Fork lightning cut the warm air as far away as the eye could see. It began to rain big drops as Bill Hardcastle drove up Sallie's driveway.

By the time they pulled and pushed her out of the car, Lily had the tears oozing down her face. There was no doubt in the mind: she should have been an actress. Within a week she would have them all at her beck and call. Far better than first class on a boat with a shipload of snobs. Far better than the hotel in Cape Town that was only interested in her paying her bill. As she waddled into her new home she thanked her lucky stars. When Sallie Barker had pitched up on the doorstep after Herr Flugelhorne had done his deed, Lily had taken her in as a future asset for the whorehouse. Not the financial manager she had so successfully become but as a whore. The girl would have made them a fortune.

"You are so sweet to me," she said, squeezing out the last of her crocodile tears. "I don't know what I'd have done without you. Just get your man to show me my bedroom and Lily will get some nice sleep."

"Won't you have some food first? A drink maybe?"

"Maybe just a little whisky."

"Bill, give us both a whisky and soda."

"Do you call your man by his first name?" she said sharply.

"It may not be done in England. But here with the Africans all around it is different. Anyway, Bill and his wife Molly are more my friends. I don't know what I would do without them. Mostly I work fourteen hours a day."

"I see," said Lily, making it quite clear she did not see at all.

Bill Hardcastle would have preferred to put rat poison in her drink than whisky. When he finally got to bed having half carried a drunk fat woman to her room he took hold of his wife's hand.

"We just brought a big, big problem into the house."

"I saw you arrive. Watching through the window. Who is she?"

"God knows."

"When is she going?"

"Only when she is kicked out. Sallie owes her for something."

"Then she'll have to pay. You can't get and not give. Even if the giving is rather more than you got. God works in mysterious ways. Nothing comes free. The more you 'ave, the more you pay. Now go to sleep, Bill Hardcastle. The bitch won't get the better of your Molly. You mark my words."

TWO DOORS DOWN THE CORRIDOR, Lily White was drifting into sleep with a smile on her face. She was home and who would have thought it. She'd never have to lift a finger. She let out a giggling laugh and turned her face into the pillow. To hell with men keeping her. This was better.

TINA PRINGLE RETURNED home to Parktown Ridge soon after Lily fell asleep. It was late, and the man she was with let her out of the car and drove off. Albert was waiting up for her.

"Do you know what time it is?" he shouted at her after he answered a knock at the front door. "And who was that?"

"It's one o'clock and I don't know 'is name. Butch, or something. Who cares? Give us a drink, luv."

"You know, you've only just turned seventeen."

"I had my first fuck when I was thirteen. And 'e was lovely. Stop trying to be a dad. You's my brother. And the sooner you fuck that Sallie Barker the better for both of you. What 'appened to the whale?"

"Sallie took her home."

"Poor Sallie... That one's trouble."

"She started the first business for us."

"You sold it, didn't you? All got paid out according. You don't owe that fat old fart a farthing... Don't stand there like that, Albert Pringle. Get me a drink. I've something to tell you. Benny Lightfoot is taking me on a safari."

"The American?"

"Could be."

"He's fifty, for Christ's sake."

"Don't use the Lord's name in vain, brother Albert."

"He slunk off when he found out I was your brother. The bloody man was swiping my drinks like he owned the place."

"He's rich. Very rich. And divorced. Blimey, if he kicks the bucket early on in the piece, I'll be rich and single."

"How do you think he's going to marry you?"

"I 'ave my ways. Besides, he's besotted."

"I'm going to send you back to England."

"Don't be daft. Poor old Barnaby. Wouldn't touch him with a bargepole. Benny's rich. Barnaby's the last of the litter and old Lord St Clair as poor as a church mouse. Bugger his title. It's money what counts. Anyway, there's a war on over there... You going to 'ave a drink with me, Albert darlin'?"

"You're the bloody end."

"I know. But it's nice."

"Where are you going on safari?"

"Rhodesia. That's north of the Limpopo River."

"I know where it is. Met a bloke on the first boat we came out on. Farms in Rhodesia. Think his father was a white hunter."

"What's a white hunter?"

"The same as a black hunter. But he's got a white skin."

"You are daft. What's this bloke's name? Is 'e nice? Maybe we'll pay him a visit."

"Harry Brigandshaw was up at Oxford with Robert St Clair."

"Then we're almost relations... Is 'e rich?"

"Family controls Colonial Shipping among other things. They own the ship we came out on. They are a very big shipping company."

"Then I will pay him a visit won't I? And about Robert's age, you say. Is he good-looking?"

"All the girls thought so but he didn't take up with anyone on the boat."

"Then he's fussy. Good. Waiting for Tina."

"What about Benny Lightfoot?" said Albert sarcastically.

"What about 'im? We women use men, Albert. Or they do when they look like me. Ruled by their cocks they are. Never use their brains. That was a nice drop of Scotch, Bert. Now I'm going to bed. It's been a bloody hard day."

"Looked like it. Night, Tina. Sleep well. Don't let the bedbugs bite... Just keep your own head screwed on right... When did he ask you to go to Rhodesia?"

"Over dinner."

"But he left before you."

"Oh, Albert. You should know by now. I always end up with the one with the most money."

"And who was Butch?"

"One of his flunkies."


In Flanders, the shelling stopped an hour before dawn. The Pringles, Sallie Barker and Jack Merryweather's former mistress were still asleep in their beds. Jack had changed his trousers and cleaned himself with the muddy water in the trench, vowing never again to let his bowels get the better of him. They waited fifteen minutes before the order came to stand to alert on the fire-steps of the reserve trench. Twice before Robert explained to him, Jerry had given them a break and then plastered them when they were standing out of the dugouts waiting to repel an attack. Robert had made no mention of the fouled trousers. With the rain drizzling into the mud and the light showing Jack the mangled devastation, the German attack began on the front line up ahead. Vickers machine guns, perfectly enfiladed, fired without stopping.

"Poor bloody Jerry isn't going to see this Christmas," said Robert. "Surely nothing can live under that crossfire."

"Then why do they do it?"

"Some have made it personal and want their own back. Some are scared of being cowards. Some are more frightened of being shot for running away. Others want to die quickly. Most just do what they're bloody told to do." They stood in the line of men along the trench for another half an hour... "The German attack is faltering. The British Army won't need us to fight today."

"Why do you fight, Robert?" asked Jack.

"Don't even ask such a stupid bloody question. I'm here, am I not? Isn't that enough? What else can they want? Whenever England has gone to war the St Clairs have answered the call. Habit. Force of habit. Self-preservation. Keeping what little is mine. How would you like Fritz ordering you around in your own country? After a while you accept growing old is not all it's cracked up to be. We're here because someone told someone to tell the man that told you to do your duty. We're old men in this war. The kids are easier. They do what they are doing without question. Come on. It's over. We'll have one tot of what's left of your brandy and try and get some sleep. That bugle was the stand-down, if they didn't teach you that at OCTU. The duckboards are out of the water for the moment. Most nights we sleep in the mud and water. The strangest thing of all is you get used to it. Even the noise."

"I wonder if their souls went to heaven?"

"Whose?"

"The dead Germans. The ones just killed. Our men from the shelling."

Without replying Robert pushed open the heavy blankets, wet and dirty grey, that hung over the entrance to the dugout. The fact that both sides prayed to the same God was a great puzzle to him. Victory for one side was death for the other. And both sides thought God was on their side. Both sides thought they were in the right.

"I don't know," Robert answered at last. "At first I thought so. Now not so sure. Damn. My mug fell in the mud. Must have kicked it over when Jerry started his hate."

FURTHER TO THE NORTHWEST, on the other side of Mons, Captain Merlin St

Clair, in command of B Company, Dorset Fusiliers, was inspecting the five machine guns that fell under his command. Not one had jammed in the German attack. The barrels of the guns were still too hot to touch. The only point he could see on the positive side of the slaughter, with Germans tangled in the wire and spread in the mud all the way back to the German front line, was his own preservation and that of his men, coupled with the steady rise in the value of his Vickers-Armstrong stocks that he had bought before the war and were now worth ten times what he had paid for them. If he could survive the war he would be a rich man. Merlin was a realist. Promoted to captain after three months in Flanders, he was the only one left of his intake. He thought the chances of survival were minimal. But there was always a chance. There always had to be a chance or no one would go on at anything.

Neither Robert nor Merlin had any idea they were fighting within ten miles of each other. After three months Merlin had learnt not to think of anything other than the present moment. Lighting a cigarette well below the line of the parapet, he walked on down the trench to the next gun. Even though his gunners were good, he always got behind each gun to check exactly their line of fire. If he was going to survive his piece of the war, he was not going to take any chances. In many ways, it was part of his superstition. If he sat behind every gun before and after battle they would enfilade where they were meant to, and the mechanism wouldn't jam. The men relied on him. They were part of his superstition. They liked the comfort of the captain with his arse in the mud, sighting the guns. All of them knew it would make no difference to an incoming German shell, but it gave them something to hold onto. The fact they knew his first name was Merlin added to the men's superstition. If the Germans killed the captain they were all dead. If Merlin the magician survived the war, they would all go home with him. The ritual to the men was as essential as food.

THE EAST SURREY REGIMENT moved up the communication trenches to the front line on Christmas Eve. For Jack Merryweather, the comfort of his home in Baker Street might as well have been on the other side of the moon. Allocated to his platoon on the second day of action, he had not since spoken to Robert St Clair except in passing. Negative thoughts expressed in earshot of the men were tantamount to treason. Officers set an example. They never grumbled. They never questioned an order. They kept to themselves until they were needed. Fraternising with soldiers was the quickest way to destroy an army, or so a pompous brigadier had told them during Jack's course at Aldershot. What it all meant in the din of battle he was not sure. All he could do was keep his platoon as comfortable as possible in appalling conditions and hope he did not shit his pants in front of them the first time he led them over the top.

In the days since arriving in the reserve trench, they had been shelling every day and every day British shells whistled overhead searching for the German trenches. With the tangled wire and mud between them, the two sides could not get at each other's throats. It was an impasse. The Germans could not get to the coast or Paris and the Allies could not push them back into Prussia. As Jack dropped into the front-line trench for the first time he was convinced the war would go on forever.

During the night it was bitterly cold, the air gripped by the black frost which froze the mud. Men stamped all night, too cold to sleep wrapped in their greatcoats. At midnight, Jack wished the soldiers on either side of him a merry Christmas. He could not see them in the dark, only hear their stamping feet on the duckboards, now frozen to the mud and grisly remains of dead men blown to pieces in an earlier hate. Disembodied voices wished him back a merry Christmas. Then the colonel walked the trench, wishing everyone a merry Christmas, giving each man a small parcel with the compliments of the King. Next to the colonel, his adjutant's sergeant carried a sack of the parcels. Inside each parcel was a tin of biscuits with the faces of the King and Queen on the lid.

Since midnight, no one had heard a shot fired from the German trenches. The British guns were silent. The bitterly cold night gripped friend and foe, separated by less than two hundred yards of no man's land. Very lights went up from both sides to make sure nothing was really happening. All through the night Jack stamped his feet and flapped his arms over his chest, making no impression with all the clothes he was wearing. The silence of the night was worse than the noise. A premonition of death. No one spoke. Just the occasional flare fired high into the dark cold night, cloudless in parts, stars visible through holes in heaven. Leaning against the back wall of the trench, Jack found himself dreaming, asleep on his feet. When he woke there was daylight enough to see the soldiers on either side of him. Robert St Clair was shaking his shoulder and smiling at him, the smile just visible in the dawn.

"Merry Christmas, Jack."

"Same to you, Robert. Must have dozed off. Why's it so quiet still?"

"It's Christmas. We are all Christians in this fight. Maybe God is working for both sides at the same time on Jesus's birthday."

They both heard someone down the trench yell 'Happy Christmas,

Fritz', at the top of his voice. From the other side, a German boy shouted 'Happy Christmas, Tommy'. Then everyone was shouting back and forth, and men began to climb out of the trenches without their rifles.

"What the hell do we do?" whispered Robert.

"Let's have a look."

Jack climbed up the fire-step and looked out into the dawn. Germans were climbing up over the trenches. Some had met the British soldiers in the middle and were exchanging cigarettes and food. Some of the biscuit tins went across to the German side. Someone threw out a football and it bounced on the frozen surface. Below the fire-step, Robert pulled at the bottom of Jack's greatcoat.

"What are they doing?" he asked.

"At the moment, some of them are playing football. If someone doesn't do something quickly, this war is over."

"Are there any officers out there?"

"None I can see."

Robert got up on the fire-step to see for himself. "Both sides will shoot their men as deserters if we don't get them back in the trenches," he said.

"What a pity."

Down the trenches officers were shouting to their men to get back. Some, so used to orders, obeyed. They watched the football disappear into a shell hole.

By lunchtime, the Germans and British were back to killing each other, both engaged in intensive shellfire. God had deserted them all.

# BOOK 4 – BATTLEFIELDS OF LUST AND WAR

# 1

## JULY 1915

*B*enny Lightfoot was forty-nine years old and at his own best guess worth half a million pounds sterling, which was more than he could ever spend in the rest of his life. Putting together the elaborate safari to the banks of the great Zambezi River had only one real purpose: the slow, delicious seduction of Tina Pringle. Pushing fifty, he found the thing that made his hormones rise to the surface was a very young but provocative girl, full of wet juice and excitement for life. Leading such a lady astray was the only thing left in his life that kept his attention. And she really was as sexy as anything he had seen in the past years of his nefarious life.

Born in Missouri, some fifty miles from the strict rules of Kansas City, he had drifted away from the family corn farm to put some excitement into his young life. Watching corn grow and ripen year after year was as exciting as going to Sunday church, even when old Reverend Green was screaming at his congregation to give up their sinful ways and go to the Lord. Looking around the Episcopalian church, bare of any colour, the young Benny wondered more and more about those sinful ways. Finally, looking at the reverend's congregation, all as dry as a bone, old and young, Benny concluded the sinful ways had to be going on someplace else. The people surrounding the farm had all been dredged clean, though Benny thought it unlikely there was any dirt in them in the first place. The more times the preacher brought up sinful ways, the more Benny wanted some of it. At sixteen he went looking. He could read and write. Had read the Bible cover to cover, both Testaments. His mother had said he was wild and would come

259

to nothing. Though he wrote to her for some years, he never once received a reply. Drifting off to Australia after sampling the simple ways of large parts of California, he made his first real money from the brief flurry of gold at Ballarat. From Australia, he took a boat and ox wagon to Kimberley in South Africa and a whole new set of sinful ways.

With some capital and the experience in the forests around Ballarat, cheating good men out of gold claims in the big hole was easy. There was nothing simpler, separating a good man from his money, than by introducing him to sinful ways. By the time he moved to the goldfields of the Witwatersrand in 1885, he owed a great deal to the Reverend Green, more than the reverend could ever have imagined.

Soon after his arrival, Doctor Jameson led the bizarre raid of Rhodesians to free Johannesburg of Boer rule, particularly that of Paul Kruger, which ended in fiasco and surrender. Benny's timing could not have been better. The British were out of favour in the Boer Republic of Transvaal, and Benny, an American, filled the gap; hadn't they both had trouble with the British? With Cecil Rhodes, who had organised the raid, keeping a low profile for fear of losing his royal charter in Rhodesia, the pickings were many for a man with capital. By the time the Anglo-Boer War came and went, Benny was a rand baron. Strangely, he had never visited the Mansion House, so he would not have recognised Albert Pringle. Benny liked seducing women, not paying for them. The chase, he found, was far more exciting than the climax, a fulfilment was brief and only sometimes satisfactory. He never stayed with anyone for very long. They were all the same when it came to the end, which he found a pity. He had once said, rather drunk, that he had never been in love; that life would be a lot better if a man could fall in love once and for all and be done with it. The man he told was an employee who reminded him the next day. The man was fired.

Soon after the end of the Anglo-Boer War, Benny went home. Nothing had changed. His mother laid an extra place for supper as if he had never been away. Two of his brothers were running the farm. His father had finally died from overwork. There were sisters-in-law and children he had never seen before all over the place. Not one of them asked what he'd been doing. The corn was ripening and both sisters-in-law were pregnant. Everyone kept their heads down and worked. On Sunday they scrubbed up and went to church, leaving the corn ripening behind them. To Benny's amazement, the same old Reverend Green was still after their sinful ways. He too asked nothing about where Benny had been. The man had given him one queer look and probably didn't want to know. The next day he left home without saying goodbye. A week later he doubted if any of them would have remembered his visit. Maybe they could smell the stench of sin all over him. Looking back, he just hoped they were happy. He wondered if the reverend would work out who had left the envelope on the silver tray with ten gold Krugers inside. But then God, as the reverend had so often told them, worked in mysterious ways. Soon after getting back to Johannesburg as fast as possible, he made an anonymous endowment to the church. He owed the Reverend Green that much for his good advice. If he had done the same for his mother she would have thrown the money in his face. And that was the last time he found them running through his mind.

When a man has more money than he can spend and is not a fool, he grows rich and then very rich, very quickly. He had made a will as dying intestate was a messy thing. The money was to be divided between all his living relatives, which would keep the Missouri and Kansas lawyers busy for a while, unless he married, then the money would only go to them when his wife died. Unless they had a child. He had visions of his poor relations scratching out each other's eyes one way or another. There was nothing like adding a little greed to the pot of life. He wondered then what would come of all their sinful ways.

There was a white hunter he had picked up in a bar who said he knew how to kill an elephant. It was one of Benny's quirks to go into strange bars and get drunk with strangers. He could say what he liked without repercussions. The mining camp that was Johannesburg suited him. The next day the man still said he could kill an elephant when he was sober. The barman had told him which flophouse to look for the man. The man had the most plummy accent Benny had ever heard in his life; the British to Benny were something of an enigma: they had as many accents as towns on their island. The 'plummy accent' was down on his luck and the twice-yearly remittance cheque was not due from England for another three months.

"You're a black sheep?"

"Oh yes, old boy. Black as they come. Pater said I'd never come to any good. Trouble is, when the money comes in it gets blown rather quickly. Lots of friends. That kind of thing. When the money's gone so are the friends. That sort of thing."

"How long have you spent in the bush?"

"On and off? Eight or nine years. When you get in the bush you can't spend money. No friends. That sort of thing."

"Would you like a job?"

"No thank you. I've never had one."

"Putting together a safari. I want to go to the banks of the Zambezi."

"That's different. That's fun."

"Could you get me there with a party of friends?"

"Piece of cake. Train to Salisbury. Hire a wagon or two. Horses. I still have my guns. Purdeys. Never sell 'em, however broke. You can live off a gun in the bush. When are you going?"

"Next week."

"Oh good. What's your name?"

"Benny Lightfoot."

"You're an American aren't you?"

"Does that make any difference?"

"I suppose not. My name's Wally Bowes-Leggatt. My father's the Earl of Fenthurst."

"I thought he might be... Why aren't you in the war?"

"They wouldn't have me. Or they would if they caught me. I'd go to jail, not the trenches. Wouldn't mind the trenches. Can't stand the idea of jail."

"What happened?"

"I killed my wife. I was trying to shoot the rotter on top of her. Drunk of course, or I'd never have missed. Shot at Bisley for the old school. Damn good shot, if I have to say so myself. Father said it was the only thing I could do straight. The Mater and Pater don't really like me; they shipped me out of the country as quickly as possible. Do you think I could slip back into England and join the army as a private?"

"You'd have to change your accent."

"Oh! Why is that?"

Benny had shaken his head, packed the man's gear into his car and taken him home.

"Would you mind awfully if I had a haircut on the way to your place?"

"If it makes you more comfortable?"

"Oh, it would."

If asked, Benny thought the man would not know how to spell the word sarcasm.


GETTING AWAY from Johannesburg and the daily newspaper with the endless list of casualties from the Western Front assuaged some of Benny Lightfoot's guilt. In the end, America would have to go into the war. Though too old himself, he felt the looks of the British, who thought the Americans were shirking their responsibilities. It seemed in life, however you looked at it, you had to take sides.

He thought Albert Pringle was seeing his sister onto the train and then getting off. Benny's driver had been sent back from the house in Parktown

Ridge with a note from Tina saying she would meet him at the railway station in good time for the train to Bulawayo, where they were to change trains to Salisbury.

"Oh, I've got a ticket, Mr Lightfoot," smiled Albert. He had not had a holiday in his life, boat trips not included, and rich old men he trusted not a bit. Especially with Tina who was as naïve as she was pretty. Unless he helped, she would end up like all sexy young girls who went through the mill. He only had to look at Lily White, who was still living with Sallie after six months, and not a pound the lighter. Tina was going to turn out differently. The last thing he had expected was a chinless wonder in a safari suit, wearing a pith hat that would have better suited David Livingstone. It took all Albert's concentration not to laugh when he was told by Benny Lightfoot with a straight face that this was their white hunter who was going to show them the bush. The thought of Harry Brigandshaw's address in his pocket was comforting, even if he had only met the man briefly at Cape Town railway station as Jack Merryweather's gentleman's gentleman. He wanted to ask the man with the two sets of leather-cased guns why he wasn't shooting Germans. The man was no more than thirty. They briefly locked eyes and those looking across the five feet of the railway carriage were mockingly simple: 'don't be a hypocrite'.

"We're going to have a nice holiday," said Wally Bowes-Leggatt, "which is more than can be said for a lot of other people."

The war was everywhere.

Benny, smiling to himself at the confrontation of the two Englishmen, turned his attention to Tina and the long, slow delicious seduction that lay ahead, however many brothers she brought on the journey. For Benny, the seduction of a woman started right at the beginning, when he rang the girl's doorbell to take her out. In this case, from the moment the heavy train door clunked shut. The steam engines back and front puffed violently, slowly at first, then the train lurched and they were off, headed for the north and the African bush. Tina was just as sexually provocative as he remembered. Benny was relieved that after all the effort, his hormones were still screaming with delight. Even the brother on board just made the game a little more difficult but, he hoped, more satisfying in the end, like a handicap at a steeplechase. Benny looked first at Tina's open cleavage and then at her large brown bedroom eyes. The point of Tina's tongue came out and slowly went back in again.

For Benny, one of the advantages of being rich was the ability to find out the truth about anybody. A drunk who said he shot his wife, told you his name and the name of his father, had to be telling a lie. Self-preservation alone would keep a sane man's mouth shut in the case of killing his wife. He might have got away from the gallows if the rotter was really screwing his wife, but then he thought the British might just hang him by his neck. Only the French knew properly about crimes of passion. The French would have given the husband a medal and hanged the rotter. Benny always thought the French had a point.

Like all drunks in bars, Wally finally believed his story and cried real tears when he told the story of the death of Poo. From Benny's experience, there was always some truth to the stories of drunks, they were mainly embellished to make the story last longer and sound a lot better. It was part of the bar trade, swapping stories. Part of the entertainment. Mostly, the other drunk who was meant to be listening to the story was thinking of something he could cap it with from his own life. Harmless fun, and in the morning neither of them would remember a thing... It all passed the time for a man like Wally with money, even if it was spasmodic, and nothing to do when he ran short, drunks were always good at getting free drinks if they told a good story.

There were two books in the Johannesburg library listing the British peerage, and both quoted Walter Bowes-Leggatt as a third son of the First Earl of Fenthurst, who had fought and won an obscure colonial war for the British in China, parallel with Chinese Gordon who had subsequently perished at Khartoum, a victim of the Mahdi's holy war. General Bowes-Leggatt had stayed away from the Sudan after the Boxer rebellion and gone into politics. According to Benny's investigator, the general had been such a pain in the arse of the Tory party, they had made him an earl and kicked him up into the House of Lords, where he could talk hot air with impunity. The man had first been offered a barony but had turned it down. Benny thought, reading his man's report, that the general was quite well aware of how much pain he was causing in the arse of the Tory party. No money went with the earldom, only a parliamentary vote that increased the general's pension. There was, however, a big estate in Surrey, so the family must have had money. Finding out about Wally the black sheep after that was simple.

There was a rotter, and there was a Poo, though her real name was Prudence. Prudence was probably very much alive, though the rotter was equally likely dead in the trenches. By the time Benny made his enquiries the regular British Army had been decimated in France and Flanders. At the time Prudence ran off with the army subaltern, she had been married to Wally six months. It was a scandal and Wally was shipped out to the colonies. Reading between the lines of the press reports, Benny's sleuth thought the subaltern was definitely dead. Annoying a powerful general in peacetime had been one thing. The man was a rotter and the army had ways of dealing with rotters. Especially in wartime. And Wally was best kept out in the colonies.

The rest of the story Benny had found out on his own, trawling the bars frequented by Wally. Wally, happy in the comfort of preparing for the big safari, easily told Benny the names of his old haunts. Even the names of some of the drunks he drank with. Two of the drunks had known Wally up north in the bush. Both separately said Wally was a braggart and a teller of tall stories, usually about himself. They said he could shoot the eye out of a leopard at one hundred yards, and that he had learned about the bush the hard way, by his mistakes. In the bush, sober, Wally was a man they both respected.

Coupled with the fact the man had no chin, drooping wet eyes like a spaniel, and had lost his wife in six months, Benny knew there would be no competition. Benny had always been careful never to introduce competition, even in his businesses. And to go into the bush without a skilled guide would have been plain stupid. Having mentally undressed Tina three times while smiling at her, Benny finally closed his eyes. He had been glad his guide was only a cuckold, not a murderer.

Having been a stray dog most of his life, Benny liked to help others in the same predicament. In his younger days, he could have done with the help himself.


WALLY BOWES-LEGGATT HAD LOST his illusions many years ago. Being the son of a famous British general had taken him only so far and after that, he was meant to do it on his own. He knew better than anyone else in his life that he looked like a dog, which was why he kept his hair long, and his big floppy ears well covered. The commission in his father's regiment when he was nineteen years old had been little more than a formality. The colonel of the regiment had served under his father. Prudence was a girl he had met on a hike in the Lake District soon after he received his commission. To his surprise, he had passed out in the top half of his officer course and his confidence must have shown. She was the second daughter of a schoolmaster with limited prospects and took to Wally from the start of the three-day walk that had been arranged by the local churchwarden. Foolish in his youth, he had not realised she was dazzled by the general's son, not the man, even though Prudence never met his father until a month before the wedding. Prudence swept Wally off his feet and into the church in ten weeks and Wally thought himself the luckiest man in the world. With a solid, pretty wife that senior officers liked to be flattered by, there was no reason he could not make himself a good career in the army. At mess functions when the wives were invited, Prudence was always surrounded by men, and always deferred to the senior officers. Wally was happy to stand on the fringe and bask in her glory. 'You're a lucky chap, Bowes-Leggatt,' was a constant refrain. If he had known she had the same effect on men as Tina Pringle, he would have kept a closer eye on his wife. He should have kept his eyes open, but at twenty, a very young twenty, he had no idea what was going on. To him, a wife who did not want to sleep with her husband after the first try or two was normal. Wally thought she must have been pregnant. Anyway, he was not a very physical man when it came to women. If Prudence had not chased him right off his feet he would have remained a bachelor, enjoying the male camaraderie of his fellow officers in one outpost of the empire after another. The army suited him. It gave him a home. A patient, meticulous man, he was good at his job, and even though he looked like a dog, the men looked up to him for himself. Like all men married to unfaithful wives, Wally was the last to hear of it. He did find Captain Craig on top of Prudence. And both were naked. Wally did have a gun in his hand and he was one of the best pistol shots in the regiment. But he did not shoot his wife as he told everyone in Africa. As he should have done. The next day he resigned his commission. The colonel cashiered Craig. Prudence went home to her schoolmaster father.

When he had gone home that fateful night to his married quarters, he had taken back a fellow officer for a late drink after they had checked the regiment stores. There was no way of keeping the story quiet. The general, his father, had got him out of the country fast.

"A man who can't keep his wife under control is not a man. Get out. Stay out. And don't ever come back to England or darken my door. You have made a fool of me, Walter. Making a fool of yourself is your business. Making a fool of me is mine. God damn you, boy, the whole regiment is laughing at me."

In Africa, he had felt at home. There were other Englishmen in the same predicament. Disgraced, one way or the other. He had taken to the bush and nearly got himself eaten by a lion, only killing the beast in the end with his revolver, the wounded lion right on top of him. He had fired the rifle for the head and not the heart. Quickly he had grown to respect the African bush. Any wild animal was dangerous. A honey badger the size of a dog could kill a buffalo, the animal in the bush said to be the most dangerous to man. And in town, when his cheque came in, the cheque from his mother, not his father, he had taken to drinking with drifters and telling them the story of his life. How he shot his wife. Why he was not in the war.

Why the American had taken to him he had no idea. But it suited him for the moment. His cheque was not due for another two months and he never looked a gift horse in the mouth.

"I've heard about you, Pringle," he said to break the ice. The American seemed to have gone to sleep and like all women, the girl was not interested in looking at Wally Bowes-Leggatt. "Serendipity Mining and Explosives. Your shares came out when I just received a cheque from Mater. Bought a hundred shares. Had to sell them again. Doubled my money. Thanks, old boy. You must be a very clever man."

Strangely, looking sideways at the man next to him in a new light, Albert thought he meant what he said. Instead of saying something depreciating he put out his hand.

"Thank you. We are going to be friends, Wally, isn't it? I'm Albert. A bit soon maybe for Christian names but do you mind? I come from the lower classes."

"Out here that doesn't mean a thing. We're all Englishmen."

"Not all of us," said Benny Lightfoot, without opening his eyes.


THEY REACHED the big river twelve days later. Benny thought he was losing his touch. More than once he had manoeuvred Tina away from the crowd and had yet to even get a hand on her bust, let alone more vital parts. What was going to be a long, slow seduction was becoming tedious.

They had spent the first night in Meikles Hotel. The next day Wally had gone off and come back with a wagon, a string of saddled horses, and six grinning black men, whose teeth shone whiter than anything Benny had seen before in his life. It was the contrast of the coal-black skins and the perfectly white teeth.

By ten o'clock they were on the road out of Salisbury heading northwest. A mile or so out of town, Benny saw a sign to the right which said Elephant Walk, and wondered what it meant. No one else commented on the sign. Their road was just a track and more than once Benny watched Wally take their position from the sun. The earth was as dry as a bone, the sky a perfect blue, with tufted white clouds, high and stationary in the sky, throwing shadow patterns on the dry brown bush, the small hills and outcrops of rocks the size of small mountains, some balanced one on the other, their cantilever weights stopping them crashing to the ground. The rich red soil sprouted grass which came up to the top of Benny's riding boots, even as he rode high in the saddle.

By the time they camped the first night, there was game on both sides of them, herds of buck and antelope, that Wally named as they first appeared, grazing the vast expanse of the bush. The first rifle shot was Wally shooting a young female kudu that had looked up with big bat ears, and big frightened eyes, from behind a thorn bush, where she had been delicately picking off green shoots without pricking herself on the thorns. It was a good clean shot and made Benny sad, sadder than it should have done. For a brief moment, he would have turned the party around, but they had come so far from Johannesburg, and it was a safari. The poor animal tasted better than any American beef. The party had to eat. Wally had handed him the heart of the kudu, roasted in the coals, and Benny said a silent prayer for the beast's soul and thanked him for his supper, glad the others could not read his sentimental mind.

The great plains around his home in Missouri were beautiful, but as the hunting party penetrated deeper into nowhere, Benny was sure he had never seen anything like it before. He knew then he wanted to come back.

At night Wally checked their position from the stars, reading the south line of the Southern Cross. The first night out of Salisbury they heard the lion roar. By the time they reached the south bank of the Zambezi River, the seduction of Tina Pringle was some way back in his mind. Benny Lightfoot knew he had himself been seduced by the African bush.

They were going to stay a week beside the big river and made a good camp on a high piece of ground. After days of eating meat, the river bream ate well. Despite the original idea of hunting for trophy heads, Benny said he only wanted to shoot and catch what they would eat. Tina gave him a real smile and he felt good inside that had nothing to do with his hormones. Wally Bowes-Leggatt was the perfect guide, and the boys, as they were called, which was nonsense to Benny as they were all men, were equally enjoying their paid journey into the bush, chatting away to each other nineteen to the dozen. To think that nations were slaughtering each other thousands of miles away was impossible to comprehend in the omnipotence of the African bush.

"And they call that civilisation," Benny had drawled, that first night on the banks of the river, thinking of the slaughter far away. No one replied. Wally understood.

With the fire down, there was layer upon layer of stars in the heavens, the splash of the Milky Way almost close enough to touch. Only when a leopard coughed behind them somewhere in the bush, away from the tall river trees, did Wally signal one of the black men to stoke the fire, sending sparks flying up to the stars, dancing through the canopy of the tall trees that covered their camp. After they had gone to bed, Benny woke each time someone stoked the fire. In the morning it was cold.

TINA HAD READ the sign to Elephant Walk. In Johannesburg, where the lights were often dim, and good clothes made an old man's body look better than it was, Tina had been happy to play with Benny Lightfoot. In the bush, he was an old man and there was no way of changing it. The sight of him taking an early morning swim in the river, with Wally on a rock, standing shotgun against the crocodiles, made her laugh. His thighs were thin like sticks. He was swimming in a long pair of shorts. His knees were knobbly, and the little floppy belly rather sad, as it wobbled above the leather belt that kept up the shorts. She wanted to laugh out loud and had to put a hand over her face, making a choking sound. Benny turned around from the water just at the wrong moment and they caught each other's eyes. Having first been annoyed by her brother, she was now happy he was there, stuck as they were in the middle of nowhere. Twice they had seen villagers on their journey out of Salisbury and then no sign of human habitation. She wondered why. Wally, the poor thing that looked like a shaggy goat, with sloppy big eyes that followed her everywhere she moved, was good at finding his way in the bush but fending off the old voyeur would be another thing. For the rest of her life, she would never again put herself at a man's mercy, no matter how much money he had in the bank. Looking at the old man climbing out of the water made her feel sick. She much preferred to be surrounded by lots of men, all vying for her attention. There was safety in numbers. She could play them all without fear of retribution. She would have to think before she did things next time.

The water dripping off the old body looked obscene. She got up from where she was sitting on the ground and climbed into the wagon. The sooner they all went home the better. Straight back to Johannesburg. If there wasn't a war going on, straight home to England. A flash with a face passed through her mind. It was Barnaby St Clair. For the first time since they had been forced apart, she missed him. Life had been a lot less complicated when they were kids, before that first time in the horsebox down at Swanage. Or was it Poole, she asked herself. So much in her life was sliding together, men and more men. Rows of them. All smelling her heat. Playing with them in more ways than one.

Getting out of the wagon with a handkerchief, she wondered how it would all end. Taking the bull by the proverbial horns, which Tina thought in her mind was appropriate with so many wild animals all over the place, she walked across to Benny with a pre-made smile on her face. He was dressed again which made it easier. Long, lightweight khaki trousers and a blue shirt that hid his pot belly. He had combed his hair carefully again to hide the bald patch on his pate. Wally was still on his rock with the rifle, staring down the river. Her brother was reading a book. The blacks were in a group off to themselves.

"Did you have a nice swim, Benny?"

"Very nice, thank you. Never swam a river full of crocodiles before."

They were being so damn polite to each other she could scream. Surely he could see they were going nowhere together.

"Did you see a sign on the road just out of Salisbury that read Elephant Walk?" she asked.

"Sure. What does it mean? The walk for the elephants or elephants please walk?"

"Something like that originally. Wally told me. Every twenty or thirty years the elephants do a great migration. And they always take the same route. An early hunter who stayed to farm saw the migration going through his land and called his farm Elephant Walk. We know the family. Or Bert does. You want to go visit, Benny? You're not shootin' for horns or heads. It's nice here but a bit lonely. What you say, luv? We pack up an' go visiting. The worst they can do is give us a cup of tea and tell us to bugger off."

"Hey, Wally," shouted Benny, "get off your rock. We're going back to make a visit."

"Where are we going?" drawled Wally, taking his eyes off a pair of fish eagles, motionless on the stump of a dead tree, looking hawk-eyed into the slow brown flow of the river, fishing. He would have liked to have sat with them all day.

"Elephant Walk."

"Harry Brigandshaw?"

"Have you met him, Wally?"

"Yes, briefly, and I know all about the family. His father was a legend in these parts. One of the first hunters with Selous and Hartley. He ran away from England. Or was shipped out by his father... We can pay them a visit. Albert met Harry once, so he said. Sebastian Brigandshaw's wife is still alive. Harry's mother. Mrs Brigandshaw would be about your age."

Wally, having missed the entire point of the safari had put his foot in his mouth. Benny smiled to himself. At least the man was honest. Maybe his days seducing young girls should be over.

"Sounds a good idea," said Albert, joining the conversation. He wanted to get back to Johannesburg. To the explosives factory. There was a war going on. If he was still in England they would be sending him to France. Like many other Englishmen in Africa, he was beginning to feel guilty. He was getting the same feeling that sent his brother back from Australia.

Within half an hour, they had struck camp. Going back was easy. They followed the path crushed by the iron wagon wheels.

THAT NIGHT, there was pandemonium when Wally woke next to the dead fire. There was no moon and cloud had covered the stars. One of the black men had been taken in his sleep by a lion, pulled from under his blanket, screaming out the last of his life. Wally had a gun out but it was too dark to see. The lion was running fast, the screams running away with him into the night. Horrified, all they could do was stand and listen. They heard the last, terrible cry for life and then the depth of silence.

The next day there was cat spoor all around their camp. Lions and lionesses. Wally blamed himself. For once the fire had been allowed to burn out. Away from the river, they had let down their guard and one of them was dead. They tracked the kill all morning, following the trail of human blood that ended with a pride of lions. The big, black-maned father, three lionesses and seven cubs. One of the cubs was chewing on a human hand.

"Let them be," said Benny. "It is the way of life. The cubs had to be fed."

The Purdey fired three times, the first shot killing the male. Systematically Wally shot down the pride, hunting them to the death on horseback with the help of the blacks. When they were satisfied, they rode back to where Benny stood. Albert had stayed in the fateful camp with Tina.

"I told you not to do that," said Benny. He was seething with anger.

"Oh, it's not as easy as that, old boy. These chaps look up to us. They wanted revenge. Their friend will rise to the spirit world to his ancestors. But most important those lions won't stake out a native village and eat the villagers one by one. The father was teaching his cubs. As he should have been. But we don't want them growing up with bad manners, old boy. You want us to skin the carcasses?"

"Leave the poor things where they are. I feel bad enough as it is."

"Now that is a waste. You wanted to go on safari. You found me in a bar. This is real life. The real jungle. I made a mistake with the fire and will have Jackson on my conscience all my life. I wonder where he came from? What was his real name? None of the others seems to know. No, Mr Lightfoot.

We're going to skin those lions and take them home. Maybe next time I won't make such a stupid bloody mistake."

AT THE TOP of the escarpment the next day, Benny Lightfoot looked back over the Zambezi Valley, the trees looking smaller and smaller as his gaze ran down to the valley floor. From their height, the grazing animals were barely visible. There were white fluffy clouds over the distant river. The clouds were motionless, as were their shadows on the valley floor. The trail had wound up for hours, the six oxen pulling the wagon. Jackson's horse was tied to the back of the wagon on a long lead, the saddle inside next to the wrapped skins of the lions. The heads were still attached to the skins. Wally had covered them with a tarpaulin to keep off the flies.

After ten minutes they rode on, following the old track of their wagon wheels. No one was talking, the blacks quiet next to the riderless horse. Some ten miles away a bush fire was hazing that part of the valley. Benny could smell the woodsmoke on the wind. Tina was riding next to her brother and Wally was off alone in one of his silent moods. For him, the safari was over, another piece of his life come to an end.

Benny looked at Wally for a long moment, wondering what would become of him next. Ships passing in the night. There had been many in Benny's life. Sometimes he could see their faces, rarely remember their names. He felt the pain of loneliness for those parts of his lost life. Down in the valley, he had left nothing else behind. The seduction trip had been a failure. With all his money, he wondered if the same could not be said for his life. Giving a wave to the valley, he turned the head of his horse. He was still not yet fifty. He would remember that. Maybe there would be something else for him to do with the rest of his life.

BY THE TIME they reached the signpost to Elephant Walk a week later, Wally Bowes-Leggatt had made up his mind. He was going home. He was going to England. He was going back to his regiment. In the depth of the war, he didn't think they would give a damn about his wife's indiscretions. What his father thought of him would have little effect on his life in France. He was a trained soldier. He couldn't keep a wife but he could keep the respect of his men. He would divorce the bitch as bitch she had to be to place horns on his head. He may have a funny-looking face. But the rest of him was sound.

"This is where we part ways," he said to Benny Lightfoot. After the killing of the lions, they had not been the best of friends. "I'll take the wagon on to Salisbury and leave your excess luggage at Meikles Hotel. They have a parcels office for farmers to centralise the delivery of their shopping. Deduct the wagon, horse and oxen deposit from your cheque. I'll pay off the boys and return the equipment. Can't say I've enjoyed the trip but that's how it goes, old boy. Not much of a safari. I'll keep the lion skins, seeing you don't want them. It would be nice if you found out who Jackson was and give his family some money. But you rand barons probably don't have time for that sort of thing. I'll try my best when I'm in Salisbury. Oh, and just for a tip, old chap. She is young enough to be your granddaughter, just in case you think I missed the point."

"That's exaggerating."

"You know what I mean."

"What are you going to do?... I'm sorry."

"Shoot Germans instead of lions. Most of the regular officers are dead now. Even the colonel, if he's alive, won't have any objections. And if my father, the famous general, had any he can go to hell... I have written down every detail for your cheque. I presume the Standard Bank in Salisbury will honour your signature."

"I expect they will," Benny said sarcastically.

"When are you Americans coming into the war?"

"Soon. I rather think soon."

"Will you come over?"

"I'm nearly fifty."

"So what the hell."

"Maybe... You think I'd make a good soldier?"

"Yes. I think you would."

"I'll take that as a compliment."

"It is, Mr Lightfoot."

"How are you going to pay your passage back to England? By your own report, your mother won't be sending you money for another month."

"I'll sell the lion skins."

"Then their lives won't have been wasted... And I will find Jackson's family. You can be certain of that. One of the benefits of being a rand baron. I have some clout... And yes. You are right. She is too young. Men never think they are too old with women until they make fools of themselves."

"You didn't make a fool of yourself."

"Nearly. Very nearly."

Tina and Albert were two hundred yards down the track towards Elephant Walk.

"This won't be a long visit," said Benny, looking at Albert and Tina. "Albert wants to be back in Johannesburg."

"You never know."

"Those skins stink by the way."

"They do, don't they? There's always a price to pay for everything."

# 2

## JULY 1915

*E*mily Brigandshaw had been widowed at the age of thirty-seven by an elephant. Ever since she had been dead. No light in her eyes. No care for herself. Just the daily chores and her children, Harry, Madge, and George. Even her father Sir Henry Manderville living on the farm had been of little consequence. Every day she went through the motions. No one on Elephant Walk ever saw her smile. What went on in her mind was a secret. Even Harry had given up trying to help her while he went about the business of running the farm.

She had known Harry's father, Sebastian, most of her life. In the early years, she had lived with her widowed father in genteel poverty at Hastings Court in the south of England, the family fortune having dwindled to the old house that had stood on the same piece of ground for centuries. Nearby, Captain Brigandshaw, founder of Colonial Shipping, had built The Oaks. They had been inseparable as children, Emily and Sebastian. In the grotto, they had seduced each other without understanding any of the implications. She had just turned sixteen, Sebastian seventeen. Neither of them knew another world even existed. Left on their own they had been the only thing in each other's lives. But like so many other things in life, Emily was to find out later it was not to be. The Captain, whom many in his erstwhile employ called the Pirate, for the origin of his wealth, a lot of it stolen, they said, in his early years on the high seas, coveted Hastings Court and the antiquity of Sir Henry Manderville's baronetcy that went back to the time of the Normans. And all the money in the world (and as Colonial Shipping grew there was plenty of that) could not buy the old Pirate respectability. He was certain everyone thought him as common as dirt. All they were after was his trade. His money. Somewhere he had read a family could become gentry in three generations.

The plan he hatched was for his grandchildren. He could buy himself a hereditary title by donating large sums of money to the Tory party. He could leave his family rich. What he could not do was leave bluer blood in the veins of his descendants without some outside help. He made Sir Henry do a deal with the devil. In exchange for the hand of Sir Henry's daughter in marriage to his eldest son, the eldest son who would inherit the title he was going to buy, the Pirate would purchase the falling-down Hastings Court, which would be restored, and bequeathed to the eldest son of his eldest son. The Pirate's grandson would have wealth and the respect of ancient lineage. Arthur, the eldest son of the Pirate, debauched and living off his father's fantasy, fell in with the plan. Sebastian, the Pirate's youngest son, was shipped out to the colonies to get him out of Emily's way. Emily, struck dumb by the secret knowledge she was pregnant with Sebastian's child, fell in with the plan. To a point. She refused to sleep with Arthur, who merely chortled with glee. Not only was the stuck-up little penniless aristocrat not going to give him trouble with his mistresses, but the prissy little thing was also pregnant, pregnant, Arthur was sure, by brother Sebastian, a lovely joke on their father. All Arthur had to do was sit back and enjoy his life. Everything had been done for him. Even the breeding of his son, who wasn't his son but still his father's grandson. Arthur Brigandshaw regularly laughed himself to sleep.

The grandson, Harry, was born at Hastings Court. Sebastian, getting wind of the timing of the birth, later came back from Africa, ran a ladder up to the nursery window at Hastings Court and kidnapped his son, Arthur's wife Emily and, for good measure Alison Ford, the boy's nurse. Arthur was delighted. All his troubles had gone out of the window at the same time. Leaving the countryside and Hastings Court to the birds, he went back to his life of debauchery in London.

Not so contrite, the Pirate threw a fit and had his youngest son pursued for kidnapping. If caught, Sebastian would have been hanged. Deep in the African bush, they had finally been left alone, husband and wife in everything but name, until Arthur died of drink and obesity at the turn of the century. If Harry had not been declared a bastard after his mother's marriage had been annulled for lack of consummation, he would have inherited Colonial Shipping. That is if he knew, which he didn't. Even that part of Emily's responsibility had passed her by.

After Sebastian had been killed by the Great Elephant, nothing had seemed to have a point for Emily. What did it all matter? Their love was dead, ended by an elephant. Nothing, she said to herself, mattered anymore. And now Madge had gone off with Barend Oosthuizen to the other side of Elephant Walk to start another section. Even the one-time nurse of Harry, Alison, Barend's mother, had gone with them. George, her youngest son had come back from school in Cape Town and then gone to England, so he said, to go to Oxford like his brother Harry before him. It had been six months and no one had heard a word.

The sound of strange horses coming into the compound made Emily's stomach sink. George was dead. They were coming to tell her. And she wanted to scream. Why did nothing good ever come to her in life?

Emily stood in the dining room behind the window that looked onto her veranda. There were three riders. One was a young girl. Praise be to God, she said out loud to herself. It's not George. Then she saw her father come out of the third house in the compound and walk across the tree-dotted lawn towards the strangers. Emily let the lace curtain fall back into place and walked through the dining room into the kitchen. Her black cook was working at the sink.

"Better get Tembo to kill a chicken. Three more for dinner. Ask the gardener to dig up some more potatoes. And cut some vegetables."

She knew how to run the house. That was routine... She watched the cook boy dry his hands on his apron and go off to look for Tembo. It was three o'clock in the afternoon. Harry would be back from the lands when the sun went down. Even now Emily thought she could do with a drink. Three hours to sundowner time. She could wait. That was the one big rule on Elephant Walk. No drinking before the sun went down. Not even on Sundays. Not even at Christmas.

With the cook out of the kitchen, she made sure the kettle on the hob was full of hot water. Just before he made the tea, the cook boy would stoke the fire and bring the water to the boil.

In winter she didn't mind eating hot food for supper. Once the sun went down the temperature dropped quickly. Someone once had told her the reason was that they were three thousand feet above sea level. By seven o'clock they would need a wood fire burning in the lounge. The family of Egyptian geese, that had once been wild when she first came to Elephant Walk, took off noisily over the balustrade that surrounded the family compound for the river, disturbed by the horses. There were now four separate dwellings, the last a small rondavel with bath and kitchen her father had built for Peregrine the Ninth. His old wagon was still parked in the yard. Clary and Jeff, the wagon donkeys, had been put out to graze down by the river. Surprisingly to Emily, neither lion nor leopard had eaten either of the donkeys. There was something about the kick of a mule. It had to be. Predators kept away from donkeys and mules.

So relieved the horsemen were not bringing news of her youngest son from England, she opened the inside door to the veranda to go out and greet the guests, to trip over the female ridgeback lying on the reed mat. The dog gave her a look of 'mind where you're going' and closed its eyes. The three dogs were sprawled on the same large mat that covered most of the veranda floor. Only when Emily opened the fly screen door to the garden did the dogs take any notice of the horses on the pathway through the compound. Then they all got up and put their front paws on the low windowsill to see what was happening. Not greatly interested, they went back to the mat and their sleep. From the inside windowsill to the dining room window that opened into the long veranda the ginger cat watched the dogs carefully. When the dogs flopped back on the mat, the cat went back to sleep. There would be time enough to jump into the dining room if the dogs got up and snapped at him. The cat and dog war had been going on all his life. He was used to it. If the dogs had looked at him carefully, they would have seen a thin slit of yellow eyes. The cat never let his eyes quite close on the dogs.

It was always pleasant for Sir Henry Manderville to have a conversation with strangers. They were more isolated on Elephant Walk than most people on earth. After nearly two years of Peregrine the Ninth living with them in the compound, the two old men had run out of new conversation, and like with a good book, they were going for a second and third good read. The last of the three riders was a lot older than the young couple in front. Even though he was sixty-three and celibate for longer than he could remember, he could still see the girl was as pretty as anything stored in the memory of his mind from the long past of his life. He would have to be dead, he told himself, before he did not appreciate a good-looking woman.

Only when he walked closer to the horses did he see she was only a girl. The older man spurred his horse and rode forward.

"It's a bit of a cheek, I'm afraid," said the man. "We don't have a letter of introduction. You see, we went on safari and saw the sign back there, and Albert once met a Harry Brigandshaw on the boat, so we thought you wouldn't mind the intrusion, so to speak."

The man was speaking English in an accent Sir Henry had never heard before in his life. "You don't have to explain. Sort of Rhodesian tradition.

Travellers always welcome. Harry's in the lands but will be back by sundown. I'm Harry's grandfather, Henry Manderville. You'll stay for supper, of course. And there's always a bed."

"It's roast chicken," called Emily walking across the lawn to join her father.

"That's Emily. My daughter. Harry's mother."

"How do you do, ma'am. Benny Lightfoot. This is Tina Pringle and Albert Pringle."

"Welcome to Elephant Walk, Mrs Pringle," said Henry formally.

"I'm not married. Bert's m' brother."

"I'm from America," said Benny, not sure why the old man's eyes lit up.

"Oh good," said Sir Henry. "My cousin lives in Virginia. He is my heir actually. Funny things happen with titles in England."

"He won't be able to use it in America."

"I suppose not. Never thought of that. There's no money. Just the title. Poor Cousin George… You can leave your horses for Tembo."

"He's killing a chicken," put in Emily as she reached the men.

"Chickens die quite quickly. I'm quite sure Tembo will make the cook pluck and gut. Been with us for years. His privilege, you see," said Henry.

"Is it Lord Manderville?"

"Oh heavens, no. Just plain Sir Henry. Goes back a bit. One of my ancestors came over from France with the Conqueror… William the Conqueror," he added when Benny failed to register what he was saying.

"Man that built the Tower of London?"

"So you know. Jolly good. Come and have some tea, old chap. Offer you a drink but it's too early. You can all have a wash. Did you shoot anything? Where are the porters? Oh well never mind. Tie the steeds to that tree. Em's house is the place for tea. We all have our own. Harry will be so pleased to meet you."

Then Benny understood. The look of interest had not been for the old boy but for his grandson. Everybody seemed to be looking for something. Then he looked at Emily again. She had the most beautiful green eyes with orange flecks that smiled at him. He did not have to be told she was a beautiful woman when she was younger. Pity she didn't know how to dress. How to do her hair. Quite frankly, he told himself, the woman looked like she had walked through a hedge backwards. Benny thought it was a pity.

As he got down from his horse, four dogs burst out of the big house and rushed at him across the well-kept lawn between the trees that were ringed with flowerbeds. Standing his ground he looked the dogs in the eyes. Then he got down on his haunches and smiled at the dogs from their own level. The bitch of the pack began to lick his outstretched right hand.

"A dog can always tell," said Emily.

"What, Mrs Brigandshaw?" Benny was still watching the dogs carefully for any sign of aggression.

"A nice person. When the dogs growl at someone on first meeting, I never trust that person again... Ah. Here come the geese again. You frightened them."

"We didn't know... Dogs, will you please get out of the way," he said to the four ridgebacks. The dogs looked hopefully at the geese landing on the lawn. Then they began the afternoon chase around the trees and the flowerbeds. The ginger cat watching from its sill inside the veranda closed its eyes and went to sleep.

As with all visitors to Elephant Walk, they were first taken off to see Henry's house, that boasted the pull-and-let-go toilet invented by Mister Crapper. Henry explained in detail how he had mastered the water supply with a series of windmills pumping water up the pipe from the Mazoe River; then up into the header tank on its tall wooden stand that provided the water pressure for the house. He promised Benny Lightfoot he would show him the whole system down to the river when everyone had washed and had their tea.

"I'm a bit of a crackpot but it keeps me amused," said Henry. "The children encourage me but I think it's more indulgence. For years I've heard them say I'm potty. Why is it children think old people are deaf? I hear perfectly well. Much better than the kids when someone asked them to do a job. Not so much now. When they were younger. You'll like my grandson, Harry. Well, there it is. I'm boring everyone as usual... Those damn dogs make one hell of a noise. Maybe Miss Pringle can use the bathroom first. Jolly good. Well, I'll be off for tea. Later we'll have a snort or two. Oh, if you see a very old man that looks like Methuselah, it's our Peregrine. Takes a nap around about this time so you should be all right. I'll show you the tobacco tomorrow. The house with the long veranda. Where the dogs raced out from. Come and have a cup of tea. Toodle-oo... Damn those dogs. They ruin my flowerbeds... Dogs! Shut up!" he yelled leaving Benny Lightfoot smiling at the door to the bathroom shut behind Tina Pringle.

"What a delightful old chap," he said to Albert Pringle.

The old man raised a hand still with his back to them. He had heard as Benny had intended. He had not become a rich man without using subtle praise as a tool for his trade. He had found out early in his life that there wasn't a single person on earth not susceptible to flattery.

"I can only stay one night," said Albert. "Business. Been away too long. Sallie can cope but she always needs help. I've taken advantage of her for long enough on this trip. You don't have to rush."

"You may be right. There's something about this place," agreed Benny.

"Can you look after Tina on the way home?" Albert asked.

"It will be my pleasure."

"Thank you," said Albert without smiling.

"I know you don't like me, Albert. Frankly, in your position, I'd be the same."

"Tina wanted to come. My sister has a strong will. I had never been in the bush."

"I'll get a message to you when I'm back in Johannesburg. You and I can talk business, start all over again. And you are all right. She's a darling but far too young."

"Who's a darling? Who's too young?" asked Tina letting herself out of the bathroom.

"You, my dear... Your brother wants to go home tomorrow."

"But we only just got 'ere. Blimey. What was the point?"

"You can stay if you want, Tina. It's Sallie," said her brother.

"I can stay! Good. That's settled. Hurry up in the bloody toilet you two. I want a cup of tea. At least this place serves tea. Now that's civilised. We must be in the middle of nowhere."

THE ONLY TOBACCO on the farm at that time of the year was in the shed, the samples left over from the first crop that had flourished better than Henry Manderville's best expectations. They had made a mess of the first two cures but when the third came out of the barn they had pumped steam onto the dried-out leaves which they had hung from poles tied in clumps of six. Instead of the dry leaves breaking up, the leaves were soft, pliable, and slightly oily. Henry had even thought they smelt like tobacco, so he made up a small parcel and sent it to Imperial Tobacco in England, marked on front and back 'Product of Rhodesia'. Not a word was heard for weeks. The great piles of leaves stacked in bunches of six one on top of the other stood on a tarpaulin on the dirt floor of the shed staring at him. For the first time in his life, he was depressed. Everything had come out according to Cousin George's instructions, except that the crop was five times bigger for the acreage than expected.

For Henry, it had been a case of the chicken and the egg. Which came first? He had to grow the tobacco and send it to the cigarette company. To write and say he was growing a crop would not have found any interest. Months went by. War was declared in Europe. The tobacco stood looking at them when anyone was brave enough to go into the shed. Harry even grew worried about his grandfather. The idea had been so good, and with tobacco selling at sixpence a pound in America, even Emily's maths showed they were onto a good thing. By her calculations, they would receive nine times more money for tobacco than maize. And unlike the cattle, that suffered deadly tick-borne diseases and the regular attention of the lions, tobacco seemed to grow straight and pure without a blemish. For a country locked away in south-central Africa, the value to weight ratio made tobacco the perfect crop. A few wagonloads of dried out, cured tobacco was worth a fortune.

The war changed everything, though they did not know it on Elephant Walk at the time. For a man in uniform, much of his time is spent sitting around waiting for something to happen. He is bored and scared at the same time, long before he hears a gun go off in anger. In civilian life, bored men full of tension took to drink but drink was not allowed in the army on duty. The only sedative to calm jangled nerves was tobacco, tobacco that could be stuffed back in a pocket at a moment's notice. Cigarettes in small packets. With tens of thousands of men joining the colours, the demand for cigarettes multiplied sevenfold. Not only did the price of American tobacco rise sharply, but there was also a risk factor. It had to be shipped to England across the Atlantic, where German underwater boats were waiting for the merchant ships in packs. Men were soon dying bringing tobacco to England. It was far safer to sail a boat from Cape Town, South Africa, to Southampton than from Norfolk, Virginia to Liverpool. And the British could pay for tobacco in pounds sterling and not American dollars.

The parcel sent to Imperial Tobacco in London caused a stir considerably bigger than the size of Henry's parcel blaring at them 'Product of Rhodesia'. Admittedly it had taken the chief chemist five minutes to find Rhodesia on the map and another week to test the tobacco and nicotine content and tar. They would need to blend the new African tobacco. There was a difference in taste. But there was a war going on. Men in the trenches wanted cheap cigarettes. Under the bad conditions, the men would soon grow used to the new taste. They would even like it. The stuff was genuine tobacco grown in another place. With the mud and the noise, the chief chemist doubted anyone would notice the difference in the first place.

In a letter that had gone with the parcel, Sir Henry had explained in full detail the extent of his experiment, asking the company to send him more good seed. He also wanted to know how many acres to plant.

With a large wooden box full of fine black tobacco seeds the company had brought back from America for research at Kew Gardens, a man was sent to Africa to make sure no one was playing a practical joke on Imperial Tobacco. If the product was genuine, it would be worth millions of pounds to the largest cigarette maker in the world. It would also save the lives of seamen. Or free up space on the ships to bring to England more lethal loads from the factories of America. Even the Americans would not mind. The demand for their tobacco was far in excess of the supply.

HARRY BRIGANDSHAW HAD BEEN out in the lands all day supervising the clearance of the trees. The man from Imperial Tobacco had given them an advance of one thousand pounds to build another twenty curing barns that were to be half the height of a church steeple. By the time they were given the money on Elephant Walk, it was too late in the season to stump out the new lands and build the tobacco barns. A grading and storage shed had to be built. Before any of the buildings could go up, bricks had to be made on the farm from the gestated soil they would dig from the great anthills that dotted the farm. Water pipes had to come up from the river. Metal flues had to be manufactured in Rhodesia's capital, Salisbury. Special fire clay had to be imported from England to make the long ovens that would protrude into the barns at ground level to heat the air inside, and drive the moisture out of the leaves hanging in tiers one above the other, the hot air rising and drying all the way to the top. Even if all the maize lands had been used for tobacco, the curing barns and sheds would not have been ready for a crop grown in the 1915 rainy season.

Harry checked the buildings rising in straight lines. He went down to the brick kilns that were burning the brush from the trees he had torn out of the soil the previous year. Everywhere he found intense activity. The long seedbeds had been prepared in a closed off area, sanitised by burning more of the brush over the turned soil to kill insects and worms that would otherwise eat the tobacco seedlings. The sun was almost down, and some of the labourers had already gone back to the village of grass huts that had sprung up on the banks of the Mazoe River a mile downriver from the family compound. The big, wide-brimmed hat had kept off the sun all day but his sweat had soaked the grey-green felt of the hat. His face was filthy from all the times he had wiped the sweat from his brow. His shirt was soaked through with perspiration, and the part of his legs between the bottom of his khaki shorts and socks was covered in the fine red dust of Elephant Walk. The socks had sunk unnoticed to his ankles long ago.

Climbing up onto his horse for the last time that day, he turned to go home, the idea of the first drink already screaming in his head. The stallion broke into a gallop, sensing the end of the working day. From the cluster of newly thatched huts down by the river, the drums began to play. Only in years to come was Harry to know that when the drums stopped beating there was trouble on the way.

By the time Harry reached the family compound, there was no warning of the visitors. Tembo had taken the three horses down to the stables for a rub-down and a feed of oats. Giving comfort to strangers included their horses.


TINA PRINGLE SAW him for the first time through one of the screens she had watched earlier being slotted into place down the veranda by a black man in a white shirt and shorts and no shoes. The lamps had not been lit. With the fly screens in place, she was invisible from the outside, even though she stood with her face close to the screen. Everyone seemed to be off doing something and no one took any notice. He had got off the horse without any semblance of effort and handed the reins to a black man who went off in the opposite direction with the horse. Even at that distance across the lawn looking through the flowerbed-ringed trees, she sensed they were friends rather than master and servant.

Tina had no doubt in her mind it was Harry Brigandshaw striding across the lawn, slapping his bare legs once to rid them of the red dust. Halfway across he took off the big, wide-brimmed hat and she could see his face. His hair was long. Even in the last glow of the sinking sun, she could see his face was burnt the colour of mahogany by the sun. He was tall, probably close to six feet, she thought, and slim. But most of all he was lithe. Everything about him was easy. The walk, the knee slaps, the sureness of tread, the expectant smile on his face.

Then the screen door was pushed open and they were facing each other, the smile on Harry's face turning from expectation to astonishment. She thought he even shook his head slightly to make sure. Their eyes locked, as a shaft of light burnt through the screens as the sun found a small gap in the clouds, before quickly sinking towards the horizon. Neither of them could speak. Then her brother came through from inside the house and the spell was broken.

"Hello. You won't remember me and it's all my fault."

"Of course I do," said Harry, finding normality. "You worked for Jack Merryweather. Did well for yourself. Albert Pringle, isn't it?"

"You have an amazing memory," said Albert.

"Not really. You're quite famous, you know. Even though we're in the sticks, we do sometimes read the Joburg papers."

"This is my sister Tina. We're on safari. Tina, this is Harry Brigandshaw. He's the boss around here."

"Don't you believe it. My mother runs the show. Doesn't miss a thing... Now there we go," he said looking over his shoulder. "The sun is officially down. Light the lamps and let's have a drink. I've been parched for a whisky for an hour. Been in the lands since the sun came up... You're staying with us, I hope?"

"Yes we are," said Tina sweetly, licking her lips with the tip of her tongue.

It was the first time in her life she actually felt weak in the knees in the presence of a man. He was the most gorgeous thing she had ever seen. And when he bent over to light the first lamp with a long match he had found on the table she could see his eyes were blue. Which was when she sat down with a plonk to save herself any embarrassment. The room filled up and she was able to watch him from the safety of the couch. When he caught her looking at him she winked. She had recovered her composure. She was back in control.

When a very old man came onto the veranda with Henry Manderville and took over the conversation, Harry sat down next to her on the couch.

"Your brother says you can only have two drinks. Here's the first one."

"Oh, does he? We'll see about that, old cock."

"I've met your mother and father. Stayed with Robert St Clair in '07. We were up at Oxford together. Albert was then in London. A brother in Australia. Where were you, Miss Pringle?" His blue eyes were smiling at her, full of mischief.

"In and around... Don't you remember the little girl with Barnaby?"

"I remember Barnaby had a friend."

"That was me. I was about nine then. Grown a bit, don't you think? Has anyone told you you're plain gorgeous."

"Not that I remember," he said, laughing to cover his embarrassment.

"Well, you are... You goin' to show Tina the farm tomorrow?"

"If you like."

"Oh, I'd like all right... Just the two of us... Mind if I call you Harry?"

"Not at all."

"That's good... That's nice. Cheers, old cock. Down the 'atch... Now what the bloody 'ell was that?" The sound from the night which Tina knew well enough, still made the hair stand up on her neck.

"A lion. Probably a mile away. Sound travels far in the bush."

"Who's the old geezer?"

"Peregrine the Ninth."

"Funny name."

"He's actually the ninth Earl of Pembridgemoor. Grandfather got it out of him."

"Try and tell that to my brother. The bloody old earl you're talking about is a fat old sponger. He's on the board of Serendipity Mining and Explosives Company. Bert needed his name."

"Now that is a bad coincidence. Forget what I said. You're probably right. The old man over there has been telling tall stories."

"There goes the lion again!... It's quite nice when you know what it is."

"And a mile away." She had moved up an inch closer to him on the couch. She could feel the heat from his bare knee.

Across the room, Harry's mother was in deep conversation with Benny Lightfoot. Tina thought the old lady had tarted herself up a bit. The hair was in place, and though the dress was out of fashion, Tina could see it had come from an expensive shop. Then Benny and Harry's mother were coming towards them and Harry got to his feet.

"This is my son, Mr Lightfoot," she introduced, "my son Harry. Mr Lightfoot's an American, Harry, but he lives in Johannesburg. Been all over the world. Quite fascinating. I see you have been introduced to Miss Pringle. We're going to sit down to supper tonight. At the dining-room table. I had your grandfather open the red wine, Harry. Not often we have company in these parts. It's so nice to talk about something other than the farm and the war in France."

From across the room, where he had been trying to catch his grandson's eye picking up the wink for some time, Henry Manderville gave Harry a wink.

It was going to be a party, Tina thought, picking up the wink.

THE LONG DINING-ROOM table had been made by Sir Henry Manderville from a piece of bush timber that was now known as Rhodesian Teak. The colour was a rich brown and shone from years of polishing. It had been made with loving care when Henry was trying to make himself useful. The Africans called the wood mukwa and it was as hard as nails. Henry remembered; he had done as much saw sharpening as wood cutting but the result still pleased him. Emily was at one end of the long table with Benny on her right. At the other end, Harry had the girl Tina on his right. Madge might be pregnant with Barend Oosthuizen's child on the new section seven miles away but Henry wanted a son by Harry to cement the new Rhodesian dynasty. The third generation in Africa would make them permanent. The girl was possibly too young and spoke with a dreadful Dorset accent, but that would change. Her brother, now in high finance, with a company listed on the London Stock Exchange, had most likely once spoken like his sister. In the bush where there was no one to raise an eyebrow, Henry found the directness of the girl a pleasant change. It had all happened rather fast, starting on the couch on the veranda during sundowners. He had never seen people more aware of each other from such a short acquaintance.

Peregrine had eaten his food, excused himself from the table, and gone off to bed, followed by Albert, who was making an early start in the morning. Peregrine could only manage two small glasses of whisky and a little white wine with the roast chicken. Henry was not looking forward to getting old. Mostly, Peregrine sat in a chair with his eyes shut, or he went to bed. It was good he had people to look after him. His days of living in the bush alone were finally over. Henry had walked his old friend to the new rondavel and then came back for a second helping of roast chicken. Tembo had been sensible and killed two birds. If there was anything over they would have it cold for lunch.

A message had come back from his granddaughter Madge, saying she was not feeling well, and if she felt better they would come over in the morning. Henry hoped nothing was going wrong. The marriage had been rushed. As soon as Alison had arrived from Cape Town, leaving her daughter Katinka behind in the Cape, they had gone off to the new missionary at Uncle Nat's old church and had him read the banns of marriage. Three months after Barend came back from the wilderness he was married. Now he was going to be a father. It was all too fast for Henry's comfort. A man didn't change from being a wanderer overnight. For all intents and purposes, the man had been a vagabond. And now with the diamonds sold he was going to stay put in one place for the rest of his life and be a farmer. Henry could only hope and pray. The poor boy was being smothered by two women, his wife and his mother, competing for attention.

If no one came over by lunchtime, he would ride over and pay his granddaughter a surprise visit. It was all right for grandfathers to pay surprise visits. Part of their duty, he rationalised as he poured himself another glass of red wine. They had visitors. It was a dinner party. There were not too many yards to walk to find his bed. Being a little drunk was also good for grandfathers. For good measure, he gave Harry another wink. He left them to talk to each other. Harry to Tina. Emily to Benny. He was quite happy with his memories. It was enough for him to be part of the family. He had rather hoped Alison would be at the dinner party but he couldn't have everything. He would definitely ride over in the morning. Pushing his glass away, he quickly got up from the table and left the room.

BAREND OOSTHUIZEN HAD COME in from clearing the lands for breakfast. The idea of sending his breakfast out to the lands to eat watching the blacks never entered his head. If they didn't do what they were told he boxed their ears when he came back, so watching them all day was a waste of time. He would leave that kind of farming to Harry Brigandshaw.

He had never been quite sure how much of Elephant Walk had belonged to his father. There was talk he had sold his share when the family had moved to the Cape and bought the farm Kleinfontein in the Franschhoek Valley that had been confiscated by the British after they hanged his father for treason.

He had managed to sell the diamonds with the help of Harry, and Emily had had the surveyors out from Salisbury to divide the farm. He had title to his six thousand acres of land, half what had been the farm Elephant Walk, capital enough to employ a gang of black men and build a house, and still not have to make a profit for five years. He had Madge, the only woman he thought he had loved in his life. He had a son or a son it surely would be. He had his mother living under his roof to assuage his guilt for running away from her. And it felt like they had put him in prison. Despite the wide open space, he was claustrophobic. He wanted to run away. Be on his own. But mostly, he did not want any part of the responsibility.

Dawdling over coffee on the veranda of the bush timber new house he had built with the gang, he saw the old man on his horse from a long way off. Coming to see what was going on. Why they had not ridden seven miles for dinner. The wooden floor was uneven in parts but it served his purpose. If he moved his chair he could stop it rocking on three legs. Why people couldn't leave them alone he would never understand. Ungraciously, he got up from the chair when Sir Henry rode in and dismounted in front of the veranda. Barend was wearing long black trousers held up by braces. Over the braces, he wore a black waistcoat with the buttons undone. His big feet were covered by thick socks and the right sock had a hole in the heel. Since returning to Elephant Walk with Peregrine the Ninth he had put on weight and given up shaving. Shaggy hair, the colour of dirty sand, covered his face. Only the slate-green eyes commanded attention. He was a married man. The house was his. What did it all matter? They had finally trapped and caged him. Rudely, he waited for the old man to speak first.

. . .

ALISON HAD WATCHED from the kitchen and her heart sank. It had all seemed so wonderful at first. The son back from the wilderness. The young love come to fruition. The farm and the money from the diamonds. Madge so happy. So happy to be pregnant.

She watched her son get up from the chair in his stockinged feet, not bothering to put on his boots, which were next to him, not thinking of buttoning his waistcoat. The son she had loved was breaking her heart. He looked more like a caged animal than a man just married, expecting his first child. The man was miserable, plain to see. And there was nothing in the wide world she could do about it. Only the father they had hanged so long ago could make her son the man she wanted him to be. Only Tinus could have made him happy. Instead of going out to greet their guest, she began to cry. Not even her daughter was there to give her comfort. At the age of not yet fifty, she felt more like a hundred.

Remembering there was more to life than feeling miserable, Alison went into her bedroom to powder her nose. Even if he was Emily's father, she was still a woman. Then she heard Madge retching from the bathroom and smiled. There was a grandchild of hers on the way. Tinus's first grandchild. It made it all worthwhile. Checking in the mirror that her eyes were not puffy, and patting her hair, she took a deep breath as she prepared herself to face the morning.

MADGE, hearing her grandfather's voice from where she was squatting in the bathroom, got up and washed her face. Even though her stomach was sick from the baby, her face was radiant. She even loved being sick in the mornings from the baby. She was so in love that everything around her was beautiful. If the sky had fallen on her head she would have found in the clouds exquisite joy. She was blind to anything but happiness. Keeping her stomach under the power of her will, Madge left the bedroom to join her family. All her life she had had a special place in her heart for Grandfather Manderville. She knew to him she was special. She was his only granddaughter. Father's liked to have sons. Grandfathers liked to have granddaughters. That was what he had told her when she was five years old. He probably told the boys much the same in reverse. But she loved him just the same. If only her father had not been killed by a rogue elephant her life would be perfect. She was luckier than any woman alive. They were going to call their farm New Kleinfontein after the one confiscated by the British. Barend thought it would lay a ghost to rest.

ALISON HAD HAD the cook boy make a pot of tea and bring it to the veranda. Like all Rhodesian houses, the veranda ran the length of the house and was used for entertaining. She politely shook hands with Sir Henry Manderville. She made signs to Barend to put on his boots and button his waistcoat. The boy needed a good haircut and his beard trimmed. He reminded her of his father. She had seen the hole in the sock and would reprimand the wash boy for not having it darned. Maybe it was a new hole. She hoped so. She had been a servant herself those long years ago. Harry's nurse at Hastings Court, the ancestral home of the Mandervilles, bought by the Pirate, Madge's other grandfather, now long dead and buried. And here she was entertaining the current Manderville baronet whose blood would be mixed with hers when Madge's child was born. There were so many complications in life. The cup rattled a little as she gave Sir Henry his tea. She was in awe of the man's ancestry, rather than the man. When he thanked her for the tea he looked her straight in the eyes. In someone else, she would have understood the look. She would have offered the baronet a second cup of tea but she knew her hand would be shaking.

Madge, not understanding the problem, poured her grandfather the second cup. She had taken his cup and saucer to the sideboard, which looked out onto the bush and the track that led to the family compound on Elephant Walk. The new house was in a hollow close to the Mazoe River where it flowed towards the distant hills. The farm was in a valley, ringed by a low range of mountains covered in msasa trees. It was the prettiest spot on the whole farm and she had chosen it herself. The bitch at Elephant Walk was with pups and soon three of them would be brought to New Kleinfontein. Her very own cat had refused to move to her new home. They had tried three times. Each time the cat had walked home the seven miles unscathed.

As she picked up the saucer with her grandfather's second cup of tea her eye was caught by a horseman galloping fast down the track from Elephant Walk. Standing and staring, with the cup and saucer still in her hand, she recognised her elder brother. She put it down the on the tray and waited. She had never seen Harry ride so fast.

"What are you staring at, darling?" asked Henry Manderville.

"Look. It's Harry. His galloping like a maniac."

Sir Henry got up quickly and stood next to his granddaughter. There was a dust trail behind the horse.

"Oh, my God," said Henry.

"What's the matter?" asked Alison, joining them.

"It's George."

"No, it's not, it's Harry."

"It's George."

Barend had also got up to have a look. All four of them watched the rider and the galloping horse.


HARRY CAME off his horse before it stopped and ran the last few yards. The horse was blown.

"Grandfather, saddle up and get home," he shouted.

"Is it George?"

"Yes, it's George. There's nothing you can now do for George. Any of us. It's Peregrine. When he read the cable from the War Office he had a stroke. Please hurry. He's going to die. He knows it. He just wants to see you before he dies. He is mumbling about a letter. Do you have a letter? What letter, for God's sake? What can a letter do to help? And I've decided. I'm going over. Can't stay now. Should have gone before George. I'm going to join the Royal Flying Corps. If nothing else, I can get some revenge."

"It doesn't help," said Barend. "I know. Oh, do I know about revenge. It eats into your guts. Never stops. You have to be dead before it stops. If you were going to join the Germans I'd come with you right now. Revenge. You go and take your revenge. Enjoy it. They wouldn't even let me have that pleasure. I was going to join the uprising that Botha, the traitor, put down. They didn't even give me the chance. And now where am I?"

# 3

## JANUARY 1916

*F*ay Wheels woke screaming from the pictures in her dream. Men, some whole, some mangled, some dead, some alive, all screaming, flying up into a sky filled with darkness and rain, lit by flashes which went unheard amid the shattering noise of exploding shells, and mud, mountains high, beyond her dreaming, screaming vision. The baby was shrieking and there was banging on a door.

Then she was properly awake, the baby in the cot screaming its head off, and the hammering on the door, the same door in front of which they had left her mother's chest of gipsy lore, and the key pushed through the gap into the flat in Sutherland Avenue where she was shaking from her dream that stayed and stayed in her mind. The sweat of fear was oozing out of every pore of her body and her hair was soaking wet, the room pitch dark. And there in the heart of the carnage, amongst the mangled, screaming dead, was the father of the screaming child, and she was sure with all her gipsy sight he was dead, mangled in the blood and torn-off bones and floating eyes, with the smell of old carnage blown up with the new, seeping deep into her air-starved lungs. Then she retched, and her screaming stopped, and a dead man's voice was shouting at her through the door and she retched again and again.

"Fay! *Fay!* What's going on? Why are you screaming?"

To hide from a dead man's voice she hid under the vomit-soaked blankets, the baby quiet all of a sudden.

"Fay! It's me. Jack. I've got some leave... Did I hear a baby cry? Fay! Let me in. What's the matter? For God's sake let me in."

Outside Jack Merryweather had lost the key to his mistress's flat. He was cold, and the long overcoat down to his ankles could not keep out the east wind. There were no lights down the Paddington street for fear of a Zeppelin raid. All the windows were dark and fast asleep in the middle of the night. He was hungry and the wound in his left arm hurt more than it was meant to hurt. He would have to find a hospital when the light of day came up. In France he had told them all his wound was fine and taken up his leave, walking back down the wet cold muddy communication trenches to the reserve line, and then further back, trudging through the dark till he found the slope. Then up above ground for the first time in months, if he excluded the raids over the top into the German lines. The thought of England, Fay and their new baby took him through the night to a backward command post where they found him transport to the coast. Even the seething lurching swells of the English Channel could not take the smile from his face. He wasn't sick, not even once. The Calais–Dover ship had docked in time for him to catch the last train up to London but the line was blocked and the train arrived late at the station, and he had walked to the flat in the cold, with the wound in his arm hurting so much he had to concentrate his mind to stop the stumbling. There had been no taxis in the middle of the night. There were not meant to be any trains.

Then he fainted on the doorstep and slid to the ground, wondering if he was about to die, the pain too great for bearing.

Fay found him on the steps the way she found her mother's iron-bound chest. Abandoned. She knew, of course, he was dead. Knew who he was without seeing his face in the dark and creeping fog. She looked at the crumpled figure on the step for a long moment. Having considered her vomit and the banging on the door for a long time in the silence, she had got up and taken a look outside. The soldier at her feet was skin and bones, the army overcoat having fallen open. The body began to stir. Her gipsy mind began to understand. This was not Jack. This was another soldier come to tell her of his death. The messenger of death.

She grabbed the man by both arms and began pulling him into the hallway of the flat. The man screamed in pain, so he wasn't dead.

"For the love of God, Fay. Be more careful. My left arm was shot right through... You smell of vomit. Are you all right? Oh, I see. The baby was sick all over you. Sorry. I fainted from the pain in my arm. I don't know what you did to it by pulling but it's better now. What a way to come home. Dragged through the door by the mother of your son... How are you, Fay? Why are you crying? It's me. Jack Merryweather. If you can help me up off the floor, you can show me our son. Before I passed out I heard you screaming and then the baby cry."

"I had a terrible dream."

"We all get those. You get used to them in the end."

"The dream told me you were dead."

"Well, this time your gipsy feyness was wrong, my Fay. I'm alive, on ten days' leave. Not much, true, but enough. We three are going to have a wonderful time... Now show me my son and then give me a drink. Something strong. It was cold out there and the boat was going up and down... Now, will you please stop crying?"

"I wrote you there was a child, Jack. You have a daughter."

"Then show me my daughter! But first, give me a kiss."

"I'm covered in my own puke. Sick from the dream."

"I don't care, Fay. Probably don't smell too sweet myself. It doesn't matter. We are the ones alive in all the horror. We have a daughter. Covered in sick, to me you look quite beautiful. I'll give you a good idea. Let's take a bath together. Then we'll make love. Then I will sleep for the rest of the day. This uniform I came home in shall be burnt. My tailor can run me up a new one. The new one will look much the same in a week after I get back. But that doesn't matter. When I escort my Fay round the town I don't want those dreadful women handing me white feathers so I shall be in uniform... To the baby. To the drink. To the bath. In that order."

"I'll have to change the sheets."

"Then the sheets shall be changed."

"Does your arm really hurt that badly?"

"Not anymore... And that's the last time you and I shall talk about the bloody war."


THE DOCTOR at the Paddington hospital was so old, Jack thought at one stage the man had gone to sleep while peering at the wound in his arm, which the field hospital in Flanders had patched up as best they could.

"Not the slightest trace of gangrene. You are a very lucky man, Captain Merryweather. Straight through the flesh of the arm. You'll have a scar on both sides but nothing much more. The heat of the bullet sterilised the wound. The nurse will put on a new dressing. Keep an eye on it. Come back if you think you should."

To celebrate, Jack took Fay to dinner. He used his years of patronage to get a table at Simpson's on the Strand. She was prettier than he ever remembered, and excited to be seen in public with him for the first time.

They had gone to his house in Baker Street for clothes. Bradford, the valet, burnt the old uniform, and Jack paid a visit to his tailor in Savile Row.

For the night, he was dressed in civilian evening clothes, though his left arm was kept in a sling. He could use the hand well enough but when the arm was allowed to move around the wound hurt.

A young woman standing at the entrance to Simpson's gave him a white feather for his trouble as they got out of the taxi that had brought them from the Baker Street house. Their child had been left to an astonished Bradford to look after while they went out to dinner. It was the first time they had visited Jack's house. Jack gave the woman with the feather a sweet smile, tipped his hat and put the feather behind his right ear.

"You should be ashamed of yourself," said the woman, annoyed by the way Jack flaunted her feather, the white feather of cowardice.

"So should you," spat Fay.

The doorman, who had known Jack for twenty years, raised his voice for the first time.

"Welcome home, Captain Merryweather. Hope the wound is not too bad?"

"Thank you, Fred. Anyone in the restaurant I know?"

"The Honourable Robert St Clair. He is dining with one of his brothers."

"Didn't know any of them could afford the place."

"I believe the Honourable Merlin St Clair took a large position in Vickers-Armstrong just before war broke out."

Without looking back, Jack took the feather from behind his ear and handed it back to the young woman.

"I'm sorry," she said.

With Fay on his arm, Jack walked through the door held open by Fred into the crowded restaurant.

ROBERT ST CLAIR had started with a cheese soufflé, which was much to his liking. The second course, a partridge, had been hung just enough, high to the taste but not quite rotten. The red wine and port sauce over the bird were, to Robert, perfection. Where they had found the new peas and new potatoes in winter he had no idea. The menu he had been given showed no prices and Robert asked no questions. He was Merlin's guest.

"Where did they get the vegetables from at this time of year?" he asked.

"Someone's hothouse, most likely. You can get anything, even now, if you have a lot of money. Well, here's to the old Vickers machine gun."

"Please, Merlin, don't bring up the war."

"Do you know that chap over there? The one with the pretty girl. He's been trying to catch your eye ever since he sat at his table."

"Of course I do. That's Jack Merryweather."

"Then why don't we join them for supper?"

"Don't be silly. He'd be terribly embarrassed. That's his mistress. You wouldn't want to be recognised if you were dining here with Esther."

"Esther, I'm afraid, went off and married a corporal."

"Oh. I'm sorry, Merlin. I hope she'll be happy."

"He's dead."

"Then she can move back into the Barbican flat."

"I'm looking for another mistress."

"I'll have the roast sirloin if you can afford it, Merlin," said Robert, breaking the awkward silence.

"They say Vickers makes a machine gun every two and a half seconds, which they sell to the British government at a nice profit. The average lifespan of a machine gun is ten days. And they are strung out from coast to coast along the Western Front... Frederick has joined the army in India. They're sending him to France. Probably on the water by now. Penelope and the girl are staying behind."

"Does Mother know?"

"I'm going to tell her tomorrow when we go home," said Merlin.

"What are we going to say to Lucinda?"

"Give her a hug, I'd say."

"Did you meet her fiancé?"

"No. Don't even know his name."

"Poor old Cinda," said Robert. "Terrible to end up an old maid. She should have stayed in Africa with Harry Brigandshaw. Far away from this bloody war. There are going to be a lot of old maids left by this carnage. What a waste of life. All those years with nothing to do. No purpose. I think the fiancé was the lucky one."

"Barnaby should be all right. They've posted him to Palestine. It's a two-year posting. Granny Forrester cried when she heard. Doctor Reichwald, who now calls himself Doctor Smithers, has one son left alive. Do you remember when you had that flu? He was good, saved your life... He's coming over."

"Who?"

"Your friend Jack Merryweather."

"Then that makes it different... Hello, Jack. How's the arm? Didn't see you come in, old chap... You alone?"

"Come and join us, Robert, for coffee. You know who she is as well as I do. Shown you her photograph enough times over there."

"Why no uniform?"

"Burnt it. New one is ready tomorrow. I have a daughter."

"Jolly good... Did that woman catch you at the door?"

"Fred saved the day."

"Good for Fred, whoever he is. I can't afford these places myself."

FAY WATCHED Jack make his way back to her with pride. He had lost a lot of weight in the trenches but there was more purpose in his walk. As if he had something to do that was important. He looked older than his thirty-five years but so did they all. None of them would ever be the same, even if they came out of the war alive. It would live with them forever. She smiled up at the father of her daughter who still did not have a name. She had been waiting for Jack. Only if he had been killed was she going to do something on her own.

"They're coming over for coffee and a brandy. Met Robert in Africa... I'm going to take you to Africa when all this is over. You've heard me talk of Harry Brigandshaw? He came over and joined the Royal Flying Corps. They're teaching him to fly Sopwith Pup biplanes. Best of our fighters. He's a lieutenant. That was one of the letters I read this morning when we went to the house."

"Are you really going to take me to Africa, Jack?"

"I said I would. When all this is over. A celebration."

"When will it be over?"

"Not for a while. Jolly good of Harry to come over and help. He's a Rhodesian. English stock of course. They're growing tobacco out there for the troops. Saves bringing it across the Atlantic from America. And it's cheaper. Harry says America put up the price of tobacco a month after war broke out. Someone always makes money in a war. Merlin, Robert's brother over there, has made a small fortune having the nous to buy Vickers-Armstrong shares just before war broke out. They make the machine guns that kill most of the Germans. In Germany, the lucky chap was the one that brought Krupp shares. What Herr Krupp makes kills us. Silly really. And we all pray to the same Christian God out there. There never has been any sense to war. Just every now and again it has to be done. As I said, rather silly but there it is."

Together they listened to the dance music in silence.

"What do you want to call our daughter?" Fay was trying not to cry about the war.

"Oh, Mary. Definitely. My mother's name was Mary... What do you call her now?"

"Baba... You want my child named after your mother? I'm your mistress, Jack, not your wife."

"Doesn't make her any less my daughter... There's a new clause in my trust. Or will be. Jared Wentworth's out in the Atlantic with the Royal Navy. He is my stockbroker. There's talk of convoys for the merchant ships. The Huns are sinking far too much tonnage. Underwater boats. From the depths, they fire torpedoes... Jared's office will change the trust. You and Mary will always be all right, Fay."

"She won't be without a father, however much money."

"Don't pooh-pooh money. Money is important. Or rather it is not important when you have it... The one thing I can never understand is where Robert St Clair puts all the food. He's as skinny as a rake... He's going right through the menu. We had better dance. It's going to be a while before they come across."

"I can't dance," said Fay.

"Don't worry. The dance floor's so small and with so many couples we just sway to the music. Just an excuse for people to hold each other."

"Do you need an excuse, Jack?" She was smiling again.

"No, I don't. Come on. It's a waltz. A slow waltz. Not one by that Austrian Strauss."

THERE WAS no one on the platform at Corfe Castle railway station and the weather was bleak. Merlin pushed open the door to the waiting room. It was freezing inside. No one had lit the fire for days. The grate was full of old ash. He had a slight hangover from the previous night. After doing the right thing with Jack Merryweather, drinking coffee with a snifter of brandy, Robert had kicked him under the table on the shin. They left the happy couple, and went on to a club, but did not find any girls even though he and Robert were in uniform. Neither of them tried very hard. Seeing Jack and Fay look at each other that way made little sense of casual acquaintances.

They had caught a cab back to Merlin's empty flat in the Barbican and Robert had slept on the couch. They travelled down the next morning to their ancestral home in civilian clothes. There were two women at Waterloo Station handing out feathers. In passing one of them, Robert went into an elaborate limp. Ten yards further on he walked up straight and the women began running after them. They changed trains twice before getting off at Corfe Castle. The last part of the journey they spent alone.

"Well, I'm not going to walk," said Robert. "Fun in the spring. Even pleasant in summer. But not in the winter. When Harry Brigandshaw first came down I made him walk. Lucinda was in love the moment she clapped eyes on him. She was only fifteen. Poor Cinda. I've told Harry to come down here if he gets any leave, so you never know... Not even a sign of old Pringle. Do you remember how Mrs Pringle used to make us those sandwiches? There was always a pickled onion. Then we'd bring her a chicken. Nothing will ever be the same."

"Stop moaning, Robert. Nothing can ever be the same twice, or it wouldn't be the same now would it?... You did phone Father? Well, we walk. And fast. Marching pace of light infantry. We'll be home in less than two hours. Come on. No one will steal our luggage from the waiting room. They've all gone."

"What happens if someone takes the high road and we're walking along by the river?"

"We leave them a note, stupid."

"I hadn't thought of that."

"Why they made you a captain, I have no idea."

"Neither have I... By the bye, thanks for supper last night. Not sure when we'll get a slap-up meal like that again."

"Don't be morbid. You can always rely on Mother and Granny Forrester... Best foot forward. March."

"And the note!"

"Of course."

"Now how they made you a captain is an even bigger point of contention."

"Do you have a pen?"

"Of course I have a pen. I'm a schoolmaster."

They had not gone fifty yards when they heard the horse and trap. Lord St Clair, their father, was holding the reins. They were all very cold when they reached the manor house.

· · ·

LUCINDA'S FIANCÉ, they found out, was John Heynes, a lieutenant in the Irish Guards. He had died on the third day after reaching the Western Front, blown apart by a German whizz-bang. There had been nothing to bury. They hugged their youngest sister but everyone was restrained. The brothers were due back in Flanders in four days' time. Robert wondered if the fear was not greater for their mother. No one mentioned Frederick on his way to France. His ship was to dock at Calais, so there was no home leave. Too many men needed to be replaced quickly. No one mentioned the family doctor was now Doctor Smithers for fear of bringing up the deaths of his two sons, with a third still alive and fighting. If the family had not emigrated from Germany as Reichwalds, the three sons would have been fighting on the other side.

Annabel was at home with nowhere else to go. Her impressionist painter, Geoffrey Winckle, had swapped his paintbrush for a rifle. He was a corporal in an infantry regiment. Merlin was now sure he would never see the ten pounds he had loaned his brother-in-law. They had not had any children. They had been happy for the short while. Merlin rather envied them in a way. The day after Robert and Merlin arrived back at Purbeck Manor, a letter arrived from Geoffrey Winckle saying he was now a sergeant. Someone, he said, for a reason he did not understand, had put him in for a medal. With the letter were four canvases he had done in charcoal. Robert and Merlin shuddered at the reality. Their brother-in-law was very good. All four canvases depicted the hell in the trenches. Robert even smelled the dead bodies by looking at the pictures. It seemed a pity to use good canvas for charcoal but what else could he use in the trenches?

Genevieve was away in Norfolk living with her mother-in-law. Her father-in-law, who had once been a professional soldier, was back in France commanding a battalion. Her husband was in the same battalion. Robert and Merlin read one of their sister's letters. It was as bleak as the Norfolk winter. The two women were trying to farm the family estate. They had recruited four young women to help them. All the young men from the village were away or dead. It was the same at Purbeck Manor. Two land girls from Corfe Castle and Lord St Clair looked after the pigs. The cows had been sold, as no one knew how to milk them except Lord St Clair and his fingers were bent with arthritis.

Merlin gave his mother fifty pounds without telling his father or anyone else. When the war was over he would buy some more cows. Two of the family portraits in the hall gave him a smile. He was sure of it. Their eyes followed him. Twice he smiled back at them. One of the portraits was over three hundred years old and dark with age. The eyes were alive. The eyes were smiling. Merlin stopped going into the hall, preferring to go outside through the French doors in the lounge. He knew more than anyone else the meaning of his name Merlin. He even knew he was going to survive the war. He never thought about his brothers for fear of finding the truth. Like Fay Wheels, he saw things others never saw.

GRANNY FORRESTER WAS certain all the boys were going to die but never said a word. She blamed herself for loving one man and marrying another. She missed Cousin Potts more than she could ever have imagined. They were companions, comfortable in silence, feeling safe and whole together. If his first posting to an obscure colony in the South Seas had not been so sudden it might have been different. Cousins they might have been but they only found out about each other for a week. Potts had proposed. Gave her hours to make up her mind. Her father had put his foot down firmly. No first cousins were ever again going to marry in the family. The bloodline was too intermarried as it was. And much later had come Richard, her eldest grandson, and the flaw in the family genes again came to the surface. In their old age, they had been together under the same roof. Maybe it was not living in sin. They were too old for physical comfort. The Reverend Reichwald, the family doctor's brother, now Smithers, frowned at them in church sitting next to each other in the St Clairs' family pew. It was their silly gesture. If they could not have it when they wanted it, they would not marry at all. Granny Forrester was certain that all sins were punished. She would be punished. God would kill her male grandchildren.

HER DAUGHTER, Lady St Clair, was permanently tired from worry. The moment she stopped worrying about one of the children she began to worry about another. It was all so silly as there was nothing she could do. Once they went away from home they were outside her protection. She prayed a lot but then she had prayed a lot for Richard and he had died from a fit.

And the food was running low. No milk or butter without the cows. They would buy some more cows if they had the money. Then she would learn to milk. Robert and Merlin were going to shoot as many hares and rabbits as possible. The weather was cold enough to let them hang for weeks without going too rotten. Somehow it would all be better after the war but she could not see how. The St Clairs were out of money before the war. Only Sir Willoughby Potts gave them an income. When he died his pension died with him. Not having money was the second worst thing in her life, after the war.

She had no idea what she would have done without Merlin's fifty pounds. Maybe he would save their bacon if he wasn't killed in the war.

The idea of saving bacon made her smile for the first time in weeks. The one thing they were not short of at Purbeck Manor was pigs... Her husband definitely had a way with pigs. She could not remember the last litter of fewer than fifteen piglets. She would have to ask Robert to visit Mrs Pringle at the railway cottage. Edward, the seaman in the Pringle family, had gone down with his ship bringing munitions from America, sunk by what she heard they were calling *U-boats*. They had a new word for everything that was nasty. And there she was worrying again. That was three out of Mrs Pringle's children taken by this terrible war, she told herself. First, Walter who had come all the way from Australia to die. Now Edward. Worst of all, with her worrying, she could not for the life of her remember the name of the third boy who had died in France.

She had told Mrs Pringle in no uncertain terms to tell Albert to stay in South Africa. They never talked of Tina for fear of talking about something both of them would rather leave alone. In her plea to keep Albert safely in South Africa was the unspoken hope that Tina would stay there too. There could never be a marriage. Both understood. As a regular soldier, if he survived, a wife from Tina's class would have him thrown out of the regiment... And not a very good regiment either. To live in a top-class regiment, Barnaby would have needed money. A private income. No, Tina was out of the question. Barnaby had to stay in the army after the war to make his living... Why did it always come back to money? Then she began to worry about Barnaby in Palestine. The Turks killed Englishmen just as willingly as the Germans, even if they were not so efficient. For a moment, she thought of the Australians and New Zealanders that had died at Gallipoli.

Lady St Clair knew she was cursed with too vivid an imagination. Her husband could think about his pigs for hours on end without any intrusion into his mind. She wished she could do the same. No, she decided thinking back. She would have to ask the old cook to learn how to milk a cow. Even in poverty, there had to be appearances. It would never do for the lady of the manor to become a milkmaid. The people in the village would think the whole country was going what they called broke. It had given them comfort for centuries to know the lord was in his manor. When the lord was strong, the people were safe. They might not like some of the rules but that was how it worked. In every society, someone had to give the people protection.

Turning her mind from the past to the present, she hoped the boys would not mind eating pork for the next four days for supper. She doubted if Robert would notice. And Cook had made a plum pie for him, knowing it was his favourite. They had even added a little of the saved-up sugar to make it an occasion. The fruit had been bottled when the Victoria plum trees were heavy with plums at the end of the summer. Before her youngest son went away to war.

And then she was worried all over again, going round in a circle, starting at the beginning.

MERLIN WAS WOKEN that night in his room by the silence. Unbeknown to him, Robert was also awake in the next room, staring out of the open window into the winter night. They were both used to sleeping with horrendous noise. The wind shifted and Merlin listened more carefully. It was the guns. Someone was having a hate. Probably both sides. Merlin opened the window wide, making a noise.

"Can't sleep either," said Robert from the dark. There was only one wall between them and with their windows open they were able to whisper and hear each other. Neither wanted to wake anyone else in the family.

"Can you hear the guns?"

They both listened for a while in silence. There was no sound from the nearer blanket of silence. The guns were an overtone. From hell. Even at home, the war was in their bedrooms.

What sounded like a dog barking came from close to the hen run, followed by the squawking of the chickens. Used to putting boots on fast, they were out of the doors at the same moment, and running around the dark, familiar corridor, not caring if they woke the devil himself. Both had thrown overcoats over their pyjamas. Robert had his boyhood .410 shotgun in his hand, the nearest weapon he had found to snatch; Merlin was going to kick the fox to death if it did not run away. A box of cartridges banged in Robert's greatcoat pocket. Down the main stairs more by falling, turning in the dark to the kitchen by instinct, and out the back door, racing across the hoar-frost grass, Robert put a cartridge into the single barrel of the gun, spurred on by the sound of mayhem coming from the hen run. There was something of a moon and the stars were bright, the hoar frost showing them a pale white layer on the ground. There were a fox and two vixens in the run. Dead chickens and feathers everywhere. Merlin got in one good blind kick and the predators were gone.

"You wouldn't have done that to a leopard," said Robert.

"We don't have leopards in England... What's the damage?"

"Looks worse than it is. My word. Poor Mother would have had a heart attack if she had lost the chickens. That's what happens when the hunt is cancelled. You and I will wait up tomorrow with torches and twelve-bores. I find sleeping for long impossible. We can make ourselves a thermos flask of coffee. If we don't get that darn fox we'll get ourselves a rabbit. We used to do this often as kids. You remember? It's fun... Two of Mother's chickens are dead. The rest have had their feathers ruffled... Now we really have woken up the family."

The electricity installed with old Potts's money was springing up all through the house. Lord St Clair was leaning out of his window in his nightshirt.

"What's going on?" he called.

"Foxes in the hen run," called back Merlin.

"Much damage?"

"Chicken for dinner tomorrow."

"Make a change," said Lord St Clair.

"We're going to wait up for them tomorrow."

"Good idea. Who's with you, Merlin?"

"Robert. We were at our bedroom windows listening to the guns."

"Just as well. I'm rather partial to an egg for my breakfast. Good night."

"Good night, Father," they both called in unison.

Back in the house, with the chickens flopped onto the kitchen table, Robert poked up the fire in the Dover stove and waited for the big copper kettle to boil. Neither of them would be able to sleep. The tension of being out of the front line not facing the inevitable was worse than being in the trenches under bombardment. It was their only world. The foxes and the chickens would be gone like a puff of wind, like the whole of their leave. There was something about the inevitable for both of them that made the rest of life unimportant. There wasn't any point in anything when you were about to die. And there was nothing they could or wanted to do to stop it. Not to go back was unthinkable. The small portion of the rest of their lives was over there in the mud and cold, the noise and fear. They may be still alive but knew they had been sucked into eternity. The inevitability of their lives was right in front of them.

The kettle boiled and Merlin poured in a little boiling water to warm the big brown family teapot before putting in two spoons of tea from the caddie. There was no milk or sugar. They would drink it black.

They were more comfortable with each other than at any time in their lives. They sat with the fire door to the cooker open, with the chickens on the white-scrubbed table. Even inside with the door closed, they could hear the guns.

"You imagine how many of our ancestors went to war for England from this house?" asked Robert.

Merlin thought for a moment, sipping his hot tea. The fire was warm and he was enjoying his brother's company.

"And from the castle," he replied at last. "So long as someone survives, it's all right. The family goes on. England goes on... Jack Merryweather is lucky to have a daughter. Even if he dies, there's some of him left behind."

"And Frederick has a daughter."

"That's good but he must have a son. After so many centuries, for the main line to die out would be terrible. Father to son. Father to son. Been like that since the first baron."

"Maybe she's pregnant."

"Who?"

"Penelope."

Merlin suddenly got up and opened the back door of the kitchen and looked out at the night. He listened for some time.

"You're causing a draught," said Robert.

"Thought I heard that damn fox again."

"What was the real matter? You bolted for the door."

"Fred... I had a premonition. The men think I have the sight. It's not Captain St Clair. It's Merlin the Magician. Maybe Mother and Father knew something about me. When I was born. It's a curse. Father's a romantic. Never got past the legends and his reading. Why Richard was Richard. Richard the Lionheart."

"Mother preferred Arthur for you. Father won. I like Merlin. It makes you different. There's nothing different about good old Robert. Or good old Bob. Plain and simple. Don't read too much in a name and please close the door properly... I can just hear Cook tomorrow when she finds wet tea leaves in the pot. 'One of life's little mysteries,' she'll say."

"You ever feel the presence of our ancestors?" asked Merlin, not wishing to be side-tracked.

"Of course not."

"Well, I do. And those portraits in the hall are alive. The eyes follow me. Especially one old fellow. And the look changes. Today his eyes were smiling."

"Good portrait painters have that ability to make the eyes follow you. And I don't want to hear any weird stuff about Fred. He is going to be quite all right. We are all going to be quite all right."

"You don't believe that, do you?"

"Am I going to die?" asked Robert after a long time.

"How the hell do I know?"

"Merlin, sometimes you contradict yourself... I wish I had stayed in Africa. She married Barend but that does not matter. You would have liked Madge. There was so much peace in Africa. In the bush. Wild but peaceful. Empty, I suppose. Empty of people. Animals just kill to feed themselves. They don't blow millions of people to pieces."

"What about that fox? He'd have killed every chicken in the coop and taken just one home for supper."

"The genet does that in Africa," said Robert sadly. "Kills for the fun of it too."

"No. Man is territorial. The Germans want to expand. We want to stop them. They envy the empire. Man defends his hearth and home."

"Or rapes and pillages. We are the survivors, according to Darwin. The part of rape and pillage that evolved."

"Amazing how much nonsense we talk in the middle of the night," said Merlin.

"It's true. How do you think our ancestors got their hands on this place without a bit of rape and pillage? And if we don't stop Fritz, he'll do to us what he did to the Saxons. And the Saxons were from the Germanic tribes. History going round in a circle. No, we'll have to stop Fritz."

"There isn't much here to rape and pillage," said Merlin.

"What about the girls? The villagers? It's not only us they're after. We poor fools in the aristocracy are meant to keep the place safe. And we will. Even if it kills us. For now and forever. We owe them that for our years of privilege. This is payday for the St Clairs. Every time we fight a war it's payday."

"No. This time we're just machine gun fodder like the rest of them," said Merlin.

"They look up to us."

"In a funk everyone looks for a leader. If you go out to Africa and take up some barren land, if you don't kill off the locals like the Americans, they'll breed under British law and modern medicine, and want the land back again. Stay in England. There are too few of us English to control the world much longer. The Romans found out the same. Even if you run the place far better than they can run it themselves, they want it back again. Some orator promises them the earth, kicks you out and treats his own people worse than you did. But everyone will pretend to be happy as they are being starved and murdered by their own people. Once the orator gets power, he won't give it up unless you kill him. So they will kill him. We haven't had a civil war in England since Oliver Cromwell. And you only have to go up the valley to look at the ruins of Corfe Castle to see what Cromwell thought of the St Clairs. No, Robert, stay in England. Teach history. Find a wife. Stop dreaming."

"First, we have to get through the war."

"There's that."

"You think we should go down into the cellar and look for a bottle of old Potts's special brandy?"

"Why not? There's a torch in the drawer of the kitchen table. First I'm going to pluck those two birds before they get stone cold and the feathers are difficult to pull. You want to help?"

"Of course. We have all night. By the bye. Thanks for being my brother."

"Didn't have any choice. But if I had, I wouldn't have changed any of you."

When they finished there were feathers all over the table and floor. The birds were naked from head to feet. Merlin gutted them in the sink and threw the unwanted entrails into the fire. The wet intestines sizzled. He cut open the gizzards and worked out the grit under the tap in the sink. He hung the birds by their heads from a hook next to the sink. Then he looked for the torch in the kitchen table.

"Are you coming?" he asked.

Robert had found the remains of the leg of pork from supper in the meat safe and was cutting himself slices of bread. Instead of butter, he used the dripping from the roast pork that Cook had scraped into a pot and left in the meat safe.

"The smell of that offal makes me hungry. I'm going to have a sandwich. And please use all your Merlin magic to find the brandy. Nothing better than a good pork sandwich and a balloon glass weeping up the inside with Napoleon brandy. Look in all the spots. Whatever you find we'll drink. I'll have the fire stoked up. Now off you go."

"You're impossible."

"A man has to eat. And there's only one torch. By the time we've had a few drinks, it will be breakfast time."

From inside, the old house was completely silent. From outside, they could still hear the guns from France.

"Poor sods," said Merlin as he left the kitchen.

# 4

## JANUARY 1916

$\mathcal{A}$t first sight, Fishy Braithwaite's resemblance to a codfish was uncanny. The same flattened pointed face with wet fishy eyes. He had been known as Fishy from prep school and very few ever found out his christened name was Mervyn. The second sight showed the cold, killer fury behind the wet eyes, with the blond invisible eyelashes. He was thirty-one years old, a major in the Royal Flying Corps, seventeen confirmed kills to his name, Military Cross and Bar, with a burning hatred for the whole human race that for so long had looked at his face and laughed. Now, no one laughed at him in France. They called him sir, kept the first smirk to themselves, and avoided his company even in the officers' mess, a French farmhouse the British rented at exorbitant cost, along with the farmer's field for the aircraft. The irony of paying rent to defend another man's country was lost on the French, but not on Fishy Braithwaite. He hated them as much for their exploitation as the Germans for shooting down his pilots. Major Braithwaite was commanding officer of 33 Squadron, Royal Flying Corps, and he ran the show efficiently, like a tyrant. The new pilots went from inner laughter at his facial appearance to bowel-melting fear in thirty seconds. But for all of his nastiness and discipline, he kept most of them alive, for which they were grateful. He told even his senior officers he was there to kill Germans and not to make friends.

Most of the hatred and malice stemmed from Sara Wentworth's disdain. To love a woman for so long without reward had eaten away all the goodness in his soul. And when Harry Brigandshaw was posted to his squadron as a raw pilot out of flight training, the request for the transfer had come from Major Braithwaite. Fishy Braithwaite was going to have his rival killed. When the war was over and Brigandshaw dead, she would marry the war hero he now was, and he would take his revenge for all the years she scorned him, fifteen long years of ridicule. Even their engagement so many years ago had become a mockery of marriage.

And now, on his last leave, she had made excuses not to see him. He with two Military Crosses. He who was still officially her fiancé.

He, the eldest son of a family of great wealth. How dare she deny him what she had agreed to do? That their parents had wanted the marriage as much as Mervyn had nothing to do with her final agreement. All that running off to Africa, that had worried Sara's father so much, should have brought her to her senses instead of making her wild. And now she was running around in a nurse's uniform close to the reserve trenches instead of waiting for him at home when he came back on leave. She mocked him and he would not be mocked. Why did his face have to freeze her heart? They told him even in prep school it was impossible to judge a book by its cover. And he was not a wet fish. No, he was not, his mind screamed at him. And every time he shot down a German, he screamed out loud, 'See, I'm not a wet fish! And you're dead!' The other pilots thought he was laughing at the kill and shunned him all the more.

HARRY BRIGANDSHAW HAD CONTACTED the Wentworth home in Warminster at the end of his first week in England. A man had answered the telephone, demanded his name, and then gone off somewhere after Harry asked to speak to Jared. They had kept in contact by letter for years and Jared had given Harry the family phone number in one of his sporadic letters. The correspondence had been with Jared, though Sara's name always appeared in the letters, with the throwaway line about her still not having got around to marrying Fishy Braithwaite. Harry had read nothing personal into the references.

He could hear voices talking some way away from the telephone and then the mouthpiece was picked up followed by a pause.

"Hello," he said expecting Jared to come on the line.

"This is Mrs Wentworth, Jared's mother. Are you the nice young man from Africa?"

"I live in Africa, yes, Mrs Wentworth. May I speak to Jared?"

"You could if he were here but he is not. My son joined the navy."

"Yes, he told me so in a letter. So he's not there?"

"No, he's not."

"When will he be home?"

"I have no idea."

"I'm here in England you see."

"Oh, Sara will be glad to hear you're in England."

"Well, then, is Sara there?"

"Then you wanted to speak to Sara?"

"Yes, if Jared is not there."

"Then I'll tell her. She'll be very pleased."

"But she's not there?"

"No, Sara is in France. She is a volunteer nurse. FANY, that's the First Aid Nursing Yeomanry. Won't you come down to Birchdale still this weekend?"

"Will Jared be home?"

"No. But Sara will be home on leave. She wrote to me from France. You don't have relations in England."

"I do, actually. My grandmother and my uncle, Sir James Brigandshaw. He's the managing director of Colonial Shipping."

"How very nice for you. But I still think you should come down to Birchdale all the same. Sara often talks fondly of you, Mr Brigandshaw."

"Hasn't she married Mervyn Braithwaite?"

"No, she has not. How do you know of Mr Braithwaite?"

"Well, from Sara, really. But Fishy, I mean Mervyn, was up at Oxford at the same time as myself and Robert St Clair. Robert met Sara and Jared at Elephant Walk in '07, I think it was. Might have been '08."

"Then you will come down this weekend. I insist."

"Well, if you insist."

"After so much hospitality Jared and Sara received in Africa, yes, indeed, I insist. Telephone when your train will arrive at Warminster station and I'll have the chauffeur meet you. Goodbye, Mr Brigandshaw. I shall look forward to meeting you."


FEELING guilty at not visiting Granny Brigandshaw in her London flat, Harry had taken the train to Warminster on the Friday afternoon and was met by a large motor car of a type he had never seen before. The chauffeur turned out to be Sara Wentworth in her civilian clothes. They had not seen each other for nearly ten years but Harry would have recognised the long brown-red hair anywhere. It was still down to her waist. The feet, as he remembered, were surprisingly small. Harry thought she would now be in her early thirties. She was strikingly good-looking but what was most striking was the way she greeted Harry, as if her whole world centred on their meeting. It was only around about Saturday lunchtime that Harry realised the poor girl was head over heels in love with him. This made Harry very nervous. Explaining that Granny Brigandshaw was expecting him that night, he fled Birchdale for the railway station, this time with the chauffeur at the wheel of the car. It had all been very embarrassing, Sara convinced in her mind that after all the years alone in Africa he felt the same way as she did. In the end, he had to tell her in plain words and there had been a scene at the end of the rose garden next to the lily pond.

"Then who are you in love with?" she demanded.

"No one."

"Then why not me?"

"Sara, we haven't seen each other in almost ten years."

"There's another woman!"

"No there isn't. Anyway, I thought you were engaged to Mervyn Braithwaite."

"I hate him. His face looks like the face of a wet cod."

"But you agreed to marry him."

"Only after Mother and Father threatened to cut me off without a penny. Either you marry me and get me out of here, or I break the engagement and get thrown out onto the street. Or I marry Fishy. And I'd rather die than do that."

"Doesn't he love you?"

"Of course he does. Follows me around all day with those wet eyes. Gives me the creeps... You've got to help. You're my hope. I love you, Harry. From the first, forever. Please!"

"Sara, we don't really know each other. On the farm, there were always four of us together. I rather thought you were more interested in Robert St Clair."

"He was just after my money."

"Well, look, old girl, this really is a pickle. And I have to get back to London to see my grandmother."

"You never before mentioned your grandmother."

"I did on the phone to your mother. And my Uncle James. And he's not the only one. There's Uncle Nat. They just made him a bishop, so I should see him too, and then the Flying Corps want to see me in Farnham on Monday."

"You're making excuses."

"Not really, Sara. Please, I had no idea you felt this way for so long."

"It's horrible, Harry. Horrible... And it hurts."

.   .   .

Harry had told his grandmother later the same day he had never been more embarrassed in his life.

"Should 'ave married years ago, grandson."

"There aren't that many opportunities in Africa, Granny Brigandshaw."

"Not by sound of it, lad. Not by sound of it." Granny Brigandshaw had still not lost her north country accent that had come with the poverty of her birth. Harry thought she liked to put it on a bit now she was Lady Brigandshaw, widow of a baronet. He liked her better for it and for not living at Hastings Court, where his Uncle James was now ensconced with an entourage. He had heard the family say Granny Brigandshaw had always been on her own and preferred it that way.

He had left her reading a book, with a pair of spectacles lodged on the end of her nose. For a moment, Harry thought of asking her the truth about his birth, which was when she had picked up the book and the spectacles. How she always knew what he was trying to say, he never understood. After the war, he made up his mind to get the truth from his mother once and for all.

Ten days later he made his first solo flight in a trainer aircraft that had been built before the war. The small plane had an undercarriage made from parts first intended for bicycles. Harry's lifelong friendship with aircraft had begun, even though his first landing nearly ripped off the bicycle wheels. To Harry, the rest of the aeroplane frame seemed to be made of painted cloth, string and wire struts. But it flew. Flew him up into the high blue heavens and the cotton wool clouds. He had never been so happy in his life and completely forgot about Sara Wentworth and her chronic obsession. And the war he was about to fight.

To add insult to Fishy Braithwaite's injury, his twin sisters were the toast of pre-war London society. When they came out, the twins were given a ball by their father in the family townhouse in Park Lane. The carriages and new motor cars had lined up right down Hyde Park as the girls were launched into society. Where Fishy was plain ugly his sisters were beautiful, one dark, one fair. They were not identical twins. Mervyn, the eldest, was seventeen months older than his twin sisters. Where his eyes were wet and fishy with no visible eyelashes, theirs were round, wet and seductive, with long soft brown lashes that they had learnt at finishing school in Switzerland to flutter like the wings of a butterfly. Where his face was squashed, theirs were round and in perfect proportion. Where his shortness on a man was unfortunate their smallness on a woman was petite and drew the desire of every man's protection.

At the ball, in his boiled shirt and tails that exaggerated his long thin face, he danced every dance. With all his family wealth, the mothers of that year's debutantes had placed his name on their daughters' dance cards, but not one of the girls had ever looked him in the face or asked for a refreshment at the end of a dance while younger brother Hal, who had just turned eighteen, was followed by a small group of giggling girls wherever he went. And Sara had made an excuse and stayed at Birchdale with a cold.

By the end of the evening, Mervyn knew what was ahead of him for the rest of his life... And he hated them.

The war, when it came, was a godsend. With goggles and flying helmet, and seated in a small plane armed with a machine gun mounted in front of him on a swivel, he was an invincible killing machine. And for the first time in his life, people stopped laughing at him. And Sara, whether she liked it or not, was going to be his wife.

The leave, when they awarded him his first Military Cross, was to be the one when Sara would run into his arms. He went down to Birchdale in a new car and a new brown uniform, with his wings and the ribbon of the Military Cross stitched on his left breast. He had worn his flying helmet and goggles in the open car on the journey from London where he was staying in the family townhouse.

She had not even appeared at the front door. Mrs Wentworth had to coax her out of her bedroom. Instead of flying into his arms, she had stood halfway down the stairs, holding the wooden banister while she glared at him.

"How many did you kill this time?"

"Seven," he said proudly.

"Don't you feel ashamed of yourself?"

Then she had walked back up to her bedroom. Mervyn had driven back to London with his tail between his legs, feeling much the same as he had as a child when his father verbally put him down. He had learned later Sara had joined the FANY the next day. And ever since, she had refused to see him. There had been one letter, saying the big diamond ring was in a safety deposit box in a Cox & Kings bank in the Mall: enclosed was the key.

The key had reached him in France one morning just before the dawn patrol. The German he shot down that day might have landed his crippled plane behind British lines and been captured. Mervyn had followed the young, defenceless pilot almost to the ground. The boy had waved at him and smiled. Mervyn had swivelled his Vickers machine gun and shot the young German to death. Back at the temporary aerodrome none of his pilots had spoken to him. And he didn't care. Killing was satisfying, like the sex he had never had. Not even with a whore.

HARRY BRIGANDSHAW HAD FIRST SALUTED and then put out his hand. The wet eyes stared back at him without recognition. Unperturbed, Harry kept his hand out. It had been a long time.

"Harry Brigandshaw," he said. "Oxford, '04 to '07, remember? My roommate, Robert St Clair. You remember, Mervyn?" Harry only just choked back 'Fishy'. The man in front of him was his CO. He deserved respect.

"It's either Sir or Major Braithwaite, Brigandshaw."

"Yes, sir."

Calling a man his own age, who had been up at Oxford with him, sir, was about as absurd as calling his mother Mrs Brigandshaw. Harry waited for the stern face to crack and laughter to follow. Above everything, they were fellow pilots. His right hand was still out, now stared at pointedly by Fishy Braithwaite. Harry did know some of the British took themselves too seriously. He had read about Hal's death in the *Times*. The paper had mentioned Captain Braithwaite's brother, the flying ace. Hal had been killed on the Somme leading his company in an attack. He was going to say to Mervyn how sorry he was.

Instead, he pulled back, stood rigidly to attention and saluted. Then he turned and walked quickly across to the officers' mess. They had been outside the CO's office in uniform with their hats on, so it had been correct to salute. Harry had shrugged it off by the time he reached the small bar in the mess. He thought nothing of it. He was new to the military.

It was getting dark. There would be no more flying that day. He ordered himself a large whisky. Sundowner time!... He would first fly into action tomorrow... Africa seemed a long way away. When the other pilots trickled into the bar he was shocked at how young they were. Half of them didn't even have to shave.

No one said a word to him. They all looked through him as if he was already dead. He asked the mess steward to give everyone a drink and put it on his card. It took Harry three rounds to get a smile out of anyone, which was wiped clean when the CO came into the bar. He looked at no one and no one looked at him.

"Can I buy you a drink, Mervyn?" asked Harry, now they were hatless in the sanctuary of the bar.

"I told you outside it's Sir or Major Braithwaite, Brigandshaw... My usual, Corporal. Give me Lieutenant Brigandshaw's mess card... That is not possible! No man can drink this amount in a day. Has the officer been buying my pilots drinks, Corporal?"

"Yes, sir."

"And you know it's against my rules?"

"Yes, sir, but..."

"There are no buts. Cut those stripes from your uniform and give them to me."

"But, sir," began Harry.

"You did not know the rule, Brigandshaw, now you do. The corporal knew, so he will give me his stripes, and from tomorrow receive the pay of a private. Now, is that clear to everyone?"

"Yes, sir," called the pilots together.

Harry had kept his mouth shut.

"Is it clear, Brigandshaw?"

"Yes, Major Braithwaite." Harry looked him straight in the eye. He had thought the Germans would be the ones to hate him in France. And then he understood. Sara Wentworth. The posting had not been a fluke after all. The man hated him.

"Oh, my God," he said barely aloud. "Better give me a drink, Corporal," he said louder. "A large one."

"He's not a corporal," snapped Fishy Braithwaite.

"He is until tomorrow if I heard you rightly... Sir."

It felt like being alone in the Zambezi Valley without a gun. He would have to watch his back.

He was woken the next morning by his newly appointed batman, just before dawn. The nine aircraft took off for the dawn patrol over the Somme, led by Major Braithwaite. Harry had felt safer with his foot halfway down onto a puff adder. He had never had a real enemy before. But like everything else in life, he told himself, there was a first for everything.

THEIR JOB WAS to stop the Germans shooting down the observation balloons that were spotting for the British artillery. There was a minor British hate on one section of the front, a probe, Harry thought, to take prisoners in a night attack to find out the German intentions.

Soon after take-off, they had split into three patrols. Harry was flying to the back and left of Fishy Braithwaite, maintaining the leader's altitude as they climbed above the Western Front. By the time they reached a position above the reserve trench, the false dawn had given way to broad sunlight at ten thousand feet. Below, everything was dark. All the time Harry, in the cockpit of his de Havilland biplane, moved his head around. He was as comfortable as riding his horse on Elephant Walk, the Vickers machine gun on its swivel no different to his Purdey. For the first time in many years, he was hunting. And being hunted.

Harry said a short prayer for his brother George, who had died down below, and left his flesh and bones rotting in the mud far from home. When he said his prayer he could make out the Somme River, then the Allied and German trenches.

"In the bush, Harry, always trust your senses. The buffalo, the lion, they are animals. So are you. We sense each other when in tune with nature."

Harry smiled at the voice of his dead father in his head. Even now he was giving him guidance.

"A good hunter has good senses. He knows when he's being watched. He knows by instinct he is being stalked. Get into tune with nature. Survival. That's all we are about. Survival of us. Survival of our family. Survival of our species. It's your job to make sure we survive, Harry."

Some had said before that Harry's peripheral vision was so good he had eyes in the back of his head. From years of watching his back in the bush, he had trained his eyes to pick up movement directly behind, even when he was looking forward.

"Never drop your guard, Harry. Never let your mind go to sleep when you are hunting. A leopard can drop on you from a tree quicker than you can bring up a rifle. Feel the cat tense before he drops and you will have time to gut-shoot him in the belly. No, don't just take my word. Ask your Uncle Tinus. You only have to mess up once in the bush... And all animals are dangerous. A honey badger the size of a dog goes for the balls of a buffalo, the one vulnerable spot. A honey badger can kill a buffalo. It can kill you. Have a look at his teeth... In the bush, a man feels alive."

They flew another hour up and down no man's land, looking for German aircraft. Then they headed for their airfield and breakfast. His mind still crystal clear, Harry had never felt colder in his life. His three-point landing on the rough turf of the field was perfect. He noted Braithwaite kept his goggles on even when he climbed down from his aircraft. His mechanic had taken control of the machine, gunning the engine to taxi the biplane towards the camouflaged canvas hangar. Twice the field had been attacked by the Germans. Regularly the camouflaged hangars were moved on their wooden poles.

Harry was hungry. The grey sky was weeping a thin drizzle. The third pilot in their trio caught up with Harry and walked alongside. Both of them had taken off their helmets and goggles but not their flying gloves.

"What's the matter with him?" asked Harry.

"The major is quite mad."

"You sure?"

"We all are. Too long in the air. Too many kills. Nerves snap. He's been gone a long time. Not the only one. But he's good. You wait and watch him fight... Thanks for the drinks last night. We should have told you. Most of us live off our pay... You have a farm in Africa... Sorry, sir. Money."

"Don't call me sir. We're the same lowly rank."

"It's the age bit, sir. How long you been flying?"

"Less than four months."

"Good God. Watching you up there and land, thought you'd been born in the cockpit."

"In the saddle. To the son of a white hunter."

When the third flight landed there were only two aircraft. Five minutes later the third one landed, pieces of cloth flapping under the right wing and from the fuselage behind the cockpit.

Major Braithwaite strode across to the aircraft.

"Poor old Bunty," said someone looking up from his bacon and eggs. "Some say it's better to let the Hun kill you than bring back a damaged plane... Can someone pass me the butter?"

Outside in the cold, the pilot of the damaged plane was receiving a roasting. Making the gestures and shouts of the small major more bizarre, was the fact he had not taken off his goggles. Harry watched the man through the window of what once had been the farmhouse dining room. The man was like a bantam cock in a blind rage.


THE LEADEN SKY settled down just above their heads for three days and rained on them. There was no more flying. The grass airfield was waterlogged and visibility down to one hundred yards. From the air, they would be able to spot nothing on the ground. If they flew into clouds, they could lose themselves and never find clear sky. They were grounded.

Harry learnt to avoid Fishy Braithwaite. Any conversation they had would be military. If the man wanted to behave like an idiot, that was his business. Because the other pilots were so much younger, he found himself mostly on his own. Which was how he liked it. Harry Brigandshaw had never been lonely in his life. The solitude of the bush was his joy. Like flying alone high in the sky. When the youngsters talked to him he joined the conversation, the kind of conversation he remembered from his days at boarding school in the Cape. At Bishops, life had been one long leg-pull. Even playing cricket. His fellow pilots were slightly overgrown schoolboys and he envied them their innocence. Getting killed was no different to getting a duck at cricket. Mostly, he left them to their small talk, their innocent practical jokes. Even the three captains in the squadron were in their teens. In a war with appalling casualties, any survivor rose quickly in rank. Harry, mostly, read a book or thought about home.

More than once the picture of Tina Pringle appeared in his thoughts. If George had not been killed and sent him running to Europe, he wondered what might have happened. He couldn't remember meeting a sexier woman in his life. She was alive, dangerous, and knew what she wanted; and that was never going back into the class system of England. He could still feel her eyes looking at him and sending a signal straight to his balls. Just the picture of her in his head had the same effect.

Even at the time, he had known that there could be no casual affair with Tina Pringle. Unlike the few girls he had known in Cape Town when he did not go back to Elephant Walk for the school holidays. When he stayed with schoolfriends. Or at Kleinfontein with Barend Oosthuizen.

The first had been a woman on the beach between the rocks, where a wet bed of sand had been washed in by the sea. She was the nurse for the younger siblings of his schoolfriend, the only reason he could still remember his friend, Francois Botha's name. The woman, he thought subsequently, was in her twenties. Harry had just turned fifteen. Gently, she had made a man of him. He would always remember her but never knew her name.

"Always cradle a woman afterwards even if you don't want to. She wants that. Even the most casual of sex has the meaning of life."

"What's your name?"

"No, Harry. Just remember me. You are going to become a wonderful man... Just remember me the same, so for you, I will never grow old. When I am old and grey, I will think of you thinking of me, young and beautiful. Then I will be young and beautiful again. Sun, beach and me. Enjoy the rest of your life, Harry. I wish us both to have a wonderful life. Just treasure my memory for me. It's going to be precious to me."

Harry had wanted many times over the years to find out her name from Francois Botha, but he had always kept the promise. And she was still as young to him as the day so long ago they had made love together on the wet sand of the beach, hidden from any other world than their own. Even now in France, wet and cold, fighting a war, he could see her smiling up at him. And she would never grow old as long as he lived. The beach was called Llandudno, that much he could remember. And it was in the Cape, not in Wales. And he had never been back to the place. And never would. The memory was too precious to break.

THE THIRD DAY was more leaden than the first, visibility down to fifty yards. Away from the other pilots by the window, Harry picked up the sound first. He had never heard the engine note before but he knew it was not coming from a de Havilland. The CO was not in the farmhouse they now called the officers' mess. He had not been seen all day, not even at breakfast. One of the flight leaders had stopped talking. Then everyone listened.

"Shit," cried one of the pilots. Ripping open the door, he raced over the field towards the hangar and his aircraft.

Harry could now hear the distinct chatter of machine gun fire. Then he saw them. Three enemy aircraft were flying down the grass runway six feet off the ground, having hopped over the hedge. The running pilot stumbled and fell thirty yards short of his aircraft still in the camouflaged hangar. He did not get up. An aircraft engine fired from the hangar, and the major's aircraft came out, the engines running as he taxied the plane to face the Germans. Then, solid on the platform of his aircraft on the ground, he fired at the oncoming Germans who were shooting up his airfield, swinging his Vickers back and forth across their line of flight. The Germans were flying directly to the officers' mess. They were after the pilots, planes being easier to replace than trained pilots. One moment the three German planes were steady on their approach and then they broke, two of them flying into the ground, the third pulling up over Fishy Braithwaite, the downdraught shaking the de Havilland biplane on the ground. It was over as quickly as it started.

The pilot who said the one word 'shit' was lying dead on the runway. It was the same boy who had thanked Harry for the drinks.

In the middle of the grass runway, well short of his aircraft, Harry felt the rain dripping down his face. They could all clearly hear their CO shouting now the noise of the engines had gone. The two German aircraft were burning on the ground. Ground crew were trying to pull out the pilots. One was still alive.

"I'm not a wet fish! And you're dead!" shouted the CO over and over, gunning his engine. Then he got down from his aircraft, pistol in hand, and began to race across the soggy field towards the German pilot who was still alive.

"Oh, my God," said Harry, and began to run. He was lightly clad from the time he was reading his book in the mess. Fishy Braithwaite was fully dressed for winter flying. Harry caught him short of the German, who was now kneeling on the ground. Harry tackled Fishy low, as he had been taught at school, pushing the major's face down in the mud. The sergeant mechanic who had pulled the German pilot from the burning wreck was standing with his mouth open. The pistol flew from the CO's right hand and Harry struggled up and trod it into the mud.

"Sorry, sir," Harry said looking back. "Following you. Must have tripped. Jolly good show. Two of them. Very brave. The one chap's still alive, you'll be pleased to know. Won't be flying in this war again. Can I give you a hand?"

"You did that on purpose, Brigandshaw."

"Why on earth would I do it on purpose? You saved our lives. They were going for the officers' mess... Sergeant! Bring the prisoner to the officers' mess. Poor chap needs a drink... It is over, Fritz," he said to the kneeling German.

"I speak English," said the German. "He had a gun in his hand. He was going to shoot me."

"Nonsense, old boy. Running to help. We both were... Are you wounded?"

"I'm not sure."

"We'll have the MO give you a once-over. The weather was clearing your side of the lines, I suppose. How you jumped us."

"Yes, it was."

"Almost caught us napping... You are now a prisoner of war. The other chap's dead I'm afraid. So's one of our chaps. Silly really, isn't it?"

"Where are you from?" asked the German.

"My accent, I suppose... Africa. Rhodesia. You chaps killed my brother, or I'd still be over there."

When Harry looked around, Fishy Braithwaite was walking away in the opposite direction still wearing his goggles. Harry waited for the sergeant to escort the German to the mess. Then he walked across and picked up the gun, slipping it into his pocket. He did not think anyone had seen him. Then he began to shiver from the cold. And fear. If there had been a senior officer anywhere he knew he would have handed in the gun. What Fishy Braithwaite was going to do was murder in Harry's book. Even in a time of war. As he walked to his room behind the officers' mess, the gun was heavy in his trouser pocket. Then he put on his army greatcoat and went for a walk in the rain. There was a pond half a mile away. Harry checked he was alone, took the pistol from his pocket and tossed it out into the water, where it sank out of sight. Fear, cold fear, had a firm grip on the inside of Harry's stomach. He was no longer so sure he was coming out of this war alive.

THE WEATHER CLOSED in again and it was unlikely they would fly the next day. The rain intensified. The airstrip was deeply waterlogged. Harry took himself off to the only bathroom in the old farmhouse and soaked in a hot bath. Fishy Braithwaite had gone off in his open sports car despite the rain. He was still wearing his flying goggles. The senior captain, still in his teens, a boy, gave the order to post machine gun crews at each end of the runway, the guns mounted on stands so the gunners could fire up into the air.

Harry thought it should have been done before, as today had been the third attack on the makeshift aerodrome. Good officers planned ahead. Good officers out-thought the enemy. Heroics were one thing. Prevention was another.

Letting his mind drift, he went back into the comfort of the bush. Everything was simple in the bush. Dangerous but more predictable. One lion behaved much like another. Animals had their habits and rarely strayed. They drank from the same waterhole. Mostly emptied out yesterday's food at the same spot with the whole family. Birds nested every year at the same time. Trees flowered when they were meant to flower. The migration of birds happened every year. The bush was predictable. Nature was on time. Inside one lion's head were the same thoughts and instincts of any other lion. Unless the lion was sick. Had an abscess. Was in pain.

When it came to man, the worst thing to do was judge another person by what one would do oneself. Inside every man's head was a different set of thoughts. No man was quite certain what was in another man's head. To try to work out the next move of a rational man was hard enough and mostly a calculated guess. What was going on in the head of Fishy Braithwaite was beyond Harry's comprehension. In normal times, his ranting at the crashed German aircraft, heard by nearly everyone on the station, would have had him carted off to an asylum.

THE FIRE in the room with the bar, which had previously been the parlour of the French farmhouse and the most comfortable room in the house, was burning high, competing with the storm outside. The big guns were silent. The machine gun and rifle fire from twenty miles away were muffled by the distance and the storm. The corporal who was now a private was still behind the bar doing the same job for less pay. If he had complained he might have been sent into the trenches.

After his third drink sitting alone silently at the bar, the senior captain sat down next to him on a bar stool. The barman was at the end of the bar.

"Did you pick it up again?" he asked.

"Yes."

"Do you have it?"

"No. Threw it in the pond…"

"Quite a tackle."

"What are you going to do?"

"Nothing… You knew him at Oxford. Did you ever call him 'Fishy' to his face?"

"All the time."

"Oh, dear God. No wonder he looks at you that way."

"It's worse. There's a woman. Once his fiancée. She thinks she's in love with me. Braithwaite knows. I think he is going to let me get myself killed. Where is the prisoner?"

"We sent him back straight away."

"Look out. Our CO has just walked into the room… Don't worry about me. And no, I don't love the woman in question. Fact is, she's about as obsessed as Braithwaite."

SARA WENTWORTH RECEIVED the letter the next day. It was still raining over most of France. All the casualties from the last hate had been sent back to the hospital in Calais. For the first time in a week, the tent was empty of wounded soldiers. Sara was smoking a cigarette, something she had taken up on arrival in France. The cigarettes calmed her nerves. The one doctor was also smoking, sitting in a canvas chair next to the bucket fire. Both of them were frozen at the back and warm in front from the fire. Inch-wide holes let the heat from the coals warm her feet. She took the letter from the runner and recognised the handwriting. Her first instinct was to throw the whole thing in the fire. She kept it in her lap for when she was alone.

"Don't you read your mail?" said the doctor. He was sweet on her. She smiled at him now and turned the envelope on its face. To stop the doctor looking at her she pushed her index finger under the flap and crudely broke open the envelope.

MY DEAR FIANCÉE,

*You will be pleased to hear your friend from Africa is now under my command.*
*You should not have mentioned his name.*
*Your loving Mervyn.*


THE KEY to the safety deposit box had fallen out onto her lap.

She slipped the key into the large front pocket of the white apron and
threw the rest on the fire. Then she went outside the tent and was sick in the
mud and the rain. Her feet were quickly icy cold.

Down the line towards Amiens, the British guns started up again. There
was a new exchange of heavy artillery. A new hate.


BY THE TIME they were able to fly again from the airfield, it was the last day
in January. It was the second time Harry had taken off to fly into action.
They had waited until three o'clock in the afternoon. Only three aircraft
took to the air, led by Major Braithwaite. They had not flown for five days.
The leaden sky had gone. There were a few white fluffy clouds, with some
blue high in the sky. The leftover water on the ground was already
beginning to freeze. By the time they came back, the mud would be frozen
hard. If it wasn't, they would probably tip over on landing, with the front
wheels stuck in the mud.

Harry had never taken off before in such conditions and twice taxied his
plane around pools of water. He knew Fishy Braithwaite was looking at him,
though he could not make out the man's expression behind the goggles. The
third pilot was the senior captain who had ordered the machine guns to be
placed at both ends of the runway.

They took off badly, Harry just clearing the mounted machine gun. Then
they were up in the afternoon sun, dodging around the big clouds, making
for the front line where the new hate had been going on for two days. With
the weather clearing, the spotter balloons had been cranked up on their
cables into the sky. Harry forgot the airfield he had left behind. All his
instincts were concentrating on keeping alive, his head moving constantly as
he searched the sky. He was flying his biplane thirty feet to the back and left
of Fishy Braithwaite, keeping his eye on the major as much as the sky. The
British balloons below were halfway up to their spotting height, the ground
crews laboriously cranking up steel cables. They flew for half an hour to the
limit of their patrol line and turned, curving over the German front line at
six thousand feet. Even if he had wanted to look down, Harry kept his eyes
on the surrounding sky and his CO. There was now little wind at six

thousand feet and the higher clouds had expanded, squeezing the pockets of blue sky.

At the moment his hair rose on the nape of his neck, Harry kicked left rudder, scudding his biplane to bring it round onto 'the belly of the leopard'. The German tracer passed harmlessly through the air where he had been flying. The enemy craft had the same black tailplanes that had shot up the airfield earlier in the week. There were six of them. Gaining height as he had been taught, Harry flew into a cloud, flying blind for half a minute. When he came out he was alone in the sky. The sun was down on the horizon, straight in his eyes. Shielding the sun with his gloved right hand, Harry found his bearings, much as he had done in the bush, and headed for their airfield. He was the first to land on the hardened mud, the daylight almost gone.

The pilots and the ground crew waited on the ground, listening for the sound of the de Havilland engines. When the sound came the pilots cheered. The CO's plane landed first, down the wheel line made by Harry during his landing. Only the top of the mud was hard. When the captain landed to the left of the CO it was too dark to see where he was landing and too dark to make a circuit and land in the CO's tracks. The biplane cartwheeled halfway down the field and burst into flame, the captain still strapped into his seat. The man burnt, screaming.

Harry was quite sure he was not going to make it through the war.

"Why did you run, Brigandshaw? First bit of action and you run for the cloud." Fishy Braithwaite was laughing. "Thought you big game hunters were tougher than that. You'd better keep on getting lucky or it'll be all over for you. The idea is to fight the Germans not run away. But you Rhodesians wouldn't understand that now would you? Colonials are all the same. Wrong backbone or they wouldn't have left the island in the first place... Maybe you will fight next time. We shall see. We can only hope."

"Would he have been your pilot choice if he had not sighted the machine guns at each end of the runway?" asked Harry.

"I don't know what you're talking about."

"I hope not, Fishy, I really hope not."

"*Don't call me Fishy*," screamed Braithwaite.

"Sorry, sir. Just slipped out."

The pilot, now free of the burning wreckage, was still screaming, though he was lying on the ground. Harry was not sure if he wished for the captain to live or die.

# 5

# NOVEMBER 1916

*S*allie Barker finished the newspaper article and wondered if there was any civilisation left in man. She questioned whether humanity learned anything from the journey out of the primaeval slime.

She got up from her desk in the downtown business district of Johannesburg and looked out of her fourth-floor window. In the distance she could see the yellow mine dumps, the tailings brought up from the bowels of the gold mines deep in the belly of the earth. A highveld wind was blowing loose soil in clouds towards the city. Above, a bright blue sky dotted with small white clouds belied the thunderstorm that wet Johannesburg most afternoons in November at around four o'clock. The balance sheet she had been reading before her secretary brought in the *Rand Daily Mail* was covered by the discarded newspaper. The company, Serendipity Mining and Explosives, had increased profit by a multiple of ten. She was richer than she could ever have imagined.

The price of gold had risen the moment the war in Belgium and France bogged down into trench warfare. Albert Pringle's contact with Frederick St Clair had sent large quantities of fuses and percussion caps to India and the mining empire of Frederick's father-in-law. Benny Lightfoot, having returned to Johannesburg, now bought all his explosive supplies for his mines from Albert. The two of them had become friends. Tina, miffed, was usually left out of the conversation. But above everything else, the war and munitions had made them rich. Making shells to explode among Germans was where the money came from. Sallie shuddered. The battle of the

Somme, generally regarded as finished by the journalist she had just read, had killed half a million British troops. Between the French battle at Verdun, and the British offensive on the Somme, both going on for months, two million young men on both sides of the war, the best of Europe, had perished. And very largely, according to the article Sallie put down in sickening disgust, the armies were in much the same place they started from.

Turning from her sightless stare out of the window, Sallie looked for the company profit and loss account, which was attached to the balance sheet hidden under the morning newspaper. The small newsflash at the bottom of the front page caught her eye.

'Rhodesian pilot receives second Military Cross in nine months. See page seven.'

Sallie turned the pages and on page seven, a man in flying gear looked back at her. He was somehow familiar. Forgetting what she had been looking for in the profit and loss account, she sat back in her chair and picked up the newspaper from her desk.

It was headed, *Pilot's eighteenth confirmed kill in nine months*. She began the article.

*THE SON of a well-known white hunter has turned the skills he learned hunting lion and elephant in the African bush into hunting German aircraft in the sky. Harry Brigandshaw, son of famous hunter Sebastian Brigandshaw, who was killed by the Great Elephant, has now shot down more than any other Allied pilot in the first nine months of 1916. 33 Squadron, led by the legendary 'Mad' Major Braithwaite, has shot thirty-seven of the enemy out of the sky. There is talk in the Royal Flying Corps, soon to be renamed the Royal Air Force under General Trenchard, that the mad major and Captain Brigandshaw are racing each other for a Victoria Cross. The mad major has twenty-five kills, far less than Major Ball, VC. But if the war goes on long enough, and Braithwaite and Brigandshaw survive, they could both receive the supreme honour from the King. When Brigandshaw first joined Braithwaite's squadron in January of this year, Braithwaite had seventeen confirmed kills with the Military Cross and Bar. Brigandshaw is catching up. It is the stuff of men like this that will win us the war. This journalist salutes the both of them.*

THE ARTICLE, Sallie read, had been copied with permission from the *Times* of London. Taking a pair of scissors from her desk drawer she cut out the article to give to Albert Pringle. Then she thought again. In some ways, it would be like giving him a white feather. And the last thing Sallie wanted was another rush of conscience and Albert running off to war. The Pringles had given enough sons to king and country.

Sallie carefully folded the article and put it in the drawer with the scissors. She remembered the name well from the SS *King Emperor*. Just the photograph had looked different. On the boat out from England, Harry had been a man shrouded in innocence. Now that had gone. She was now glad not to have had any brothers. Or a husband, she thought, thinking back to her first introduction to Harry on the boat. When they had both been innocent. When she had never even heard of a whorehouse.

For the first time in months, Sallie thought of her mother. In her mother's hunt for a suitable husband for Sallie, she had found out something odd about Harry Brigandshaw's birth. That he was heir to far more than a farm in Rhodesia. After racking her brain for a few moments without success, she picked up the set of accounts and went back to work. They were sitting on far too much cash. Cash in the bank was good but idle. Money was made to invest.

With difficulty, she removed her mind from the immediacy of the war and thought how business would look when it was over. All wars came to an end. Even the hundred-year war in Europe. If this one lasted that long they would have killed the European race. What could she do with an over-expanded explosives factory once the war came to an end?

She was still worrying and not finding an answer when her secretary knocked at her closed door. A moment later into the room was ushered Mrs Barker. Sallie had not seen her mother in nearly ten years. The woman looked dreadful. Rather like Lily White when she had arrived back at the end of her tether. Though where Lily White was as fat as a pig, Mrs Barker was as thin as a rake. Had thinking of her mother brought the devil through her door? For the second time, Sallie shuddered.

"Hello, Mother," Sallie said wearily, not getting up from her desk. There was no point in asking what she wanted. They all wanted the same. Money. It was the downside of being rich Sallie knew one day she would have to accept.

"Darling, how are you?" gushed Mrs Barker in her cheap clothes, trying her best.

It was hard for Sallie to imagine that once, in another world, she had suckled at this withered old woman's breasts. But she had. And the woman was still her mother. Forcing away all her revulsion she got up and gave her mother a hug. Sensibly, the secretary had closed the door.

"So you work here?"

"No, Mother, I own the place. With Albert Pringle. But I'm sure you know all about that."

The revulsion had washed over her in a drowning wave.

"We'd better go out and get some lunch," she said, pulling herself together.

"That would be nice, darling. Very nice."

"Do you have any luggage?"

"Not really, darling. But does that matter now?"

"No, it probably doesn't."

As she reached the door handle she had a brief flash of fat Herr Flugelhorne raping her as he farted, a picture she knew would never go away. The third shudder was the worst.

SHE TOOK her mother to the main restaurant in the Grand, staring down the head waiter who sniffed at Mrs Barker's clothes. At the end of the meal, she signed the bill adding ten per cent for the tip. The man was only doing his job. If every patron brought their destitute mothers to lunch the place would get a bad reputation. All through lunch she had let her mother tell the story of her humiliation. The Flugelhorne relations were never mentioned. Nothing else was mentioned other than how badly Mrs Barker had been done by, starting with Sallie's father and ending with her last job as a housekeeper. The small severance pay from that job had paid the passage to Africa. Sallie was her mother's last chance.

WITH LILY WHITE still ensconced in her house like a returning duchess, Sallie wondered what would become of her private life. But in a strange and true way, she owed both of them her life. They made her cross and she would have to bear them.

When they finally reached her home in Parktown it had begun to rain. Bill Hardcastle, who ran the house, helped Mrs Barker out of the open Bentley tourer. Then they all heard the thunder and went inside. By the time she was through the front door, it was clear Mrs Barker thought she owned the place.

The only pleasure Sallie reaped from the day was the look of panic on Lily White's face when Sallie introduced her mother. Bill Hardcastle kept a blank face. Inscrutable. But under the inscrutability, Sallie knew Bill was having a laugh. Not at her. At life. How the past so often came back to haunt the present. The idea of marrying Albert Pringle was no longer so obscure. He may not make her sexually crave the satisfaction. She did not love him in the sense that other people understood. She was not even sure she could imagine the two of them in bed together. Yet, Albert was reliable. Albert was always there. He was her friend. Never once had she not been pleased to see him. Maybe that was worth far more than all the excitement... Try though she did, she could never quite make herself agree. There had to be excitement. There had to be a gut-wrenching rush. There had to be the desire to never take her hands off a man. To make love for a week... In some ways, her life seemed to be so simple. She had tried with a man. Several times. But it never lasted; she always remembered, always afraid. And afterwards, life was worse than before. To find and lose life's satisfaction so quickly. It was cruel. Something in her private life had to last, other than Lily White and her mother.

AT THE TIME Mrs Barker was ordering Bill Hardcastle to bring tea out onto the veranda, not far away, Tina Pringle was reading the newspaper. Her brother had brought it home with him. Diligently she read the front page but did not pick up on the newsflash about the Rhodesian pilot. Reading the newspaper was part of her new education. Since the reading had become easier, she enjoyed some of what she was reading.

Soon after they returned from their safari more than a year ago, Albert had broached the subject of her education and where she should be going with her life.

"Being a magnet for men is one thing when you are young. But keeping them is quite another thing. You only have to look at Lily White. I can tell you from first-hand that when she first met Jack Merryweather she had the same power over men as you. Now look at her. She couldn't sell herself in the old Mansion House if she tried. Not even sure with all that weight if it's still possible."

"She let herself go," Tina had said, not in the least bit interested.

"It would not have made any difference."

"Why not?" said Tina with the confidence of youth.

"All women get old. After twenty-five, their power diminishes."

"Nonsense. Once you got it, like, you never lose it. Sex appeal stays. Mark my words. And talkin' of sex, when are you goin' to bang that Sallie Barker? You look at 'er like she is the bloody Queen but she's a woman with the same under 'er pants as the rest of us. Bang the bloody woman, or stop lookin' at 'er with them sheep eyes."

"She's not interested."

"You can still bang 'er. Surprising what you find after a bang. The ones what looks the worst out of bed are sometimes the best in the sack." Tina smacked her lips.

"You have a filthy mind."

"Why does the truth always hurt, brother Bert? Bang 'er. Take my word."

"You're getting me off the track."

"I know."

"You can't even read properly let alone add up. You need an education like I got at Sallie's instigation."

"There you go again. Bang the bloody woman."

"I'm being serious. If you want to really get on in this life you have to have an education. Look at me."

"All right, Bert. What's the problem?"

"I want you to be someone. Not a Lily White."

"I'm not a whore."

"You behave like one."

"I'm looking for a rich husband."

"Rich men do not marry illiterate women. They make them their mistresses and kick them out when they've had enough... You don't think Benny Lightfoot would have married you?"

"He might have done."

"In your dreams, sister darling."

"What you 'ave in mind, Bert?"

"A teacher. A Miss Pinforth. Reading. Writing. Arithmetic. Decorum. How to walk. How to dress."

"You're serious! Blimey!"

"You need to be taught how to behave yourself. But most of all, how to speak properly. Dammit, Tina. We are not going back to England. That railway cottage doesn't have to come with us. I'm rich. Alongside me, you can marry who you want in Johannesburg. But first, you've got to learn how to behave."

"Are you knocking our dad and our mum?"

"I love both of them. You know that. We've a chance to get off the bottom bloody rung. Growing up in that old cottage was lovely. Crowded but lovely. But I want more. So do you. For heaven's sake, I was a 'gentleman's gentleman', a bloody valet. Now look at me. And had it not been for Jack Merryweather making me read proper, and write, and speak proper, I'd a still 'ave been in the gutter so to speak."

"You just dropped an 'h', Bert."

"I know I did. And that's what I mean. It's still skin-deep in me but it won't be in my kids."

"Better bang 'er first, Bert."

"Oh shut up and listen... Do you want to make something of your life?"

"Yes I do," said Tina very quietly.

"Good. Miss Pinforth moves into the house tomorrow."

"You banging 'er, Bert?"

"She's fifty-seven. A severe fringe. Glasses. Very plain I'm afraid. She would probably have killed to have had your sex appeal. Though at fifty-seven that doesn't even matter. No, I'm not 'banging' Miss Pinforth. And when you see her tomorrow you'll know exactly why... I want mum and dad to be proud of you. What with Walter blown to bits and Edward drowned. Never found nothing of Billy."

"I'll do it if you promise me one thing. You don't go and join the army. I don't want you dead too, Bert. Please. I can't 'andle another. There's three of my brothers dead in this bloody war and they can't take the last of you. Promise me that and I'll do anything you want."

BRINGING her mind back to the present, Tina noticed the rain had stopped as quickly as it had come. She could still hear thunder rumbling over towards the Magaliesberg Mountains. From the veranda on Parktown Ridge, she could see the bush going far away, to where the rays of the sun were breaking through the black thunderclouds moments before the sun would sink for the day. Miss Pinforth preferred a small cottage at the bottom of the garden where the flowers were plentiful and she could be at peace on her own. Being at peace was a large thing in Miss Pinforth's life. Surprisingly to Tina, the woman was happy. She never mentioned family or friends. Only the flowers and the birds in the garden, and the books she read.

Tina had turned nineteen the week before and when she concentrated she managed not to drop letters all over her speech. She had even begun to put the words in their right sequence. Adding up, she said to Albert, was now a 'piece of cake'. Why it was a piece of cake Albert did not know but he understood what his sister was saying. She was learning. There was even a better quality of men on the veranda when Albert came home to his house. And quite often the same people. Sometimes the men brought girls but none of them appealed to Albert. Only when Sallie came over to the house did his face light up. There was nothing he could do. As the years went by he only wanted Sallie. And if he couldn't have Sallie he'd end up like Miss Pinforth, at the bottom of the garden with a book.

To Albert's surprise, there were no visitors drinking his booze when he had come home with the paper. He had put it down to the rain. Later, he was standing with his hands on the iron wrought railing looking out from the ridge, when he heard his sister take a sharp intake of breath.

"It's him," she said deliberately. The 'h' in place was so affected it made Albert smile. He had found the same problem. In the end, it came naturally. "It's Harry Brigandshaw. Got to be. Air force. That's right. Look at this, Bert. Our 'ost up in Africa's a bleedin' hero."

"You'd better not let Miss Pinforth hear you put it that way."

"But he is. Look. I'm right. There's his name under the photograph. Harry Brigandshaw. Now, he's lovely. Don't know what I wouldn't have done to him if he hadn't run away. He's gorgeous. What was the name of his farm?"

"Elephant Walk."

"That's it. The funny name. That's what started it. I could marry him, Bert. The others are mostly a bunch of twits. Harry Brigandshaw is a man. Too bad he ran away."

The doorbell rang from the hall and Tina put down the paper. The entourage was late, thought Albert, but there had been the rain. The sun gave out a last flash of light and sank into the African bush. One of the black servants was wheeling in the drinks tray. Albert smiled to himself. There were always plenty of friends when there were free drinks. And Tina... Harry Brigandshaw. He thought she had forgotten him months ago. The babble of voices was building up in the hall. Waiting until the last moment, he turned to greet their guests. No one was ever invited but that did not matter. There were seven of them. Two women. Neither of them was Sallie.

Albert made himself a stiff whisky and turned back to look out over the distant bush. Most of the colour had already gone from the sky. There was a new light in Miss Pinforth's cottage. Behind him, Tina was doing her thing. Later he was sure one of the men would escort her out to dinner. Or the crowd would all go together.

Making an excuse, he took his drink to his bedroom and sat on the balcony that led out from the bedroom. He kept the lights off to keep away the mosquitoes. There was no malaria in Johannesburg. The canvas chair was comfortable and Albert fell asleep when he had finished his drink. He would have liked another drink but did not want to talk to the guests. It had been a long, hard day in the explosives factory, making certain all the safety precautions were being observed. Giving orders was one thing. They had to be checked.

The banging front door woke him. His empty glass was on the floor next to the chair. He would have one more good one in the quiet of the night on his own. Then he would go to bed. He was not hungry.

To his surprise, the small light was still on over the drinks tray and Tina was using it to read the newspaper.

"Didn't you go out with them?" asked Albert.

"He's a hero. Eighteen kills. Military Cross and Bar. Whatever the Bar means."

"Who?"

"Harry Brigandshaw."

"So that's why you didn't want to go out."

"Yes... It is... You think he'll be all right, Bert?"

"Of course."

"They say it's all the hunting he did in the bush. His father was a famous hunter... Why did he leave to go to war?"

"The Germans killed his brother... I should go."

"You promised, Bert. Please don't go. You do more for the war effort in the factory. By far. Have another drink and come and talk to me. I couldn't be bothered with all the chatter tonight."

"You'd better turn off the light or the mosquitoes will eat you alive."

"Then we'll go inside. I'll make us a sandwich. Have a good chat, you and me."

"We haven't done that for a long time... You're not tired, are you?"

"Not anymore."


THE NEXT DAY, and just past eleven o'clock in the morning, on the other side of Parktown, Lily White, born Lily Ramsbottom in south Wigan, was watching Mrs Barker like a cat watches a snake, ready to strike if the danger became real. Lily had eaten four slices of fruitcake for her elevenses and the pangs of hunger and loneliness had gone away for the moment. Mrs Barker was ordering poor Mrs Hardcastle, the cook and housekeeper, left and right. It was hard for Lily not to chuckle out loud. She knew the story. Not so long ago, the high and mighty Mrs Barker was a housekeeper herself, a servant, ordered about from pillar to post. Watching Mrs Barker lash Molly Hardcastle with her tongue, Lily wished someone would order the old bitch to a post on the other side of the world... And just when it looked like she was settling in nicely to the home that would be hers for as long as she wanted. Lily sighed and wondered what she would have to do to get the skinny little rake out of the house. Bill Hardcastle had found an excuse to go shopping. Even though he had not said a word, they understood each other.

At least she, Lily, had started the process that had led to all the money. All Mrs Barker had done was give herself to a man, but what man could ever have wanted to dip his wick in a spitting viper, Lily could no way comprehend. The poor man had done the sensible thing by killing himself. That much she did know.

Lily didn't want a man any more. She had satiated her lust on a string of lovers, all of them rich, some of them nice, one of them, Jack Merryweather, she had thought once she even loved. It was not the lack of men that worried Lily, even though she was barely forty; there were enough good memories to last her a lifetime. If she wanted a man she would lose her fat and go for the really old men. Fat came from eating. All she had to do was stop eating. No, for Lily it was not the lack of men or even being the centre of male attention. It was loneliness. However much money she still had stashed away from the old whorehouse, it was being left alone that worried Lily White the most. She was terrified, utterly terrified of being left alone. And Sallie Barker was the answer to her prayer. A nice home. Good food. And company every time she wanted it.

"Would you like a piece of cake, Mrs Barker?" she said sweetly.

"Haven't you eaten enough?" snapped Mrs Barker turning her attention from the hapless Molly Hardcastle.

Sallie smiled and said nothing. When Mrs Barker turned back to her first victim, Lily gave Molly a wink. The trick, Lily thought, was to make allies. As many as possible.


THOUSANDS OF MILES away Robert St Clair would have given anything for just one piece of Lily White's cake. The rations came through but never a good meal. Canned meat. Canned vegetables, mostly carrots. Canned fruits, mostly plums. Canned corn kernels, big yellow globs that Robert had never seen before in his life. All were stamped made in the USA. Anyone over there with a canning factory was getting rich.

There had been a lull in the fighting for a week. Both sides were exhausted. It was rumoured the Somme offensive was over. The only thing in abundance on the Western Front, other than machine gun fire and high explosives, was rumour. Soon the rumour would change, and he would lead his men once again over the top of the trenches, through the freshly cut British wire, into the mud and shell holes of no man's land, waving his swagger stick for how much good that would do and, like a man in constant pain, hoping a bullet would kill him and get it over with.

Jack Merryweather had been made a major and gone off to another regiment that somehow had more need for a major. Robert was still a captain. He was good at doing the right thing, but not very inventive. Caught out in the open in a shell hole, Robert was more inclined to stay where he was and crawl back to his trench in the dark with his men. Three times he had lived for days in the forward German trench with no idea of what to do next, alone with a few men cut off from orders. He had done what he knew best and eaten the German sausage, which was better than anything in a can from America. He watched his men die and blanked his mind to save his sanity.

On the last attack, the colonel had been killed. A new colonel had arrived the previous day. The man had drooping wet eyes like a spaniel's. Not the first sign of a chin. Been in India, they said. Robert kept to himself. The rumours had already started. The new CO had once resigned his commission. Left the regular army. The only 'regular' army Robert had met were well back from the front line with red tabs on their uniforms and red bands around their staff hats.

Robert was hungry as usual. He missed the company of Jack Merryweather. They had fought side by side for months on end. And it was better not to make friends with the new officers. None of them had lasted very long. The trick, Robert told himself, was to stay in his own cocoon, and if the gods were with him, one day the guns would stop and some of them would walk away alive. Robert forced himself to stay in the moment. Never the past. And never, never the future.

The men had been stood down, with sentries on the lower fire-steps looking out over the drizzle and mist that covered no man's land. The old hands knew long before an attack. There had not been a German spotter plane for days, even when the rain had stopped. At night they watched more carefully for German patrols. Double sentries at night. Like every job Robert had done in his life, there was a pattern.

Robert was duty officer, standing at the bottom of the trench below the sentry who was looking through his binoculars, searching the shattered earth for signs of life. Every ten minutes Robert went up and had a good look himself. From months of experience, his eyes could discard the 'normal' in the mangled landscape. He was looking for a straight barrel. Domed shape of a tin hat. A mound that was not there before.

Robert looked at his watch. Ten o'clock in the morning. Time for his hourly tin mug of sweet tea. His feet were cold, his hands cold, the gas mask heavy on his chest under the coat that was meant to keep out the rain. Robert forced himself not to look for Private Lane and the hot tea.

"Right behind you, sir."

"Give it to Jones up top." Robert had not turned around.

"Two mugs, sir."

"Thank you, Lane."

"The mail came up, sir. Three for you. On the table."

The table was in the dugout with the tarpaulin over the top that was meant to keep out the rain. Robert had been wet through for months.

"The colonel, sir," whispered Lane.

Robert turned. The new colonel was walking down the trench with his adjutant. They were never alone, Robert thought. No one was ever left alone. Putting his tea carefully on the fire-step, he made himself ready to salute. They had seen each other twice but never spoken. Robert thought they were probably about the same age. Saluting none too well, he reported nothing happening as he was expected to and waited for the colonel to pass on down the trench.

"You have any more of that tea, Private Lane?" asked the colonel.

"Yes, sir." Both Robert's and his batman's face registered surprise at the new colonel knowing Lane's name.

"Carry on up the line, adjutant," said the colonel.

Robert waited for the tea and the new colonel to speak. His tea was getting cold on the fire-step so he picked it up and drank. What did you say to someone who had the right to speak first?

"Not like Africa," said the colonel.

Robert was sure he had heard right but could think of no answer.

"I got as far as the signpost to Elephant Walk. You stayed there, I believe... Thank you, Lane... They were a bit short of officers so they let me back into the army. Not the same regiment of course. My father saw to that. While we drink our tea, you can tell me every bit you know about this part of the front. It's the first time I have commanded a battalion, so I need your help, Major St Clair."

"Captain St Clair."

"No, I changed that. I want you to be my adjutant."

"But what about..."

"He's going back to England. Poor chap's a bit shot through. That sort of thing."

"He's wounded, sir?"

"Not exactly. Needs a rest."

"And I'm not shot through?"

"You're not the type, St Clair."

The adjutant who was 'shot through' came back from the end of the inspection. Robert drank the rest of his tea and went up the fire-step to have another look. He had never been singled out before. And he didn't like it.

Later Robert read the mail from home. There was one from his father. There was one from his mother. There was one from Lucinda but this time no mention of John Heynes, her dead Irish Guardsman. They were all numb. The whole family. Most of the men had letters from wives and girlfriends. He would have liked that. But what worried him most at the moment was why Colonel Bowes-Leggatt wanted him as his adjutant. One of Robert's secret claims to fame in life was always keeping himself out of the way. No one at school had even thought once of making him a prefect. His trick was to be always there, but always invisible. It was the best way for Robert to go through life. And how the hell did the colonel know he had ever been in Africa let alone on Elephant Walk? It made him uncomfortable. He did not like surprises. And he didn't like people knowing things about him they were not meant to know about. He had never heard of a lieutenant colonel with an adjutant the rank of major.

WALLY BOWES-LEGGATT WAS NOT sure whether the army was trying to get him killed or give him the chance to remove the block from his father's escutcheon. The war had certainly killed off Captain Craig, the rotter who had run off with Poo, and through Wally made a fool of the great General Bowes-Leggatt, first Earl of Fenthurst. Smeared the reputation of a great British regiment by seducing a fellow officer's wife. That much Wally had found out back in England at the end of August '15, after he had sold the lion skins with the lion heads still attached to them to a taxidermist in Johannesburg, the lions that had killed Jackson, at what proved to be the end of Benny Lightfoot's African safari and his sexual pursuit of Tina Pringle. Craig had been put on the front line the moment hostilities broke out and had lasted a week. Wally, back in the army, had lasted over a year, but how he wasn't so sure. Though like everyone in life, he told himself, there had to be a percentage of luck. And up till then, luck had not been his in any quantity.

The old regiment had turned up their noses at him, but after the fiasco at Gallipoli and the decimation of the British regular army in Flanders, by September 1915, when Wally reapplied for his commission, the army was so short of trained officers they would have taken him back for a far worse crime. To Wally, the East Surrey Regiment was as good as any other regiment, and now he was a lieutenant colonel, commanding the 2nd battalion, having spent the last year with the 1st battalion outside Amiens.

The army had even given him a Military Cross for his afternoon alone in a shell hole surrounded by dead soldiers, using one of the dead soldier's .303 rifle to pick off German soldiers on their abortive way to the British front line in the counter-attack. Wally's platoon had been killed in the British assault leaving Wally stranded in the shell hole. Some said he should have been put up for the Victoria Cross, but they were the ones who knew nothing of Poo's indiscretion and the embarrassment of Wally's father the general. Six months later the army had promoted him to major. Now he was an acting lieutenant colonel. If he won them the war they might just forgive him his trespasses. Anyway, he told himself when they gave him the Military Cross, at least the years drinking his way around Africa had not been totally wasted. He could still shoot the eye out of a leopard at one hundred yards, even if the leopards wore grey uniforms and tin hats. An eye was an eye, whatever was wearing it. The yellow eye of a leopard or the blue eye of a German.

Someone had found a man prepared to say in court he had committed adultery with Prudence. They had been booked into a London hotel together and the concierge was in on the perjury. Wally had received his divorce, and Poo had gone back to live with her schoolmaster father in the Lake District. Wally doubted if she would marry again. Her youthful flash of sexual attraction had gone by the time Wally saw her again in the divorce court. He had not spoken to her. He had not felt sorry for her. He had felt nothing. A stranger carrying his name and then losing it. He had not even felt sorry for the rotter, dead for more than a year.

But even up to the very end the regiment's name came first. He had not been allowed to cite Captain Craig as a co-respondent. It had been the army condition for letting him join the East Surrey Regiment.

But one thing he had not done was to go home and see his father. His mother he had met in London to thank her for the remittances she had made to him in Africa. He had not even bothered to make contact with his brothers. In everyone's eyes but his own, he was wrong to have lost his wife. It was his fault. And to them, it always would be.

After the war, if he survived, Wally had made up his mind to go back to Africa. Only this time he would not drink. He would offer himself for hire as a white hunter. Back in England, deposited in the Naval and Military Club, were the two cases of matching Purdey rifles. He was going to pay his dues to England and the army. Then he was getting out. They did not want him except in the hour of need, and that for Wally Bowes-Leggatt was too much of a one-sided bargain.

What made him smile as he sat down in his own dugout after appointing Robert St Clair his future adjutant was the man's complete non-recognition.

"Pass the hash, Jim," he said to his adjutant, "and don't start arguing again. You need a rest. Your bloody hands shake. You jumped when Mortimer put down the tin plate of hash. I told you. Shot through. Nothing to be ashamed of. You earned the rest."

"I'm still a good officer."

"That I don't deny. At the moment. The mind can only take so much, Jimmy boy. I know."

"Why on earth St Clair... The only miracle he's performed is staying alive."

"I have my reasons. And staying alive is not the worst of talents... He was a schoolmaster at one point in his life."

"Is that in his army report?"

"No, it's not, as a matter of fact, old boy."

"When do I go back, sir?"

"An hour before dawn tomorrow morning... What did Mortimer put in this bloody hash?"


THEY HAD all been drunk when they met and paralytic drunk when they parted. One of the rules of a drinking companion was not to have a memory. The end of the evening was still a blur and where he slept that night a mystery to Wally Bowes-Leggatt. Whether anyone would equate the unshaven drunken bum with a half colonel in the East Surrey Regiment was debatable.

He had been out of money as usual. His mother's cheque was always sent to a bank in Johannesburg and he was still in Salisbury. The other two were booked into rooms at Meikles Hotel. They were not going back to Elephant Walk that night. Using his charm, Wally had insinuated his way into their company. There was more than one white bum in the downstairs bar of Meikles Hotel and everyone knew Harry Brigandshaw. Some of the night was still hazy in his memory. He had even remembered the man's name. Most of that night, he remembered he had talked to Robert. Learned the story of his life. Said nothing about himself in return. In those days, it was Wally's payment for his drinks. A stranger listening to a stranger's problems with life.

Maybe one day he would tell Captain St Clair they had met before. But he doubted it. He knew the man intimately from that one night of opening up his soul. And Wally had liked what he saw... The man knew himself and his own limitations. And just maybe Robert could teach him the secret of surviving the war... For all of them.


TWICE THAT NIGHT the battalion came to full alert. Flares were fired along the line, white light vividly defining the smashed earth, tangled barbed wire and body parts. A hand, frozen, had been sticking out of the mud for weeks, thirty yards from Robert's fire-step. They all hoped it would be blown away. No one knew if the hand was German or British. Just the hand with six inches of a bare arm and no part of a uniform. Someone had fired a machine gun at nothing Robert could see and then the flare had gone out and the night was pitch black. In between Robert slept in a dugout on a raised length of duckboard. He even had one brief dream but when he woke to the stand-to he could not remember a thing. Each time he woke he was hungry. Each time he went straight back to sleep after the stand-down.

In the morning, he was told to report to the new colonel. What he knew about army administration was limited. Filling in forms had never been one of his priorities. In triplicate. Why always in triplicate he never understood. Most of the equipment got blown to pieces in the end and nobody counted the carnage and sent back a form.

He was on his way down the trench that zigzagged, so a successful German attack could only fire twenty yards each way, each zigzag defendable even if Fritz was just around the corner. Private Lane was behind him. Each carried their own equipment. Some officers made their batman carry everything. Robert could see ten yards ahead in the gloom of first light. The drizzle was still coming down, the sky heavy and low, just above their heads. They had not yet had their breakfast. The heavy guns were firing at each other again. Robert could hear the shells bursting high above his head. Today, he thought, the gunners are firing at each other. Or trying to. They were both just out of each other's range. Maybe supplies were coming out for both armies. They were shooting at the supply line. Robert doubted if anyone on either side knew what they were doing.

Both sides increased the ferocity of their bombardment. The lull was over. New supplies of heavy ammunition had replenished the stocks of both armies. Discarding the high flyers, Robert trudged on, slipping once off the duckboard into the mud and filth. The smell no longer nauseated. The rogue shell came from the British guns. Robert picked out the sound a fraction of a second before Private Lane and threw himself onto the half-frozen mud at the foot of the trench on the British side. The explosion blew Lane and the duckboard high in the trench, high up into the new day, high above the devastation, pulling apart the higher the pieces rose and then came down. Robert was covered from head to foot in the body parts of his batman. Shells were still passing overhead. Someone shouted for the stretcher-bearer. All the time Robert kept telling himself he had not had his breakfast. His right foot began to hurt, and when he put his hand down to find out why, there was nothing there. Then they lifted him onto a stretcher and someone gave him morphine. Then he passed out.

By realising quickly enough the shells were coming in from the British guns, and diving into the corner of the trench nearest the British reserve trench, he saved his own life. The shell had been incorrectly filled at the factory and had come down a mile short of the gunner's target.

Robert never became a major in the British Army. He never became Wally Bowes-Leggatt's adjutant. And he never found out that the drunken bum he had spilt his heart out to in the middle of Africa was the colonel in charge of his last battalion.

When Robert reached home in the spring of 1917 he was unable to walk without a pair of crutches. Lucinda met him at the railway station. Again, as so many times in the past, he was the only passenger to disembark at Corfe Castle. Old man Pringle was nowhere to be seen, though the flowerbeds had been recently turned and weeded. Yellow crocuses were growing on the grass bank behind the waiting room. The sun was watery, but it was out. The train puffed up and wearily pulled its way out of the station on the way to Swanage. Robert could see his younger sister was crying.

"Thanks, Cinda. Can't walk home this time, even in the sunshine." He was trying to make a joke.

Lucinda burst into heaving tears. Silly, Robert told himself. All of John Heynes had gone forever. All Robert had lost was his right foot. Once the stump had healed properly they'd give him a wooden foot with a hinge. They had shown him one in the hospital. Someday he would walk again the lanes of England. Slowly. But he would walk again.


ACTING LIEUTENANT COLONEL BOWES-LEGGATT died a week after Robert came home on a hospital ship from Calais. When they told his father, the great general smiled. His son, after all, had died a hero. No one had besmirched the family name.

Halfway through the smile, his wife slapped his face in front of one of the servants. The servant reported the words of the Countess of Fenthurst, as the earl stood dumbstruck, feeling the stinging side of his face.

"She said, 'Now are you satisfied?'" the servant had said in the servants' hall. "What do you think she meant?" The man had just joined the servants' hall, badly gassed in the Somme offensive. The rest of the servants, the men too old to go to war, kept their thoughts to themselves. They were more interested in keeping their jobs, the good food and the comfortable rooms. If his honour meant more to the old general than his son's life, so be it. They did not have to like the man for whom they worked.

"Never, ever repeat what you just said," ordered the butler.

"Yes, sir," said the young man. Then the chlorine damage in his lungs made him cough and cough. He went on coughing, tears clouding his eyes from the effort. When he wiped his eyes, the rest of the servants had left the hall to go about their daily work.

By the end of the day, he had forgotten all about the slap across the general's face. They had told him in hospital after the gassing that he would cough for the rest of his life. But he was alive. Which was more than could be said for the general's son. When the butler saw him again he was whistling away to himself as he cleaned the family silver with silver polish and an old toothbrush to clean out the pattern of a bunch of grapes on the silver rose bowl. Next to the bunch of grapes, the silversmith had forged a cherub. He managed to keep control of his chest until he had cleaned out the dirt around the cherub. Then he began to cough again, heaving up his intestines, right up from the ring of his rectum.

# BOOK 5 – PERSUASION AND RETRIBUTIONS

# 1

## APRIL 1917

*H*arry Brigandshaw thought he was going to die every time he took to the air to fight. He had talked to God about it and received no reply. There was only silence to his aching question 'why?' If he was going to die why was he born? What was the purpose? If he had had a son he could have seen some of the purpose. A daughter. Something that could go on forever and ever to the end of time. He had never married and now he was going to die.

The de Havilland biplanes had been replaced by Sopwith Triplanes, the successor to the model on which they had taught him to fly. The latest Sopwith was faster, better in the turn. The German aircraft were getting better too, their biplanes replaced with triplanes. They turned better too. Slowly, through the months and years of the war, they had systematically killed each other. If they had met as young men they would have gone off to the beer hall and drunk together. If they had met their sisters they would have married them. For all intents and purposes, they were the same people.

Harry had long forgotten his revenge. Not his brother George, but his revenge. He had assuaged his brother's death by killing twenty-three young Germans like himself. Now all he wanted to do was survive and go home. Back to Africa. Elephant Walk. The bush. He wanted to hear the roar of a lion, not the snarl of an aero engine.

Every request for leave had been turned down by Fishy Braithwaite.

"I don't go home and leave my pilots, the young pilots who will be shot out of the sky if I don't show them how to fight. Why should you go on leave?

Anyway, your home is too far, and if I let you go there you would never come back again. Leave denied, Captain Brigandshaw."

They never spoke of Sara Wentworth but she was always there between them. Harry knew his nerves were shot to ribbons. Like his plane's tail when he had come back the day before, half its rudder missing. He had been in combat over a year.

"You really don't like me do you, Colonel Braithwaite?"

"No, I don't, Captain Brigandshaw. No, I don't."

The spring day was warmer than it had been all year. A perfect day for flying. The squadron, in three flights of six, Harry commanding A Flight, took off from the same airfield the Germans had strafed when he first arrived. The war in the trenches had heaved around in the mud, grinding away at the youth of France, Germany and England. There were colonials, too. Australians. Canadians. South Africans. New Zealanders. Men from Newfoundland. Rhodesia. And Ireland. Ireland after the Easter uprising in Dublin in 1916. Still, the men of Ireland came to fight for their colonial masters, England. Volunteers. The cynical said for lack of Irish jobs.

Harry flew over them all every day, and they all died the same, wherever they came from. And now the Americans had finally entered the carnage. Always turning his head, listening to his instinct, Harry cleared his head of everything other than the sound of his single engine, the sky above, the ground below. Over the front lines, the squadron split into individual flights. Harry led his five pilots on the dawn patrol. Below there was a hate on. Explosions. Men moving out of the trenches from the German side, a cloud of chlorine smoke drifting in front of them towards the British lines. Wagging his wings, Harry pointed down. They were going to strafe the infantry out in the open. It was all over quickly. One minute he was pointing down, the next his engine took machine gun fire and the propeller came into his vision, turning slower, dead. The Germans had been waiting for them. It was to be the start of the biggest German offensive of the war. Harry knew he was going to die. Waited for the second burst of machine gun fire. Instinctively, he banked the Sopwith Triplane to fly back over the British trenches. A German pilot waved at him. He was alone on the glide and concentrating. If he missed the landing there would be no coming around again.

"I'm still alive," he shouted.

A line of British five-ton trucks came into his flight path. Then he was over them almost touching a canvas roof with his fixed undercarriage. One of the trucks was an ambulance. When he woke he was inside the ambulance. In the field hospital, all they could find was a concussion and a broken leg from the crash-landing.

"Take six, eight weeks," said the doctor. "I've strapped it. Nice and clean. Enjoy England. I always love England in the spring." Then the doctor moved quickly to the next patient.

LADY ST CLAIR had been through them all, worrying about them. Lucinda moping about the house for months, never smiling, never doing anything unless she was told. The girl was twenty-five, not fifteen! She was not the only one in England with a dead fiancé... Robert upstairs, stomping around on a wooden peg before they would give him a foot that would at least make him look as if he was in one piece... Barnaby writing he was dressed as an Arab and blowing up Turkish trains with some Colonel Lawrence. Dashing all over the Arabian Desert. She had tried to find Aqaba on the map and failed... Genevieve's father-in-law dead, shot in the head by a German sniper at the age of fifty-six. Men had no right to be fighting wars at that age. And her son-in-law standing next to his father when he was killed... Annabel, married to a sergeant who painted pictures, and pregnant with her second child whose chance of ever knowing its father was almost nil. Who was going to support the little mites the Lord only knew... At least Penelope had given birth to a son, though the date of Frederick's home leave was a bit wobbly so she did not want to worry her way down that route. Penelope, for goodness sake! The straightest young girl in England. The war! It was the damn war. Whether they won it or not, England had fallen to pieces. Everyone just did what they wanted without a thought for other people. Just as well there wasn't a way of making certain the father was Frederick. One day the boy would be Lord St Clair, Baron St Clair of Purbeck. And if her poor husband did not stop worrying about not having any money, he would kill himself. And if the Germans had their way, they would kill Frederick. And then the little bastard would be the eighteenth Baron St Clair of Purbeck. And, when his grandfather died, rich. The Lord worked in mysterious ways! She just hoped the young heir to the barony would have some resemblance to a St Clair. And there was still an outside chance the boy was Fred's.

"I must stop worrying," she said out loud, walking into the entrance hall where the telephone was ringing. "Lady St Clair!" she bellowed into the mouthpiece, still not believing her voice could travel down a piece of wire.

"This is Harry Brigandshaw."

347

"Harry Brigandshaw. Harry Brigandshaw. I've heard that name before… Don't you have something to do with Africa?"

"Is that Harry Brigandshaw?" called Lucinda from the morning room where she was meant to be writing letters.

"Yes, it is. If you know him, you'd better come and speak to him. Now, what was I saying?"

"That you must stop worrying about us, Mother."

As she picked up the two pieces of the telephone, she gave her mother a kiss on the cheek. Then she put the speaking tube to her mouth. "This is Cinda, Harry. Where are you? Are you all right?"

"London. Smashed up my plane. Broken leg. Can I come down?"

"I'll ask Mother."

"Of course he can," said her mother who had been listening. "He's that nice young man from Africa you went to visit. Tell him Robert's here with his foot blown off."

"I know, Lady St Clair." Harry could hear the two voices but only talk to one.

"Give us a ring from the station," said Lucinda.

"I can't walk, you know." He was smiling down the phone.

"I had the same problem with Robert."

"It's strange," said Lady St Clair, walking away to do something she had already forgotten about. "The one person I never worry about is Merlin."

"Harry is coming to stay with us, Mother."

"That's very nice, dear… Now, what was it I was going to do?"

ROBERT ST CLAIR was stumping up and down the platform of Corfe Castle railway station. The new car made by Ford in America was standing on the other side of the station building. Robert hoped Harry would know how to get it started again. The car had been bought as a gift for the family. Jug Ears had died of old age and Merlin thought it time his family joined the mechanical age. He was amazed how few of his Vickers-Armstrong shares he had had to sell to buy the motor car. He had bought the black car on his last leave and shown Lucinda how to drive the thing. Cranking the car to start was the biggest problem, and sometimes when the ignition was turned off the engine went on running, the whole car doing a dance while it waited for the engine to finally stop. Lady St Clair had refused to get into it. Lord St Clair would not come within one hundred yards. When Lucinda drove it around the lanes it frightened off the rabbits, of which there were too many now the men had gone off to war. The fox had not once gone again for the chickens. There were too many rabbits to eat. Burrows all over the hills and dales. They got into the vegetable gardens at the Manor. Cook had said every time the lettuce was eaten, 'If it isn't one thing it's another. The hens or the lettuce. Now that certainly is not one of life's little mysteries.' They didn't go away for long, the rabbits. Just ran down their holes. When the noise of the car was gone they came out again. The whole family was sick of rabbit. Rabbit pie. Rabbit stew. Even Cook's famous stuffed roast rabbit with all the herbs and garlic was sniffed at by family and staff.

The train was late. Old man Pringle was sitting on a bench in the sun. Robert had brought him a chicken for Mrs Pringle, the bird gutted but not plucked. Even if he didn't need any sandwiches. And Mrs Pringle had more money than she knew what to do with, thanks to Albert in South Africa. But it was the thought that counted. Robert didn't mention any of the dead sons. He liked the sight of old Pringle sitting in the sun. It brought back his childhood and Mrs Pringle's big thick sandwiches and the pickled onions. Old man Pringle didn't have to work but there was nothing else for him to do. Sitting at home, he got under Mrs Pringle's feet. And since the boys had died they didn't like talking to each other about the good old days.

Lucinda had her hands planted on her hips with the elbows sticking out. Waiting for the train. Robert hoped she would not be disappointed with Harry Brigandshaw once again. And his foot hurt. The one that had been blown off by a British shell exploding in his trench. Maybe when they gave him a wooden foot it would not hurt so much. Slowly the old steam train puffed its way into the station and cranked its way to a halt. One carriage door came open and they waited. A small case was lowered onto the platform with difficulty. Then the crutches were pushed down to feel the hard earth of the platform before Harry swung himself down from the train. Old Pringle was still asleep in the sun. The train, as it always did, puffed off towards Swanage. They all gave each other a hug. When they left the empty platform, old Pringle was still fast asleep next to the unplucked dead chicken. The first daffodils had come into bloom in the station flowerbed.

Holding the front of the bonnet and standing on one leg, Harry gave the cranking handle a solid jerk. The Ford started the first time. Easier to start than cranking the propeller of a Sopwith Triplane. Then they were off to Purbeck Manor in style, Lucinda driving.

Both Harry and Robert were remembering the first time they had done seven miles together. Walking. Harry was twenty-one. He felt like an old man. And Lucinda had been just fifteen. She had met them, ambushed them before they reached the old house. Now she was a woman with a dead man to remember for the rest of her life. There were rabbits everywhere, Harry noticed. Scurrying away down the burrows.

THE TELEGRAM REACHED Sara Wentworth in the tent where the doctors were operating on the mangled bodies that somehow seemed to stay alive. She put it unopened in the big front pocket of her apron. A young man was put on the bench in front of her. She held him down while the doctor sawed off what was left of his legs. Before the doctor finished the man died. A male orderly took the dead man's head and Sara the torso. They heaved him off the bench onto a trolley. The orderly took away the body. On the other side of the waist-high bench, another young man was placed from a trolley onto the operating table. He was still alive when they took him away. The doctor had stuffed his intestines back into his body and sewn him up.

Just five miles away the German offensive had overrun the British front line. The reserve trench was holding, they were told. There was no time to move the big tent. If the Germans broke through, the doctors and nurses would stay with the wounded. She had been working non-stop for seventeen hours. The doctors had not slept for two days. She thought the telegram was from Fishy Braithwaite and did not care. The man's paranoia had paled into insignificance, faced with the war.

An hour later she looked from right to left. There were no more bodies on trolleys. The doctor told her to go and eat. He would call her if the flow of men began again.

In the canteen, she read Jared was dead. Her brother had gone down with his ship. The telegram was not from Fishy Braithwaite. Then they were evacuating the field hospital. Sara sat in the back of an ambulance. She began to scream and the doctor put his hand over her mouth. Only when she stopped thrashing around did he take his hand away.

"You're going home, young lady." He was a kind, old man. Well over seventy.

"My brother."

"I'm sorry, Sara. But what can we do? And now the Germans are advancing."

"I can't go home."

"You can and will. Then you can come back if there is anything to come back to."

"There's nothing to go to, either."

"There is. There always is. I know. There has to be. Otherwise, humankind would not have survived."

Sara landed at Dover a week after Harry arrived at Purbeck Manor. She landed from the same hospital ship that brought Harry from France. She called her mother at Birchdale from the FANY headquarters in Dover. There was no reply. In desperation she phoned the temporary aerodrome of 33 Squadron, Mervyn Braithwaite had given her the number. She spoke to a captain who said Harry had been wounded and was in England. The man gave her a phone number in Dorset. She gave the man her phone number in England in case he phoned his squadron. What she did not know was that Fishy Braithwaite had overheard the conversation. She wanted to tell Harry Jared was dead but it was not the most important phone call she had to make. Jared had had many friends.

An hour later, 33 Squadron was ordered to evacuate their airfield. When they landed at the designated airstrip further back from the advancing Germans, they had lost contact with their commanding officer. In the confusion, two of the new pilots had landed at the wrong airstrip. Everyone thought the CO was with them, shielding the new pilots. His absence was not reported. At dawn the next day the squadron flew strafing attacks on the German reinforcements. There were three stray pilots flying with 33 Squadron who could not find their own squadrons. One was a major who took command. They returned to their new field three times that day for fuel and ammunition. By the third day, the German offensive had been checked. Colonel Braithwaite was reported missing, presumed killed. One of the young pilots rejoined his squadron. No, he had not seen the colonel go down in the confusion.


GRANNY FORRESTER HAD WATCHED them for a week. The pilot and the granddaughter. And this time she told herself not to interfere. Paying the passage to Africa had brought Lucinda nothing but tears when she came back to Purbeck Manor with Robert. She had been an interfering old woman and told herself not to do it again. With anyone. If Bess wanted to worry herself to death, let her worry. If Ethelbert wanted to spend more time with his prize pigs than his family, let him be. If Lucinda thought Harry Brigandshaw was being more than a good friend after John Heynes, then she should find out herself. For Granny Forrester, it either worked the first time or it did not work at all. Making do with something because the right person had not come along led to a life of excuses. Making a marriage work was the biggest lot of rubbish she had learnt in her life. And despite her granddaughter smiling for the first time since the Irish Guardsman was killed, she could see no future in the daily walks. Slow, very slow, as the pilot lifted both feet forward at a time. Sometimes they took the new car. Mostly they walked down the weed-strewn path through the tunnels of climbing roses that had not been pruned for ten years. After the fourth tunnel, they were out of sight from Granny Forrester's bedroom on the second floor of the old house from where she watched. They never looked up at her. Or at Robert's bedroom on the same floor, where her grandson spent most of his days alone.

Beyond the arched roses was a lily pond, an arbour protecting a wooden bench from the wind where the bench caught the morning sun. Once it had been theirs. Hers and Potts's. It was a place for lovers... Then she went down on her knees and prayed for all of them.


ROBERT HAD GIVEN up worrying about his sister. He let his mother do the worrying. The only surprise was Granny Forrester saying not a word. Everyone in the family was waiting. For something to happen. From wherever it came. Like so many houses in England.

The way out for Robert was writing. He could live in his own story and make his characters happy. His only lifelong interests had been history and his family. And reading books. On Elephant Walk he had read all of Henry Manderville's books. And they had talked about their respective families going back to the time of the Conqueror. Both the St Clair and Manderville families had come across from Normandy with William the First. They might even have known each other, those first St Clairs and Mandervilles. During many an evening, the two of them had swapped family stories, most of them passed down from father to son. Or found on the gravestones. In the family churches. The family tombs. No one in either family had ever written it down.

"One day when you have time, Robert, you should write a book," Henry Manderville had told him. "It would have to be a historical novel as so much of your family history is hearsay. Like ours. Maybe you could start by introducing the St Clairs to the Mandervilles before the Battle of Hastings in that year of 1066. I did tell you my old home in England is still called Hastings Court. Harry's uncle lives there. But that's another long story and one I'm not proud of. How the Brigandshaws own my ancestral house."

Without a foot, without a job, with a small army disability pension, Robert had begun the book. For the first time in his life, he was fully absorbed and happy. Whether it was any good or not he did not care. He had found something to do with his life. When he was writing, his missing foot was irrelevant.

. . .

THAT MORNING ROBERT had watched them go off in the car after breakfast, his favourite meal of the day. There had been fried duck eggs, to which he was particularly partial and so different to hen's eggs. Cook had made Harry and Lucinda a picnic basket with hard-boiled eggs, a green salad, and cold, home-made pork sausages. Little bags of salt, twisted into greaseproof paper, and a bottle of Cook's home-made salad dressing, thick with herbs from the garden. Two flasks of tea and a small cake Cook had taken out of the oven just before she packed the wicker picnic basket. Robert had watched the packing and wanted to eat one of the sausages.

The spring day was perfect. Full of sun with no sign of April showers to be seen anywhere in the blue sky. The birds were trying out their voices for the summer season. A little envious, Robert had gone up to his room and was soon absorbed in his writing, to the exclusion of everything else. The day was quiet. Not one sound of man or woman. Only the birds and insects. Robert had made himself a pile of sandwiches, which he ate his way through during the day. He, too, had a flask of tea. He'd gone into an ancient world and stayed there in his mind. The window to his bedroom was wide open to the spring, his writing desk pushed up against the windowsill. He had not heard the constant ringing of the phone far away in the entrance hall. The first thing he knew was a banging on his door. For a long moment, he was unable to bring his mind back into his body and the present.

When he wrenched open the door he found an agitated Cook. He was about to be brusque but changed his mind. For Cook to be flustered there had to be something wrong. And now he could hear the guns from France.

"What's the matter, Mrs Mason?" normally he would have called her Cook but there was something more serious than the family dinner.

"There's a young woman on the phone, Mister Robert. Hysterical, she is. Wants to speak to Mr Harry Brigandshaw. Now how would she know he is here? Says she's going to kill herself if he don't come up to London. Gave me a name and address and made me read it back. I told her the young man had gone off for a picnic with Miss Lucinda and that set her screaming. I told her to hang on and I'd get you. Says she knows you from Africa. All these people from Africa, I just don't know. You'd better come down. Don't want no one killing 'emself on account of me."

When Robert reached the telephone in the hall the line was dead. The London address was on the pad, which hung from the phone, with a pencil attached to a piece of string. There was no return telephone number. It was

Sara Wentworth, Jared's sister. He rather thought she had not liked him because he did not have any money.

Upstairs again, and as hard as he tried, he could not restart the book. His characters refused to talk to him.

"Well, there's nothing I can do as I don't know where they've gone and I only have one foot... Damn. And the book was going so well."

He had had enough worrying about other people, so he lay down on his bed. Soon he was fast asleep. The wind had changed and the sound of the guns had gone away again.

THEY HAD EATEN everything except the last of the salt in the twisted little bags of greaseproof paper. They had gone deep into the woods, the car pushing through the bracken that grew on the side of the bridle path. The oaks were big, hundreds of years old, gnarled roots hunched out of the earth, covered in green lichen and moss. They could hear the lazy sound of summer insects worrying the spring flowers. Lucinda had cleared a patch of last year's acorns from the soft ground and put down the rug from the car. They were truly alone and said not a word.

"Will you make love to me, Harry? Please. I want something to remember. John said he wouldn't until we were married and now he can't. Oh, I know you'll never marry me. I'm not sure I can leave England. Comfort me, Harry. Make love to me. Is that too much to ask? We're hidden here from the world. For a short sweet moment, it will be us. I can keep that memory forever. I won't be so alone when I'm old. I do love you even if you don't love me. Please, Harry. Give me a memory. Something to hold onto."

GRANNY FORRESTER WATCHED them come home and knew immediately. They were holding hands. It was almost teatime. Then she heard the commotion and went downstairs to find out what was going on.

Cook was standing in the hall, her lips pressed together. Robert was stomping round and round on his peg leg. Lucinda was looking horrified and about to burst into tears. Harry Brigandshaw, the pilot, was standing looking at a torn off piece of paper. His face was white as a sheet.

"Barnaby!" cried Granny Forrester and her daughter Bess joined the throng.

"No," said Harry. "A friend of mine, of Robert and Cinda's, is threatening to kill herself if I don't go up to London... How on earth did she know I was here?"

"You're not going," said Cinda.

"I'll have to. We owe that to Jared."

"That was the man's name," said Cook. "He went down with his ship."

"Oh, my God... We'll all go," said Harry.

"Not me, old chap," said Robert. "Bloody foot hurts."

"Cinda, can you drive the car as far as London? The address is the Wentworths' London house, Jared wrote to me from there many times over the years. Lady St Clair? Would it be all right?"

"Yes," said Granny Forrester, running with her intuition.

"You can't go now," said Lady St Clair. "Tomorrow. Poor girl. Where is my husband?"

"Down at the pig pens," said Robert.

"You don't have to stay in London more than a night," said Granny Forrester sweetly.

"I've never driven that far," said Lucinda, recovering her composure, "but I'll try." Gritting her teeth, she told herself love was not going to fly out of the window that fast. And a night in London. They'd sort out Sara quickly. Go to the theatre. Have dinner together. Spend the night together. They would tell the hotel they were married. There was a war on... Putting the smile back on her face, she began to make all the plans... She could still feel Harry deep inside of her. She had not been a virgin. They both knew that. Lovers, she thought, should never tell each other of the past.

FISHY BRAITHWAITE HAD LANDED the aircraft on the wrong airfield with deliberate intent. He told a sergeant mechanic the engine was backfiring badly and needed an overhaul. Then he requisitioned a motorcycle to get him into the new airfield for 33 Squadron. He was a colonel and no one in the chaos was senior enough to question him.

For an hour the mechanic tried to make the engine of the Sopwith Triplane backfire. Then he gave up. The engine purred like a cat. He left the plane at the end of the airfield and reported to the senior sergeant. Minutes later panic spread and everyone was told to clear out. The Germans were less than two miles away. There was no one to fly out the colonel's aircraft and, having looked around, no transport for himself. A shell came in close to the airstrip. Running back to the stranded aircraft with a still turning propeller waiting for the engine to backfire, the sergeant climbed up into the cockpit. He knew everything about the aircraft but had never been allowed to fly. His take-off was perfect. With no idea of navigation, he flew the plane until it ran out of petrol. Gliding down he tried to land in a field, cartwheeling the plane onto its back where it exploded close to a British Army observation post. The mechanic was burnt beyond recognition. The observer who normally went up in the basket of the balloon took down the markings of the aircraft.

"That was Colonel Braithwaite," he said to the two privates, who were not sure what to do now they were surrounded by advancing Germans. "Worst bloody landing I ever saw. Poor sod must have been dead in the cockpit before it came down... There's three of us, a bloody balloon and a regiment of Germans. Put down the guns, mates, and put up your hands. I'll give my last report and tell 'em."

"Better ask 'em," said the Tommy. "Don't want being shot for desertion."

After the observer cranked up the field telegraph he reported their position.

"Surrender, Corporal."

"Who are you?"

"Captain Middleton. Good luck."

"Colonel Braithwaite just killed himself. Crashed and burnt."

"Are you sure it was Colonel Braithwaite?"

"Certain. Reported 33 Squadron many times. Three yellow stripes on his plane's tail. The rest of them had three black stripes. Are we losing the war?"

"I have absolutely no idea."

Ten minutes later the three of them were smoking German cigarettes.

BY THE TIME the corporal was sent off on a train back to Germany, Fishy Braithwaite had landed at Dover from a ship. He was still in uniform and had bluffed his way ashore. Then he took the train up to London. If she was going with Brigandshaw he would be there to stop them. She had been given Brigandshaw's phone number in England. She was going to ask him up to London. In case Brigandshaw contacted his squadron he had overheard the man repeating the phone number of the Wentworths' London home. So he knew where she was. His fiancée! Asking for another man.

When he got on the train his flying goggles were still hanging around his neck. No one spoke to him. One glance was enough to avoid conversation. He had not even eaten since taking the motorcycle.

WHEN SARA WENTWORTH eventually phoned for Harry Brigandshaw in hysterics, she was frightened for her life. After staying in the London house for a day, she had gone to Birchdale to be with her parents, where she had slept for twelve hours without waking. Once properly rested she wanted to rejoin the FANY and find out where they wanted her to go. She took the train from Warminster back to London and reported to the FANY headquarters for duty. The old doctor had left instructions that Nurse Wentworth was to stay on leave for a fortnight. She had gone to the London house. Going back to Birchdale would have been too depressing. Jared was dead and there was nothing more she could do for her parents.

The townhouse was on the Bayswater Road in Holland Park. She had seen a man sitting on the bench with his back to the iron railing that ran along the length of Holland Park. The bench was on the other side of the road to the small gate and steps that led up to the front door of the Wentworths' three-storey house. The house was in an attached row of ten similar houses. There were people walking the footpaths on both sides of the road. She noticed the man on the bench was wearing goggles and wondered idly what he had done with his motorcycle. The man was wearing a brown leather overcoat of a type she had never seen before. She had let herself into the house and thought no more about the man on the bench.

There were no servants in the house as her father had taken the only one left to Birchdale. The men had gone off to the war. There were white dust sheets over the furniture and everything reminded her of Jared. Often they had stayed in the house together without their parents after they came back from their trip to Africa and their stay at Elephant Walk. She had watched her brother becoming an unwilling stockbroker and entertained his clients, including Jack Merryweather. The three of them had talked for hours about their adventures in Africa. She had liked Jack and asked him more than once to send her love to Harry if he was writing a letter to Elephant Walk. He was good-looking enough but not her type. There had sometimes been a girl with him. For Jared, not for Jack. She and Jack were always looking for a nice girl for Jared to marry.

She had wandered around the house all afternoon and when it came to teatime there was no milk. There was plenty of tea and biscuits but no fresh milk. It was then she looked out of the lounge window to see if it was raining. To her surprise, the man was still sitting on the bench and seemed to be looking at her through the goggles.

She went downstairs, put on her coat from the stand in the hall, and picked up an old umbrella. London was full of odd people, and if they wanted to sit on a park bench across the road from her house, they had a perfect right to do so. Maybe the man had come and gone while she was making her bedroom comfortable and folding up the dust sheets. When she went out to get the milk she was not sure how long she had been thinking back on her life with her brother. The man wearing the goggles was still on the bench when she stepped onto the street. And when she came back with the milk and a loaf of bread, he was still in exactly the same spot on the other side of the road.

Inside, she closed the curtains to the street and turned on the electric lights. She made herself tea and opened a tin of butter and a jar of Gentleman's Relish. On the fresh bread, she spread the butter and relish, took everything into the lounge with the drawn curtains, and sat down in an armchair for tea. She read a book for some time until her eyelids drooped and then she took herself off to bed. The old doctor was right. She was worn out.

She looked down from her third-storey bedroom onto the dark street before closing the curtains. For some reason, she had not first turned on the lights. She could not see whether anyone was sitting on the bench. She fell into a soundless, dreamless sleep that went on all night. She was woken by the birds singing in the park, the dawn chorus. As always, winter and summer, she had slept with one of the bedroom windows half open. The first thing she remembered was that Jared was dead. She lay thinking of him, the covers drawn up to her chin. Then she took a deep breath, jumped out of bed, and ran to open the curtains. It was freezing cold in the early spring morning.

She had forgotten the man outside but when she looked down onto the bench he was still sitting in the exact same position. Sara shivered before running back and jumping into her warm bed. The man had still been wearing his goggles. She wondered if he had frozen to death. She didn't think so. It was the end of April. Trying to put the war out of her mind, she went back to sleep.

When she woke late in the morning after the best sleep of her life the sun was warming the room, and Sara was ravenously hungry. She dressed quickly and only then looked out of the window. The man on the bench was not dead. He had taken off the goggles. Even from the third storey and looking down across the Bayswater Road she was quite certain. She would know that squashed face and those large fishy eyes anywhere. On the bench was the man she had been forced to accept as a fiancé but never married. It was then she understood the implication of her phone call to 33 Squadron. An innocent phone call to report her brother's death had turned into a nightmare.

In a panic, she rushed down to the telephone and called the number 33 Squadron had given her. She knew she was quite hysterical. The woman on the other end of the phone had repeated back her address. She checked the bolts on the front and back doors. After closing all the windows, she holed herself up in a cold funk and waited for Harry Brigandshaw. There was no doubt in her mind. The madman on the bench outside had overheard her phone call. She had been told Harry was recovering in England from a plane crash. She had wanted to tell him about Jared. They had all been friends. The fact that she wanted to hear Harry's voice again had only been part of the reason for phoning the squadron.

Only much later did she wonder if she had done the right thing by calling Harry Brigandshaw. And when she looked out of the top window before the daylight went and saw Fishy Braithwaite was no longer sitting on the park bench she was not sure whether to laugh or cry.

In the afternoon the following day, she heard the ring of the front doorbell. She was embarrassed. What was she going to say to Harry, dragging him all the way up from Dorset? She had let her imagination run wild. Now the man had gone from the bench she was not so sure it had been Fishy Braithwaite. Harry would think she was chasing him again. The hysterics and threats to kill herself were more than expected from Jared's death. Everyone was losing someone in the war. No one she knew had killed themselves with grief. She patted her hair, put a brave smile on her face and lifted the bolts from the front door.


OUTSIDE HARRY and Lucinda were glad to hear the footsteps from inside the house. The drive had turned out a pleasure with the top down all the way. Lucinda was a good driver, and the twisting, narrow English country lanes a joy to drive through in spring. The sun had shone most of the way. Granny Forrester had been right as usual. To rush around the lanes in the dark would have been looking for an accident. In the morning, there had been no more panic phone calls and Harry was of a mind to call off the trip. He had wondered if Sara had created all the drama to make him pay her a visit. He was still wondering how she knew he was in England.

That morning, they all enjoyed a good breakfast, with Robert eating two of the large duck eggs, too rich for Harry, who had stuck with the chicken eggs. He even suggested to Lucinda they give up the drive to London. Robert had given both of them a funny look and Granny Forrester had a smirk on her face. Was it that obvious, thought Harry!

"We can have a nice lunch on the road at a quaint old inn," said Lucinda.

"Good idea," said Granny Forrester.

"Jared would expect you to make sure his sister is really all right," said Robert, looking at the remains on his breakfast plate.

Only when they had had their lunch just outside Guildford, and were on a piece of straight road, did Harry have the first, terrible rush of panic. It was worse than when he thought he was going to die with his engine cut out and the German coming in for his kill.

"It's Fishy Braithwaite," he said out loud, suddenly understanding. "Sara must have phoned the squadron and asked for me and been given your phone number."

"What's between you and Sara?" asked Lucinda, with the new authority born from their half hour in the woods.

"She's obsessed. Fishy's obsessed. It's a love triangle that doesn't exist."

"You'd better explain, Harry."

With his right hand stroking her knee, Harry told her everything. Including his posting to 33 Squadron. Sara sending a key to the safety-deposit box where she had deposited her engagement ring. Colonel Mervyn Braithwaite sending it back again. The man had even bragged that no woman would ever break off an engagement to him.

"Do you love her?"

"Of course not. A friend, yes. As is Jared. We enjoyed their company on Elephant Walk. Robert was the one after Sara, not me."

Lucinda had parked the car in front of the Wentworths' London house. Harry had a good look around before painfully getting his legs out of the car and himself up onto the crutches. It was teatime. People were walking up and down both sides of the Bayswater Road. There were cars going up and down both ways. It was a typical London afternoon in spring and the trees in the park on the far side of the iron railing were lush with young green foliage.

"I've only got a broken leg," he said to Lucinda, who hovered at his elbow.

The small gate was opened for him by Lucinda. The steps up to the front door made him concentrate on what he was doing. He had his head down. Lucinda had a proprietary hand on his elbow. Neither of them saw Fishy Braithwaite vault over the iron fence from his hiding place in Holland Park, dodge through the traffic, and pull his service revolver out of his flying coat, a long, brown leather coat that kept him warm at night. He was wearing his flying helmet and goggles.

As Sara opened her front door to apologise to Harry for all the fuss, she was surprised to find him standing there with Lucinda St Clair and briefly felt annoyed. Then she smiled.

"Harry, I'm sorry. I thought I saw Mervyn and panicked. You know us women. How kind of you to come."

Mervyn Braithwaite came over the now-closed small gate in one leap, his flying coat open, his uniform visible, and ran up the steps, the gun firing at Sara as she stood in the front door. She was dead before she collapsed on the floor.

"*I am not a wet fish! And you're dead!*"

Fishy Braithwaite screamed on and on until Harry hit him across the throat with the wooden end of his right crutch. Lucinda was kneeling next to Sara. Two men were holding down Colonel Braithwaite and a policeman was running towards them down the road.

"She's dead, Harry."

"It's a bloody war. You can't kill and kill and kill and stay sane. Poor sod. Mad as a bloody hatter." Bending down with difficulty, Harry covered up his CO's RFC uniform by closing the flying coat. The goggles were still on his face.

"When you get him to the station, call General Trenchard at the War Office," he told the constable. "He'll want to know about this right away. I'm afraid the girl's dead. We'll be in this house for as long as you want us to be."

"What happened?" asked the constable.

"It's a very long story and it started very long ago. At school, kids being mean to kids... Look after him. He was a damn good pilot."

Only inside the house did Harry begin to cry. For all of them. The dead and the living. Then he pulled himself together and phoned Birchdale. Mrs Wentworth answered the phone and before he could say anything thanked him for calling about Jared. Then he told her Sara was dead. Shot by Mervyn Braithwaite.

Outside a crowd had gathered at the sight of another person's adversity.

"It was my idea," she said.

"What was, Mrs Wentworth?"

"Mervyn marrying Sara. Now I have no children. Nothing to leave behind. I'd better go and tell my husband. I won't ask you why you are there, Major Brigandshaw. Such a coincidence has to have a reason. If she had not gone off to Africa with Jared this would never have happened. Sara would have been safely married with children. You do know the firm Braithwaite and Penny? Very big firm. I hope you're proud of yourself, Major Brigandshaw."

The phone near Warminster went dead. Harry stood for a long time. If it was somehow his fault, he could not see why.

· · ·

361

HARRY AND LUCINDA stayed the night at the Savoy in separate rooms. It was as if someone had thrown a cold bucket of water over them.

Harry never saw Colonel Braithwaite being taken away. When the ambulance arrived to take away Sara, Braithwaite was gone. The crowd was still there. Bigger than ever. People at the back standing on tiptoe to have a look at the dead girl on the top of the steps. One woman lifted up her child to have a better look.

They waited another two hours in the house. A senior policeman came and said they could go. He took their names and Harry told him the dead girl's family had been told. The blood had been cleaned from the steps. The policeman took the key to the house. They parted with the policeman in the street. Most of the crowd had gone.

The Ford fired the first time and they drove to the hotel. They ate supper in the Grill Room but neither of them was talkative or hungry. Harry thought it better not to drink champagne so soon after Sara's death.

The next day they drove back to Purbeck Manor. The magic had gone. Harry stayed the next night and made his usual excuse about visiting Granny Brigandshaw in her Kensington flat. Lucinda drove him to the railway station.

"Was that all it was?" asked Lucinda, dry-eyed.

"I don't know."

"Try not to get yourself killed, Harry. And give my regards to your grandmother."

"I'm not going to visit her."

"I know."

"Thank your mother for me again."

"Will I hear from you again?"

"Yes, I'll write... I didn't tell you but Mrs Wentworth blames me for Sara's death. For Sara going out to Africa. For Sara not marrying Mervyn and having a brood of kids. Ever since I can remember it has always been my fault."

"We all say that. It's much better for Mrs Wentworth to blame someone else." Then the train arrived and took him away. At a complete loose end, Harry phoned his Uncle James at Hastings Court. His uncle sent a car up to London for him.

"It'll be my first visit to Hastings Court."

"You were born here, Harry. You could have owned Hastings Court. You still could."

"What do you mean, Uncle James?"

"Ask your grandfather. Ask your mother. It's not for me to say."

. . .

IN THE OLD dining room at Hastings Court, where unbeknown to Harry his grandfather Brigandshaw, the Pirate, had died a lonely death, Harry, sitting at the breakfast table, read the previous day's *Daily Telegraph*. He was alone in the vaulted hall of a room that had watched his mother's ancestors eat for centuries. The obituary was prominent, next to some old lord who had died peacefully in his sleep. Harry read it twice and left his last cup of tea to go cold. His leg was mending fast and he only needed a stick.

He found what had once been his grandmother Brigandshaw's favourite bench overlooking the ornamental lake. And let his mind think.

Colonel Braithwaite was reported killed by ground fire.

*EVEN IN DEATH, the German air force had not been able to shoot him down. Colonel Braithwaite probably dead in his cockpit when he crash-landed his Sopwith Triplane with the three distinct yellow stripes, in front of the British observation post. The corporal who reported the crash said that the body was burnt beyond recognition. Soon after, the corporal's position was overrun by the Germans. A report in a German newspaper stated Colonel Braithwaite had been given a military funeral after the British corporal identified the charred remains.*

*Colonel Braithwaite was engaged to Miss Sara Wentworth, a brave nurse who gave her own life saving British lives in the same German advance that has since been checked and reversed.*

*There is talk Colonel Braithwaite may be posthumously awarded the Victoria Cross, the highest award of valour the King can bestow. Colonel Braithwaite had just turned thirty-three. He was the commanding officer of 33 Squadron. This newspaper salutes a brave man.*

A MONTH LATER, Harry Brigandshaw returned to France as commanding officer of 33 Squadron. He phoned Lucinda the day he left England to say goodbye. What he did not know was his feelings for Lucinda. What he did know was 33 Squadron would never be told by him what really happened to their first commanding officer.

Shortly afterwards the Royal Flying Corps became officially the Royal Air Force, with Trenchard its first air marshal.

# 2

## OCTOBER 1917 TO JANUARY 1919

*T*he lion was old, mangy, and the black tuft at the end of its tail dragged in the dust. There had been no rain since the end of April and the lion had not eaten for a week. With difficulty, the cat walked down to the Mazoe River and drank. The river was still flowing but only just. Every joint in the lion's legs hurt from the shoulders down to the toes. The old gash that had almost taken his right eye throbbed, the fight over the lioness long forgotten. The eyes were big and sad and did not see very well. The lion had been on his own for a long time. Still hungry with little prospect, the black-maned lion pulled itself up from the bottom of the riverbank, climbed slowly to the top and lay down under an acacia tree that had been growing in the same place for centuries, reseeding itself. Soon the old lion was asleep and dreaming of better days. Above, and near the top of the acacia, a giant eagle owl was also asleep. The air was hot and dry, filled with the scent of wild sage. Across the river, a fish eagle was watching the water, hoping for something to catch. The bird had been motionless all morning on the same stump of dead tree... Even the crickets had fallen silent in the African heat.

SIR HENRY MANDERVILLE had ridden out with the dogs at dawn when it was cool. In the hot, humid month of October, which the old Rhodesian hands called suicide month with an air of propriety, the butterflies were easier to catch and chloroform in a similar jar to the one he had used as a boy at Hastings Court in England. Then it was mostly cabbage whites, not the magnificent butterflies in rich blues and reds with long tails like Chinese kites. The best specimens were pinned into glass-topped trays, packed carefully and sent to a collector in Kent. They had been corresponding for seventeen years.

Sir Henry, now sixty-five years old, was very pleased with himself. The man in Salisbury who added up the figures had said the tobacco crop made two thousand pounds sterling the previous year. Imperial Tobacco in London had asked him to double the size of the crop as they slowly introduced the new tobacco to their blends. For the first time in his life, he had actually made some money. He had promised himself a ride to New Kleinfontein to tell Alison Oosthuizen once he had bagged ten good butterflies. If he could only remove the twenty-five-year age gap from his mind he would propose to the girl.

His daughter Emily had been blunt.

"Father, she may be young but she's lonely. You may be old but you're on your own. You like each other. You chatter away all day long to each other given a chance. I don't know what's happening to Madge and Barend. They married, so that's that. Nothing I can do. Nothing Alison can do. Parents have to stand back from their children and let them make their own mistakes. You know that... You could have a lot of fun, you two. There's money now from the tobacco. Marry her and take her on a trip."

"You can't be serious. I'm old enough to be her father."

"So what? Have some fun. You never know what's going to happen in Africa. And I'm so sick of worrying about Harry in France and I am permanently tired. Happiness doesn't come too often in life. So what if it only lasts five years? Anyway, you'll probably outlive her. I've never ever seen you sick once in your life."


THE OWL HEARD the ridgeback dogs first and woke with big eyes. The fish eagle on the other riverbank took no notice. Sir Henry had not seen a worthwhile butterfly all morning and was about to give up, ride over to New Kleinfontein and ask Alison for lunch. The dogs were ranging, sniffing the air. The lion woke, smelt the dogs first and then heard one of them bark. The dogs could not get the scent of the lion as the wind was in the wrong direction. The horse was trailing Sir Henry at the end of the long lead; walking slowly forward, the net poised, Sir Henry was about to bag a butterfly he had never seen before, his mind fully concentrated as he walked towards the dappled shade of the old acacia tree, the dry grass bent and brown at his waist.

With difficulty, the old lion pulled itself up on its haunches to find out what was making the new noise. He kept his ears flat and his head down below the top of the old grass. Near the top of the tree, the owl's eyes were as big as they could be as the bird watched the crouching man walk straight towards the crouching lion. The lion's tail was now twitching as best it could, as the old lion wound itself up to spring. A curl of wind brushed around and down off the tree. Fletcher, the largest male in the pack of dogs caught the scent and turned, growling in his throat, making Sir Henry straighten up from his approach with the big butterfly net. He now looked straight into the old, sad eyes of the lion twenty feet in front of him.

Fletcher took off for the lion as the cat sprang, going straight for the throat. The lion chopped him away with his right paw, breaking the dog's neck. Sir Henry turned the net and held the pole rigidly, pointed at the open mouth of the lion as the pack of Rhodesian ridgebacks hurled themselves forward. The old lion sank under their weight. The owl flew off away from all the noise. Sir Henry pulled his service revolver from its leather holster and, aiming carefully so as not to hurt the dogs, shot the lion through its mouth. Then he went across and bent down next to Fletcher, stroking the dog's head on the other side to where the lion's claws had torn out the flesh.

He had dropped the horse's lead but when he called, the horse came up from the river. Sir Henry put Fletcher over the front of the saddle and rode back to Elephant Walk, the three dogs following. Behind them, next to the dead lion, lay the broken butterfly net.

Before the sun went down the vultures were circling the carcass. The hyenas and jackals were still frightened by the smell of the lion.

Sir Henry buried Fletcher next to the family plot. Standing with his daughter Emily and Tembo, he had never felt so lonely in his life. All afternoon the two remaining dogs and the bitch had looked for Fletcher. Even the wild geese were quiet. Both of them were thinking of Harry in France.

"You're right," he said, "I'm going to ask her to marry me. Life is too short. Too short."

They were both crying for Fletcher, now buried deep in the red earth of Elephant Walk.

THEY WERE ALONE in the family compound and alone in their own houses. Before the sun came up, Emily could hear her father getting ready to go out into the lands. By the time the light was good enough to see what they were doing, the metal plough disc was hit with a metal rod. The insistent clanging brought the labourers out of their own compound of thatched huts a mile downstream. Tembo brought the saddled horse from the stables and her father went off to work wearing a wide-brimmed brown hat against the power of the African sun. He wore a khaki shirt with long sleeves and long khaki trousers to keep the sun from eating his skin. Everyone had a two-hour break in the middle of the day when the heat was intense. They worked all day, six days a week, planting, weeding, suckering, reaping and grading the tobacco. For five months at the end of the season, everyone on Elephant Walk worked only in the mornings. The season began with planting the seedbeds and keeping them moist with watering cans. A cut grass mulch was laid on the seedbeds to protect the green seedlings, the only green to be found on the farm in October other than the family vegetable garden. Only when the rains came would the seedlings be planted out in rows in the newly prepared lands.

Most days Emily saw her father come home in the dark and go straight to bed. The routine of sundowners on her screened veranda had been long broken by Madge's marriage to Barend and the boys going off to war. She even missed old Peregrine the Ninth. Even with Alison and the grandchildren on the farm New Kleinfontein, that had once been half of Elephant Walk, the families never visited each other without good reason. Barend, the boy she had loved, had become Barend the son-in-law that made her want to weep for her daughter. Madge had given birth to a girl in February 1916, a boy in February 1917, and was pregnant for the third time. Madge looked thirty, not twenty-five, and the light of happiness had long gone from her eyes.

Barend ran his farm from his veranda, shouting orders to his black foreman, who did more than shout at the labourers to make them work. The crops, when they came, were sparse and barely fed the men and women who lived on New Kleinfontein. The meagre wages, paid in kind (maize meal, salt, sometimes dried beans), were doled out through the foreman, who never left his hut without a rawhide whip in his big fat hand. Whatever was meant to go into the soil (seed and fertiliser), or into the mouths of the labourers, was first taxed by the foreman. Barend and his foreman were the only two fat men on the farm. To Emily, who now ran the maize and cattle sections on Elephant Walk, it was a recipe for disaster, a catastrophe waiting to happen. Alison, the one-time nurse for Harry as a baby, brought to Africa by Emily when she fled England with Sebastian Brigandshaw, was treated by her son as a servant.

She had thought about Alison marrying her father, long before she had suggested it to him. The looks between them had been going on for a long time. And when Harry came back from the war she would have him talk to Barend. Madge said nothing to her, loyal to her husband and the rapidly growing brood of children. Emily thanked God every night on her bended knees that Sebastian had been a good man in every sense of the word. What made a man grow to hate and bully she never understood. What made a man make everyone around them miserable she never understood. Maybe when the children were old enough they would protect each other and their mother. She wondered if Katinka, who had stayed in the Cape, had seen her brother for what he was and kept away. All the man did was sit and drink and shout and bully. Emily was quite sure Barend knew what his foreman was up to. They were made by God from the same rotten material. They were the devil on earth and she prayed for them every night before she went to bed. For what good it did.

HENRY MANDERVILLE HAD RARELY BEEN LONELY in his life, except at boarding school in England surrounded by other boys torn from their families. It was Emily who was lonely and there was nothing he could do. All her children had gone. Little James dead as a child. George dead on a battlefield. Madge to her husband. Harry to a war he would likely not come back from, despite the Americans joining the Allies at last. His daughter was forty and everything good in her life was in the past. Just an old, tired father to talk to of an evening. A woman needed a family to run, not a cattle and maize farm. And if he really thought about it, marrying Alison would probably do the poor girl more harm than good. A marriage should mean children, a family, cats and dogs, and above all, youth. Should they have a child, he was far too old to bring it up. It would not be right. Like Emily, Alison had had her children. Like Emily, one, Christo, had died as a child. 'There's no fool like an old fool,' he told himself. 'Fooling oneself is one of the more stupid accomplishments in a man's life.' He was an old man with his books, who collected butterflies and grew tobacco. He should be satisfied with what he had. His wife, like Emily's husband, had died. And that was all there was to it. Life was a mosaic. Bits fitted together to make up a life. Some bits blissfully happy. Some bits content. The rest was life itself. He was sometimes content. He had had a good life. Much to be thankful for. He would just have to let his daughter's generation sort out their own problems and not become a meddling old fool. The strangest part of it all, he was not sure if he even wanted to start life all over again. There were too few moments of happiness. Too little content. Too much war and too many arguments.

. . .

HARRY BRIGANDSHAW LOOKED down on the manufacturing might and manpower of America. He was patrolling behind the Allied lines. The Royal Flying Corps had complete command of the sky. He saw trucks loaded and grinding forward, some towing guns. Teams of horses towing guns. Men marching. Roads clogged with the means of war all pushing to the front. From the French ports to the front lines were American men and munitions. It was inevitable. If Fritz could see what he could see they would give up the war. Down below, the slowly flowing tide was too powerful for anyone to stop.

The light was fading though sunlight still caught the propellers of the biplanes. Their fourth sortie, and they had not seen a German aircraft all day. One German observer had tried to put up a balloon during the dawn patrol, cranking it up as fast as possible, the observer in the small basket below. A Flight had incinerated the balloon when it was halfway up in its bid to see what was happening with the Americans. The observer had jumped but he was too close to the ground for his parachute to open.

Harry lifted his right gloved hand and signalled 33 Squadron back to base. Harry was still looking for danger up till the moment he cut the Sopwith Camel's engine at the end of their old airfield. They were once again back where they started from. The Germans were now sending boys to fight at the front to fill their manpower gap. The old French farmhouse was still there. All that was missing were Fishy Braithwaite and many of the pilots who had come and died. Harry was thirty-two years old with a dead German pilot to his name for every one of the years he had lived. He felt neither brave nor victorious. Just a survivor.

The mess steward brought him the message at the bar. Harry opened the official envelope. He was posted. To Military Headquarters. To liaise with the flying wing of the American army. To teach them what he had learnt... And then it dawned on him. His war was over. He had survived. All the conversations with his father to watch his back, to watch the clouds, watch what was coming out of the sun. His father had saved him day after day, talking in his head, keeping him alert. His nightmare of killing and surviving was over. He stuffed the envelope into the pocket of his uniform and turned to the barman, the same barman, back with the rank of corporal.

"Give everyone who comes into the mess tonight a drink on my card. They've posted me, Corporal. I won't be flying anymore."

Harry put his glass out for a refill. His whole body was numb. It was over. He was going to see Elephant Walk again after all. The corporal was smiling and they caught each other's eye. The corporal had understood the meaning of the posting.

"Have one yourself, Corporal. Now, with me. Let's break another rule."

Both men laughed to break the tension.

A MONTH later Harry met Jack Merryweather. Three days later Merlin St Clair walked into the officers' mess at Military Headquarters. It was not such a big war after all. They had given Harry the Distinguished Flying Cross, made him a lieutenant colonel, and for some reason left him in the army uniform with red taps on his lapels, and a red band around his hat. It was something to do with the Americans not having their own separate air force. To make them feel at home. He still wore the wings on his right breast pocket with the DFC ribbon, the MC ribbon with the two studs on it depicting the two bars. So there it was and every American had to be told what the ribbons meant. Three Military Crosses and one Distinguished Flying Cross. Most of the Americans had enough feelings not to ask him to his face the number of kills, but they all knew.

And there they were, the survivors with their red taps, their new ranks, and an influx of American bourbon to drink to a now certain victory. Jack's arm had healed and left no outward scars. It was only when the Americans looked into their eyes they saw the distant stares. And then they looked away again. The Americans had yet to fight the war.

THE STRANGEST THING had happened to Jack Merryweather. The moment they had taken him out of the trenches and the danger was gone, he was bored again. The job had been done and now he was back to waffling, being social, telling the Americans it wasn't that bad after all. Telling them what they wanted to hear. He had gone from reality to the old ways of an educated man. Saying the right thing. Playing down any idea of hardship. Never mentioning the real friends he had made and lost. What people thought was the real world, Jack now knew to be one long pretence. All the years of polite talk lay ahead of him and it made him want to scream.

MERLIN ST CLAIR had sold every one of his Vickers-Armstrong shares a week before the Americans came into the war. He had managed the impossible. Buying at the bottom and selling at the top of the market. The machine gun he had orchestrated so effectively to kill Germans had made him rich. One hundred and twelve thousand pounds sterling. Enough to never work again in his life. Lloyd's of London could kiss his arse. Cornell, Brooke and Bradley could kiss his jolly old derrière. Someone had to be a winner in a war. He would buy his father the best herd of cows money could buy. He would set the builders onto repairing Purbeck Manor. Then he would sail around the world as slowly as possible and thank God every day that he was still alive. Then, and only then would he think what to do with the rest of his life. He was rich. For the first time in more than a century, a St Clair was stinking rich.

GLEN HAMILTON COULD NOT SEE one good reason why his fellow Americans had come into the war. If the Europeans wanted to bury themselves in mass graves it had nothing to do with America. He had no idea why they all went to war in the first place, and he doubted if any of the troops, dead or alive, had any idea either. His editor in Denver had said something about the balance of power. Germany building a navy to challenge the British. Treaties of alliance: an attack on one country would be considered an attack on all the Allies. So the whole of Europe had fallen into the same pit in a matter of days. Which was fine for the Europeans if that was what they wanted but it still had nothing to do with his America.

"Well go and get the story and try not to get yourself killed." Matt Vogel was editor of the *Colorado Telegraph* and what he said was law. They could argue but what he said, in the end, was law. So Glen had sulked.

"You want the real reason, Glen Hamilton? The real, real reason why we are going to kill a whole bunch of young American boys that I hope very much won't include you? Money. It's the money. If the British and French don't win the war we don't get our money back. Fact is, if the Royal Navy had not been there to stop us, we might have shipped the war materiel to Germany and Austria. Then they would have owed us money and we'd have gone in there to fight the British and French. Every war in history has been about money. Whatever they say about right and wrong and going to war with God on our side. They're talking shit. Never been any damn difference since man came out of the primal slime. After this war, if we get our money, we'll be the richest damn nation on earth. We didn't bleed none up to now. And that was smart. They'll put you in the army. In uniform. A captain. So off you go and get the money, Captain Hamilton. That's where our interests lie."

"It can't be that poor."

"Oh yes, it can."

He was a journalist attached to British Military Headquarters, where his job was to interview the British liaison officers who had been pulled out of the front line to tell the Americans how to fight a trench war. It was Harry Brigandshaw's unnerving stare that first gave him the shivers.

"You don't talk like the other officers. Are you Australian?"

"No, a Rhodesian."

"Where's that?"

"A little jewel of a country in south-central Africa. I'm a farmer. My brother was killed so I came over. Revenge sounded good six thousand miles away."

"You did all right, sir."

"But they didn't, Captain. Every man I killed could just as easily been my friend. And none of this 'sir' business in the mess. Chances are we're the same age. Both colonials but you won't admit to it. All the product of mother England, who was a product of mother Germany, if you include Saxony, who was a product of I don't know where. Or like my friend over there, Merlin St Clair, a product of mother Normandy which is now a province of France... You must have a lot of factories in America. I flew over the product. If the Germans could see what you've sent they'd give up now."

"But they won't."

"No. Not yet. Now it's pride. Desperation. Hatred... And please don't try and interview me for your newspaper. I don't want to talk about it."

"How did you survive?"

"My father was a white hunter. One of the best. He talked to me when I was alone in the air. He is dead, you see. Killed by an elephant."

"Can you talk about Africa? The bush, I think you call it."

"Anytime."

"Do you still hunt?"

"Only for food. And once for revenge. I have a friend at home who believed in revenge. The British hanged his father for going out with the Boers. His father was a Boer but lived in the British Cape. We sowed the seeds of hatred, as we are all doing so well right now."

"I'd like to visit Africa."

"Maybe you shall. After the war."

"Can I visit with you?"

"Everyone is welcome at Elephant Walk."

"What's Elephant Walk?"

"My farm."

"What squadron were you in?"

"I said no interviews, Mister?"

"Glen Hamilton. Denver. Colorado."

"How d'you do? Now, will you excuse me?"

"You knew Colonel Braithwaite." Glen Hamilton knew perfectly well Harry was 33 Squadron.

"He was a great pilot. An officer and a gentleman. Sadly missed."

"He's alive. They've got him in an asylum. Did you know?"

"Colonel Braithwaite was shot down by ground fire. Rifle fire to be exact. He was dead at the controls when the aircraft crashed. His plane was positively identified by a British corporal who had more than once identified the individual markings of the CO of 33 Squadron. I had hoped he would have been awarded the Victoria Cross posthumously. It is the only decoration we have that can be awarded to a dead man."

"You were at Oxford with him."

"Yes. That's common knowledge. Why he had me posted to 33 Squadron."

"And you knew his fiancée who died as a nurse in the same German advance."

"Sara was a lovely girl. I'll buy you a drink in the mess if you stop trying to interview me. You are trying to make a story out of nothing. Why ask me my squadron when you knew perfectly well?"

"You were there when he shot her."

"Where are you trying to go, Mr Hamilton?"

"I'll have that drink... Research. Not for my newspaper. Every journalist is a frustrated novelist. The policeman talked in a pub. Said he had a good idea for a book he was going to write after the war and because he can't write he told me. The truth is always crazier than fiction."

"I'll ask you one thing now. Keep your mouth shut. When the war's over, come to Elephant Walk. Men and women do things in a war they would not do otherwise. Quite frankly, Mervyn was as mad as a hatter. But a great pilot, who trained many other great pilots. If your personal greed for sensation writes such a story you are as sick as Mervyn Braithwaite."

"I'm sorry."

"Good. And British policemen don't write books. Or think about writing them. There is an Official Secrets Act... Now, the drink. And there is Merlin. Fighting a war from a forty-bedroom French château is absurd," Harry said looking around at the luxury. "And there is Jack Merryweather."

"You British all seem to know each other."

"The ruling class, I'm afraid, are a small brotherhood. My grandfather is a baronet from the days of William the Conqueror. As is Merlin's father, though his father is a baron. His eldest brother and heir to the barony was killed in action yesterday. His sister Lucinda's fiancé was killed. His sister Genevieve's father-in-law and husband were killed within days of each other. They were both in the same regiment... This great château with all its finery and regimental silver, its fine wines from old cellars, its permanent dance of good manners, all this is the product of the upper classes, who have ruled England and the empire for a thousand years. This last pirouette in such fine surroundings is the end of them, for better or for worse. Probably some good will come out of it. I don't know. But please, Glen Hamilton, let our skeletons rest in their cupboards in peace."

"What are you going to do after the war?"

"I'm going home. To peace. To solitude. To the sound of the bush. To the most wonderful place in the world to live. Africa... Merlin, come and meet an American. He'll want to interview you but say no."

The next day Merlin went forward with an American major as far as the reserve lines. They were shelled the day after and the major asked to be taken back to the château. After that, no one asked to go out to the front before he was sent. They sat at tables explaining everything to do with war. How to set up a machine gun. How to draw the lines of fire. The only thing Merlin could not teach them was how to stay alive.

Three weeks later the major was killed in the first American offensive on that part of the front. By then Merlin could not remember his face. There had been so many of them, so eager to learn.

The one permanent American was Glen Hamilton, the American newspaperman from Denver, Colorado. Harry had avoided him after that first drink. Then his leave came up at the same time as Merlin's and they arranged to go to Purbeck Manor together. By then the Allies were advancing right across the Western Front. Like the Battle of Waterloo, when the Prussians had come to help the British at the end of the battle, the American intervention was too much for the Germans. The irony was not lost on Harry.

Merlin was going to be home for Christmas. Glen Hamilton had been away from America for six months. The *Colorado Telegraph* wanted him to go to London to interview senior British generals at the War Office. Merlin asked him down to Purbeck Manor for Christmas. Merlin wanted Glen to read the book just finished by his brother Robert. The family wanted an opinion from a professional before the manuscript was sent to a publisher, to save any embarrassment. Had it not been for the small boy born to Penelope, he would have been heir to the barony. In her letter, his mother had written that everyone except Barnaby would be home for Christmas. The sergeant married to his sister had been badly gassed and was out of the war. Merlin wondered if he was going to get back his ten pounds. Not that it mattered anymore. With luck, Harry would propose to Lucinda, and one of the girls would have a life and a fully functional husband. Barnaby was now in Syria with General Allenby.

GLEN HAMILTON HAD NEVER INTENDED to write a novel. And war stories sent back with hundreds of other American journalists were not going to get noticed. Not going to make him famous. He was a journalist who wanted a story no one else had, not a reporter of state news that was forgotten in twenty-four hours. Some in Denver called him a snooper but he never cared what other people said.

Matt Vogel would have called it luck but it wasn't. He had been in London before the American army began pouring into Europe writing back potboilers for the *Colorado Telegraph* when he had the idea to write about the people who had fought the war so far and not the places and battles and tally up the dead. He wanted to put faces to the battles and the mangled remains strewn across France and Flanders, so he started asking questions. Going to the pubs the British so often frequented. Buying drinks. Looking for smashed up men who had a story to tell which was mostly all of them. He told the men he bought them drinks because of what he was doing. Looking for a character. Someone larger than life.

The sergeant mechanic was drunk, and like all drunks talked too much and regretted what he said in the morning. He had seen Colonel Braithwaite leave his Sopwith Triplane on the edge of the airfield and take the motorcycle. All the squadrons were in disarray and scattering in front of the German advance. When he read later his colonel was killed in his own aircraft he knew it was a lie. He also knew the CO was as mad as a March hare, along with everyone else at 33 Squadron. But the madman was good at keeping his young pilots alive and that was all that mattered in a war. That, and killing the enemy. The next day he regretted his indiscretion and hoped the American with the flush wallet was equally drunk. The sergeant had forgotten that right at the beginning, the American had said he was a journalist.

The American had got him reminiscing about the squadron. He was drunk by then and said with that drunken fondness that the CO was mad.

"How do you mean, mad?" Glen had asked. He was completely sober but acting drunk.

"The other pilots said when he killed he yelled at the top of his voice the same words over and over again."

"What were the words?"

"'I'm not a wet fish. And you're dead.' Don't know what the word fish was about but the last bit was clear. We had a ground attack one day on the airfield. The CO was the only one to turn his plane at the end of the airfield to face the three German aeroplanes. Cool as a cucumber, our CO shot from still on the ground. The one Fritz died on impact, the second came out alive. The CO ran at him with his service revolver yelling the same words. Even I heard that day. If it wasn't for Captain Brigandshaw who tackled the CO it would have been murder. Saw Captain Brigandshaw pick up the fallen pistol and put it in his pocket. I was looking out of one of the temporary hangars. They got Fritz off the station the same day, back to Blighty to go in the 'cage'. The CO saved my life that day. Those three planes flying straight at me with their guns firing. The one broke off and got away. The CO shot the other two out of the sky. The officers' mess was going to be next. More important to kill the pilots than smash up their aircraft on the ground. You can build a new aeroplane but you can't build a new pilot so quickly. Those Germans knew just what they were doing."

"What happened to the CO?"

"That's the funny thing. The War Office said he was shot down by rifle fire. They recognised his squadron and personal markings. But he wasn't. He scarpered on a motorcycle. Ran away. Then months later I was back on a week's leave and having a pint in the pub on the Bayswater Road with a couple of squadron mates, and we were talking about the squadron and one of us mentioned Captain Brigandshaw too loud, and one of the locals came over. Said there'd been a murder on the Bayswater Road. The bloke was one of the crowd that had gathered. There was a dead girl on the steps and a man in flying gear on the ground with a crutch pressed into his throat. The local heard the copper take the names. One of 'em was Brigandshaw and the man the copper arrested was Braithwaite. A few days after I'd seen the CO leave his aircraft and the girl was killed, the colonel was reported killed in action."

Knowing when to stop when he was onto a good thing, Glen Hamilton bought the sergeant another drink and left.

Finding the police officer in the Holland Park police station who took down statements was easy. He confirmed Harry Brigandshaw and Lucinda St Clair had seen the girl killed. Gave him the name of the dead girl. Then told him to go to the War Office to find out what happened to Mr Braithwaite. The policeman was quite open, even talkative. The War Office was not. They said they knew nothing about a murder on Bayswater Road.

"They should have done," said the friendly policeman on Glen's second visit. "When the army took the poor sod away from the station he was still yelling, 'I'm not a wet fish. And you're dead.' Bloody bonkers. The army was welcome to him. And there's more to it, I would think. The dead girl was engaged to Braithwaite and she had visited Brigandshaw in Africa. All in the statements. The dead girl had called Brigandshaw in a panic. The army told us to drop the case. We do what we are told."

Glen Hamilton's deliberate lie to Harry Brigandshaw about the hearsay of the policeman was to keep up the charade of writing a novel. The invitation to Purbeck Manor was a bonus. He would ask Merlin's sister out of the blue what she knew about the killing of Sara Wentworth. Once he found out where they had hidden the flying ace, he would break the whole gory story right across the world. He would be syndicated. He would be famous. And to hell with the British and their upper class. The sheer bloody cheek of Harry Brigandshaw, to call him a colonel made him want to spit. He was an American... He had his story. To hell with them. The fact he was accepting hospitality for Christmas under false pretences never crossed his mind. Or the fact that he was going to fall in love with Lucinda St Clair.

For Granny Forrester, there was nothing to celebrate except Christmas. She had helped to tuck sprigs of holly behind the old pictures that littered the house. Most were dark faces of the ancient dead, nameless and sometimes crashing down from the old walls, to be put back with a renewed screw or another length of picture wire. They were found in the mornings, fallen on the stairs, or ready to be trodden on down the dark damp corridor, waiting for help. Some were grime-covered pictures of lifelong dead. Fox hunts with splashes of red coats. Men with feathered hats and old guns. Landscapes. Seascapes. Horses. Dogs. And no one knew the painters' names or cleaned away the grime of centuries. She had the feeling they were all about to take their last bow, finally swept away by war and poverty. Not that any of it mattered. When the old died, a picture here or there made no difference to their death. Memories faded like the pictures.

The child, of course, was not a St Clair or any of her family but they would see. The boy was only six months old. Richard. Richard to replace the idiot Richard. She thought, whenever looking at him silently as was her wont, that the father had Turkish, Moorish blood. The knowing eyes that fixed on her own were coal-black and mocking. The hair was curly dark. No one had ever found coal-black eyes in a family portrait, despite the soot of years. Of course, no one mentioned it. Rather fitting. The end of the old. The beginning of something new. Maybe that was it. But she was rich, Penelope, and that was all that mattered in the world. Poor Frederick. Poor Penelope. Damn the war, and all the wars before them, and the wars to come!

She wore mittens on her hands, and two pairs of woollen socks on her feet and the chilblains burnt, as did most of the joints in her old body, that once had had so much promise. The draughts came at her from under every door in the old house. Sitting in front of the fire was warm in front but cold at her back. She quietly wondered if she would make it through the winter. Not that it mattered. She had had her life. A good one. A few good years with Potts. Watching the children. Helping her daughter. There was always a time to die, and though she tried to believe her Christian religion, she was never quite sure. The idea of heaven was good and comforting. The idea of seeing Potts again was wonderful. She didn't really believe it. Earthly words for deathly comfort. As much comfort for the living left behind and waiting their turns of life... None of it really mattered. The earth would take her bones. If her soul floated away, what would it do on its own? Could souls recognise each other? Live together for all eternity? And where? And why? And what would be the purpose?... She would have this Christmas, and then wait to find out... She never spoke to the others. They had their problems, the only ones that mattered to them, and those she tried to help them solve. Her own problems were never important to other people.

She had never met an American before and doubted if she ever would again. And there was a problem she could see with her old and rheumy eyes. Poor Lucinda. Trying so hard with the nice young man from Africa she had wanted from a child and briefly had. The American wanting her and Harry lost in a world he would never escape. She caught him often staring into space. Seeing none of them. Remembering... She hoped the distance of Africa would bring him comfort. Strangely, she was sure the tension between the two men had nothing to do with her granddaughter... She was going to celebrate Christmas and hope for the best, in the here and now. Barnaby was safe in Damascus. Her Barnaby. Then she smiled to herself. She would have to live through the cold of winter to see him back again. The American had said they would win the war in 1918.

"What is it, Grandma?" asked Genevieve.

"However terrible life may seem at the moment there is always something in the future that will make you smile. Try and remember that, my child. I have felt your pain. Tried to take away some of it. In the end, there is always something to smile about."

"Do you think Lucinda will marry Harry Brigandshaw?"

"No, but I'm not really sure."

"Why?"

"Because I don't think he loves her. Likes her, yes. Good friends. But none of the power of love."

Genevieve, her granddaughter, burst into tears and ran out of the room where they had been sitting around the fire.

"You're an old fool, Nettie! An old fool."

She would ask Doctor Reichwald, who was now Doctor Smithers, to give Genevieve something to make her feel better, if there was such a thing. Then she stoked the fire with a log of wood and used the poker to stir the embers. The flames came up again and warmed her, so she fell asleep in the old armchair.

When she woke her daughter was offering her a glass of sherry. Then the room filled up with her family and she smiled. Penelope put the black-eyed curly-headed heir to the barony in her lap and she smiled again. In the end, he would be what they wanted him to be whatever colour his eyes. Lord St Clair, Eighteenth Baron St Clair of Purbeck.


THEY HAD GIVEN Glen Hamilton a room on the third floor down an old, dark corridor with pictures on the walls too dark to see. The room had no bathroom attached, and when he asked the doddering upstairs maid where he could find one, she pointed to the side table with a large enamel basin and in it a large jug of cold water. On a rail to the left of the wooden stand was a towel. A metal dish held a cake of soap. He had been in England long enough to know that the bathroom to them was a place for a bath. Usually, the toilet was in a separate small room with a tiny window. He asked where he could find the toilet. Between the maid's broad Dorset accent and his American, they were largely speaking a foreign language to each other. He asked again. Very slowly. The old woman pointed under the bed, which seemed unlikely. He again looked bewildered. With pain written all over her face, the old woman bent down by half leaning herself on the big, four-poster bed. The curtains were drawn. The woman triumphantly hoicked a huge potty from its hiding place. He had not seen one since he was a child and then it was much smaller.

"Potty," she had said and left the room leaving him gazing at the thick enamel chamber pot with the big curly handle. On one side, though he did not know it, was emblazoned the St Clair coat of arms.

When he looked up at the tall ceiling there were cobwebs in the corners. The air was stale and despite the bitter cold, he opened the windows onto the bleak winter afternoon. Most of the big trees were leafless. It was drizzling. One of the trees almost touched the bedroom window. When he put his hand inside the bedcovers it was warm. Someone had aired the bedding in a room with a fire. Then he saw the bedroom fireplace freshly laid. Despite the warm bedclothes and the fire ready for a match, the whole house gave him the creeps. He was sure it must be haunted. He would not be the first or last journalist to put himself in harm's way while pursuing a good story. More than anything else, Glen Hamilton was scared of ghosts.

The next day was Christmas Eve when he found himself alone with Lucinda. She was aloof, ice-cold, but more attractive to him than any hot-blooded, full-busted Southerner. He was used to women reacting to him favourably; they met each other's eye and understood what they were about. Sometimes he followed up with the silent look. With all the travel and cynicism of a journalist, he had never married. Only when he could not have a woman did the idea of marriage enter his head. He had a strange thought that any woman who rejected him would reject the advances of other men. The idea of a faithless wife was an anathema. The fact that he himself played around, and would always do so for as long as women found him attractive, was to Glen Hamilton the male privilege of life. The more Lucinda froze in his presence, the more he wanted her. And when they were at last alone he smiled his sweetest smile and asked her to take him for a walk in the garden. The trees were still dripping water but the rain had stopped.

THE REASON LUCINDA agreed to walk out alone with the American had nothing to do with the bright eyes of Glen Hamilton. She wanted to teach Harry a lesson. Get his attention. Make him jealous. They had not resumed their love affair. Harry always seemed to be somewhere else in his mind, staring, always staring into the distance of the past.

"What's the matter, Harry?"

"You don't want to know, Cinda. That burden is mine. I'm sorry. Not very good company. Please excuse me. I'm going to borrow Robert's horse and go for a ride."

"Can't I come with you?"

"Not where I'm going. I have to be alone to think. Please, Cinda, leave me alone."

"I will, Harry Brigandshaw, I will."

"And if the American wants to know about Mervyn Braithwaite, don't tell him."

Why the American should want to know about Mervyn Braithwaite she had no idea. A newspaper at Purbeck Manor was a rare intrusion. After what Harry told her about his CO and the murder of Sara Wentworth, she presumed the colonel had been committed to an asylum. She had not been told of his reported death. She now even wondered if Mervyn Braithwaite had not been right. That Harry and Sara were lovers. Why Harry was so peculiar.

When Glen Hamilton had been rebuffed and firmly put in his place they had walked over a mile along the bank of the river. She had waved at Mrs Pringle and called out Happy Christmas. When the American gave up his amorous quest and asked her about the murder she told him everything she knew. Including the contest for Sara Wentworth between Harry Brigandshaw and Mervyn Braithwaite... Harry had made her bitchy, which was not normally part of her nature. She was hurt. When she got back from the walk and after again fending off the boorish American, she went up to her room and had a good cry.


IT WAS GOING to be the biggest story of his life. A certain Pulitzer Prize winner. Syndicated all over the world. The New York and Washington newspapers would ask him to name his price. *Time* magazine would ask him to contribute. From what he gathered from a gullible Lucinda, Braithwaite had tried to murder Harry Brigandshaw by hanging him out to dry. As a novice pilot, by using their connection at Oxford University to post him to 33 Squadron, Fishy tried to get Harry killed and out of the way of his fiancée who had sent back his engagement ring. The great British air ace was a bloody psychopath. No wonder he enjoyed killing Germans and yelling at their deaths. The last pass Glen made at Lucinda had been to disguise his real purpose. Upstairs in his room, he lit the fire and settled down to write the most important article of his life. All this British upper-class nonsense he was going to break into pieces. He hated the upper classes. He hated the people who had lived on the same land for nearly a thousand years. He hated their polite snobbery that allowed him into their home, and if the Lord of the Manor's daughter wanted to reject him, what else could an American expect? Those so-called aristocrats were the same as everyone else and he was going to show the world. As Matt Vogel had once said in a state of mild intoxication when they were talking about the class system, 'every man looks the same under a bus'. The fact that Matt was referring to Americans who had made more money than they could spend in ten lifetimes had gone right over Glen Hamilton's head.

Having finished the best writing he had done in his life on the table that first held the bowl and the vast jug of cold water, he brought the one easy chair up to the fire and planned what he was going to do next. He was impatient to get away, and if the following day had not been Christmas, he would have made an excuse and bolted for the railway station. Even if he had to walk all the way to Corfe Castle. His mother stopped him in his head. 'Once you accept an invitation you never break it when something better comes along. However tempting. You hear, Glen Hamilton, or I'll box your ears again and get your father to give you a good thrashing.' He still feared a tongue-lashing from his mother. So, like a good boy, he put away his papers, put the fireguard in front of the fire, and went downstairs. What he was going to do when he got back to London was find out where the British would have put such a high-profile maniac. Then he was going to get a photograph of the dead Colonel Braithwaite very much alive. And in all the hullabaloo that would break out from his revelations, he would have a follow-up article, with him interviewing the once-dead hero. When he met Granny Forrester at the bottom of the never-ending staircase he was metaphorically hugging himself with excitement.

"Oh, Mr Hamilton. How nice to see you. You will join us for a glass of sherry in the sitting room? I was going to send Harry to find you. How was your walk with Lucinda? Such a nice girl but of course losing her fiancé was a tragedy. Thank goodness Harry is out of the battle at last. They have known each other for ten years and I think she might go out to Africa with him when the war is over."

"He's going to marry her?" said Glen, taken by surprise.

"I don't know, but I hope so. Harry is very shaken by his experiences in the war but once he goes home he'll be his old self... Now there is just something else I want to talk to you about. You're a journalist, so you're a good wordsmith, and we want your valued opinion. They say a writer can recognise a good writer after reading a few pages so it won't be so much of an imposition. You see, my grandson Robert, who lost a foot in the war, wants to write historical novels, and none of us here have the ability to judge his work properly. Family are always the last to recognise genius in one of their own. Come and meet Robert, Mr Hamilton, and please, as a special favour to an old woman, ask to read his book."

"It will be my pleasure, ma'am." He was so full of his own article, he would have kissed a horse's arse. Of course, he thought it would be a load of rubbish but that didn't matter since he had nothing to do for another full day.

He had wondered why they had invited him down for Christmas. And now he knew... When he went in to join the family he was having a good chuckle with himself. No one ever did anything in this life without a selfish motive. Not even the British aristocrats.

WHEN STANDING STILL in long trousers, the new wooden foot filled Robert St Clair's right shoe like any flesh and blood foot and no one could see he was crippled. It was a tradition in the family for some reason that the young in the family drank a glass of sherry standing up. They had all gathered for Christmas Eve. The big Christmas tree that normally stood in the Great Hall had been cut down to a manageable size. England was still at war, presents were difficult to find, and everyone had stopped giving them since 1914, using the war as an excuse. They were all there except Barnaby, Frederick, and Robert's right foot, if you only included the flesh and blood family. Young Richard had been put to bed upstairs. If the heir to the house cried, Robert knew that was just too bad as no one would hear. He was in a tough locking cot and the only harm he could do to himself was to be on his face and suffocate. Even though the cot was older than anyone knew, so far as the folklore of the family went, no harm had come to anyone sleeping in it. Every now and then a female member of the family would take a look. In the good old days when the family was rich, a nurse slept in the room with the children, but there wasn't any money for a nurse. Even with Penelope's large personal fortune, she was glad to let her son bellow his lungs out unheard. Pampered children, she told anyone who would listen, grew up with too many vices. Children should be seen and not heard. Robert rather thought there was something to be said for the sentiment. Given the chance, little children were the worst little extortionists in the world, especially when they played sick.

Robert had to smile. Penelope was playing up to the American, talking about India, and hinting her father was very rich. He even heard her mention to the American her son would one day be Lord St Clair. Someone must have told her Americans, living in their republic which forbade such things, were susceptible to titles. The girl was looking for a new husband, which was probably not all bad. The unheard screamer upstairs needed a father in his life. And with so many British killed, an American was probably the next best thing. They spoke English and were not so far away as the Australians. And there were not enough Rhodesians. Robert smiled to himself.

His father had read the first paragraph of the family saga and had seemed surprised Robert could write at all.

"Jolly good, Robert. Jolly good. Keep it up."

"But I finished the book, Father. I'd like your opinion."

"If the rest is as good as the first paragraph, I'm sure it is very good."

"Won't you read it, Father?" He was pleading.

"Don't be silly, Robert. I haven't read a book since I was at school. If it were not for the farmers' weekly newsletter and the occasional newspaper, I'd have likely forgotten to read by now. Do you know they made me read the whole of *Vanity Fair* at school? And that was punishment enough. I don't know how people sit down and read a book, let alone write one. You must be very clever, Robert. Don't know how an old clod like me had a son like you. Jolly good. Jolly good."

His mother had not even read the first paragraph, saying she had broken her reading glasses. Merlin changed the subject of writing so adroitly, Robert found himself off at a tangent without knowing what had happened. Lucinda was too full of her dead fiancé, and Harry Brigandshaw, to want to read. Annabel's husband, fellow artist, professional painter, the sergeant with the Military Medal, had tried to read but the damage done to his lungs by the mustard gas had welled up into convulsive coughing, and Robert had had to rescue his manuscript from the flying remains coming out of his brother-in-law's lungs.

No one in the family wanted to touch the thing and it made him hate the lot of them. It was probably a load of junk but at least someone could give it a read. Had he worked so hard to just make a fool of himself?

Robert went off to stand by the fire and sulk. He was a failure. All his life had been a failure. He couldn't even get himself properly killed like the rest of them.

EVERYONE EXCEPT ROBERT knew what was going on. Penelope, on cue, had engaged the American in a light flirtation. She owed the St Clairs an explanation, but often, when explanations are needed, the explanation did more harm than good. She knew the dates as well as they did. Frederick's last, wonderful leave and the miraculous birth of her son. However many fingers they used, and whatever the medical possibilities of a very late birth, the only father Richard could possibly have was Frederick St Clair. Despite the distraction, despite the opportunity, and the knowledge the boy she was dancing with would probably die within a month, Penelope had never been unfaithful to her husband. And knowing the racial snobbery of the English, she had not dared explain the dark, curly hair and the coal-black eyes of her son sleeping upstairs. Her grandmother's mother was an Indian, with more ancient blue blood in her veins than all the St Clairs from the time of

William the Conqueror. But that explanation which should not have had to be given as an excuse would have led their minds in a host of new directions. Instead of protesting too much as had been done in Shakespeare, she kept quiet. She knew that was all that mattered. So when the family wanted her help with Robert's book, she gave them all a good look at the temptress they thought she was. When she took Glen Hamilton across the room to the fire and Robert standing alone she had mixed feelings. She was being made part of the family but would her action make them think young Richard upstairs was even more of a bastard? She could only hope that when the boy grew up, the genes of his father's families would shout out loud and clear. That what he did in life would squash any bad rumours from the time of his birth.

"Why don't you tell Mr Hamilton about your book, Robert? Mr Hamilton is one of the most famous journalists in America."

Knowing flattery always worked on a man, she left them shaking hands at the fire to go up into the dark, cold house of Christmas Eve to check on her son.

"Maybe not yet," she heard the American say and wondered once again at the conceit of some men. She was gone from the room when Glen turned round.

Merlin from the other side of the room watched with approval. He had started the ball rolling, as he liked to say when he was home on his last leave and had sneaked day after day into Robert's study to read the book without his brother knowing. During Merlin's brief leave, Robert was constantly being plucked away to strange places by the rest of the family. When he reported the book was astonishingly good, but who was he to judge as a family member, he had been tasked with finding a suitable reader. A whole chapter had been temporarily removed from the manuscript for Robert's parents to read. The problem they all came to was bias. Was the family biased? The writer was family. The story was family. Would they be making fools of themselves, and give Robert the worst let-down of his life, and that included losing his foot? Though they all appeared so disinterested in Robert's writing, they were all excited. And they knew how much it meant to Robert. So when Robert left the fire and the room to go and get his manuscript for the American they all held their collective breaths. The one thing Merlin had found out for certain about Glen Hamilton was his reputation as a journalist. Though Glen Hamilton was unaware of it, his fellow journalists held him in the highest esteem as a writer and had been glad to recommend him to Merlin as the man to read the St Clair manuscript.

When Robert came back and gave Hamilton the large pile of paper, Glen Hamilton put it on the coffee table saying he would take it up to bed with him after dinner. With everyone in the family trying not to look at the manuscript on the table, they filed out of the sitting room and into the dining room with the fires at both ends and the old, long, wooden table that the family had fed from over the centuries. To everyone's surprise but Cook's and Merlin's, a side of beef was roasting on the old spit at the exact right angle to the fire. Merlin had also brought down with him three cases of French red wine. Despite the undercurrent of absent friends and the book in the sitting room, everyone set about enjoying themselves. And it was Granny Forrester who went upstairs to check on Richard after everyone had eaten too much roast beef. Mysteriously the manuscript had gone from the table, which she found a great relief. She had pushed open the door to have a look. Whether, of course, the American would read the book was another thing. All she could do was hope. Back in the dining hall she drank a whole glass of wine and felt quite tipsy for the first time since Potts died... They were all wearing silly paper hats. In the end, Robert was quite drunk and had to be helped up to bed.

They were all sound asleep, except Glen Hamilton, when the midnight chimes brought them Christmas. Thinking the book would send him quickly to sleep and expecting the worst, he had picked up the first chapter and began to read by the small new electric light over his bed. He was still reading when the dawn came up and the cocks began to crow.

The old maid brought him breakfast on a tray. He could smell the coffee, the coffee Merlin had specially bought for him. Unaware he was the only one in the old house drinking coffee, he carried on reading. When he finally finished, it was almost time for the big family Christmas lunch. Having used all the bathroom facilities, he dressed in the tweeds he had bought in London and went down to join the family. He was not sure what to do with the potty, so stuck it back under the bed. He wondered in the old days if they just tipped it out the window!

He could never have been more wrong in his life. If he lived to be a hundred he would never match the book written by Robert St Clair. By the time he reached the bottom of the great winding stairs, he had decided to offer himself as Robert St Clair's literary agent. He was smiling to himself. It was better to get ten per cent of the lot than one hundred per cent of a little. He kept them all in suspense through Christmas lunch. Then he told Robert.

"But you can't have read the book by now," exclaimed Robert.

"I haven't slept since you gave me the book. I finished at eleven o'clock this morning."

"Is it really any good?" asked Lord St Clair, dropping his façade of disinterest.

"Oh, yes."

Then the family were all clapping and Robert was crying.

"Do you think someone will want to publish?" he managed.

"I'll see to that. I'll see to that... I give you a toast. To the new author and his next ten books."

After cracking nuts with the men over a glass of port, Glen found himself alone as the whole family went off for an afternoon sleep. The air in his room was remarkably clean, which he put down to leaving the window wide open. When he plucked up the courage and pulled the potty out from under the bed, it was as clean as a whistle. The English really were a curious race. Then he fell into a deep sleep that had been a long time coming. It was a Christmas he was to remember for the rest of his life.

GLEN HAMILTON LEFT the Manor the next day in a hurry. It was Boxing Day when the servants received boxes containing their Christmas presents. While Glen was standing at Corfe Castle railway station with Merlin, the ancient upstairs maid was staring at the five-pound note she found tucked into the handle of the water jug. There was a note but she was unable to read. Cook read her the message.

"This is for the lady who cleaned my room. For services beyond the call of duty. Thanks from the American."

Cook smiled and gave the old woman the large, white five-pound note that had been folded four times.

"More than I spend in a month on food for everyone at Purbeck Manor. Better ask Lord St Clair to open a bank account for you in Swanage. You can earn three per cent a year. That's two shillings a year, Meg. Not to be sneezed at. Once a month you can have yourself three gins at the Greyhound in Corfe Castle and raise the glass to the American. They must be real rich in America. Fancy giving you five pounds. If you were fifty years younger I'd worry about the last piece of the note. What you think he meant?"

"I've no idea," said Meg, clutching her five-pound note.

It was cold but not raining on the station platform. Glen Hamilton walked up and down impatiently. The train from Swanage was late.

"You think the book's that good?" said Merlin, misinterpreting the man's hurry and impatience.

"What book?" said Glen, stopping in his tracks.

"Robert's book. He is going to call it *Keeper of the Legend*. He told me this morning."

"I can hear a train. Thank God. Why does nothing ever work on time in this country?"

"What's all the hurry? Why the rush? You seemed to enjoy your Christmas lunch."

"I have work to do. Work! A lot of work. The biggest story of my life."

"So it had nothing to do with Robert's book, all this haste? I rather hoped it was. Is the book any good, Glen? Or were you being the polite guest?"

"Kept me up all night... Oh, don't worry about the damn book. It's my article I want to get out. You know that war hero Braithwaite? The air ace. He is alive. The man's a murderer. What a story. I'm going to find him and splash his face over every newspaper in the world."

"So that's why you agreed to come down to the Manor."

"Of course. I'm a newspaperman. Smelt a big story... What are you laughing at, Merlin?"

"The machinations of man. We're all the same. The reason I wanted you down for Christmas was to read Robert's novel."

"So that's good. You got what you wanted. And so did I. Now that doesn't often happen in the schemes of life."

"And you are going to find a publisher?"

"Definitely. Probably in America. They love all that shit about old families as we don't have any of our own."

"And you don't care about Braithwaite?"

"Why the hell should I... You know he wanted to kill Harry?"

"That I didn't... Harry wants to protect him. Something about the other pilots. The dead and the living."

"You don't happen to know where they put Braithwaite?"

"Try the Banstead Lunatic Asylum. It's near Epsom in Surrey. Don't tell Harry I told you."

MERLIN DROVE the trap back to Purbeck Manor in troubled thought. He knew he had been wrong to give away the whereabouts of Mervyn Braithwaite. Harry had warned him about Glen Hamilton. He was so surprised to find out from Harry the CO of 33 Squadron was still alive, he had asked where he was if he wasn't in his grave.

"Banstead Lunatic Asylum. It's a long, sad story, Merlin, and you don't want to know about it."

So often, he ruminated as he drove along the bottom path by the river that was only just passable with the trap, things one didn't want to know about had a bad habit of telling their own story. And with Harry about to marry into the family, if Granny Forrester had her way, it became a problem that belonged to all of them. If he had not been so happy for Robert he would not have blurted out the name to Glen Hamilton. In some way, it was his trade, the fact he was rich and whole that made him want to make his crippled brother a successful author, something Robert could do for the rest of his life without a right foot.

The horse picked its own way down the bridle path while Merlin worried about his dilemma. It was not Braithwaite he gave a hoot about but Harry Brigandshaw's confidence. He did not have to be told that the last person to know where the War Office had hidden the one-time hero was a newspaper reporter.

He could now see the old chimney stacks with the tall brown pots looming over the trees and he was glad he had the money to repair the house. The land, the old house and the even older building material that had gone into the house were core to his being. For the family to survive, the house had to survive. He was just someone in a long line of family who had come down the old centuries and would pass down the new. He was just a link in nature's chain, a chain he never wanted broken. It gave him his sense of belonging. In the here and after and before.

Where the garden started, he found Geoffrey Winckle, painting away at a wide canvas that included the old house. The easel was standing at the same spot where Lucinda had first met Harry walking from the station with Robert on his first visit to the Manor. Lucinda had pointed out the spot more than once. Merlin stopped the horse and got down from the trap to watch. His brother-in-law was so engrossed in his work, Merlin and the horse went unnoticed. The ex-sergeant was not even coughing. The painting from thirty yards spoke to him of centuries past. He stood watching for five minutes.

"It's for the cover of Robert's book," he said without turning around. "In exchange, he's going to give you back your ten pounds when he gets his advance."

"You hadn't forgotten!"

"A man should never forget a debt."

"It's very good."

"Thank you. You think that American is genuine? He was after something but it wasn't one of the girls."

"Can you keep a secret?"

"No. So don't tell me. Wars have been started by the same request... I'm going to do portraits. Where the money is. Rich old factory owners from the north. Where there's muck there's brass! Fat ugly wives, they want to be remembered forever. Ugly and rich. They go together."

"Aren't you cold?"

"It stops the coughing. Round a fire I start coughing my guts up... In a way, the gassing is a blessing. A small pension for life. Not many painters have anything to live off."

"What about the rich industrialists?" Merlin decided he liked his brother-in-law.

"Yes, there's them... And it isn't fatal. They say I can go on coughing like this until I'm ninety. You go on in, Merlin. And don't worry about your ten pounds. And that Yank's after money, whichever way you look at it."

Instead of getting into the trap, Merlin led the horse by the head to the stable. He knew he should tell Harry what he had told Glen. Let Harry warn the War Office. Then he felt a cold shiver run up his spine and decided to forget the talk at the railway station... There were muffins for tea around the fire in the sitting room. He quickened his pace.


MERVYN BRAITHWAITE KNEW he was as sane as the next man. The trick was to make everyone think he was quite mad. Till the war ended. When he knew they would not give a damn about war heroes. At the moment, everyone wanted him insane. Everyone believed his little outbursts. He was preaching insanity to the converted. After the war, they would throw him to the wolves. Yesterday's hero. No longer any use to the war effort. They would hang him just as easily as declaring him insane. So he was going to get out and go to South America. Lose himself in the Amazon. Find a dark young girl and make her his mistress. Discard her. Find another. He was going to have a string of women in his life to prove them all wrong. He had money which he would send out of the country before they found out he was gone. There were cargo boats sailing for the Americas every day from Liverpool. Looking for hands. Never asking questions. He had read about it in the paper. He could put on a north country accent. Wear a cloth hat.

The only regret he would have was not killing Harry Brigandshaw with the same pistol. He hated the man. Had hated him ever since Oxford University. Everyone liked Harry Brigandshaw. Everyone wanted to be his friend. Wherever he was, a group gathered around, with Brigandshaw, good-looking Brigandshaw, the centre of attention. Men and women. Old and young. Students and dons. Even the servants. The bulldogs. It had made him sick. And then to add insult to injury, when he was meant to die in the first week of joining the squadron, the damn man could fly an aeroplane better than anyone. And Sara loved him. Even Sara had been taken away. He wished he had killed both of them. Then he thought of another good idea. When he had been away for a few years and they had all forgotten him, he would take a boat to Africa. Find Harry Brigandshaw. And kill him. Then he would be able to rest in peace and enjoy all the women.

A male nurse was approaching the old wooden bench where he sat so often and made his plans. He began to roll his eyes to make them vacant. He let his jaw hang down. There was a tall man in uniform with the male nurse. A type of uniform he had never seen before. The man carried a camera that he set up in front of the bench. Mervyn had on his best vacant look when the man put his head under the hood, put up his arm and pressed a button at the end of the wire. Mervyn, concentrating like he had done so often in battle to stay alive, maintained his idiotic expression. He didn't know why they were taking his picture but he did know he had to look mad.

When the man began to ask him questions, Mervyn went into his well-rehearsed gibberish. The man had an American accent. When he was done and the nurse was helping carry the photographic equipment away the American leaned close to his ear.

"Harry Brigandshaw sends his love, Fishy."

For a moment, all sign of his madness left him, and he glared at Glen Hamilton.

"As I thought, Colonel Braithwaite. You're as sane as me." The vacant expression and the gibberish had come back again. When he was alone again Mervyn made up his mind to go as soon as possible. The American's eyes had been laughing at him. The way he had laughed at all those Germans when they died, going down in flames.


THE FIRST THING Harry heard about the story in every newspaper was a phone call from the War Office. He was still at Purbeck Manor and he had still not proposed marriage to Lucinda St Clair despite everyone's expectations. He was due back in France at Army Headquarters on the third day of the new year. The man who called was the ADC to Trenchard.

"They found him. Bloody American. Goofy photograph of Braithwaite in every English-language paper in the world. Trenchard wants you back at 33 Squadron. To command the squadron again. Question of morale. You'll have to tell them the truth. The good news is the photograph in the papers makes Braithwaite look as mad as a hatter. You're to report to your squadron immediately. And we're having a big hate on Jerry."

"I must go today?"

"Now."

"Was the American Glen Hamilton?"

"How did you know?"

"He's being staying with us at the Manor."

"Did you tell him anything?"

"Certainly not where he could find Braithwaite. I told him to mind his own business. He'd been snooping before he came down here."

"Someone told him. Definitely not good for public relations. People like their heroes not to have clay feet. Is there somewhere we can land a plane? Trenchard is not amused."

"There are plenty of big fields."

"Then wait. I'll send someone down... Why can't people keep their mouths shut? You yourself said the man was insane. Hamilton interviewed Braithwaite. Says the man's insanity is faked. The police want to know what's going on. But that's not your problem. Those pilots deserve a proper explanation."

The line went dead at the other end and Harry found himself staring at an old gentleman in a wig across the hall. The eyes looked straight back at him from the portrait.

He was back in the battle. Fishy Braithwaite would still have the last laugh. His hands holding the mouthpiece and earpiece of the telephone were shaking. Quickly he put the telephone back on the hook. He was frightened for the first time and looked for somewhere to run. Down the long corridor. Out the bay window. Through the side door in the big Gothic door. Back to Africa. Safety. His legs would not move. His mind numbed. His jaw set and the moment passed, to be strangely replaced by excitement. Over there were all his friends. They needed him. It was his job to make sure all of them came through the last part of the war alive.

By the time he walked back into the sitting room to tell Lucinda, he was smiling.

THE FIRE WAS WELL BANKED in the sitting room and Granny Forrester was half asleep in her big chair. Outside the long windows that came down to a foot from the floor, it was cold and windy, the boughs of the trees whipping in the wind. Inside it was warm and cosy, and soon her daughter Bess would come in and draw the curtains, and they would all take tea... She had had a good life with few regrets, and the pain in her side was not as bad as it had been in the morning. She knew she was dying but at her age, it did not matter anymore. That morning she had plucked up the courage to confront Penelope and she liked the idea of an Indian princess having something to do with her family. It was fitting for so big a colonial power to mingle its blood with the colonies. Whether the girl was a princess mattered not a jot. What mattered most was Frederick going to his early grave without horns on his head, the horns of a cuckold. She believed the girl and hoped with her for the future young Richard to show some of the St Clair traits. The girl had hugged her at the end and she had liked that.

When Harry came into the room, all smiles after taking his phone call, she was happy for Lucinda. This was going to be the day. Lucinda could not take her eyes from the boy's face, a gentle smile of pure happiness. She was in love, that much Granny Forrester could see as plain as a pikestaff.

"I'm afraid I've got to leave you all," he said. Everyone else in the room came fully awake. Lucinda's expression turned to panic. "Trenchard is sending down an aeroplane. They'll land on one of the fields. They want me to command 33 Squadron again." The household, not receiving a newspaper, had not read Glen Hamilton's article.

"When are you going?" asked Granny Forrester.

"Oh, not for a couple of hours."

"They can't land in the dark," said Lord St Clair.

"You're right. I wasn't thinking. Then tomorrow."

"Are you going to fight?" barked Lord St Clair.

"I rather think so, sir. That's the idea of a fighter squadron. There's a hate on. With the Americans on our side, we are now going to win the war."

Lucinda got up and ran out of the room.

"You'd better go after her, Harry," said Granny Forrester.

"Yes, I had hadn't I? She seems upset. I was going to ask her to marry me as a matter of fact. With your permission, of course, sir. Till I got the phone call. Well, the war will be over soon. Then everything will be back to normal. It's been such a wonderful Christmas. Excuse me. I'll go and find Lucinda. And write my mother a letter... I just hope my father's still talking to me. Thank you all for giving me a nice time."


IN THE MORNING, when they came in a twin-engine bomber aircraft to take Harry back to the Western Front, they found Granny Forrester dead in her bed with a smile on her face. He left the family in disarray and climbed up into the aircraft with a small bag. The rest of his luggage he had left in his room.

When the plane was out of sight and out of sound, Lucinda went into his room to look at what was left of her life, the bits and pieces of another man she loved and was about to lose. And now there was no Granny Forrester to go to and cry on her shoulder.

Merlin followed her into the room.

"He'll come back," he said.

"How can you know?"

"Cinda, I know these things. I know. Weird, but I know. Like Barnaby, he won't have a scratch. One day you'll be mistress of Elephant Walk and your children will live there for many generations."

"So you can see down the generations."

"Well, maybe not quite that far. I've never been to Africa. Come and give your brother a hug and we can both have a cry together for Granny Forrester... Now there was a woman I really loved."

"Me too," said Lucinda, crying... "Are you sure about Harry?" she said in a small voice on his shoulder.

"Certain. So was Granny Forrester."

They silently cried together for a long time, holding each other for comfort.

"Did you buy the cows?" she asked at length.

"All seventy of them. They arrive this afternoon and Father still doesn't know."

"Did Granny Forrester know?"

"Of course."

"And the big bull?"

"And the big bull."


BY THE TIME the bureaucratic wheels had turned sufficiently, and the civil police arrived at the Banstead Lunatic Asylum, Mervyn Braithwaite was on a boat to Demerara, that would first call at Mobile in North America, where Mervyn intended to jump ship. He had no intention of being landed at a British colony, however far-flung the outpost. Like Glen Hamilton, he had bribed the male nurse. The American had searched the newspaper archives and come up with a photograph of Mervyn receiving one of his medals. The well-bribed male nurse had taken Glen Hamilton to his quarry in less than ten minutes. Another large sum had stopped the nurse reporting his absence after Mervyn climbed over the ten-foot-high red brick wall behind the apple orchard. There the nurse had a motorcycle waiting, full of petrol. Money could buy most things, he had chuckled to himself. The man had known from the start he was sane. There was always money to be made from a rich man's adversity.

Soon after the police found he was gone they lost interest. After the war, the male nurse bought himself a small farm in Cornwall and married a local girl. Everyone was satisfied.

The big hate that was now killing Americans by the thousands took up the headlines in the papers. Glen Hamilton's story was lost. No one remembered it. Yesterday's hero had already been forgotten. The manuscript of *Keeper of the Legend* was also forgotten at the bottom of his old sea trunk. The war continued to consume everything. Men, materiel, and wealth. The so-called civilised world was smashing itself to pieces with every new means of destruction at its disposal. Glen Hamilton went back to reporting the war with the rest of the journalists. He avoided Merlin and was glad Harry had gone back to his squadron. Jack Merryweather gave him one nasty look and everyone at Army Headquarters in France went their own way.

ON RETURNING TO 33 SQUADRON, Harry found the weather good for flying and the Allied hate at full intensity. He flew straight into battle, three to four times a day for a week. No one had said anything to him. They had lost two pilots while he was away and lost another to German ground fire during the week. By the middle of January 1918, the British had shot most of the German aircraft out of the sky. Then the weather came down and they were grounded.

He ordered all the pilots into the briefing room and told them the truth, right from the first years of Colonel Braithwaite's life when a small boy had noticed his face resembled a cod, the wet, squashed face of a fish with bulging, wet eyes. The small boy who was ten years old nicknamed Mervyn Braithwaite 'Fishy', and it had stuck for the rest of his life. Harry explained how he too was guilty of hurting a good man by calling him 'Fishy' to his face at Oxford. How so small a thing to some people had festered into so much hate. How so small and insignificant a word had caused a good man so much pain. And, finally, how the women had laughed at his squashed faced, including his own fiancée, the fiancée he had shot in front of Harry Brigandshaw. He told them how he had met the girl and her brother in Africa, and made friends with them, but nothing more of the girl's obsession with him, even though she was engaged to Mervyn Braithwaite. Of the returned ring. Of their first commanding officer successfully proving to everyone at 33 Squadron that he was the best pilot of them all. How it had made it worse when the woman he wanted to marry still scorned him.

"We are all insane at moments in our lives. We are all hateful. We can all be foolish. As the friend I should have been to him and wasn't, I ask you all to forgive him killing Sara Wentworth in a moment of insanity. To remember him as the CO of the squadron. Why many of us are still alive because of the training we received from Colonel Braithwaite. I have heard he is no longer in the asylum, gone no one knows where. There is no scandal. Only a war. And a small boy with a facial impediment who made himself one of the best pilots in the Royal Flying Corps. I want you all to remember him as a pilot and forget the rest. I call for three cheers. Three cheers for Colonel Braithwaite."

Some months later, after the Allied breakthrough, 33 Squadron left the old French farmhouse and its fields. The aircraft and the guns went forward. The ghost of Mervyn Braithwaite stayed behind with the ghosts of the dead pilots, German and British.

THE WAR DRAGGED on and Robert St Clair went from euphoria to the depths of despair. Even his right foot still hurt even though it had been blown off two years earlier. After weeks of excitement at the ring of the telephone and the sight of the postman, he had withdrawn to his room a broken man. Food was no longer an obsession. Sleep became difficult to find. Depression, the trough into which he had fallen. The few pages of the sequel to *Keeper of the Legend*, taking St Clairs to the Crusades, was left at the bottom of the drawer as punishment. He had his small army disability pension. With the family roof over his head, there was enough money to live. Mostly he stayed in his room, looking out of the window, seeing nothing. He told himself he was thirty-two years old with nothing to do for the rest of his life.

WHEN MERLIN, on a brief leave, told him the real purpose of Glen Hamilton's visit to Purbeck Manor for Christmas, his whole life fell apart.

"How can people say things they don't mean?" he had asked his brother.

"He wanted to interview Lucinda after Harry refused. Even found out from me where the authorities had hidden Braithwaite."

"Mendacious bastard. Emotionally, I would have been over it by now if I'd been told it was rubbish. And Father was so excited. You said it was good... And Hamilton's got the only copy. I'll never trust another person in my life. I knew in my own heart it was no good, as who was I to write a good book when so many others have failed?"

Merlin had decided Glen's last words of praise were better left out of it.

The man had then sounded genuine but having done nothing, it had been another lie. He thought the man might rewrite the book. Change the names. Publish under his own name. But he kept his thoughts from Robert. The book had gone. That was the end of it. No one would know. At least gambling on the stock exchange had been something he could follow from beginning to end. He was in control. The American had probably thought it easier to throw the manuscript in the dustbin than explain it was no good... What did the family know? They were amateurs. Maybe it would have been all for the best if the damn man had not raised Robert's hopes so high. America was thousands of miles away. Once the war was over, the chance of anyone in the family meeting the man again was nil. Personally, he wished the man would leave Army Headquarters. They never spoke. He would never ask about the book. When they saw each other in the mess they passed as strangers. Well, they had asked him a favour. Invited him down to the Manor under false pretences. So what could they expect? In the end, the deceit had worked out for only one of them.


ROBERT HAD WATCHED his sister sink into the same despair. She feared to answer the ring of the postman at the side door. Hated the ring of the telephone. And Harry, his best friend, was a lousy letter writer. Barnaby wrote more letters, which was not saying very much. He once said Tina Pringle was writing to him, which was strange.

His mother missed her mother, as did everyone else in the house. Genevieve for some reason had gone back to live with her mother-in-law in Norfolk and never wrote. Maybe she wanted to be near someone who had been near to her husband. Annabel was living in Manchester with her husband but what on no one understood. His painting for the cover of *Keeper of the Legend* stood in Robert's room with its face to the wall. If his brother-in-law had not done the painting with so much love he would have burnt it long ago. Artists really did have a hard time!

Spring came at him from outside the window, and for the first time, he ventured out to look at the new pedigree herd of cows and had to run away from the bull. He was much better on his wooden leg and managed to get over the sty at the top of the ten-acre field before the bull could insert its horns into his backside. He had laughed nervously, the first laugh after Merlin had told him Glen Hamilton was more than likely a lying bastard. Mendacity personified. That evening he ate his meal with relish. The next day he found the few pages of the sequel in the bottom of his drawer and read them through. It was better than he imagined. Two more pages were added before he knew what he was doing. The first book had gone forever but there was nothing to stop him from writing the second.

Within a day, he was cracking jokes with the family. Without him realising, the whole family let out a collective sigh of relief. The same day Lucinda received a long letter from Harry Brigandshaw. She let them all read her letter. Between the lines, and despite the censors, it was clear the war was going to be won within months. By the time the month of May was out, Harry Brigandshaw arrived on the doorstep in uniform and unannounced. He had flown in alone, landing on the field next to the cows.

Cook answered the side door in the big front door.

"May I see Lord St Clair?" said Harry.

"Don't you want to see Miss Lucinda?"

"No thank you, Cook. Lord St Clair."

"He's in his study."

"That's very good and I do know the way."

"Shall I tell Miss Lucinda?"

"Not yet, Cook. Not yet." He was grinning from ear to ear until he reached the door to the study. Then he felt like a schoolboy, not a group captain in the newly-formed Royal Air Force. With his peaked cap under his arm, he knocked on the study door of his future father-in-law.

"Come in, Harry."

The Lord of the Manor had watched him land some time ago. He had heard the conversation in the hall and just had time to scuttle into his study and close the door. From the top of the stairs, unseen, Lucinda had listened as well, expecting to run down the wide flight of curving stairs into his arms. Then she ran back to her room and waited. It was all a lot of rubbish but she loved every moment. Harry Brigandshaw was formally asking her father for her hand in marriage.

By the end of August, Glen Hamilton was convinced that if Shakespeare had submitted Hamlet to every American publisher it would have come back each time attached to a printed rejection slip. He had no idea what he was going to do with *Keeper of the Legend*.

The Russians had surrendered to the Germans, giving away Poland and Lithuania, and gone back to war, this time with each other, Red Russians killing White Russians in a Bolshevik revolution. With troops released from the Eastern Front, the Germans reached to within seventy kilometres of Paris. Backed by American troops, the Allied counteroffensive looked to Glen decisive. The Germans had finally shot their bolt, as he put it to his

*Colorado Telegraph* readers, smashed to pieces by their own offensive. He predicted in the paper German surrender in weeks rather than months.

The cynic in Glen reported the sending of American and British troops to help the White Russians fight the Red Russians was a way of keeping the slaughter going for the rest of the twentieth century. He questioned whether man ever learned a lesson when there was greed involved and the chance of killing each other. Europe was a mess, and America had fallen into a quagmire from which she would never get out. With the big Pacific one way and the Atlantic the other, he asked readers what they were doing in Europe. After running away from the wars of man and the wars of religion to find freedom, why had they run back into the mess? In the euphoria of potential victory, he was told afterwards Matt Vogel had censored most of his vitriol... If nothing else, he had enjoyed getting it off his chest. It just made him a little more cynical: the motives of men were rarely what they wanted them to appear to be.

For weeks, the manuscript at the bottom of his sea trunk burnt his conscience. He kept away from Merlin St Clair and Jack Merryweather and was glad Harry Brigandshaw had gone back to the real war. After the non-event of his great exposé, lost in the greater fog of war, he found he was jealous of Robert St Clair's writing, something that would probably live forever and not sink without trace within days. Deep inside of him, like most journalists, he knew he was a frustrated novelist, that the story of Mervyn Braithwaite should have been turned into fiction. But hindsight was easy after the Pulitzer and his writing career had sunk with his article. Whether he could ever write a full-length novel was another question for his self-debate. Deep down, he doubted it. Certainly not now at the age of thirty-three.

No one had even told him Braithwaite had escaped. If they had he would not have been interested. The story was dead. He was a hack journalist and that was all there was to it. For the rest of his life... And it was then his conscience got the better of him.

The first job was to have the manuscript typed to make it easier to read. Long typing jobs he knew were done for love and not money. The English girl at Military Headquarters had the strange name of Wendy Wallop. She thought she was in love with him and eked out the typing of Robert St Clair's book for as long as possible. Glen was sure she loved the idea of America more than she loved Glen Hamilton. The British had the idea every American was rich back home. They were targets. When the corrections in the manuscript were done, he slept with her twice, found the experience hopelessly unrewarding, and kept away from the girl's place of work.

Reading the book through for typing mistakes had convinced Glen again. The book was an even better read the second time. There was far more to the characters in the fast storyline that pulled them along together.

He took the typescript back with him on the boat for his annual home leave, and personally called on the biggest New York publisher of big fiction, thinking his name as a journalist, his recommendation, would get the book read quickly, and in print long before the Germans surrendered. They had never heard of him. When he called on the editor on his way back from Denver as his boat left for New York, he was told the man was out. The man had previously refused to take his phone calls. After kicking up a rumpus at the reception desk on his third visit, three hours before his boat was due to sail for France, he was given back the manuscript by the receptionist in the same brown paper wrapping found in France. The only reason anything happened at all was due to his uniform. It was well worn. He was no new recruit to the war.

"Mr Klausberger says the book was very nice but not for our list." The receptionist by now had her defensive back up. She had a know-all look on her face.

"Bullshit. He never read a page. Tell Mr Hamburger from me, to be a man and enlist."

"Mr Klausberger is a German."

He just had time to drop the manuscript off at a second publisher, giving a friend at the *New York Times* as the return address.

The book then spent four months doing the rounds of New York publishers. No one wanted it. The friend read the book and confirmed what Glen knew. With the right publisher and the right publicity, the book would be a runaway bestseller. And better still it would go on selling for a long time.

Having avoided Merlin St Clair for one reason concerning the book, he avoided him again. How could he keep saying the book was wonderful without finding a publisher? In Merlin's eyes, he had been a hotshot reporter seconded to Military Headquarters. The only good part in his return from America was to find the posting of Wendy Wallop. Feeling something like a fraud and a thief, he hoped he would never see the girl again. She had been a virgin, something rare in wartime France.

After three phone calls to his friend in New York, who by then had read the book, Glen put it out of his mind. Apart from using Wendy Wallop, his conscience was now clear. He had done his best for Robert St Clair. Secretly, he was now glad he had not become a novelist. Until then he thought a good book would always find a publisher.

Then it all stopped in a train when an armistice was signed. The war was over. The Germans agreed to pay vast reparations. They marched back to Germany with their guns at the slope. With the same amount of glee they had used at the start of the Great War, everyone around the world celebrated the end. Germans, English, French and Americans prayed to the same God and thanked him for their salvation.

The mangled poppy fields grew neat white crosses, scored with the names of men. Row after row, field after field, all in neat straight lines. People started digging for unexploded ordnance. Cows in search of grass blew themselves up on the hidden mines and unexploded shells. Many of the crosses bore the names of men but not their bones in the rich earth beneath.

And finally, as Glen was about to write his last article under the silent winter sky of France, he had a telephone call from his friend in New York.

"Fifty pounds advance, Glen. Better than nothing. At least the book will get into print. Shall I write the author or will you?"

"You write, Max. By now that family would cut my throat. Thanks a million."

"You're welcome."

Glen had never heard the name of the publisher. He was tired. Tired of war. Tired of people. But most of all he was tired of himself. And now, as a war correspondent, he was out of a job. At Calais, he took the ferry to Dover, with the intention of spending what was left of his money in London. Mike Vogel had given him a severance cheque and a letter of recommendation. Like so many at the end of war, he had no idea what he was going to do stateside. If only Wendy Wallop had known. Her rich American would arrive home flat broke. He was thirty-three years old and, having come to the end of his great writing career, he would have to go home to his mother and father, as financially naked as the day he came out of the womb.

Then he thought to hell with it. Something always came up.


ON THE FERRY boat was a beaming Jack Merryweather making his last journey as a soldier. He was going home to marry Fay Wheels and see his daughter Mary. The idea of boredom had flown up into the sky. For their honeymoon, he was going to take his whole family to Africa, to Elephant Walk. Harry, Robert, Lucinda, and Merlin had booked him with them on the SS *King Emperor*. Harry and Lucinda were getting married for the second time in Harry's Uncle Nat's bush church in Rhodesia though without the bishop, but that did not seem to matter as the bishop, Nathanial

Brigandshaw, who had once been a missionary in Rhodesia, had officiated at the first ceremony in the small church near Corfe Castle.

"Now there you are, Glen," said Jack. "We've been looking all over for you. Wonderful thing you did for Robert St Clair. The whole family owe you a big debt. A twenty thousand print run they say. A lot for a first novel. Robert's dedicated the book to Granny Forrester and has looked all over the place for you. To thank you. It's a new beginning for all of us. What are you going to do now the war's over?"

"Get drunk in London till my money runs out and then go home. There are a lot of correspondents looking for a job right now."

"Nonsense. You'll come with us to Africa. We sail next week on the SS *King Emperor*."

"I can't afford it, Jack. I'm near to broke."

"The Brigandshaws own the bloody ship. We'll get you a return ticket. Where's your adventure? All of us from HQ and Lucinda. When one door closes, another opens. All that sort of thing. My word, am I glad to see you, Glen Hamilton."

"I'm a manipulating bastard, Jack. You know that."

"So what? You kept your word. To us English, that is the most important thing of all."

## 3

# FEBRUARY 1919

he British Army demobbed Barnaby St Clair in Cairo on the same day Jack Merryweather and Glen Hamilton disembarked at Dover. He had turned twenty-one three months earlier. The pale-skinned Englishman who had joined the army at the age of eighteen could have been mistaken for an Arab in the streets of Cairo, were it not for the piercing blue eyes and the well-cut linen suit with a Panama hat. The tailored suit and wide-brimmed hat were Barnaby's gift to himself when he left the army. The years in the Arabian Desert, first with Colonel Lawrence and then with Allenby into Damascus, had scorched his skin and added three years to his age.

Port Said at the Mediterranean entrance to the Suez Canal was full of ships, most of them on their way to the ports of Europe. Barnaby had one thing on his mind, and it all concerned Tina Pringle and the slithery wetness of her hands on his genitals. He was obsessed. What he wanted was a ship down the east coast of Africa with a call at the port of Lourenço Marques in Portuguese East Africa. From there it was a day's train journey to Johannesburg. He was going to surprise her.

On the second day of his quest, he found a coaster and took the ship.

MISS PINFORTH WATCHED the long thin bill of the sunbird penetrate the inner sanctum of the yellow canna and shuddered. She had turned sixty the previous week and had never been entered by a man. Storm clouds were boiling in the west but overhead passive white clouds patterned the blue sky over the north of Johannesburg. It would rain later, a long, ten-minute cloudburst of water that fed her garden and made it grow in lush profusion. The scents of many flowers mingled around her deck chair that sprawled comfortably under the canopy of a Brazilian pepper tree, planted by Albert Pringle soon after he had bought the house in Parktown Ridge. Her cottage had come later. Now, after three years' love and care, her garden was a constant joy and revelation. Birds of all sizes and colours. The grey lourie with its distinctive 'go away' call, big with a proud crest. The tiny, lesser double collared sunbirds, brilliant metallic red, blue and green, that had woken her senses briefly. No one had looked at her body for a long time and not with any great interest even then. Now she was pale, grey and colourless, even her eyes that had never been much. The bird hovered at the mouth of a red canna, dipping deep for the nectar. She smiled, happy as always, and smiled again as her protégée, more than her pupil, walked down the steps from what they called in South Africa, the stoep. The girl was utterly beautiful, as perfect and colourful as the sunbird now deep in the mouth of the canna.

The puppy fat had gone and the girl had grown. The luscious mouth prevailed with the luscious body, but more refined, and the strong burr of the Dorset accent had gone forever, lost in hours of elocution lessons. The spoken words were natural, unlike her brother Albert who would never quite be able to hide his humble birth.

"Well, you've done it with Tina," he'd said. "Not a trace. Doesn't matter for me. I like to be reminded of where I come from every now and again. And I'm proud of the Pringles of Dorset, even if we come from a railway cottage and not a manor house. It's what we are that counts, not what we appear to be. But that's for men. Money and power. Women need good looks and the right manners to get anywhere. They are part of the male display. One day it may change but that is how it is for the moment. Silly but Sallie with all her brains and money is still not accepted in the male world of business, let alone their clubs. Thank you, Miss Pinforth. You have done the perfect job with my sister. She looks beautiful. She speaks well. She reads. But best of all she thinks for herself. Other than Sallie and Tina, women have a habit of repeating what menfolk tell them. Not one original thought... And please remember, the cottage is yours for the rest of your life. Do you know how much pleasure I get from looking down over your garden from my veranda? You have invited in every bird and insect from the whole Transvaal. When Tina marries, you must stay, I insist."

"You are kind but sometimes foolish. When my most beautiful bird flies away I will go away. To look for another young girl I can nurture. It is what I do. What makes me happy. They are my family, strung back over the years."

"Do any of them contact you?"

"No. I forbid it. I want to always remember them young... And if life fails them I don't want to hear about it. Rich husbands can turn from a catch to a catastrophe."

Smiling at the memory of their conversation, Miss Pinforth watched Tina Pringle walk down the last steps to the garden path, between the herbaceous borders, past her rose garden and across the small patch of lawn that grew under the pepper tree. The girl was bubbling with excitement.

"Do you know there are going to be three hundred guests at my twenty-first? And every one of them has sent a written acceptance. I'm glad we waited until the war was over to have the party. It'll be so much more fun without that hanging over us."

"I'm so happy for you... Now all you have to do is pick yourself a husband."

"Do you think it's as easy as that?"

"I don't know. I never tried."

"Why didn't you marry, Miss Pinforth?"

"For the very simple reason that nobody asked me. And it wasn't for me to do the picking."


NOW THE WAR WAS OVER, the guilt returned for Albert Pringle. Three of his brothers had died. Safe in South Africa, he had made his fortune from the war. And as the young men came home, many of them broken in body, no one knew what horrors were churning inside of their minds. Quietly, he wondered how many human lives his shells had blown to pieces. The night they searched their consciences on that one was the night they first made love to each other. To comfort each other. To burn out the guilt.

"I, Albert Pringle, do hereby ask Sallie Barker to be my wife," he had said the next morning in her bed.

"Don't be silly, Albert. Just because we had a fuck doesn't mean you have to marry me."

"Darling, I've never heard you use that word before."

"And I've never heard you use that one directed at me. But, we used to run a brothel, remember. Whatever we might have called the Mansion House, it was still a damn good whorehouse."

"Will this be the only time?"

"I hope not. I'm not afraid anymore. It just goes to show what I've been missing. You're one hell of a lover, Bert. One hell of a lover... Oh, and Benny Lightfoot is coming to dinner tonight. You'd better be here. Better leave Tina at home. He has a new girlfriend even younger than Tina. It's such a true saying. There's no fool like an old fool."

"He likes young girls and young girls like money. That's not making a fool of himself. That's getting lucky." He was annoyed with Sallie changing the subject.

ALBERT LEFT through the back door, hopefully unseen. He had a meeting at nine o'clock. Sallie watched him wistfully from her bedroom window. She was thirty-one and tired. Tired of business. Tired of being a woman in business. Tired of sorting out everyone else's problems.

Tired of body, but strangely satisfied, she drew herself a bath and soaked in the warm water, trying to make her mind go blank. When there were too many things to think of, it was better to blank the mind and think of nothing. Men, she knew, in a similar pursuit, got drunk. Then she dressed for work and wondered what to say to Albert when they met in the office.

Her mother was already at the breakfast table. Lily White took her breakfast in bed when she woke, which was rarely before ten o'clock in the morning. She said to Sallie that long sleep shortened her day, and as she had nothing much to do, that was an advantage. And that when she dreamed, in her sleep she was young and beautiful. More and more often she said she dreamed of Jack Merryweather.

Mrs Barker's eyes were snapping as Sallie sat down to her breakfast table. She drank down half of her glass of orange juice. Molly Hardcastle was in the kitchen and gave her a wink. 'So everyone knows!' she told herself wearily.

"Did that man stay the night in your bedroom?"

"Yes, Mother."

"He's as common as dirt."

Sallie poured herself a cup of tea, which she drank without sugar. She was never going to be fat like Lily White, that much she had made up her mind.

"Whores behave like that." Her mother was high on the horse.

Sallie looked long and steadily into her mother's seething eyes. The epitome of righteous indignation glared back at her. She thought of bringing up cousin Flugelhorne and how he had raped her. She thought of bringing up how her mother had deserted her and disbelieved her story. She thought of telling her mother to her face that she was a selfish bitch and to get out of her house and life forever. She would even enjoy it for a few days after, getting all the bile and vitriol off her chest and out of her mind. But she didn't, because none of it would have penetrated her mother's thick skin. In her mother's mind, her mother was always right. She would even righteously thrive on being thrown into the gutter by her rich daughter. But most of all, whatever happened, she would never change the fact that the woman waiting for an answer at her breakfast table was still her mother.

"I hope you're not going to marry him. Your father would never have approved."

The fact of needing approval from a man who had gone bankrupt and killed himself made Sallie even smile briefly.

"No, Mother. I'm not going to marry Albert. We are just good friends."

"Then what was he doing in your bedroom? Think what the servants will say."

A snort came from the adjacent kitchen and Sallie had to look away from her mother. She had not been able to hide the flash of laughter in her eyes. She ate a piece of dry toast, drank the cup of tea, got up from the breakfast table without saying a word, and left the room. Then she drove herself to the office.

Strangely, Albert greeted her as if nothing had happened and it made her annoyed.


BARNABY ST CLAIR knew perfectly well the date of the party. Tina's last three letters had been full of it. By the time his train reached Johannesburg, he could barely contain himself. His instinct had been to rush to the house on Parktown Ridge and throw himself into her arms. They had known each other all their lives. Loved no one but each other. Had exchanged the smallest secrets from the age of five. It was almost too much for him but he knew that what he was about to do was crucial to the future of his life. He waited. He booked himself into a cheap hotel on the other side of Johannesburg. He drank. He fidgeted. He walked away from people in mid-conversation. He only had one thing on his mind but he waited one whole week.


THE PARTY WAS the first big social event in Johannesburg since the end of the war. A marquee had been set up on the big lawn in front of the veranda to the right of Miss Pinforth's cottage and garden. As if the gods were on the side of Tina Pringle, it had not rained for three days. There had been no boiling thunderclouds grouping on the horizon every afternoon. Only blue sky and white, waterless clouds. At night, for three nights, the great canopy of heaven had domed above Johannesburg, the Milky Way clear and splashed across the night skies, the Southern Cross pointing the way for travellers in the distant bush, three layers of stars in the great heaven.

Albert had hired the most expensive caterers, imported a string orchestra from Cape Town, and employed a small army of servants to tend to the guests at his sister's twenty-first.

"Mum and dad would have liked all this," he said to her before the first guest arrived. They were looking down from the long veranda to the lawn and the marquee and all the coloured lights.

"No, they wouldn't. Mother would have said it was a waste of money."

"Have you a man in mind? Someone to marry you?"

"Oh, it's all a gamble once you know they have money. And yes, I want to marry money. Living in a railway cottage was all right but I much prefer this house. People who say money is not important are usually those who will never have a chance of putting their hands on lots of it. If I can't have it, it can't be any good. Sour grapes... Do you like my dress? You haven't said a word... Are you lovers?"

"Yes."

"And about bloody time. When are you getting married?"

"She won't have me. And that's the first guest arriving. And that dress makes you look even more smashing if that's possible... Now, stand straight, sis. Be prepared to meet your guests. This is the night Tina Pringle is presented to Johannesburg's society... Where's Miss Pinforth?"

"I'm here, Mr Pringle."

"You look beautiful in an evening gown," said Tina.

"My dear, I've been telling you for three years not to tell lies. But thank you. May you have a wonderful life, my Tina. A wonderful life."

There had been one late letter of regret delivered by Bill Hardcastle and left on the silver tray just inside the front door of the house on Parktown Ridge.

'Miss Lily Ramsbottom regrets she will be unable to attend the ball on the occasion of Miss Tina Pringle reaching her majority.'

Mrs Barker had not been invited.

Sallie arrived among the first as she had promised and went to stand between Tina and Albert to receive the guests. The orchestra was playing a Strauss melody in the marquee where a wooden dance floor took centre stage. Waiters in white jackets offered the guests drinks. The buffet had been set up in the sitting room with its furniture removed. If it had rained they would have danced in the sitting room on the polished floor. Miss Pinforth had arranged the flowers in every empty corner of the house. The flow of cars came and went on the gravel driveway, the chauffeurs parking the cars in the streets to let the new arrivals spill into the ball. With the flow of drinks, the sound increased, giving small groups their privacy. By nine o'clock the guests had been received. Tina was taken away by a young man who would inherit millions. Albert led Sallie down the steps onto the lawn and into the marquee where they danced.

"Why did Tina give me a filthy look when I arrived?" she asked.

"Better ask her."

"Did you tell her?"

"What about?"

"Stop being obtuse, Bert."

"You look lovely, Sallie."

"And stop changing the subject."

"What subject?"

By ten o'clock the whole house was seething in people and Tina was sure some of them had not received an invitation. Many of the faces she had never seen before in her life including a man in a linen suit who had just come in through the front door. The doorman was given a Panama hat and was trying to throw the man out of the house. Whether invited or not, guests were required to wear evening dress. The man was tall, broad-shouldered and his face was tanned the colour of mahogany by the sun. Ignoring the doorman, and giving him what looked like a five-pound note, the gatecrasher moved into the house. Tina moved forward in full sail to throw him out. The man was looking around him at the guests, while Tina was swallowed in the crowd. Then she was on the other side looking into piercing blue eyes, and she was running. By the time Barnaby caught her she was clean off the ground. He put her down gently. Everyone in sight had stopped talking. The doorman froze on his way to throw out the intruder.

"The Honourable Barnaby St Clair, at your service, ma'am."

Then they were laughing with joy.

THE ROUND AFRICA voyage of the SS *King Emperor* brought Harry Brigandshaw and his party to the port of Beira in Portuguese Africa. They had left Tilbury docks in the Port of London seven weeks earlier. The rains were over; the bushveld was green and the air comparatively cool. When their train climbed out of the lowveld to the high plains of Southern Rhodesia, it was autumn, the best time of the year.

Mr and Mrs Jack Merryweather were the first of the passengers to disembark. The rails of the ship were crowded with passengers and crew. All were smiling and clapping. The ship's orchestra was playing Mendelssohn's wedding march. Captain Hosey, the Manxman from Castletown in the Isle of Man, his full grey-flecked beard perfectly clipped, smiled down on the bride and groom he had married an hour before the shipped docked. As captain of the ship, he had the power of the civil authority to throw a man in irons or pronounce a couple man and wife. It had been a good voyage from England, with good winds around the Cape of Good Hope, the 'Cape of Storms', the two great funnels belching black smoke in a steady line most of the voyage. Their only storm had been in the Bay of Biscay, soon after leaving the English Channel. It was the first time he had performed a marriage on board. And the first time he had seen a tiny daughter dressed as a bridesmaid at her mother's wedding. The seamstress that had run up the little dress was well commended. Mary, Jack and Fay's three-and-a-half-year-old daughter made not a sound throughout the wedding. Harry Brigandshaw had given away the bride. Robert St Clair had been the best man. The reception was going to take place in the dining car of the Rhodesia Railways train taking them into Salisbury. There were now eight grown-ups in the party, Merlin having attached himself to a young girl from Chelsea travelling alone to Salisbury, on her way to a posting as secretary to the Governor of Southern Rhodesia, a shipboard romance that had started soon after leaving the shores of England.

Glen Hamilton helped Robert St Clair down the gangplank. His book was due out in the spring lists. Lucinda followed behind her brother, hand in hand with Harry. Merlin and his new girlfriend came next. From the dock, Fay turned back to look up at the ship. When she caught sight of Lucinda, her hands went wet and her mouth went dry. Her mother's iron-bound wooden trunk with its studs was coming down the service gangplank on a sailor's shoulder, not ten feet on the other side of Lucinda, and for the moment of her shudder, Lucinda's head melted into the trunk where the sun caught them both from behind.

"What's the matter, Mummy?" asked Mary.

As the child asked, the sailor stumbled, the small wooden trunk fell from his shoulder, going over and over, until it hit the dockside below and shattered. Her mother's gipsy clothes, the long earrings, the pointed shoes, a myriad of bracelets, broke out of the smashed trunk and scattered on the dock. They watched in horror as a sailor ran down to gather up the contents of the broken trunk, helped by a Portuguese policeman. It was the most dangerous omen she had ever witnessed in her life. All that was her mother was exposed for all by the glaring African sun. Breaking away from Jack, she ran to the dockside and retched into the narrow stretch of water between the wooden dock and the towering metal side of the SS *King Emperor*.

BAREND OOSTHUIZEN HAD KNOWN for weeks when Harry was coming home. If he was going it had to be before Harry arrived. What he hated more than anything that had happened in his life was being stuck on a farm in the wilderness with a pack of screaming children and a mother who watched him every moment of her day. They all knew the old man wanted her to warm the old man's bed, but even living on the other side of what had been the whole of Elephant Walk with Sir Henry Manderville was too far away from her darling son. And Barend knew better than anyone he was no darling, that the right thing to do was kick the thieving foreman off the farm and do the job himself properly... He hated farming. The slowness. The hours in the sun. The months between planting and reaping and seeing if all the work had been worthwhile. He hated always watching the sky for rain and when it rained for a week on end, watching for the sun. He was hemmed in. Claustrophobic. With all the space, there was no space for him. And Madge, taking all the horrible things he did without giving him a good slap on the face. She was not his childhood companion. His muse. His love. His friend... She was his lackey wife, and he hated it.

The stores he would need for a ride back to the Namib Desert and the search for his diamonds were locked in a shed with the two new saddles. The two horses he would take had been well fed and groomed. He had had the farrier out especially from Salisbury, much to everyone's surprise. He was ready. All he had to do was tear himself away from his family and ride for his life away into the bush.

The one thing Barend Oosthuizen hated most in life was any kind of responsibility. Though he never admitted it even to himself.

MERVYN BRAITHWAITE HAD CALLED three times on the Salisbury office of Colonial Shipping to find out the progress of the SS *King Emperor*. He had been in Africa for three months, waiting his chance now the war was over. He had found a room close to Annie's Shack, a whorehouse in central Salisbury, and the whores he despised, seeing their outward smile and their inner content. The passenger list had been a surprise and the thought of killing all of them warmed his heart and calmed his craving. He hated the

American for knowing he was sane. He was ready, like a good pilot, to pounce on his enemies from out of the sun.

The night before the boat train was due into Salisbury from Beira, he indulged himself with one of the whores. She was black. Very black. The owner catered to all tastes. The place was run-down. Seedy. The carpets pocked with burn marks from cigars and cigarettes. The rooms were all the same. One cheap band in one big bar.

Mervyn had found nothing in his wanderings. Only loneliness. The young girls in South America had been no more interested in living with him than Sara Wentworth. And she haunted him. More than all the dead German pilots put together. The service revolver waiting for him in his room was a Webley, similar to the one that had flown with him during the war.

The girl, when he left her, locked her door, shivering uncontrollably. For two hours she was sure the man with the wet eyes was going to kill her. He had not even paid her a bonus. She heard his feet echo down the carpetless corridor and made up her mind. Despite the money, despite the rich men who wanted her, she was going home to her rural village. Before the pig of an owner found her dead in her bed and tossed her into the street for the stray dogs to gnaw upon.

Before Mervyn Braithwaite reached his anonymous room she left Annie's Shack for the last time, running in the night for her life, calling on all her ancestors to give her protection. Before the sun came up she was three miles out of Salisbury on the same winding path of the road that led to Elephant Walk. She neither saw nor heard the leopard as it dropped out of the tree as she passed underneath in her flight. Razor-sharp teeth tore out her throat before she could scream... The leopard dragged her carcass deep into the bush. She was a small girl, and the big cat carried her in his mouth, only her shoeless feet trailing in the grass.

When the sun came up most of her flesh had been eaten away.


JACK MERRYWEATHER MADE up his mind as the boat train pulled its way across the big veld four thousand feet above sea level deep in the African bush. It was the most beautiful countryside he had seen. The sky was powder blue. White, motionless clouds. Lush bush, green still from the last of the rains, watered with rivers, and streams. Game every which side of the train he looked. Ranges of distant mountains, hued a rich pink by the rising sun, later shimmering in the new heat of the day. He had forgotten how beautiful it was. Out of the carnage of battle, it was a balm to his soul. Beside him, Fay's eyes were shining at what she saw passing outside the carriage window. His daughter Mary was silent, taking in the herds of game, her thumb clamped in her mouth in rich contentment.

"Why don't we make this our home?" he said.

The American opposite had his eyes closed and was either asleep or did not hear. Harry Brigandshaw gave Jack a broad smile and squeezed Lucinda's hand. For some reason, Robert chuckled. Merlin was in another carriage with his new girlfriend on her way to work for the governor.

"Good," said Fay.

He waited a long moment but that was all she said. Just the one word. Good. He smiled past her to again look out of the window at the rolling countryside. The clacking of metal wheels on metal rails sang in his ears. All the horror was behind them.


AN HOUR before the boat train was due at the station, Sallie Barker was walking back from her doctor's rooms to the Johannesburg offices of Serendipity Mining and Explosives Company. In the one block walk either way her life had changed forever. She was going to be a mother. Her one was going to be two. There was a person growing inside her she loved already with a passion she had never known before.

Back in the office of her company, she walked straight to his door and threw it open without so much as a knock.

"Hello, Dad!"

Albert looked up. Then it dawned on him as she grinned stupidly. Slowly he rose from his chair, the smile rising on his face.

"We'd better get married, Bert!"

"Today or tomorrow?"

"Maybe we can give it a week."

"Are you sure?"

"The doctor is."

"Special permit. Right now. Before you change your mind."

"All right," said Sallie Barker. "You know, I never thought I'd have children."

"Neither did I. Not with you, anyway... My mother said to me the best things in life are worth waiting for. As was so often with my mother, she was right... And tomorrow we'll both take the day off."

"You think we should?"

"When you're Mrs Pringle, you'll do as I say."

"Like hell I will."

. . .

THE OOSTHUIZEN CHILDREN were running riot on the platform ten minutes before the boat train was due at Salisbury Station. Everyone was there except Barend: Emily, excited to see her son after so many years of war; Sir Henry, glad of the chance to talk to Alison. The third child in a pram watched over by Madge. Everyone was fidgeting, the months of expectation coming to a head. The three-year-old girl was dodging in and around the legs of the large crowd waiting to meet the passengers.

"Mother, please help. She'll get on the track... Now where's she gone?... Please help! And Tinus! Come here. Please, Tinus."

Alison, ever good with children other than her own, caught the boy by the hand, and then his sister. The boy howled with rage. His grandmother took no notice now she had him in a firm grip.

The afternoon sun was hot. The women wore big floral hats. Outside the station building, a line of motor cars was intermingled with tethered horses, traps, carriages and bicycles. A strong smell of horse manure mingled with the ladies' perfume. Black porters with two-wheeled trolleys waited patiently.

Someone at the end of the platform gave a shout and everyone turned to look. Emily heard the puffing from the train and held her breath. Then the train came into sight around the long curve in the railroad, the cowcatcher front of the engine black and powerful.

Tembo left the horses where they were and joined the crowd as the train puffed its way into the station. He stood at the back, a large grin on his face. He and Harry Brigandshaw had known each other for most of their lives. The train gave a sharp whistle before grinding to a halt. People in front were shouting greetings to people on the train.

HARRY AND LUCINDA had the carriage window down and were leaning out looking for the family. Glen Hamilton had got up and was looking over them. Merlin, leaning out of his own window in the next carriage was shouting over the noise at his sister. Robert was still sitting, keeping the weight off his wooden foot for as long as possible. Fay had picked up Mary to look out of the window. Jack Merryweather was smiling at his family, planning the cattle farm he was going to buy and the great house he was going to build.

Harry saw his mother and shouted louder than everyone. The family was still twenty yards up the platform but they heard. Harry saw his grandfather take off his bush hat in salute. Then he saw Madge and waved. There was Alison, his old nurse, his sister's mother-in-law. He had never before seen his sister's children. Harry had the catch of the door open and pushed the heavy door. He got down first, putting his arms up to Lucinda for her to come down to him.

Glen Hamilton saw the face and wondered why something was so familiar in a crowd so far from anything he knew. The man's eyes were bulging and wet, the face squashed. The man was looking straight at him from twenty feet. Even before the gun came into view Glen knew what was happening. The gun fired twice in quick succession, the bullets hurling Lucinda back into the train. Glen fell back against Jack as a third bullet crashed into the back of the carriage. When Glen recovered to look out, Mervyn Braithwaite and his gun were gone.

Harry had not even seen who fired the shots that killed his wife.


FOR THE FIRST time when he killed, Mervyn Braithwaite had not said a word. A black man had him from behind, arms around his throat, but nothing else mattered. He had taken his revenge on Harry Brigandshaw by killing his wife. When the police took him away he was still smiling.


THEY BURIED Lucinda on the farm Sebastian Brigandshaw had called Elephant Walk. Her brothers went straight home to Purbeck Manor after the funeral with the American, Glen Hamilton. There had seemed no reason for them to stay any longer.

The day after the funeral, Jack and Fay Merryweather returned with their daughter to Meikles Hotel. There was nothing they could do for Harry. Words were useless.

"Are you going to live here, Jack? I hope so," said Harry, trying to change the course of his mind.

"What are you going to do, Harry?"

"I know where Barend is going. I'm going to catch up with him. Only the bush can help me now. Barend and I have never had to talk too much together and that will be good."

"Will you come back?"

"Oh, yes. We both will. Here is our family. This is our house and always will be."

"What have they done with him?"

"Back in irons to England. To Banstead. To the lunatic asylum."

"But he's not mad. Glen was quite sure."

"Does it really matter now?... Did you know she was pregnant?"

"No, I didn't."

"Maybe that's something I won't tell my mother... I was going to ask her about my father and when I was born. Now it doesn't seem to matter. Nothing seems to matter, Jack. You see what I mean? You look after Fay and Mary."

THREE WEEKS later Harry Brigandshaw caught up with Barend Oosthuizen on the banks of the Zambezi River. He was going to use his geology degree, at last, to find the diamond pipe in the Namib Desert. What they were going to do with the money he had no idea. It was just something to do. To stop his brain shattering into pieces.

Three days later they crossed the big river on a raft they had made for themselves, watched by a troop of baboons. Barend had lost a father. He had lost a wife. He was not sure which was worse.

They rode on together, side by side.

CONTINUE READING the Brigandshaw Chronicles with *Mad Dogs and Englishmen.*

# DEAR READER

~

Reviews are the most powerful tools in our kitty when it comes to getting attention for Peter's books. This is where you can come in, as by providing an honest review you will help bring them to the attention of other readers.

If you enjoyed reading *Elephant Walk*, and have five minutes to spare, we would really appreciate a review (it can be as short as you like). Your help in spreading the word and keeping Peter's work alive is gratefully received.

Please post your review on the retailer site where you purchased this book.

Thank you so much.
Heather Stretch (Peter's daughter)

# PRINCIPAL CHARACTERS

~

**The Brigandshaws**
*Harry* — The central character of *Elephant Walk* and son of Sebastian and Emily
*Sebastian and Emily* — Harry's parents, central characters in *Echoes from the Past*
*Madge* — Harry's long-suffering sister
*George* — Harry's younger brother
*Sir Henry Manderville* — Emily's father and Harry's potty grandfather
*Nathanial and James* — Harry's uncles
*Mathilda Brigandshaw* — Harry's paternal grandmother

**The St Clairs**
*Robert* — Harry's university friend and son of Lord St Clair
*Richard* — Eldest son of Lord St Clair
*Lucinda* — Robert's youngest sister who is in love with Harry
*Annabel and Genevieve* — Robert's other sisters
*Frederick, Merlin and Barnaby* — Robert's other brothers
*Ethelbert, Seventeenth Baron St Clair* — Robert's father
*Lady St Clair (Bess)* — Robert's mother
*Granny Forrester (Nettie)* — Lady St Clair's mother
*Sir Willoughby Potts* — Cousin to Granny Forrester

*Principal Characters*

### The Pringles
*Albert* — Manservant to Jack Merryweather
*Mr and Mrs Pringle* — Albert's parents
*Tina Pringle* — Albert's sister
*Edward, Walter, Billy and Maggie* — Albert's other siblings

### The Oosthuizens
*Barend* — Son of Tinus and Alison, and Harry's childhood friend
*Tinus* — Barend's father (deceased) central character in *Echoes from the Past*
*Alison* — Barend's mother
*Katinka (Tinka)* — Barend's sister

### Other Principal Characters
*Jack Merryweather* — Wealthy but bored friend of Robert and Harry
*Sallie Barker* — Beautiful friend and business partner of Albert
*Lily White (Ramsbottom)* — Jack Merryweather's one-time mistress and whorehouse madam
*Doris Barker (Mrs Barker)* — Sallie's self-seeking, intractable mother
*Jared and Sara Wentworth* — Friends of Robert, Harry and Jack
*Mervyn (Fishy) Braithwaite* — Sara Wentworth's fiancé
*Ernest Gilchrist* — Cousin to Mrs Barker and Sallie
*Fay Wheels* — Jack's gipsy mistress
*Glen Hamilton* — A newspaper reporter for the *Colorado Telegraph*

# GLOSSARY

~

*Baas* — A supervisor or employer, especially a white man in charge of coloured or black people

*Bittereinder* — A faction of Boer guerrilla fighters resisting the forces of the British Empire in the later stages of the second Boer War

*Board School* — An elementary school established by Britain in 1870

*Consols* — A name given to certain British government bonds (gilts) first used in 1751 (originally short for consolidated annuities)

*Kopje* — Afrikaans for a small hill in a generally flat area

*Loop* — Afrikaans word for walk

*Potboiler* — A creative piece of work written by a reporter for the sole purpose of making a living

*Rondavel* — A westernised version of the African-style hut

*Shingle* — A small signboard

*Veld* — Afrikaans word for open, uncultivated country or grassland in southern Africa

*Very Light* — A flare fired into the air from a pistol for signalling or for temporary illumination

Printed in Great Britain
by Amazon

66106070R00255